LUCIEN

BOOK II IN THE EVE-O LUCIEN DUOLOGY

DANIELLE GOMES

AnjoOneElevenPress.com

First paperback edition June 2022
Cover design by Rafael Andres
Library of Congress Cataloging-in-Publication Data
Names: Gomes, Danielle, author
Title: Lucien [Book 2]
Description: ANJO One Eleven Press, [2022]
Identifiers: LCCN 2022909618
978-1-7365992-0-4 Paperback
978-1-7365992-4-2 E-book
978-1-7365992-5-9 Audiobook
This is a work of fiction. Names, characters, places, and incidents either are the product of the author's imagination or are used fictitiously. Any resemblance to actual persons, living or dead, events, or locales is entirely coincidental.

www.DanielleGomesWrites.com

ACKNOWLEDGEMENTS

To my dad, Dennis, who turned me into a writer with his incredible stories and who showed me the power of a good story. While you won't read this book, you helped write it by instilling in me a love of reading. To my mom, Barbara, you inspire me every single day. I'm so proud of you and your inventions. Thank you for all that you do for us and for always being my first reader! To my husband, Ben, thank you for believing in me and always making me laugh! To my boys, Jake and Zac, I love you so incredibly much! To my entire family (Mary, Jonathan, Lauren, Lexi, Aaron, Lisa, El-lie, Evie, Gabrielle, Andy, Drew, Dotsie, Mark, Dave, Maddie, Maya, and all of my family and friends) – thank you for making life so fun!

To the Wednesday Writers, thank you for being such an incredibly supportive group! To my team of editors and designers, you are magic.

To my readers, thank you for reading this book. I hope you enjoyed it!

Much Love, Danielle Gomes

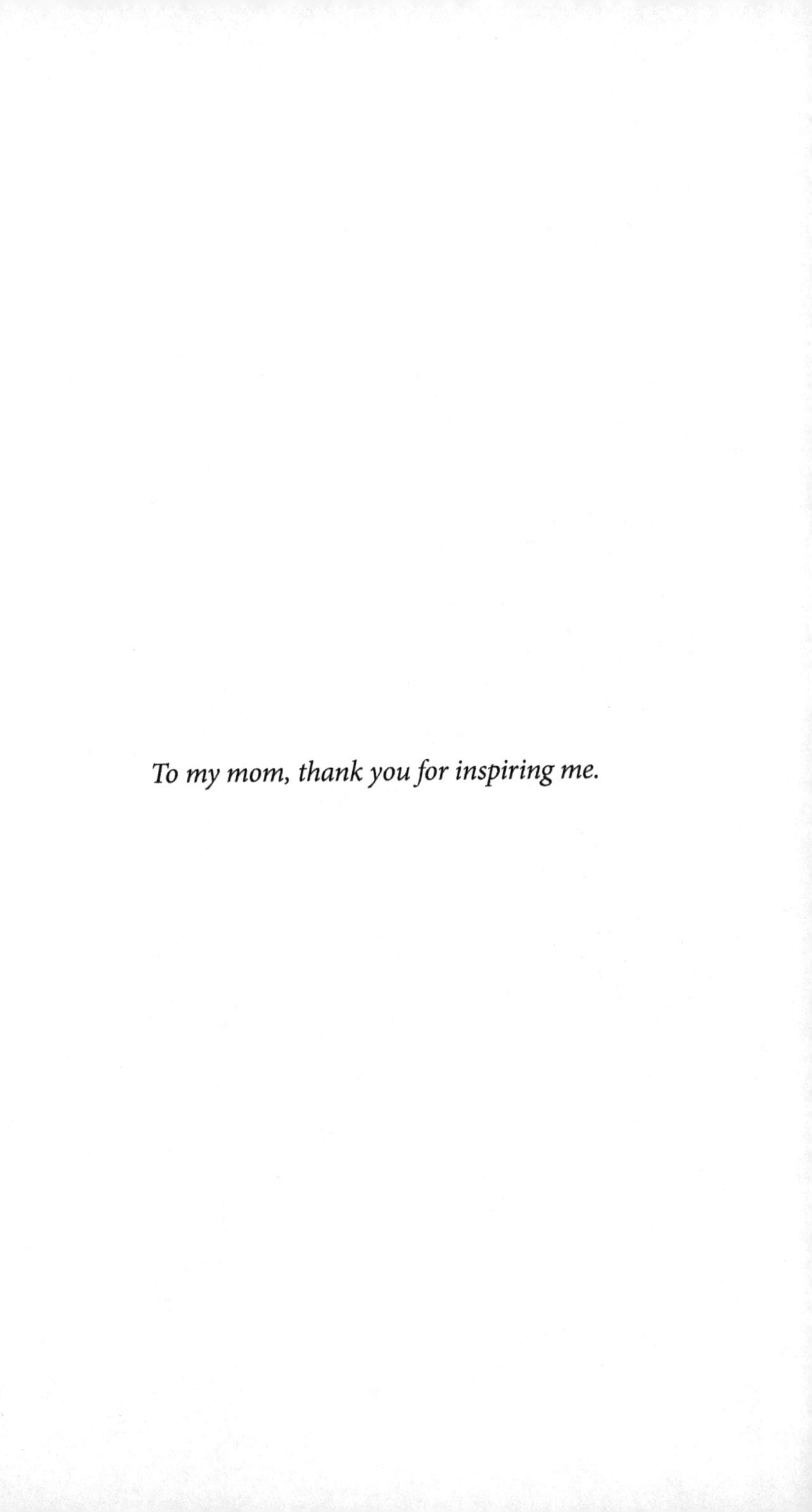

To my mom, thank you for inspiring me.

PART I

"Bad times have a scientific value.
These are occasion a good learner would not miss. "
-Ralph Waldo Emerson
*The Conduct of Life: Considerations
by the Way, 1860*

1 - IN THE GROUND

"Gabs," Chris called, "it's time. You've got to get it packed up now. Unless you want me to do it."

"No, I'll do it."

The afternoon sun was bright, but there was a soft breeze under the shade of the young kapok tree. She was comfortable in the jungle. Though a few months ago, Gabby would've never imagined she could feel at home in the Amazon rain forest. She was a Philadelphia Main Line girl; she had the greatest cities in her backyard and loved the concrete convenience they provided. Well, at least until the pandemics changed that.

Gabby played with a group of Matsés children while their families were packing up what few belongings they had in their village deep in the rain forest. Gabby had lost track of time; she was so enthralled with these young lives. They had nothing, not even clothes, yet everyone appeared happy. While their village had been shaken by the violent clash with the

AmCorps Extraction Unit, Gabby was amazed by their resiliency. So many lives had been lost. Gabby's heart ached for Trent, Kukua, and so many others. So much so, she wished she could just lay down and go to sleep until the pain subsided. But these young children were giving her a rope to hang onto. Gabby drew pictures of animals in the sand for them and they giggled, proving they weren't in shock. Gabby smiled. While the kids played, she gave them basic health checkups. They were all remarkably healthy, even though they'd never seen a doctor or gone through the rigorous practices of western medicine.

"Gabs," Chris yelled, with his hands up in frustration. He was off to the side of the village square, planning the various escape routes with Rodrigo and some of the other warriors. Lt. Christopher Silver, Special Security agent, had led the medical research team successfully into this remote area. It was a major achievement considering they'd been chased by wildlife and mercenaries alike. Even the very people who sent him into this danger zone now pursued them. Getting them out safely would be a much more daunting task.

So much had changed overnight. The loss of Trent at the hands of AmCorps—the lab he devoted the last decade of his life to—hit the hardest. Gabby didn't understand how his own team could put a bullet in him. Trent was the reason they were even there. He invented their treatment. Now, he was dead. Gabby was filled with such an awful cocktail of rage, hate, and complete and utter sadness. She wanted to either hurt someone or go to sleep for a very, very long time. She wanted to wake up somewhere else or not at all.

"Gabs, I'll do it," Chris yelled, looking in her direction.

She waved him off. "I'm going," she mumbled, then smiled and lifted the small child off her lap.

Gabby had to use all of her will to move from this spot and the welcome distraction the children provided. They had to clear out of the village by nightfall; more of AmCorps' agents would be here soon, desperate to get their hands on a viable specimen. *Specimen.* The word chilled her, for these were people, not laboratory rats. How did she get tangled in this mess? Right now, she couldn't bring herself to think about it.

Gabby had waited as long as possible. She was dreading the impending sadness that going into Trent's lab was bound to stir. It had only been a few days since her fiancé Trent died, and it still didn't feel real. There were moments when Gabby would forget and want to tell him something, only to relive the moment he took his last breath in her arms.

Trent's blood had dried to a dark red stain on the dirt floor of his improvised lab. This was the first time Gabby had been back in the lab since she kissed Trent goodbye for the last time. As she looked around, she marveled at how incredibly organized Trent was. Or *had* been, she reminded herself for the umpteenth time. He had already packed up the lab and clearly labeled everything. The only thing still out was his computer.

"Thanks, Trent," Gabby whispered under her breath.

Gabby sat down at his makeshift desk, set up on a table made of rough-cut wood. Even the papers that identified each human sample had been packed up, filed, and now sat neatly in a clearly marked folder just above Trent's computer backpack. As Gabby moved the laptop to close it, the screen flickered on.

"Hi Gabrielle."

Stunned, Gabby's mouth hung open as she stared at Trent's beautiful face on the screen.

"Well, at least I hope it's you seeing this."

"It's me, Trent, it's me," Gabby cried.

"I hope it's you seeing this and you're ok."

"I'm seeing it, Trent. Tr—"

"It's…" Trent's voice interrupted her and she immediately felt puerile for responding to a recorded message. "Not how I hoped things would go when I brought you into this. So much has changed, but maybe it's for the better."

On the screen, Trent paused and took a deep breath before continuing. "There's so much I have to tell you, and I will. But right now, you need to get out of the village. On the assumption, even likelihood, I'd be gone, I programmed this message to play as soon as my computer was touched, so you're still in the lab. When you left the camp to escape with the specimens, AmCorps issued a kill-on-sight order for you, Chris, and the others. At that moment, I swore I'd do anything I could to save you. Don't try to fight them, Gabrielle, not on your own. They are so powerful. You need to leave now. They will keep sending their military until they have what they need. Close the computer and leave now. Get everyone out of the village. Separate. Get a safe distance away, then open the computer again. I've already scrambled the encrypted location tracking and all comm capabilities from this device. When you're a safe distance away, I've recorded more videos for you. They're labeled in order. I'm going to help you, Gabrielle. I'm sorry I brought you into this. I love you."

The screen flickered off. Gabby sat there in shock for a minute. She clicked open the file tab and saw the videos, all in order. She quickly closed the computer, placed it into the backpack, carefully secured it, strapped it to her back, and buckled it. She was not going to let this bag out of her grip. She grabbed the other lab supply bag Trent had packed and headed out of the tent.

The main village was empty, so Gabby headed to the lower village. It was a short walk on a well-worn trail. She had taken the path several times with Kukua, the indigenous guide who helped their expedition when they were collecting samples from the uncontacted people in this remote area of Brazil. Their intention had been to help the world reactivate their

EVE-0 gene and put a stop to the relentless pandemics that decimated humankind. Gabby didn't realize this meant stealing these people from their homes and lives just to mine their genetic information. She never intended to capture or kill off the very people that held the key to the survival of the human race. She felt naïve for going into this mission so blindly, but she knew there had to be another way.

The thought of Kukua hollowed out her empty chest a little more. The last time she saw him, he had been shot, point-blank in the back of the head by one of AmCorps's extraction agents. They were supposed to be on the same side. Now, every time she thought of this sweet, though desperate human, she could only see his lifeless body, collapsed outside of Trent's lab. There was so much to be sad about, but the slightest twang of purpose began to sprout and she had a reason to continue on, nestled safely in her bookbag.

She found Chris in the lower village with Chief Ëpë, the shaman, Rodrigo, and the surviving warriors.

"Chris," Gabby yelled over the gathered crowd. "Chris!" The group parted so she could get through.

"Gabs, give me five minutes. We are explaining the different routes."

"No, Trent told me. He's going to help us."

The blood drained from Chris's face. "What?"

"Trent's going to help us."

Chris said something to Rodrigo in Portuguese, then pulled Gabby through the group and over to the side of the clearing.

"Gabs, Trent is dead. AmCorps murdered him. Are you…" Chris began.

She shook her head. "No, you don't understand. Trent recorded videos for me. In the first video, he said he's going to help us, but we need to leave the village immediately. He said they would keep sending their military forces until they have what they want."

"What?"

"Yeah, it's all on this computer. He's going to help us. He recorded videos of himself."

"You can't take the computer. It's a trick; a setup. That's how they're going to track us."

"No, it's not. Trent said he scrambled the encryption and deactivated all comm capabilities."

"You don't trust him, do you? You can't possibly trust him. Not after you learned what AmCorps planned to do." Chris replied, putting both hands on Gabby's shoulders and looking at her. His eyes wide with sympathy.

She didn't need to be reminded that Trent lied to her about this scientific mission, but, in the end, he'd understood that what AmCorps intended wasn't humane. "Yes, I do."

"You're not taking the computer."

"Yes, I am, or I'm not going with you."

"Gab…" Chris paused, a deep crease wrinkling his brow.

"I trust him. He saved my life. That extraction

agent was going to kill me, and Trent took a bullet for me. He's going to help us. I promise you."

Chris chewed his lip. "Fine."

"Ok," Gabby answered, "but we need to leave here now."

"Alright. Grab your things and meet me at the lab."

2 - PEACOCK INTELLIGENCE

Lucien tried to keep his anger controlled, but the heat that blazed his cheeks showed in his tone. Though his pasty complexion remained as pale as ever, an ounce of color never once graced his cheeks. A single UV ray never touched his limpid skin due to his genetic condition, xeroderma pigmentosum. Lucien appreciated the irony of his imperfect genetics gracing him with strangely perfect skin even though he was facing the dawn of his 60s.

"Why is this taking so long?" Lucien snapped at his computer.

On the screen, General Holton twisted in his chair. "As you are well aware, our best active military members were divided between the safe houses. So, we've had to pull in some others."

"I know. I've heard every pathetic excuse for your incompetency. I'm asking where the team is now."

"No one expected this outcome, including you. We've had to be very creative with reforming our extraction team. We're almost there. We have seven-ty-five members currently in decon. We did have a small hiccup. There was a breach in quarantine yes-terday and we had to clear out a pod of ten officers, but we will have a unit ready to go very soon."

"Pitiful. You're right, I didn't expect this outcome. How could your supposed elite force get taken out by a handful of untrained jungle rats?"

"We've gone over this. No one expected insur-gents. You certainly did not." General Holton let out his breath and rolled his eyes, exhaustion showing on his hollow features. His taut olive skin was now slack. His salt-and-pepper hair now had more salt. These past few months had taken their toll.

"The longer it takes you to assemble a new team, the more time they have," Lucien snapped.

"We have a small team leaving tomorrow."

"What do you think a small team is going to do?" Lucien paused. "Idiot," he said under his breath.

"We have two combat controllers with them. Their mission is simply to track the target."

"Let me know when they leave." Lucien abruptly clicked out of the communication window.

Marshall law had quickly evolved into a total lockdown throughout the United States. Necessary supplies were delivered robotically once a week. No one set foot outside of their home, for any reason, and it was working. The multiple pandemic infection rates were dropping, or at least so it seemed. There were no doctors or hospitals or testing sites to track new infection rates. Though it seemed the few remaining survivors that made up the human race had bought some time. That was the good news.

The bad news was simple: this way of life was not sustainable. Nearly a quarter of a million casualties were expected as a result of this level of lockdown. There had already been close to 100,000 reported deaths since the lockdown was decreed twenty-three weeks ago, most of which took place in institutions. The prison system had been quietly wiped out over the past several months. Incarceration rates of non-violent criminals had dropped significantly over the past decade, so only the worst offenders were jailed. Prisons went to contactless operation first, but over the past few months in preparation for total lockdown the institutions were sealed and the inmates were left with drone-operated guards and enough supplies for a year. Group homes and assisted living institutions collapsed, taking thousands of victims with them. Cities emptied out as many tried to escape the congestion of urban living in hopes the open air of the country would keep them safer. Small insurrections were quietly terminated. Successful birth rates dropped. They were at the lowest level in recorded history. The government strongly suggested pregnancies be placed on hold. If a woman did become pregnant, she might be able to scrounge up one or two virtual prenatal doctor's visits. However, she had to deliver the baby at home without medical intervention, which proved fatal for many unfortunate women and their babies. Others simply died from a general lack of healthcare.

The situation outside the U.S. was most definitely dire, though it too seemed to be leveling out, at least according to the trickle of intelligence that was available. Mortality rates in general hinted at stabilizing. Most of the First World countries appeared to be in the same situation as the former Land of Liberty. Admittedly, it was far worse in less developed countries. Drone footage indicated mass casualties with possibly no survivors across the Caribbean Island chain. General Holton called off all reconnaissance missions following these findings, deeming it unnecessary for the current situation. Furthermore, it was likely to be the same in any country that lacked the infrastructure to move to a contactless society and the U.S. was not in a position to share its resources.

In the AmCorps's Safe Houses, it was an entirely different story. The living quarters were luxuriously appointed. There were doctors on call. The sterile environment allowed the residents to begin to socialize in limited groups, in cafés and offices, libraries and gyms. Although it was drastically different sealed inside these sanctuaries, the attempt at normalcy was appreciated. It made making the necessary sacrifices a little bit easier.

The residents were not allowed to bring anything from the outside world in, which included clothing.

Millions of dollars in haute couture were left to rot at the empty mansions outside. Space was tight and sacrifices had to be made. The safe house clothing was made from merino wool and sustainable, lyocell fabric. It was naturally antimicrobial and soft. While the styles and colors were limited, no one complained. The women each had a long dress, short dress, business skirt suit, and two pants options: slacks and jeans. The men had the same pants options as well as a business suit and shorts. The clothing came in a wide variety of natural, nontoxic colors. Each client chose their palette before they went in. Lucien opted for grey. He found it easy on the eyes and universally appealing, particularly with his unique skin tone.

Lucien clicked a camera on his computer screen. A view of the community area flickered on. A handful of men and women sat around tables, enjoying cups of coffee and talking. They appeared relaxed and happy. Lucien zoomed the camera in on a woman, who appeared to be in her early thirties. Her shoulder-length blonde hair fell in perfect waves. Her features were delicate, though plump. She was beautiful by any standard but had clearly enjoyed some enhancements—a privilege reserved for the ultra-wealthy in the pandemic times. Lucien marveled at some people's devotion to their physical attributes. In the midst of several parthenogenic outbreaks and a desperate need for doctors, she still found a way to slow the effects of time.

The importance of appearance was shared across species lines. From the peacock's tail to the male deer's antlers, physical appearance was essential to the evolution of a species. Clearly, for Lucien, sexual selection was very much a part of natural selection and therefore essential to the evolution of the human species. It did, however, create quite a few hurdles for him. Defining a standard of beauty for the future of the human race was much more difficult than he'd anticipated. While it was easy for him to define the standards of beauty, when it came down to editing those into the human genome, it became much more problematic. Namely, the human race prized variety. In fact, creating a human race that was too similar would be detrimental to the evolution of the species. Some might even argue beauty was a driving force of evolution, though those standards changed so rapidly it was impossible to predict. Besides, Lucien didn't want to stop natural evolution; rather, he wanted to speed up the aspects of it that seemed to lag in so many. And in fact, science had demonstrated attractive people were around fourteen percent smarter than unattractive individuals. Researchers attempted to explain this away as a consequence of nurture versus nature: attractive people were perceived better and therefore treated better so their IQs were higher due to this reaction. However, when an entire population was smarter and less prone to negative emotions, the necessity of beauty to drive evolution would no longer be so *necessary*.

So, for the time being, Lucien had one focus: get those specimens who carried the unique EVE-0 gene which would save humanity. Or, at least, save those he recognized as valuable for his new world to come. Once his specimens were at the safe house, he'd be able to reactivate the EVE-0 gene and create his evolved species. Thus, he had made the decision to leave physical traits out of his equation to accomplish his ultimate dream: improve the human race. Besides, physical traits were easy to adjust later in life. Intelligence, according to Lucien, you were born with.

3 – RUN

The village had divided into groups. Each group had a different location they were to head to. They were directed to hide out until they received word from Rodrigo or a member of his unit. Most groupings were formed around family units with the exception of the "specimens." Only the youngest of those marked for extraction to AmCorps's labs remained with their families. The older ones joined Rodrigo's warriors, led by his first sergeant, Joao. Only the girl marked HAWA-317 and two of the young men marked for extraction were to join Gabby, Chris, Rodrigo, and their unit. Trent previously told Gabby the girl was what AmCorps considered the "ideal specimen," so they decided it was best for everyone to keep her as protected as possible.

Though before they could go, Gabby and Chris had to remove the chip implants from everyone that had been marked by AmCorps, as well as all of those that were falsely implanted to throw the extraction team off. The marked members gathered in front of Trent's lab. Chris and Gabby had to remove close to thirty chips; luckily, they had all been implanted in the soft skin between the thumb and forefinger, which made removal easy. The implants were about the size of a grain of rice, made of borosilicate glass, with a copper antenna and a battery that ran on heat from the human body. The implants transmitted both radio frequency signals and GPS signals.

A decade ago, human implant chips had been extremely popular. Brain wave chips that allowed you to telepathically control electronics, play video games, and work on your computer were the big-ticket items. However, as the pandemics began to take hold, those devices took a back seat to attempted vaccines and treatments.

While it was easy to remove the implants, all Gabby wanted to do was to get a safe distance away from the village and watch the videos from Trent. The process of pushing the tiny implant to the surface of the skin, then making small incisions to squeeze the chip through, was agonizingly tedious for Gabby. She had to take her time and make the tiniest of cuts so the process would be relatively painless with little blood and low risk of infection for the villagers.

"Ai," a young male villager said, pulling his hand away. He wore a thick red and white band around the crown of his head. His short, glossy, black hair stuck up from behind the band. He had a thick streak of red paint across his forehead and under each of his big brown eyes.

Gabby looked up from her trance. "I'm sorry. I'll be gentler." Gabby held her hand out for his and smiled.

He didn't understand her, but eventually gave his hand back to her with a scowl. Gabby carefully made tiny incisions until the chip popped out.

Out of the blue, Rodrigo ran over. He frantically spoke to Chris in Portuguese.

"What's going on?" Gabby asked.

"One of Rodrigo's guys reported an aircraft in the area. It didn't land, but we still need to get out of here. I told Rodrigo to have the groups leave now or as soon as they can. Let's hurry up and get these last few chips removed."

"I'm working as fast as I can."

"I know."

Chris's calmness irritated Gabby, but she swallowed it down and started on her next chip removal, another young warrior. He smiled at Gabby, then squeezed the chip to the surface of his skin so it was easier for Gabby to remove.

"I'm done," Chris announced as the chip popped out of Gabby's patient.

"Me too." Gabby let out a breath of relief.

"Grab your stuff, we're out of here," Chris said, then whistled to Rodrigo, Chief Ëpë, and the crew.

The village emptied out incredibly fast. Gabby

took up the rear as they marched along the deserted path. While the life that had so recently filled this bustling community had fled, the ghosts of the recent battle hung heavy. So much death left a weight in the atmosphere. Gabby could sense the extraction soldiers still running frantically. The sound of gunfire carried in distant whispers. She could almost hear Kukua call her for help. Then she heard the extraction agent's shot, and she saw Trent collapse. Dark blood poured from his abdomen. A wave of nausea left her dizzy. A sudden tingle rushed from her scalp to the base of her spine. She tripped and fell to her knees.

They paused, once again near the young kapok tree, on the edge of the village, where Trent had been laid to rest.

"Gabs, are you ok?" Chris asked.

"Yeah," she lied. Gabby was drenched in sweat. She rubbed her head. Reliving that moment was even worse. The shock that had dampened her emotion as it happened disappeared, opening the floodgate to her repressed feelings.

"Take a minute. I forgot to do something, I'll be right back," Chris said. He motioned for Rodrigo and the others to continue forward and wait inside the forest cover.

Gabby nodded her head and sat down just under the shade of the forest cover. She stared at the freshly disturbed earth that now covered Trent's body. She didn't feel any connection to this spot. It was just his body. She reminded herself she had his mind in her backpack, and that wrapped her in a bit of comfort. She turned to look back at the empty village. She could see Trent's lab in the distance. For a moment, she thought she saw Trent step out from his lab and quickly realized a strong breeze had lifted a swirl of dust. Gabby rubbed her head, hoping she wasn't losing her mind. As she lowered her hand, a big butterfly landed on her. Its iridescent electric-blue wings were outlined in black. It was the most beautiful color Gabby had ever seen. The exquisiteness of this creature was more beautiful than any painting she knew of. As it fluttered off, Gabby followed its path. She noticed Chris jogging back towards Trent's lab. She heard loud banging and sprinted towards it. By the time she got there, Chris had smashed almost everything.

"Stop!" She screamed, "What are you doing?"

"Gabs," Chris huffed, out of breath, "do you have a laptop like Trent's?"

"Stop," Gabby repeated as Chris smashed a printer on the hard dirt ground.

"We have to. The first thing AmCorps is going to do is search his lab. If they are able to easily identify what's missing, they'll know we have it. Do you have a laptop?"

"Yeah."

"Is it similar to Trent's?"

"It's the same model."

"Get it."

Gabby set her backpack on the ground, grabbed her laptop, turned it on to double-check it wasn't Trent's, and handed it to Chris.

"Here." She passed her computer to Chris.

"Are there any stickers or tags?"

"Yeah, there's barcodes. I'll switch them." She quickly peeled off the barcode stickers and replaced them. She turned on her computer one more time to double-check it was hers. She secured Trent's in her backpack.

"Keep it open and smash it," Chris said.

Gabby opened the computer and threw it on the ground. It barely cracked. She picked it up and did it again. The crack expanded. This time she picked up the keyboard, used both arms, and smashed the screen on the hard dirt. It shattered. It felt good. She jumped on the keyboard side and it bent, but not much. She jumped again and again. Finally, the keyboard began to open, spilling out its insides.

"Let me help," Chris said, driving his boot down on the computer and fully cracking it open. "Pull everything out, take the CPU, smash everything."

"I know the CPU is the main chip, but I've never actually seen one."

"It should be right around the middle, probably under a cover."

Gabby found the chip, stepped on it, and it bent. It was small but sturdy. She tossed the chip to Chris, then smashed the remaining pieces of the motherboard into unrecognizable shards. She stuck a handful of bits in her pocket and kicked the remaining pieces around the lab. Chris took the crooked chip and smashed it against a rock with the butt of his handgun. He threw a tiny fragment of it on the ground and stuffed most of it in his pocket before pulling the laptop shell apart and leaving the pieces in the lab.

The lab was a complete and absolute disaster. Everything had been smashed into thousands of shards of glass and metal. Satisfied, and admittedly feeling a bit better, Gabby and Chris rejoined the group.

4 - THE NOTHING

Gabby had grown used to moving through the jungle. The vines that once imprisoned her and snagged her every step were now no more threatening than the concrete sidewalks she had grown up with. They moved quickly. She was tired but far from exhausted. The adrenaline from Trent speaking to her powered her legs and carried her spirit. When she wanted to stop, the shaman had coca leaves, which were enough to rejuvenate her.

While the hours dragged on, the wind picked up. The breeze that had lifted dust in the village now carried debris in its wake. Gabby's eyes burned and her skin stung from the constant assault. It was becoming difficult to walk and their pace had become painfully slow.

"We've made decent progress," Chris yelled to Gabby over the howling wind. "We need to take cover until the wind dies down."

"Where?" Gabby asked.

"What?"

Frustrated, Gabby shook her head.

"We have about twenty minutes to hike from here, through the trees," Chris yelled. "Watch your head." He motioned with his hands to protect her head. She nodded.

Moments later, they broke off the path. Wind and vines formed a nearly impenetrable barrier. Gabby held her hands in front of her face and tried to walk, but struggled to move at all. She stood frozen; she couldn't open her eyes.

"Gabs," Chris yelled, "grab on to the back of me."

She reached out in front of her and felt Chris's bag. She tucked her head down and was able to follow his feet.

It was hard, but they moved slowly. After a few minutes, they stopped completely. Rodrigo yelled something to Chris.

"I don't think we're going to make it. We're going to have to get low..." A strong gust cut Chris off. Gabby heard a loud whistle pierce the wind. She looked up and saw a man and woman in the distance. They were hard to make out but seemed to be waving to them. The group began to slowly move toward them. As Gabby peeked through bursts of brutal wind, she could start to make them out. From what Gabby could see, they both appeared to be disfigured. Their flesh seemed to be twisted into knots, almost as if it was muddled by the wind.

As they came closer, Gabby could see they were badly scarred. Half of the woman's face was missing, replaced by hard, fibrous tissue. The man had massive lesions of scar tissue running up his back and covering his scalp. Rodrigo spoke to them. Gabby couldn't hear or understand what they were saying, but Rodrigo appeared nervous. Chief Ëpë seemed to urge him on and they followed the couple.

Everything abruptly turned black. The wind seemed to have blown a black snow or ash in and Gabby couldn't see anything. She reached out for Chris and found his back again. All at once, rain soaked them. Gabby couldn't open her eyes. Like a shot from the sky, the sting of hail bombarded them. Gabby crouched down to try to take cover, but Chris pulled her up. They fought their way forward.

The disfigured couple led them to the small entrance to a cave. It was close, but they would've never found it otherwise, even without the blinding storm, as it was cunningly hidden by jungle growth. The cave was surprisingly large, much bigger than Gabby's first dorm room. It was lit by the soft glow of a fire. The couple had built a crude hearth in the corner with a clever clay chimney vented through a hole they must've chiseled through the back side of the cave. There were animal skins stacked inside. Everything seemed orderly and homey. Jungle fruit was stacked along with some dried meats. There were clay bowls filled with what appeared to be a sort of grain. Coconut shells were stacked near an unwieldy pot filled with water. Gabby lingered by the door, while the others were deep in a conversation she couldn't understand.

Chris soon walked over. "Ok, we're going to wait the storm out here. They've welcomed us. Rodrigo is a bit uneasy. He said this place is known as the Nothing; they believe evil spirits live here. When members of the different tribes that live in the nearby region commit a 'crime,'" Chris made the quotation gesture with his hands, "the worst punishment is to get banished here. That's what happened to them. Her parents had married her off to an older man, and these two were caught having an affair. The older man lit them on fire to scar them. Once they were healed, they were banished here."

"That's terrible."

"Yeah."

"How long do you think we'll be here?"

"Most likely through the night. It's hard to tell. As soon as the storm clears, we'll move on."

Gabby nodded. "I'm going to look through the computer."

"Ok, but let Rodrigo prepare them first."

Gabby sat off in a corner, alone on a woven mat. She could hear the wind thrash the trees outside of the cave. She watched the group as they relaxed into the space. Chief Ëpë and the shaman sat off to the side as well. They always seemed to be quietly watching. Gabby quickly looked away, slightly embarrassed, as the shaman caught her staring. When she glanced back, he gently smiled and nodded. Gabby returned the gesture, then moved her focus to the others. HAWA-317, whose name Gabby recently learned was actually Mayalú, was the granddaughter of Chief Ëpë. The young marked warriors that came with Mayalú were Roiti and Kena. Gabby watched them talk and laugh as they sat around the hearth, struck by how young they seemed. They were teenagers. They'd been through such traumatic events; they had guns held to their heads, watched as dozens around them were gunned down, and they were marked as targets to be taken away from their homes and families, yet here they sat, comfortable, calm, and happy. Their strength and resiliency astounded Gabby, or maybe it was their innocence and naivety. Whatever it was, Gabby craved some of it, anything to take the sadness away.

Sitting in the Nothing, Gabby was overcome with sadness. She thought of Kukua, the crew, and how she had failed them. She thought of Trent and missed him. Gabby didn't want to go on; she didn't see the point in it anymore. She had watched enough people die. She laid down on the mat; she wanted to go to sleep and wake up somewhere else.

"Gabs," Chris said, sitting down next to her, "do you feel ok?"

"I'm fine, just tired," she said, sitting up.

"Rodrigo explained the computer to them. Can I watch the video with you?"

"Yeah." Gabby quickly unpacked the computer and flipped it open. The screen flickered on and Trent's face came into focus.

"Hi Gabrielle," Trent began. "I hope you're a safe distance away from the village."

A tear broke free and ran down Gabby's cheek. Chris patted her arm.

"I'm not sure where to start." Trent paused and bit his lip. "I guess I should start with the ayahuasca."

Ayahuasca was a ritual the villagers insisted they participate in, where they shared a potion that induced what the shaman considered to be a necessary spiritual experience, one that would reveal their true intentions, in order to allow them to stay in their village. It had induced visions for Gabby, to be sure. How much of it she could believe, she'd never know.

"I didn't tell you this, but I did have a... ah... an unexplainable experience. I spoke to... I can't believe I'm saying this... I spoke to my mother. I've never even met her. I only saw a picture of her once. I'm not sure how I knew it was her. I know this doesn't make sense."

"No, it does, Trent. It does," Gabby whispered.

"I know it was a hallucination, but she told me things that happened. I..." Trent paused, looking down. "I can't explain it. I still haven't come to terms with it, but it doesn't matter. It only lasted for a few minutes and then my mind was clear. I remember everything from that night. The fact is, I've known what we were going to do was wrong. In the beginning, I didn't fully grasp what was going on. I truly did want to leave the world a better place. I wanted to help and I believed Lucien. I more than believed him. I guess, looking back, I idolized him. He's a powerful person, Gabrielle. You have no idea. But that all changed, and I was trying to fix it. I wish I had been able to explain everything to you earlier, but I couldn't put you at risk."

Trent looked off-screen, a machine chimed, and something printed out. Trent grabbed the paper and glanced at it. At this gesture of normalcy, of Trent living and working, Gabby's emotions swirled into a storm, rushed out on her breath, and left her completely hollow. Her whole body drooped and Chris put his arm around her. She didn't look at him for fear another human interaction would push her over the edge.

"Sorry," Trent said as he returned his attention to the screen. "Lucien was my mentor. He was the closest thing to a father I had. I felt like I was betraying him initially, but I know this is the right thing to do. Part of me wishes it wasn't. I wish we were back in the safe house, together. But the future Lucien is creating is wrong. I will tell you more about that in the videos to come. What I need you to know now is how smart he is, how much power he has, and how driven he is. He will not stop until he has his treatment. He will kill or destroy anyone that gets in his way. I've seen him destroy lives before." Trent suddenly looked up and placed a piece of paper in front of the screen. He said something but the sounds were muffled by the papers moving on the computer.

"Sorry," he said, moving the paper, "I'm trying to buy you some time." Trent paused. "I'm sorry I tried to contain you." Still not looking at the screen, Trent squirmed in his chair, clearly uncomfortable with the subject. "I thought I might have a chance to explain everything to you. I gave Chris the codes hoping that he would tell you everything when I had you secured, then when I had a chance, I'd fill you in on the rest."

Sitting up in his chair, Trent stared directly into the camera. "I have a plan. I have a lot to tell you, but first I need you to try and initiate contact with Michaela Kelstrum. Make sure all of your comms are encrypted and scrambled. I hope you still have access to the tech we brought. Michaela considers herself a biohacker, a self-proclaimed scientist for the people," Trent said with an inadvertent roll of his eyes. "I always thought her talent was misplaced, but she's brilliant and will be able to help you. She hates Lucien. Her husband, Abe Kelstrum, was a hugely successful biochemist who worked with Lucien. They were partners and formed AmCorps. I think Lucien was threatened by him. Lucien always painted him as a problem, a threat to AmCorps. He said Kelstrum was mentally ill and a danger to humanity. I believed Lucien at the time, but looking back I can see what he did to Kelstrum. He slowly and methodically ruined him, to the point he committed suicide. Lucien tortured him and Michaela knew; she will jump at the opportunity to help you. I have so much more to tell you and I will, but that's it for this video. I've got to run. Take a break. I'll talk to you soon. I love you."

The screen flickered off and Gabby slowly shut the laptop. She bit her lip in an attempt to fight back the stream of tears trying to break free. As Gabby looked up, she could see everyone in the cave was watching her. She wanted to hide, or disappear.

"Do we have the comm tech Trent was talking about?" Gabby asked Chris.

"Yeah," Chris replied.

"Can we set it up?"

"It won't work in the cave. We'll have to wait till our next camp."

"What if I go outside?"

"No, besides being dangerous, the storm will affect the signal. You have to wait."

Gabby nodded her head. Chris was right, but that didn't make her position any less frustrating. She put the computer back in her backpack.

"Our hosts want to prepare a meal for us. Then we need to get some rest. Hopefully, we can move on tomorrow." Chris said.

"Chris…" Gabby paused, "I think we should take an antiviral."

"Really? Even with the risk?"

Gabby nodded her head.

"Isn't there like a twenty-percent chance of getting a blood clot?" Chris asked.

"Twenty-five percent, but we were exposed to a lot of people at Rodrigo's outpost. Our original dose has probably worn off and I'll give us an anticoagulant shot with the dose, which will dramatically minimize the risk. We just need to be very careful that we don't get hurt over the next couple of days."

"Okay," Chris shrugged his agreement.

The hosts prepared a stew of some sort. It didn't taste bad, but it didn't taste good either. It didn't taste like much at all. Everyone sat around on woven mats, deep in conversation. Rodrigo translated to Chris in Portuguese.

"Gabs, they're telling us about the area we're headed to. There're some groups we need to watch out for. They..." Chris stopped to listen to Rodrigo.

"*Eles dizem que esta área está cheia de maldade,*" Rodrigo said, and Chris nodded.

"There are," Chris began, but was interrupted again.

"*Pessoas consumidas pela violência,*" Rodrigo said.

"Sorry," Chris said, "they say the area is filled with evil and violent groups of..."

Chris looked to Rodrigo to translate again.

"Fill me in later," Gabby said. She stood and retreated to her mat in the corner of the cave. She watched the group gathered around the hearth. Everyone was so engaged. Gabby felt completely left out and isolated from her cold corner. She put on a sweater, hugged her backpack, curled up on her mat, and closed her eyes.

5 - EVERYTHING

Lucien sat at his computer, reading the last email Trent sent over and over again. There were not many people Lucien had ever truly connected to—possibly his mother, a childhood friend, and Trent. Although, Trent was different. Lucien remembered when Trent first came to AmCorps as a doctoral student. While the other candidates had huddled together in the break room and went to happy hours as soon as the day was over, Trent kept to himself. He was also by far the smartest in the group, but there was something that seemed broken in him. Besides the physical scar that sometimes peeked out of his sleeves, he seemed to not need any personal or emotional feedback while the other candidates craved positive feedback for their work and were hurt by criticism. Out of curiosity, and as a bit of a test, Lucien gave the group individual assignments. Before the first of these assignments, he privately criticized each candidate. However, before the second assignment, he privately praised each candidate. Without fail, each candidate's performance was directly affected by Lucien's remarks: adversely under criticism or positively by praise. All except for Trent's. His work was perfect when he was criticized *and* when he was praised.

Trent was the only candidate Lucien later hired to work at AmCorps. Over the years, and very slowly, Trent became like a son to Lucien, but not necessarily in the traditional sense. Their relationship was built on a wholly intellectual foundation. As a side note, Lucien learned about Trent's father and difficult childhood. It was unimportant to Lucien and didn't factor into any part of their relationship. It was merely interesting to him. Interesting to both of them, from a nurture versus nature perspective. What quality did Trent possess that allowed him to thrive and become successful in light of such an abusive upbringing?

As Lucien read through the email, none of it made sense. Trent said he needed to disable all communication from the field lab, they had all of the specimens, Lt. Christopher Silver and Dr. Gabrielle Gale had been dealt with, and he would be en route with the extraction team soon. Then, nearly twelve hours later, General Holton reported that the extraction team had come under attack and he suspected everyone on his team to be dead. He hadn't heard from Trent since.

Dead? Trent couldn't be dead. Trent said he had everything under control. Could those rogue agents, Chris and Gabrielle, have killed him? The thought of

Chris and Gabrielle taking something from Lucien, something that was *his*, someone he cared for, filled him with a rage he'd never experienced before.

Lucien was well-versed in dealing with anger. Through the years, he'd learned to suppress feelings of anger he often felt in the face of those sorrowful, less intelligent beings. This rage, though, he couldn't suppress. He was filled with an electric urge to destroy something. It stiffened his fingers into fists and spread through his entire body. He couldn't physically ignore it, and he could not get to Chris and Gabrielle to unleash his wrath. He tried to imagine how he would destroy them, but that just raised the temperature of his fury. Lucien needed a release. He had never been in a situation where he was mentally and physically overcome. He unzipped his pants and relieved himself the only way he could. As the electric pulses of ecstasy spread from his groin to his stomach, his ire settled to a more manageable level and he could function once again.

As he neatly folded the tissue and dropped it in the trash, his computer chimed. He clicked open the screen to see General Holton. Appearing much more relaxed, General Holton wore his casual military shirt.

"Robert," Lucien greeted him.

"Bloodhound Unit has done their first high-altitude flyover at the extraction location. They report zero movement."

"Ok, what's that mean?"

"Either the survivors are in their huts, there's no survivors, or they've left the area."

"Well, that narrows things down." Lucien rolled his eyes.

"I'm just keeping you informed. They will do two more flyovers. If they deem the area safe, they will land."

"Then what?"

"They will do a full investigation of the area and begin to track our target. Depending on what they find, they will either engage or isolate."

"I want Trent located first. We also need his equipment, including his computer. If another organization or country is behind this, they could have everything."

"I told you, there's nothing to suggest that anyone is behind this other than the natives."

"I find that extremely difficult to believe."

"No one got into Brazil after our team. We've closely monitored everything. We watched and stopped the very small IFP team. There were no others. Brazil isn't even aware of our presence there. Their immigration agents never recorded our arrival. If this was a large-scale attack initiated by another country or organization, they would've had to have been there waiting and known exactly where your team was headed, which they weren't entirely sure of themselves."

"I think the point is, we don't know a goddamned thing. You've failed and now we're in this situation."

"You're wrong. I will tell you again..." General

Holton paused, taking a breath and folding his hands in front of his keyboard. His military training showed in the slow, strong, calmness of his response. "This is precisely what we know. Soon after reaching the target village, Dr. Gale and Silver went rogue. They joined a faction of insurgents that caught our boys off guard. It's *your* people that joined and possibly incited insurgents, which indicates the failure happened on *your* side. But, this is a mission for all Americans, so I'm not going to play this useless blame game. At this point, all we can do is move forward."

"Fine. I suppose you're right, *at this point.* I want Trent found first," Lucien said.

"It will likely be his remains."

"I want him accounted for. Then we need to find his lab work and the samples he collected."

"Roger. We believe his work to either be in his lab or possibly the plane for extraction. That's where the bulk of the fighting took place. I should have some answers within the next twelve hours." General Holton promptly ended the video conference.

"Let's hope," Lucien mumbled to himself as he settled back at his desk and began looking over the data from his genetically enhanced specimens safely ensconced in his lab. At least some things were working in his favor. Several of the specimens had been born and were thriving. All postnatal tests indicated they were all healthy, normally developing babies.

Lucien didn't love the idea of experimenting on

children, and in any other instance he would not allow this. However, he was so confident in the capabilities of his work that he didn't consider this to be experimental. Plus, with the ideal humans that would result, he felt justified, if not obligated to continue his work. They would make the world a better place. They would be the leaders of the future, ringing in a new era of equality. They would be healthy. There would be no more disease.

This was nothing like the crimes some other countries had allowed in their experiments, like human-monkey hybrids. Granted, the human-monkey hybrid was created as a way to harvest organs for human transplants. Which, in theory, sounded good, but in practice, Lucien found it detestable. Farms of primates with human organs taken to slaughter seemed cruel to him. Furthermore, as a scientist, Lucien knew full well it was quite possible for the human cells to migrate to other areas, like the brain. While the media, the various lauded institutes of science, and the world at large were led to believe these experimental chimeras never made it past the early embryonic stage, Lucien knew different.

A business acquaintance of Lucien's had shown him pictures and videos of the poor, wretched creature that emerged from these experiments. Sparse, wiry hair covered his body and crept up his neck and towards his face. His black eyes were strangely human, as was his nose, though his mouth and brow protruded much farther, making it clear this creature was far from human. He wore athletic shorts and a tee-shirt. He walked completely upright, with a natural gait. Although, when he ran to catch a ball, he immediately hunched over, which was indicative of his primate nature. The most frightening aspect of this experiment was this chimera spoke. His intellect was far below average, and his speech was slow and strained, but he clearly had a degree of self-awareness. Sadly, this creature appeared sick. He had a hacking cough and visible sores on his body, breaking through patches of hair. Just thinking about this experiment gave Lucien the chills.

What truly bothered Lucien the most about this abomination was that this experiment clearly blended human and animal DNA. Though, when AmCorps attempted to isolate a single animal EVE-0 gene, those experiments inevitably ended in tragic and sometimes violent outcomes. The image of the crimson mass with his connective tissue dissolved in his hospital bed, Subject #12, was galling when compared to this successfully blended chimera. While it was hard to accept, Lucien knew these failures would ultimately lead to the best outcome. The extended time it was taking to isolate a human-based EVE-0 gene would continue to whittle down the population to the point that it would be much easier for him to rehabilitate the survivors and take a step towards, no, to take a *leap* towards the future.

Lucien pulled up a video of the first birth of one of his modified specimens. He admired the baby's strong cry and vitals. He found the sound soothing. This perfect human would usher in a better future. Lucien considered this his greatest accomplishment to date. And, as soon as he was able to isolate the EVE-0 gene, his work would be fully realized and the human race would leap into the next era.

6 – PULL THE TRIGGER

When Gabby's eyes fluttered open, the cave was almost pitch black. The only light came from the smoldering embers in the hearth. As her eyes slowly adjusted, she could see everyone was fast asleep. It was eerily quiet and it dawned on Gabby that the howling wind was no longer even a whisper. She let out a sigh of relief and stood.

As she tried to dodge the sleeping bodies in the dark, she accidentally kicked Chris.

"Gabs," Chris whispered, his eyes barely opening, "what are you doing?"

"I need to use the restroom and get some air."

"You have to use the pot, in the back."

"The wind stopped."

"What?"

"The wind stopped. I can go outside."

Chris listened for a moment. "Alright, I'll meet you out there."

"I'm fine, stay."

"I have to piss, too."

Gabby rolled her eyes. He meant well but was suffocating her.

There was debris from the storm everywhere, but the fresh air invigorated Gabby. She hadn't noticed how stuffy the cave had become. The wind had died down to a soft breeze and light rain. The first ray of light, though stunted by clouds and trees, let in just enough sun for Gabby to see the silhouette of the jungle. The canopy stopped the soft raindrops from reaching her, but made the most beautiful sound. It reminded Gabby of the sleep machine she used at home. The recording she had fallen asleep to, tucked into her comfortable bed, next to Trent, was identical to the jungle's chorus of soft raindrops, insects, and birds she now heard. Gabby let out a small chuckle at the irony of this and decided to use this moment of nostalgia as a hug of comfort. In her old life as an emergency room doctor facing the harsh realities of life and death, she was the first person to use rationality to dispel what some may take as a sign from another realm. Now, though, she saw things differently.

Gabby found a private spot to relieve herself. As she pulled up her pants, she heard Chris stumble out of the cave.

"Gabs?" he quietly called.

"I'm right here," she said as she stepped out from behind an enormous tree.

Chris smiled. "It feels good out here."

Gabby nodded, taking a deep breath. The breeze was the slightest bit cool and carried the most intoxicating scent. It smelled faintly like perfume, sweet yet peppery. Gabby took another deep breath.

"Do you smell that?" she asked, inhaling again. "It smells so good!"

"Don't ask me how I know this, but that's the tonka bean," Chris said.

"What's a tonka bean?"

"It's a bean that grows wild here and all over South and Central America. It's used as a natural perfume base. It smells like a mix of vanilla, almond, and cinnamon or cloves or something. I can't remember."

"How do you know all of this?"

"My sister used them to make a natural perfume as part of her wellness line. She started a fair-trade company and taught local women how to harvest and process them for her perfume." Chris moved closer to Gabby and put his arms on her shoulders. "Are you feeling better today?"

Gabby momentarily wanted to collapse into the warmth of his embrace, but pulled away. "Yeah. Do you think I have time to watch another video before we head out?"

"I think so. We didn't cover as much distance as I wanted to, but the storm likely delayed everyone."

"Sounds go—"

"Shhh," Chris paused, tilting his head, "hear that?"

Gabby shook her head no.

"It's a faint buzzing," Chris whispered.

"Oh yeah," Gabby replied.

It was so faint and so hard to hear, but it was there.

"Could be drones. We need to make sure we stay under the canopy today and get as much distance in as possible."

As they made their way back into the cave, everyone else was just waking up. Their hosts pulled back the curtain of leaves and the braided door they held in place with two boulders, letting in the morning light.

Chris explained the situation to the rest of the team as Gabby pulled out the computer. She clicked on the video marked #3.

"So," Trent began, "I guess I should tell you why the EVE-0 gene became inactive. Wait," Trent held up his hands in the video, "don't get upset. I know I lied to you. I'm sorry. I didn't have time to explain everything to you in a way I would've liked to. This will be a difficult pill for you to swallow, bad pun intended." Trent smiled sheepishly and Gabby remembered why she had fallen for him. He was so brilliant and strong, yet could appear so innocent at times. Gabby remembered their first date. She had recently passed his genetics class at Johns Hopkins and was wrapping up her residency. He was no longer her professor and they were free to date. She was awed by his ability to deftly hop from a deep conversation to a lighthearted chat filled with silly puns. With his sandy blonde hair that perfectly matched his stunning golden eyes, it was hard for Gabby to believe Dr. Martins wanted to go on a date with her. Though, as soon as they sat down at the bar, they felt natural. Trent's lighthearted side, and to an extent, hers too, dimmed once they found themselves on the front line of pandemic after pandemic. This was a side of him she hadn't seen in so long. On the computer screen, Trent let out an exhale and the seriousness she knew all too well returned. "Remember how EVE-0 is a sort of reader gene? It interprets messages from the environment, mainly through viruses and bacteria, and tells our bodies how to evolve. This gene operates through the immune system. That's why when EVE-0 became dormant, we faced this onslaught of pandemics. What I didn't have a chance to tell you is why this happened." Trent cocked his head and squinted his eyes. "It's shockingly simple, almost stupidly simple, but we've poisoned ourselves. Well, more specifically, we've poisoned ourselves with a variety of chemical hormone disrupters, the biggest offender being Bisphenols or plastic. I know, it seems too simple, too stupid, too ridiculous to be true, but sadly it is. Remember that massive plastic jug you carried around your residency with you after you saw it on the Today Show?" Gabby let out a loud, nervous chuckle and everyone in the cave turned to look at her.

"Sorry, it's really not funny," she said, and returned her attention to the screen.

"Everything is in plastic, and those chemicals

are hormone disrupters. We've known this and we should've seen this coming, but didn't. It's so ridiculously simple, it's almost hard to believe. When I first learned this, I almost laughed. I didn't want to believe we were poisoning ourselves into extinction, but we're not the first empire to collapse from this sort of thing."

Trent paused and looked away from the computer screen. "Leave them there and collect the next ten. Thanks, Kukua." Trent paused, watching something offscreen. "Ok, sorry, like I was saying, it's really quite simple. Bisphenol A, BPA, is actually a very strong hormone disruptor. We realized this and tried to find replacements, though they weren't any better. I know you're a doctor, a very good doctor, so I don't need to explain this to you. Though modern medicine has downplayed the true importance of hormones for decade, hormones direct virtually every system in our entire body, or at least initiate processes that affect each system. As a doctor, you know that this includes gene regulation and expression. When you think back, the signs were all there. The obesity epidemic, diabetes. Actually, endocrine and metabolic disorders have been on the rise for decades. Obviously, they've been treated with medicines fairly successfully. Though we never considered the root cause of these conditions and the genetic damage that was resulting. Now, not only is our infrastructure completely reliant on these materials, but our environment is so full of these chemicals they're unavoidable." Trent paused and bit his lip. "I should be more specific; it wasn't plastic alone. It was several things that set the stage. Things we have been trying, or talking about correcting, for many years. Think of it like this: those things like overused pharmaceuticals and antibiotics, they were the gun, whereas overcrowding, pesticides, chemicals, and other hormone-disrupters, they were the bullet. BPA and really all phthalates pulled the trigger. Believe me, I know how stupid this sounds. I wish it wasn't true, but it is. The safe houses have been constructed and operate without any plastics, which was incredibly difficult, but I'll tell you more about it in another video. I'm sure you need some time to process all of this. We've figured out a way around it, but there's some implications associated with this. I will explain it all later. Remember to take Michaela's help. I love you," Trent said directly to the camera, then the screen went black.

Gabby hadn't noticed Chris had been watching the video with her.

"That's…" Chris paused, trying to find the right words, "ridiculous. Did Trent really say we poisoned ourselves with plastic?"

"It's not that ridiculous. The Roman Empire poisoned themselves with lead," Gabby snapped.

"I mean, it's so simple and seems so obvious. How did we not stop this decades ago? Before we were on the brink of extinction."

"I don't know. Hindsight is 20/20, I guess," Gabby

said, scratching her head.

Chris looked at Gabby, and she shrugged. There was nothing more they could say. No words could make them feel any less stupid.

"Breakfast, then we need to move on. Are you packed up?"

Gabby nodded.

7 – IN THE MUD

Gabby was happy to be on the move again. Not only was it a distraction from her sadness, but she was glad to be out of the cave. The air was fresh and the coolness of the mountains trickled down to this valley, keeping the temperature warm but comfortable. It was nothing like the brutally humid days on the river when they first set off from Manaus. The thick canopy of the jungle blocked the sun enough to be clement, and the hike was bearable. About thirty minutes into their hike, they passed a few more indigenous people that had fled to the Nothing.

Chris leaned in. "Rodrigo said they're not dangerous, but don't look at them. They've been condemned."

"That's sad," Gabby said as they passed the outcast group. The group was completely ignoring Gabby and the others as they walked. It was almost as if they refused to acknowledge their presence. It appeared to be a family group. There were two teenage boys; the younger of the two boys had down syndrome. Gabby guessed he was why they had been banished. The two boys were playing some sort of game with a small boulder and a circle they had drawn in the sand. One boy would roll it and try to get it in the circle, and the other would push it back. The younger boy looked at Gabby as she passed, and she smiled. He grinned back. His brother scolded him and he quickly looked down. The mother ran over and hugged both boys. She let them keep playing their game once Gabby and her crew were a safe distance away.

A few hours into the hike, Gabby started to notice the scenery changing. The carpet of dried leaves began to dampen, then become wet. The path became darker, the canopy of leaves thicker, and everything seemed to be shrouded in shade. The trail was becoming very difficult to traverse. It was almost impossible to find solid footing and she stumbled often. Gabby's knees were covered in mud; it was like walking on ice topped with a layer of gel.

The trail began to slope down slightly and the mud became so deep it was up to Gabby's ankles. The mire clung to each step Gabby took, making it difficult to move. The jungle's vivid shades of green were now merely a variety of grey.

Soon, the mud had crept up to Gabby's calves and into her boots. The slimy grain of wet dirt rubbing against her made her skin crawl. With each step, the claws of the muck got stronger and stronger. She was exhausted and the smell coming from the mud was threatening to bring her breakfast back up. It was a combination of rotten eggs and sour milk.

"Chris, is there another path we can take?" Gabby said, breaking the silence of the group.

"No. This is the only safe way to get to our next camp. Chief Ëpë said there are some violent groups in this area that we need to avoid and the only way is to go through this."

"All day?"

Chris nodded yes. "The thick canopy is also protecting us from AmCorps."

"I can't do this much longer."

"Yeah, it sucks, literally," Chris laughed as his foot made a sucking sound as it left the grips of the mud.

"Seriously? If you think now is a good time for jokes, can you at least make them funny?" Gabby said with a sly grin.

"You think you can do better?"

"No, but your mudd-ah can," she laughed.

"No, just no," Chris laughed, rolling his eyes.

Gabby smiled and looked at Chris. "Do you feel okay today? No headaches or unusual pains?" Gabby asked.

"Yeah, I'm fine."

"Good, just checking."

Gabby suddenly felt something wrap around her ankle in the deep mud. As she lifted her leg to shake it off, the mud-soaked feathers of a dead bird clung to her calf like glue. She frantically kicked her leg, but the corpse's wings had wrapped around her and held tight. A seed of panic formed in the pit of her stomach and began to sprout, quickly filling her chest. Gabby had always had a minor phobia of birds, and the feeling of dead bird feathers on her skin was tantamount to mental torture. Gabby kicked harder with each kick, sending globs of sludge flying. A lump of mud hit her cheek and she froze. The blood drained from her face just as Chris turned to look at her. He saw the dead bird on her leg and looked as if he might vomit.

"Get it off," Gabby said.

"Let me find a stick," he replied.

"No, just get it off now," she demanded.

Chris tried to kick it off with his boot, but only managed to separate a wing from the body, exposing a pile of maggots feasting on the bird's innards. Chris immediately turned and puked.

HAWA-317 turned around at this commotion. She quickly took in the scene, walked back towards them, and easily peeled off the bird.

"Thank you, Mayalú," Gabby said.

HAWA-317, or Mayalú as Gabby was coming to know her as, smiled back at Gabby, then quickly resumed her position next to Roiti and Kena. She said something to them and they laughed.

"I hate birds," Chris said, wiping his mouth.

"That's pretty obvious, soldier," Gabby said with a slight roll of her eyes.

She had to take deep breaths to keep herself from

throwing up, but couldn't pass up an opportunity to make fun of Chris. The hike moved on. Gabby forced herself to follow, though her skin crawled. All she wanted to do was take a shower.

The team continued to plow through the afternoon. They didn't stop for a single break. By the early evening, the mud was still past her ankles and every muscle in her body ached.

"Chhh," Chief Ëpë said and held his hand up.

Everyone froze. Gabby strained to listen, but could only hear the normal sounds of the jungle—there was the high-pitched bird calls and a few howler monkeys in the distance, but that was it.

Chief Ëpë motioned an arch with his hands and the warriors surrounded Gabby and HAWA-317. Roi-ti and Kena stood on each side of Mayalú. Rodrigo and Chris took up the flank positions while Chief Ëpë and the shaman slowly moved towards the front. Suddenly, a string of arrows shot past the group, narrowly missing them. An arrow came so close to Gabby, it kicked a strand of her hair up. The team froze.

8 – SUBJECT 13

Lucien slammed his hand on the buzzer to the main lab. "Where's Osiris?"

"He's on his way up, sir," a soft female voice buzzed in.

"He was supposed to be here ten minutes ago," Lucien snapped.

"I'm sorry, sir. He had an issue with the printer," the voice calmly responded. There was a soft tap on Lucien's office door and it slowly opened.

"You're late, Sy," Lucien said.

"I'm sorry, the printer—"

"It's fine, I don't need excuses. Do you have the potential subjects?"

Sy closed the door behind himself and made his way to Lucien's desk. Dr. Osiris Azazel, or Sy, had been Trent's right-hand man for the past three years, following his graduation from Harvard Medical School. Sy was tall and fit, his muscles straining the seams of his lab coat. His perfectly formed features were complimented by his bronze skin and thick, glossy black hair. Sy laid a stack of papers down on Lucien's desk. Each paper featured a picture of an individual along with a list of vitals and personal health information.

"I have three potential subjects," Sy began. "Like you asked for, they are all guards in here."

"Ok, who do you want to pick?" Lucien asked.

"There's only one single guard. The others both have wives and children in here."

"So, it's pretty obvious who we should go with."

"It's not quite that simple. The single guard's vitals aren't quite ideal."

"Why did you include him?" Lucien frowned.

"His sugar levels have consistently hovered around 141 mg/dl which is just one or two mg's above normal. It could indicate prediabetes if it continues to rise."

"I don't like that. Are there any other issues?"

"His cholesterol is also slightly elevated. His total cholesterol is 200, which is the upper end of the normal range. However, his LDL is 129, which is borderline high."

"So, do you see the problem here?" Lucien asked. Sy nodded.

"Let's take a step back." Lucien narrowed his eyes on Sy. "Why are we running this experiment?"

"So that we have options. Ideally, we will find a treatment that does not require live human specimens with an active EVE-0 gene."

"That's correct. Tell me you understand why this

is important."

"Of course," Sy replied. "Obviously, there's a very limited supply of living specimens with an active EVE-0."

"So, you do understand why this next test is so important. Did we not discuss approaching this test differently? With ideal subjects?" Lucien asked.

"Yes."

"So?"

"Both these guards have ideal biomarkers. They are perfectly healthy. They have incredibly low inflammation levels and not only meet, but exceed, our test requirements."

"Perfect. Who should we go with?"

"Guard A has a son and a daughter. Guard B has only a daughter." Sy slid the pages over to Lucien to look at.

"Who do you want to go with?" Lucien asked without looking at the papers.

"Guard B. Statistically speaking, a girl is less likely to be affected by the lack of a father," Sy replied.

"Good choice. What are you going to tell him?" Lucien cocked his head.

"He has been chosen to be the first subject to receive this experimental treatment because of his supreme physical condition. Should something go awry, his wife and daughter will receive one million dollars and be ensured a place to live. They will remain in the safe house until it's considered safe to return to normalcy, upon which they will be provided with a home and money to live on."

"Perfect. But what if Guard B says no?" Lucien asked.

"We won't give him that option."

"What if he still doesn't agree?" Lucien pressed him.

Sy hesitated only a moment. "We use force?"

"If necessary. Oh, and tell his wife he's been removed from the population due to an undisclosed issue of utmost importance."

Sy nodded his head, stood up, and turned to leave.

"Wait, Sy," Lucien called. "Pull him out of circulation now and bring him here. Tell the lab to prep a room in the secure zone. We'll get him in tonight and start."

Sy nodded.

Lucien clicked open his computer. He checked the name of Guard B, Lt. Johnathan "Johnnie" Williams. He pulled his file up. A former Navy SEAL, Johnnie had numerous accolades and medals. Though more importantly, biologically he was perfectly healthy and genetically he had absolutely no markers for future disease. He was not just the first healthy subject they would experiment on; he was a perfect specimen.

Lucien felt good about this experiment. He had an alternate plan that would allow him to approach this issue of saving and improving the human race a bit differently. Rather than try to reactivate the EVE-

0 gene in vivo through a viral vector, he would take Johnnie's genetic material and reactivate the EVE-0 gene in vitro. Lucien would still use the CRISPR method to edit Johnnie's genes, however, he would do it in a test tube first. Lucien would then administer Johnnie's own corrected genetic material using pressurized vascular delivery further accelerated through the use of a strongly applied electrical field. Lucien smiled, impressed by his own genius. While things hadn't seemed to go his way recently, he knew that regardless, he would eventually think his way through any obstacle. Though reactivating the EVE-0 gene with the living specimens AmCorps brought back from the Amazon would remain the primary treatment objective, he would feel better with a backup plan. He crossed his arms and sat back in his chair. Then came a soft tap on his office door. And here was his backup plan...

"Dr. Sabara," Sy said, "this is Lt. Johnathan Williams."

"It's an honor, Dr. Sabara. Please, call me Johnnie." Johnnie said, smiling wide.

"Sy," Lucien smiled, "have you told Johnnie the good news?"

"Not yet. I thought you'd like to tell him."

"Great, please sit," Lucien said.

Sy and Johnnie sat down opposite of Lucien at his desk. Sy turned his seat slightly, so it faced Johnnie.

"I recently brought your file to Dr. Sabara's attention because you are one of the healthiest and genetically perfect individuals we have in here," Sy said.

"Yes," Lucien continued, "and we'd like you to be the first to receive an experimental treatment."

"Really?" Johnnie asked with a furrowed brow.

"Yes," Sy answered.

"However, as the first, we want you to be aware of some risks associated with this important position."

"Ok," Johnnie said.

"It's an untested method. You will be the first, and there are risks. You could have an adverse reaction," Lucien started.

"What sort of adverse reaction? Could I die?" Johnnie asked.

"That's not outside the realm of possibility," Sy replied.

"But," Lucien broke in quickly, "you could also be the first modern human to reactivate their EVE-0 gene and re-usher the world back into a state of normalcy—a modern era of living again. I would tell you you'll be a hero, but you already are. This will make you more than a hero; you will be like Neil Armstrong; you will be the first to take a step into a new era."

"What about my wife and daughter?"

"We have prepared a document—a contract. In it we will give you one million dollars for agreeing to take this treatment. In the small chance you experience an adverse reaction, that money will go to your wife and daughter. Furthermore, they will be guaranteed a place in the safe house for as long as needed and once we're out, we will provide them with a house that's completely paid for." Lucien passed the contract to Johnnie, pointing out that passage.

"What are the chances of an adverse reaction?" Johnnie asked.

"Very small," Sy insisted. "We have absolutely no reason to believe this will not go as planned. We've run this test on chimpanzees numerous times, and it's worked perfectly every time."

"Chimpanzees?"

"Yes," Lucien replied. "Did you know we share 98.8% of our DNA with chimps?"

Johnnie nodded. "One million?"

"Yes." Sy smiled.

"You know what," Lucien reached a hand out for the contract, "let's make it two million. The economy will be so good once we return to normal, you will want to enjoy it. Travel, buy a few nice cars," Lucien said.

"Yeah, ok," Johnnie said, grinning and handing the contract back for the correction to double his compensation.

9 - GUARDIANS

Gabby felt her neck. The arrow had come so close to her it nicked her skin and a single drop of blood trickled down, tracing the line of her sternomastoid muscle. Gabby panicked. If the arrow had been even a millimeter closer, she could have bled to death from the cut thanks to the blood thinner in her system. She frantically looked into the thick trees nearby, but saw no sign of attackers. Chief Ëpë and the shaman slowly began to walk forward with their hands up and heads bowed. Another round of arrows came terrifyingly close, yet Chief Ëpë and the shaman continued. All of a sudden, two warriors dropped from trees. The warrior closest to Gabby wore no clothes, just a draping of necklaces that crisscrossed his chest. Some were woven while others had some sort of claw laced into them. Resting on his head sat a feathered headband with the dried head of a caiman on the crown. His eyes were painted red and he held a bow at the ready. The warrior opposite of him wore tattered modern denim shorts and a torn tee-shirt with just the shadow of a worn-off logo. A bright band of feathers rested on the crown of his head. He had a bow and arrows draped over his shoulders and carried a spear.

"Lobo Mau!" Rodrigo yelled.

The warrior in modern clothes suddenly looked towards Rodrigo and his eyes widened.

"Gato é você?" the warrior yelled.

Rodrigo smiled; they grabbed each other's forearms, and the two exchanged words in a language Gabby didn't recognize.

Rodrigo called Chief Ëpë and the shaman over, and they spoke for what seemed like forever to Gabby. She was beyond relieved, but her legs were still so itchy. She didn't want to scratch them. With each itch, she pictured the rotting corpse of the bird wrapped around them. Finally, they called Chris and Gabby over. As they spoke to Chris in Portuguese, Gabby listened. Every once in a while, she picked up on a word, but didn't understand enough to make sense of the conversation.

"This is Francesco de Frances. His story is very similar to Rodrigo's. His family was killed by loggers. He trained with Rodrigo and was a guardian of the forest with him for a while. Eventually, he ended up in Peru where he assimilated with this group. They have been in the process of relocating. There is another group in the area; they want to let them know they're peaceful but they are having a difficult time making contact," Chris said, filling Gabby in.

"What do you mean 'trouble making contact'?" Gabby asked.

"There is a small but very territorial group that lives in this area. Francesco said they want to settle on the outskirts of their land, though every time they get close, this group threatens to attack. They've sent war parties that have driven them out to their current location."

"So?"

"Well, we're lucky Rodrigo knew Francesco, but now we're caught in the middle of some hostility. Actually, we're making it worse for them. Both groups will associate us with loggers, drug smugglers, or everyone that's terrorized them. We're going to Francesco's encampment and we'll figure it out from there."

Gabby was struck by an overwhelming, sudden sense of guilt at the realization Francesco wanted to help them even though it would bring harm to them.

"Stop. We can't go," Gabby blurted out.

"Gabs, what are you talking about?"

"I don't want to hurt anyone else. We've caused enough trouble for the people here," Gabby said.

"We're only going to be there for one night," Chris replied. "We need to try to figure out a plan or at least a destination."

"Gab-y-el," Francesco said, approaching them, "speak little English. Know danger. Us help friends. You come."

"You should stay away from us. There are very dangerous people that are tracking us. I don't want you to get hurt or killed," Gabby said.

"Us want help. It important. You come," Francesco said.

Chris nodded to Gabby. She relented, though the guilt did not subside.

The deep mud began to dry and soon they veered off onto a hidden trail. A thick covering of trees and brush hung low over their heads. So low, Chris had to walk hunched over. A monkey peeked through the tangled branches and vines. A tiny hand reached down and pulled Gabby's hair. She brushed it away. She was tired of animals. At this point, she was just tired. Uncomfortable. Miserable.

After nearly two hours of this cramped, uncomfortable trek, the team came to a small opening and Francesco's camp. It surprised Gabby. The opening was still covered by a high canopy of trees, though the low brush had been cleared. Rather than tents or huts that rested on the ground, this camp employed platforms and leaves so that it was built up and into the massive tree branches.

Chris and Gabby exchanged surprised looks. It reminded Gabby of a vacation her grandparents had taken her on as a kid. They stayed in tree house cabins built into the redwood forest in Northern California. It was incredible. The trip was mystical. The trees were so massive and ancient, there was something electric about them, an energy they put out into the world. At the time, it seemed like magic to Gabby.

"Wow," Chris said. "I thought I had a cool tree house when I was a kid."

"I wasn't expecting this," Gabby agreed.

Francesco told them to wait at the base while he took Chief Ëpë to meet his people and explain the situation. Gabby and Chris happily sat down on the solid ground at the base of these massive trees. Gabby rested her tired body on a soft layer of moss. It was exquisite.

Chris checked out the area. He did a quick perimeter sweep, then came and sat next to Gabby.

"Did you know trees communicate?" Gabby said, eager to break the silence and escape her own thoughts. "They have a network that's connected through small fungal filaments and they send out messages as electrical pulses. They make a crackling noise in their roots that humans can't hear, and they release pheromones and other scent signals into the air."

"Trees talk?" Chris asked, clearly happy to make light conversation.

"Yeah, in much more sophisticated ways than most people realize. I learned about it on a nature trip my grandparents took me on."

"Are you sure that's not some hippy-dippy theory?"

"I'm sure. It's proven."

"Then why didn't we learn that in school?" Chris laughed.

"I don't know, it's well-documented," Gabby said. "In Africa, when a giraffe starts eating the leaves on an acacia tree, that tree releases ethylene gas as a sort of distress signal. When neighboring trees detect the gas, they pump tannins into their leaves in such monumental quantities it can sicken or even kill a large mammal that eats those leaves."

"It's not just the breaking of the leaves that releases the ethylene gas?" Chris asked, craning his neck to try and peek up at the conversation taking place above them.

"No."

"Then why aren't there dead giraffes all over the place?"

"Because the giraffes know to not eat from trees within the range of the ethylene gas."

Chris crinkled his brow at Gabby.

"Look it up," Gabby added, "it's established science."

Without warning, an arrow stuck in the tree, just above Chris.

"Get down," Chris yelled, simultaneously pulling out his gun and scanning the surroundings.

"*Chris, não attire,*" Rodrigo yelled.

"Don't shoot, stay low," Chris mumbled.

All at once, a group of warriors stepped out from the forest. They yelled three words in complete unison. Gabby couldn't understand what they said.

The warriors were painted black. Their bodies were covered in black handprints, while their faces were all painted slightly different. There were only four warriors that Gabby saw. One warrior had his face under his eyes painted black. Another had just his eyes painted black. The third had his entire face painted. The fourth warrior had his eyes painted along with a swirl design on his cheeks. Even standing in the sun, they looked like they were consumed by shadows.

The fourth warrior abruptly looked directly at Gabby, and his eyes narrowed. They were filled with anger. His lips moved, bringing the others' attention to Gabby. The warrior with just his eyes painted black grinned and aimed his arrow directly at her. He drew back his arm. Another warrior made a loud cackling sound and they howled in unison. The warrior aiming his arrow at Gabby laughed and relaxed his arm. Then they were gone.

Francesco came down as soon as the warriors left. He quickly spoke to Chris and Rodrigo.

"Grab your stuff," Chris told Gabby. "We're going up."

"I don't feel good about bringing more people into this. Maybe we should keep moving."

"We need Francesco's help. They want us to stay."

"But..."

"We have to. We need to stop for at least a night. You can watch some more videos. We need to try to contact Michaela and we need a safe spot while we put a plan into action."

Gabby didn't budge.

"Gabs, come on."

She finally picked up her bag, and climbed up the ladder.

PART II

"Science can not stop while ethics catches up."
-Elvin Stackman
Life Magazine, January 9, 1950

10 - ACTIVE

Sitting at his electron microscope in the main lab, Lucien focused in on the sample of Johnnie's evolution gene. As Lucien focused the viewer, every part of Johnnie's DNA came into focus. Electron microscope technology had grown leaps and bounds in recent years, thanks to an increased need for gene-based medicines and vaccines. Samples no longer required stains. Electron microscope technology was able to automatically add color to the computerized image.

Lucien pulled away from the viewer and clicked a key on the attached computer. The screen flicked on showing an image of Johnnie's gene magnified one hundred million times. Each component was automatically given a color. Essentially, the computer was able to interpret the information from the tightly focused electron beam scan and convert it to this beautiful image. To Lucien, this was art. This image made Michelangelo's work look like a toddler's crayon drawing.

Lucien admired the bright blue incandescent nanoblades that carried the vrCRISPR CAS9 gene edit to Johnnie's EVE-0 gene, ex vivo. As he watched this edit happen in a matter of seconds, a quick flash of light directed the guide gRNA molecule to the targeted EVE-0 gene. It instantly cut the DNA and bound the reactivated EVE-0 gene into the cell's genome. Lucien laughed to himself. The irony of this was comical. The nanoblades that delivered the activated EVE-0 gene, with its corrected gRNA, so humans would be able to once again defend themselves from infection were borrowed from a bacteria's defense system against viruses. Lucien marveled at science's ability to redirect or repurpose nature. In nature, everything was in a constant fight. Some called this balance, but Lucien knew it was really each species, each fungus, each bacteria, each virus's attempt to take over, a position clearly reserved for humans. Which he had just proven.

This was what Lucien lived for. As he reveled in the beauty of this genetic edit, he was also working on a next-generation sequencing of a sample of Johnnie's reactivated genetic material. Before inserting this corrected gRNA into its viral vector for delivery, Lucien needed to ensure that just the EVE-0 gene was affected and there were no unwanted edits elsewhere on the DNA. Everything appeared to be perfect. More than perfect. Beautiful. Lucien was certain that this new methodology would address and fix the issues that arose in the past experiments. By reactivating John-nie's own EVE-0 gene ex vivo and using that to treat him, they would avoid all the past's unforeseen side effects. However, this methodology was not scalable to the general public. If they failed to get the active EVE-0 specimen, assuming this treatment worked, he would be able to treat himself and potentially those he considered vital, but anything beyond that was un-likely.

Lt. Johnathan Williams had told his wife he would be quarantined and out of contact for at least the next four weeks. He was currently in his state-of-the-art hospital room. He had been undergoing basic tests to ensure his vitals were still in peak condition. His vitamin levels were ideal. His basic metabolic panel — perfect. He was the ideal test subject. Lucien almost regretted his decision to run the previous tests on sub-jects that were far from ideal. They had barely been alive to begin with. It wasn't surprising that every oth-er test subject had failed to survive. And, worst of all, he would never be able to erase the image of subject #12. He had been so unhealthy; it was not surprising that his connective tissue failed.

The computer nearby flashed, *Urgent Chat Re-quest from General Holton*. Lucien let it go as the next-generation sequencing completed. No changes outside of the EVE-0 gene in Johnnie's DNA were detected. The computer dinged. General Holton sent another urgent request. Lucien reluctantly pulled his attention away from the microscope and moved over to the lab computer.

"I'm busy," Lucien said as soon as he clicked open the secure chat window.

"This won't take long. Our first unit tracked down a small group of indigenous villagers."

"Great, did they detain them? Do they know if any were our targeted specimens?" Lucien asked.

"Slow down," General Holton said, "In the process of securing them, the villagers killed themselves."

"What?"

"A group of villagers killed themselves when our team approached."

"Are you sure your team wasn't overzealous?"

"I'm fucking sure. My team is a bit shaken up. They were mostly women and children. It was orchestrated and planned out. They used spears and did it incredibly quickly."

"Dammit. So, these fucking idiot rogues have now convinced our specimens to kill themselves."

General Holton nodded.

"Our specimens that they're 'protecting themselves,'" Lucien said, making quotation marks with his hands.

General Holton nodded again.

"They're essentially, no, not essentially, they are *actually* causing the needless deaths of the people they're keeping from us. Us, who would protect them. I've never seen such pure stupidity."

"I agree. However, in the present moment this situation is presenting us with a problem."

Lucien cut General Holton off. "I know what the fucking problem is. We need live specimens. How are you going to bring me a live specimen?"

General Holton froze. "Uhh... well... um... that's what I'm calling you about."

"This is your area of expertise and you're calling me for a solution to your problem?"

"Well, we are... ah... we are going to have to ambush a group and physically seize them before they have time to..." General Holton's voice trailed off.

"And, do you think you'll be able to do that?"

"I'm not going to lie. It will make our mission much, much more difficult but not impossible. Just to be clear, you can't harvest the genetic material from a newly deceased specimen, even minutes after they die?" General Holton raised his eyebrows, betraying his confidence.

"No, the nanosecond a specimen dies, they are no longer of use!" Lucien clicked out of the chat; he didn't have time for such incompetence.

Lucien let out a slow breath and immediately resumed his position at the microscope.

His work was perfect and he was ready to treat Johnnie.

11 – SIDE EFFECT

As Gabby ascended and broke through a layer of leaves, she was overtaken by a feeling of wonder. Part nostalgia from the trip she took with her grandparents, and part sheer amazement at the structure she was in. There was a massive network of platforms and huts connected by a series of catwalks. They wove between the natural growth of branches. The structure was so much larger than Gabby thought it was from the ground. It spanned numerous trees, yet remained inconspicuous. It was a work of engineering genius.

Francesco and his people had cleared two huts for Gabby and her crew. Chris, Rodrigo, and Gabby took one, while Mayalú and her protectors took the other. Chief Ëpë and the shaman went to meet with the chief of Francesco's people. Gabby quickly found a corner in their hut and set up Trent's laptop.

"Hey Gabrielle," Trent opened the next video with. "I told you how BPA turned off the EVE-0 gene through hormone disruption. Lucien saw this coming and has been working towards this outcome for as long as I've known him. I think," Trent paused, "or I thought, what he was doing was the right thing for the human race.

"It's hard to argue against a world free of disease filled with strong, healthy, intelligent humans. Though, the further we went along the more doubts I had. I became really good at justifying them. The first time I had a doubt was when Lucien identified the gene that controlled the hormone receptor that was affected by BPA and affected the EVE-0 gene. This gene also controls menstruation. Lucien's plan is to essentially turn off this gene, so EVE-0 will remain active, allowing us to fight off infections and, therefore, pandemics. The problem with that is it's very likely to leave women unable to menstruate which means they will not be able to become pregnant naturally. They'll still be able to have children with medical assistance, but not on their own.

"I saw this as a problem, where Lucien saw it as an ideal situation. To him this provided the perfect opportunity to improve the human condition. Parents would pick their child's eye color, they would ensure they're free from disease, they're intelligent, good athletes, you get the idea. Besides, it was becoming evident there wouldn't be many survivors, so this plan was easily scalable. He sold me on the idea. Part of me still thinks in an ideal environment it would be an improvement, but I know that's impossible. I..." Trent put his head down and rubbed his forehead. "I don't know what to think. I... I hope you're doing the right thing, Gabrielle." Trent paused again.

"Anyway, putting doubts aside. I'm telling you this because it's very important to tell Michaela. I don't know if there's a way around it, but she needs to know. I also saved a file on this computer called Metatron. It has everything she will need. Send it to her. I love you." Trent ended the video quickly.

Gabby could tell Trent was becoming more stressed. It was hard to see him go through this. It was even more difficult with the guilt she carried knowing Trent died because of her. He stepped in front of a bullet meant for her. The pain ran so deep her chest physically ached. She wondered if she really had done the right thing. Life would be so much easier right now if she had just gone along with the plan. Change was never easy. And at this scale, of course it would be brutal.

"Dammit," Chris yelled.

Gabby looked over to find Chris looking over the railing of their hut. "What's wrong?"

"I dropped the hammer. I need to secure the satellite to this tree so I can raise it closer to the canopy." Chris let out a huff of frustration. "I'll be right back."

Gabby nodded. She might as well watch another video.

"I'm beginning to think I'll never see you again," Trent said, beginning video number five. "There are some things I want you to know. This happened very slow. Looking back, I can see how meticulous Lucien was. He would plant seeds and develop them over years. I thought what we were doing would cure the world. I don't know how I could've been so stupid." Trent put his head down for a moment, then looked back at the screen.

"One of the main issues we were faced with was how to improve the species while also creating a peaceful future for all." Trent bit his lip. "Ok, so years ago researchers at University College London, Harvard, and NYU identified a genotype linked to leadership that was passed down through generations, called rs4950. We obviously needed to incorporate this genotype into our work. However, if every human was driven towards leadership, society could never function.

"At that point, I told Lucien maybe we shouldn't try to improve the human condition. We should just focus on the EVE-0 gene to reactivate the ability to fight off infections. He said if we didn't make improvements, the human race would inevitably wipe itself out with more poor choices that harm the health of our species. He convinced me that if the human race didn't evolve immediately, we were destined for extinction. In that case it would be pointless to even reactivate the EVE-0 gene. To appease my doubts, he put me in charge of developing a process that would mimic nature. I had a team of computer scientists create an algorithm that would randomly distribute genetic enhancements so it was fair. Looking back, I feel stupid. Avoiding genetic diseases is one thing. But I came to realize only characteristics Lucien found suitable would be included, and obviously, it's ridiculous to think an algorithm would keep things fair." Trent took a slow breath.

"Got it," Chris said as he made his way back to the platform, but Gabby remained focused on Trent's video.

"I told you how I gave Chris the passwords to my computer so he could find out what I needed you to know. I saw you guys take off, and I asked Kukua to capture you because I knew what you had to be thinking. But when Kukua brought you in, Lucien had the chat opened. That's why I said what I said. I asked Kukua to place you in the other hut, so I'd be able to talk freely to you there. Lucien had the ability to check in on the lab anytime he wanted. But, you and Chris escaped before I had the chance to tell you this. Gabrielle, if I never see you again, know I'm on your side. None of this is your fault. I've been trying to figure this out for a very long time. Please be careful. Lucien is a very powerful person. He has some very influential people wrapped around his finger. Really, I'm not sure anyone stands a chance against him, but it's worth a try. If you haven't yet, get Metatron to Michaela. I love you."

"Gabs, I know this is hard to hear, but we did what we needed to do," Chris said.

A tear broke free. "I wanted to talk to him," Gabby said, tears now streaming down her cheeks.

Chris reasoned, "If we didn't leave when we did, we would've never been able to hold off the extraction team. He must've known. He had to play both sides and that's exactly what he did. That's why he made these videos for you."

"I feel so bad, I loved him. I could've saved him, but I was too stupid. I just did what I was told, like I always do. I should've stayed."

"Gab, he orchestrated all of this. He knew we needed to leave the village. I'm sorry he didn't get to talk to you, but he wanted you to get away from Am-Corps," Chris said.

Gabby stayed quiet. If she didn't end this conversation, she would wrongly end up blaming Chris for Trent's death.

"Gab," Chris said, "it's not my fault. AmCorps killed him."

"I know, but I wish I could've talked to him." Gabby closed the laptop. "Is the comm up?"

"Yeah, but it's not on yet. We need to do this as quickly as possible. The sat is really hard to trace, but if they do, it could point them in our direction."

"What? Should we even try?"

"Yeah, they have an estimate of where we are. The signal from the satellite comes down in a cone with about a 2,000-mile radius. So, they'll know we're somewhere around here, but they know that anyway.

We just don't want to give them too many opportunities to pinpoint it any closer."

Gabby nodded. She was so filled with guilt her body felt like a hollow shell made of concrete. Simply nodding her head took every ounce of strength she had. All she wanted to do was go to sleep. She now understood what depression felt like, and what her mother spent much of her life dealing with.

Chris powered up the comm computer. It seemed to take forever to come to life and link up to the satellite. As they waited, Chris offered, "I have an idea. I think we should try to contact the group Trent mentioned, IFP, that Paulo was potentially working for." Paulo's name hung in the air, causing the conversation to stall. Chris had executed Paulo, their river guide at the start of their journey into the Amazon, after they found out he had turned out to be a mole for another organization, some ultrareligious group, as Gabby understood it.

Gabby swallowed, then tried to break the quiet. "IFP, right, interfaith religions or something for peace—" She inadvertently gasped at the idea of peace and choked on an inhale of saliva. Once she managed to calm her coughing, she said, "But they were trying to steal the treatment. How do we know they're not as bad as AmCorps and they won't do the same thing?"

"We don't know what their intentions are, but they clearly have money and power behind them, which we're going to need."

Gabby shrugged. She couldn't handle the weight of another lost life on her shoulders. She didn't know what they should do. She felt helpless, lost, confused, guilty. She sat, her body sagging next to Chris, wondering how to discern anyone's intentions anymore. When the link activated, he quickly typed in Michaela's personal email that Trent had provided. He initiated a video call. It took a moment, but the chat began to ring. As the camera powered on and Gabby saw herself on the screen, she didn't recognize the face that stared back at her. She looked away. The chat was accepted, but the screen remained black.

"Who is this?" a computerized voice came through, clearly altered with a voice changer.

"We're trying to reach Michaela Kelstrum. Our friend Trent gave us her contact information," Chris said.

"How do you know Trent?" the voice asked.

"We were with him on the AmCorps mission, but things changed," Chris said.

"What do you mean?"

"Well, we..." Chris struggled to explain the situation.

"I," Gabby interrupted, "was in a relationship with Trent for several years. Under emergency circumstances, I joined him as the doctor on a mission to the Amazon River basin to isolate a cure for the EVE-0 gene. The EVE-0 gene is what's—"

"Yes, yes, I know all about it. Go on," the voice ordered.

"While serving this mission, we uncovered the full and very unethical intentions of AmCorps..." Gabby's voice trailed off.

Chris filled in, "We helped the people of this area defend themselves against the AmCorps forces. Sadly, Trent was killed during this. For now, AmCorps is unable to secure any live specimens for their treatment of the EVE-0 gene. We have fled the location, but more AmCorps units are tracking us."

"Trent made and left some videos before he was killed and he told us to contact you," Gabby added.

The screen suddenly flickered on and the darkness was replaced with Michaela; her short black hair was set back from her face in a wave, her dark brown eyes creased with concern. She wore a black tank top that showed upper arms decorated with black and yellow geometric tattoos.

"Trent's dead?" Michaela said, shaking her head as if she couldn't believe it.

Gabby nodded her head, unable to bring herself to say, "yes."

"AmCorps's extraction agents shot and killed him while attempting to take live specimens, the Matsés people, from Brazil. We were able to stop the first attempt, but they've sent more extraction teams and we need your help," Chris added.

The tattoos on Michaela's arms suddenly turned from yellow to dark green. She looked down at her arms.

"Just a second. I'm a type one diabetic, the tattoos use biosensing ink to tell me when my glucose levels rise so I don't have to check my blood," Michaela said. She grabbed a nearby insulin shot and easily injected it. "I was working at a startup that created different types of dermal biosensors for colorimetric metabolite detection. We're able to monitor metabolites in interstitial fluid that change colors based on levels of PH, glucose, and albumin," Michaela explained.

"That's incredible. I can't believe I've never heard of it," Gabby said.

"We underestimated the resistance we faced from the medical device industry. At the time we were trying to bring this ink to market, international diabetes device sales were $28.5 billion—"

"I don't want to be rude, but we don't have much time to talk right now," Chris interrupted.

"Right, sorry. How can I help?" Michaela asked.

"I'm not sure exactly," Gabby said. "Trent left a file for you. It's called Metatron. In his last video, he told us to send it to you. That's all we know. And we have an idea. There's an organization called Interfaith for Peace, they may be able to help. Don't hand any information over to them though, do a little digging. They used a double agent to try to obtain the treatment early in our mission. His name was Paulo. We thought they were an enemy, but those lines are a little less clear now."

Chris added, "We will check in again when we

can. I will send the file now. Thanks Michaela."

"I will do anything I can." Michaela smiled, though her furrowed brow and creased eyes remained sad.

Gabby nodded and clicked out of the chat. Chris quickly sent the file, and disconnected from the satellite communication.

12 - ELECTRIC

"How are you feeling?" Sy asked.

"Fine," Johnnie answered.

"Great. Dr. Sabara will be in momentarily and we'll get started."

Johnnie nodded from his hospital bed. His IV was in and ready. His vital monitors were on and operating well. Electromagnetic field conductors were set in place around Johnnie's bed. A curved beige arch hovered over his bed, while two beige discs curved around each side of his bed. He was also laying on a PEMF infrared mat. While never used in human gene therapy, Sy proposed that by increasing cellular activity the gene edit would be more likely to effectively take place throughout the entire system and in theory, have less of a chance to affect unwanted edits in the genome, as everything would be more focused.

The human body required electricity to send signals throughout the body. When at peak performance and when cells were stimulated, positive charges entered through an open ION channel which triggered electrical currents to turn into pulses. This positively influenced the performance of the entire human body system. While therapeutic applications had generally relied on a relatively mild form of PEMF, Sy had proposed a much stronger course.

"Good morning, Johnnie," Lucien said as he walked into the room.

"Morning, sir."

"Has anyone explained what's going to happen today?" Lucien asked.

"Not yet," Sy answered. "We were waiting for you to get here."

"I thought I was going to be the first to get the treatment. And, I thought it was just an IV infusion?" Johnnie said.

"Yes, that's correct. Although we are also doing a PEMF treatment, that's pulsed electromagnetic therapy, before and during your treatment to enhance its effectiveness. That's what these panels are set up for."

"It's very safe," Lucien chimed in, "it's been used for decades. However, no one can be in the room while this treatment is underway."

"It's also very relaxing and you'll most likely fall asleep," Sy added, and on cue the nursing staff that had been in the background busily adjusting dials and setting machinery in place, swiftly moved in and secured Johnnie's hands, legs, and waist to the table.

"That's just so you don't fall asleep and roll off the

table or accidentally pull out your IV line," Lucien calmly added.

"We're all set," the male nurse that just secured Johnnie's legs announced.

"We are going to clear out of the room and run a three-hour PEMF therapy session. We will give you a fifteen-minute break, then start the IV fusion and another six-hour PEMF session," Sy said.

"I can't get out of this bed for nine hours?" Johnnie asked.

"That's correct," Sy responded.

"What if I have to go to the bathroom?" Johnnie asked.

"An enhanced commode is built into your chair. Why don't you get him into position," Sy directed to the nursing team.

They hit a button on the side of his bed, and it moved into a partially seated position. A section of the bed rotated beneath his seat to reveal an opening with a shield that gently cupped his penis.

"You're free to urinate and defecate whenever you feel the urge. This high-tech bedpan suctions the waste directly into the sewage system. There's a water hose that will automatically clean you, as well as a UV-light disinfecting system so that everything remains completely sanitary. If you need to be sedated, we can do that as well. Although we're hoping to avoid any unnecessary medicines," Sy said.

"I can't sit here tied to this bed without being

knocked out. My nose is already itching," Johnnie said as he started to squirm.

"Unlock his arms," Lucien ordered. "My apologies. We just needed to fit you to the bed so should you fall asleep or need... want to be sedated, we can keep you safely secured in the bed. We have a large library of movies ready for you. You're also receiving intravenous hydration and nutrition, so you'll be satiated and comfortable throughout this process."

The nurse unlocked Johnnie's arms. A very thin cord remained attached to the light cuffs on his wrists, but his arms were free to move and he scratched his face.

"That's better," Johnnie said.

The two nurses finished setting the equipment in the hospital room and gave Sy a thumbs-up.

"We're ready," Sy announced.

"Great. Johnnie, are you ready?" Lucien asked.

"Yeah."

"Perfect. Which movie would you like to watch? We'll cue it up from the control room," Lucien said, turning towards the control room. "Please post the movie library on Johnnie's screen so he can choose what he'd like to watch." Lucien nodded to Johnnie and the team cleared out. The door sealed behind them.

At the center of the control room was an oversized window that looked in on Johnnie. Although, from inside the room the one-way window was Johnnie's projection television screen. Around the window were a series of computers and screens that monitored and controlled everything for Johnnie and his treatment.

"I think I'd like to watch *Apocalypse Now*," Johnnie announced, unsure of whom to speak to or what direction to speak in.

"Who put *Apocalypse Now* in the library? Is that really a smart choice?" Lucien asked, rolling his eyes.

"It's a classic," Sy answered.

"Ok, we are queuing up the movie and we are going to get your first PEMF treatment started," Lucien said while holding a key on the central computer keyboard. "You will likely feel a surge of energy; try to remain relaxed. You will hear the machines power up." Lucien nodded to Sy, and he flicked an orange switch on a large terminal. The machines immediately gave off a low, pulsing hum that slowly grew in loudness and pitch. "Don't worry, once they power up, they will quiet down," Lucien announced.

After a few minutes, they quieted down.

For the first hour, there was not much to report. Then, Johnnie began to squirm and there was a slight uptick in all of his vitals.

"How are you doing?" Sy chimed in.

"Fine, a little restless. I don't like being stuck in a hospital bed for hours," Johnnie answered.

"I understand. Try to relax and think of this as a day of rest for you."

Following the first PEMF session, every process in Johnnie's body had been elevated. Even his brain waves showed an increase in activity.

"His vitals have—" Sy began.

"Yes, I know," Lucien said, cutting him off. "Shall we?"

The PEMF machines powered down and they entered Johnnie's room.

"You did great," Sy said as they walked into Johnnie's room.

"Can I get up for a few minutes?" he asked.

Lucien answered, "No, I'm sorry. We need you to stay in place. We are starting the treatment, which will take six hours, then you will be free to move around. You should really try to rest during this."

"It feels like I have restless legs; I'd really like to stretch them."

"Sorry, Johnnie," Sy said as he quietly tightened his restraints and patted his shoulder.

"Ready?" Lucien asked.

Sy finished keying in a code on the IV infusion machine.

"Yes." Sy nodded.

"Great, try to get some rest, Johnnie," Lucien said.

They left the room, sealed it, and returned to their observation chamber. They powered the PEMF machines up and initiated the drip of CRISPR CAS-13 cationic lipid nanoparticles to deliver the active EVE-0 gene to Lt. Johnathan "Johnnie" Williams's DNA.

For the first hour, Johnnie continued to writhe under his loose restraints. He couldn't settle on a movie to watch. Eventually, he fell asleep. He slept for hours, though his brain activity became much more dynamic. Lucien returned to his office as the treatment continued. Sy sent him frequent updates, but there wasn't much to report. Johnnie slept through almost the entire treatment. Lucien sat at his desk, clicking his pen. Click…Click…Click… The waiting was frustrating for Lucien. He was accustomed to getting answers, and really anything he wanted, immediately.

With no distractions on hand, he decided to take a walk. He headed towards the maternity ward. He was one of the few people that had access to this section of the safe house, so it would be quiet. As he walked through the empty halls, his mind drifted to the Amazon. He pictured Dr. Gale, she seemed so weak when he met her at AmCorps. Trent's little toy. Now, she had taken so much from him, including time that he'd never get back. People had died as a direct result of her irresponsible actions. He pictured wrapping his hands around her neck and squeezing his frustration out with every last bit of her breath. He was suddenly stopped by the carnal scream of a woman, followed by some grunting, and another scream. A baby was being born, another one of his creations. He stopped. The anguished bellows of this woman were a welcome distraction for Lucien. As he listened, a sense of calm washed over Lucien.

Lucien returned to Johnnie's treatment room as the PEMF machines were powering down and the last drip of the IV fusion was administered. The team entered the room. Johnnie's eyes shot open.

"My head," he screamed, "ahhh, it hurts!"

"What hurts, Johnnie?" Sy asked.

"My brain, it's hot, it's burning!" Johnnie screamed.

"We will give you something for the pain. It's just a headache from the PEMF machine. Put a dose of morphine into his IV," Sy directed, and the male nurse immediately administered a dose.

"Better?" Lucien asked.

"No, it doesn't hurt. It's melting!" Johnnie cried out.

"Johnnie, we have biothermal readers on you. Your body temperature is perfect. I think you may have had a bad dream. Try to relax," Lucien said, glancing at Sy with a furrowed brow.

"I feel it dripping down, it's coming out of my ears. What did you do?" Johnnie screamed and began thrashing. His restraints were loose enough he almost grabbed the IV line. The male nurse acted quickly and tightened them, so he was fully restrained to his bed.

"Johnnie, we need you to relax," Sy said.

Johnnie continued to thrash with such force the fabric cuffs began to tear.

"Sedate him," Lucien ordered.

As the medicine began to take effect, Johnnie's violent movements softened, though he started spitting through failed efforts to talk. "Whaa…" He tried forming words but couldn't.

After a few uneasy minutes, he fell back to sleep. The nurse took a few samples of blood and gave them to Lucien in a biohazard box.

"I will be in the lab," Lucien said.

Sy nodded. "I'm going to start him on an antipsychotic. I think this episode may be a reaction to the PEMF treatment."

"Monitor him closely and keep me updated," Lucien said as he disappeared into the white labyrinth of halls on his way back to his lab.

13- PACHAMAMA

"What was he planning?" Gabby asked Chris.

"I don't know, but it seems like he's been working on something for a while," Chris answered.

"I, it," Gabby paused, "it's like he was living all of these different lives and I had no idea."

"He was, but I don't think he had a choice."
Gabby nodded.

A loud whistle rang out from the jungle floor.

"Stay back," Chris told Gabby as he peered over the edge of their tree house. "Oh shit. Come on."

Gabby peeked over. It was a young man from Chief Ëpë's village. She remembered collecting his saliva for Trent to run his DNA.

Rodrigo and Francesco reached him first and brought him up. He was sitting on the main gathering platform when Chris and Gabby got there across one of the catwalks. He was tired and still catching his breath.

Chris spoke to Rodrigo in Portuguese.

"Can I check him out?" Gabby asked Chris. He translated to Rodrigo; the villager looked at Gabby and smiled, giving her the okay.

He continued talking to Rodrigo while Gabby checked him. Francesco brought him some water, which he gulped down. He was dehydrated, but his vitals were all strong.

"What's going on?" Gabby asked.

"He was leaving the village with his family group. He went to collect some passion fruit before they left. As he was coming back, he saw an extraction team surround his family. Everyone from his family killed themselves before the extraction unit could take them. He hid and watched this happen. He said the extraction team didn't know what to do. At night he snuck out of the area and tracked us."

"They killed themselves? We can't let this keep going," Gabby said.

"Yeah, I know. But, Rodrigo said you have to understand they've been dealing with outside threats like this for decades, maybe a century. They're done. They'd rather die than give their bodies and spirits to their enemy. That's their words, not mine," Chris said, with downcast eyes.

"I understand, but we can't keep fighting Am-Corps. We got lucky once. We can't outrun them forever. And we can't let them keep killing these people. And, what if he was tracked here?" Gabby asked.

"He's sure he wasn't tracked, but—"

Rodrigo interrupted Chris and said something in Portuguese.

"They've asked if we'd like to gather in their main area. They're preparing dinner and they'd like to talk to us."

Gabby nodded. They followed Francesco and Rodrigo up a series of platforms and tiny bridges. Some of them made Gabby very nervous. One bridge had to be seventy feet up and was constructed of a meager two thick branches woven together with vines. If there hadn't been a rope to hold on to, Gabby wouldn't have crossed it. It was so much longer than Gabby expected.

Finally, they came to a vast platform, much bigger than Gabby thought possible. The platform scaled three different massive trees. A middle layer of branches had been cut out so the platform sat above the base branches, but still under the canopy. *The area could accommodate at least fifty to a hundred people,* Gabby thought. The platform was constructed of branches woven together with vines and topped with thick mats. It was incredible.

A group of women sat to one side. They were talking and working on something, but Gabby couldn't see what. Mayalú was with the group of women, while Chief Ëpë, the shaman, Roiti, and Kena were gathered in a large circle with the men of this group.

Rodrigo motioned for Chris to join him in the men's group. At this moment Gabby wanted to disappear, she was completely out of place, not part of either group and chained by a language she couldn't understand.

As Chris followed Rodrigo, Gabby grabbed his arm. "I'm going to sit with the women."

"Are you sure?"

Gabby nodded and Chris smiled.

As Gabby approached the women, they froze and stared at her, absolutely expressionless. Gabby wanted to turn around but didn't. She took another step towards the group, smiled, and gave a sheepish half-wave. They stared for another moment, still expressionless. Mayalú said something and they erupted in laughter. Then they quickly moved and made a space for Gabby to join them.

Gabby sat down and they passed her a bowl. Inside the bowl were massive snails. The shells were about the size of her two fists put together. Hanging out of the shell, the snails' bodies looked like slick, monstrous muscles. Luckily, they weren't moving so they were most likely already cooked.

The woman next to Gabby tapped her leg and smiled. She was missing her two front teeth, though the rest of her teeth were perfectly white. Gabby guessed she may have accidentally knocked them out. She was one of the older women in the group, but still far from elderly. She picked up a snail and a rock and showed Gabby how to crack the shell and pull the body of the snail out. The large slimy body made a loud sloshing sound when she tossed it into a capacious bowl in the center of the group and handed Gabby the rock while she picked up another one.

Gabby picked up a snail. It was surprisingly heavy. The woman pointed to the rock and showed Gabby where to crack the shell. Gabby touched her rock on a small section towards the back of the shell. The woman nodded her head yes and Gabby pounded the rock down on that section. The shell made a bone-crunching sound as it cracked. Once it was broken out, Gabby cleared the shell fragments off. The woman demonstrated how to stick her fingers into the section and move them around. Gabby took a deep breath and stuck her pointer and middle fingers into the shell. She could feel where the slimy body of the snail was attached to the shell. She used her fingers to break the fibrous tissue away from the smooth inner shell. Then the woman demonstrated sliding her whole hand into the opening of the shell and pulling the snail's body out.

Gabby took some deep breaths. She had done worse, she reminded herself. She'd manipulated living human tissue and bones in the emergency room and cut into the mass of internal organs to save patients. This was, well, just a snail — a massive snail, but still a snail. She reached her hand into the shell. She grabbed at the slippery body and pulled. As she freed the body from the shell, a large wad of slime dropped in her lap. She tossed the snail's body into the bowl and grabbed the slime wad off of her lap. She held it in her hand, unsure what to do with it. The woman next to Gabby held out her hand for the slime wad. Gabby happily passed it over and the woman slurped it down with a big smile.

Gabby fell into a routine with the other women. They were happily chatting away and while she couldn't understand, she welcomed the respite from everything that was going on. Gabby was impressed with her snail de-shelling skills. She easily kept up with the other women. Then another wad of slime fell into her lap. The women looked surprised and the women next to her gestured for her to eat it. The slime wad was clear and had no smell. Gabby figured it was the connective tissue that held the snail's body in place, so it was probably basically collagen and possibly very healthy. At least that's what she told herself as she slurped it down.

The consistency was absolutely disgusting and difficult to get down, but once she did there was no aftertaste. She smiled and the group giggled and smiled back. She hoped whatever she just ate was safe; the thought of food poisoning in the jungle horrified her.

As her stomach settled, Chris and Rodrigo approached the group. The women giggled as they spoke to Rodrigo, who then smiled and relayed the conversation to Chris in Portuguese, and Chris smiled.

"I don't want to know," Gabby said as Chris turned to speak to Gabby.

"The good news is you're very lucky and destined to have many babies," Chris smiled.

"I don't want to know what I ate," Gabby said.

"Nope, you definitely don't," Chris said.

Gabby rolled her eyes and took a few deep breaths.

"But, we do have something serious to talk about," Chris said, his face becoming somber.

"What?" Gabby asked.

"They want us to stay here, make this our base of operations," Chris said.

"We can't," Gabby countered.

Chris looked at her and shrugged. "I'm not so sure."

Gabby's brow furrowed and her shoulders raised. "What do you mean? We're being tracked and we don't want to subject anymore," Gabby gestured to the women sitting with her, "people to this disaster."

"'They want us to stay. They understand the risk and we could use a base…" Chris paused. "At least until we have a strong plan."

"No," Gabby said.

"Let's just stay here until we have a chance to talk to Michaela more. We won't contact her from here anymore," Chris said.

"No."

"Hear me out," Chris said, "give it a week. If we don't have any answers by then, we'll move on."

Gabby shook her head, then looked around. Everyone was staring at her. Chief Ëpë, the shaman,

Mayalú, Rodrigo, and the women and men of the tree village.

"No," Gabby said, as the weight of guilt hung heavy on her chest.

"Gabs, they want to help us, and we need it," Chris said.

"No," Gabby said as anger began to make her face burn.

"Let me put it this way, if we want to have a chance to outsmart AmCorps, we need to stay here for a bit. We need to contact Michaela and IFP. We don't have many options. In fact, we don't have any other viable options. The longer we run, the weaker we are."

Chris had a point, running was not helping them. "I realize we can't keep running. But they'll eventually find us here. And then..." She looked around at the innocent yet determined faces around her. She couldn't bear for any of them to be hurt. Yet what options did they have? "Their lives will be on you, not me," she added. But, who was she kidding? Of course, they'd be on her.

"Fine. Whatever makes you feel better." Chris rolled his eyes. "Tomorrow morning we're going to hike for most of the day. Rodrigo and Francesco know how we can throw them off of our trail if they made it this far. We can also contact Michaela while we're out which will help dissipate any signal pings they may track," Chris said.

"Fine," Gabby said, "just until we have a plan."

Chris nodded to Rodrigo, and everyone understood that Gabby had agreed. Rodrigo smiled and said something to Chris.

"They said there's some more snails to de-shell for tonight," Chris said. He started to back away, but Gabby grabbed his arm.

"Great, sit down and I'll show you how to do it."

Wide-eyed, Chris sat next to Gabby and the women erupted in laughter as Gabby showed Chris how to pull the snails from their shells.

A bit later, after the last of the snails were de-shelled, two women took the snails down to the jungle floor to a small fire pit to finish cooking.

Rodrigo came up and said something to Chris, who explained, "Gabs, Rodrigo said Chief Ëpë and the shaman would like to talk to you."

Gabby nodded, then followed Chris and Rodrigo to a corner of the platform. The shaman gestured for Gabby to sit. She sat across from the shaman and Chief Ëpë while Rodrigo and Chris sat next to her. Gabby was nervous, she wasn't sure why, but she felt as though she were in the presence of royalty. The shaman spoke to Rodrigo, who then translated to Chris.

"This is Menye Waempo, Jaguar Father. He is the spiritual guide for his people. He has spent many years learning to speak to spirits."

Gabby looked at the shaman, nodded, and smiled. He then spoke more to Rodrigo, who again translated to Chris.

"In the jungle all living things have spirit. From Pachamama, the Earth Mother herself, to xapiripë. I listen to spirits and teach our people to love all of the cosmos, to love all nature, and the spirits of all living things — the life force."

Gabby touched her heart and smiled at the shaman to show she understood. Again, the shaman spoke to Rodrigo. She had been awed by their lifestyle now for months and had admired the shaman from afar, but this was the first time he was sharing something with them.

"The whites have been coming here for many years. They kill many of us, they bring disease, they take from the forest and destroy it, they disrespect the cosmos. When the forest here dies, their world dies too. They don't realize this has created their epidemics."

Gabby looked at the shaman, her eyes wide with the realization that his understanding of the world was greater than she gave him credit for. In a roundabout way, he was right. Trent had confirmed this. Despite being so disconnected from modernity, he understood exactly what was happening in the world, even more so than she did.

"The sky will fall soon, and all will die if things don't change."

Gabby nodded as the shaman continued to speak to Rodrigo.

"Whites tell us, we must believe in their God. They

say we are tools of Satan and if we don't change our beliefs, God will burn us in fire. We don't fear white God. No true God wants to control spirit. Whites not only kill our people and our home, whites have been our enemy of spirit too." Chris held up his hand to pause Rodrigo, so he had a moment to catch up in his translation. In a matter of weeks, his Portuguese had improved dramatically. Chris took a breath and gestured for Rodrigo to continue.

"When you live in the forest, in our way, you have a deep connection to the spirits. Shamans study this connection for decades before we become a shaman. When you start adopting the ways of the white, when you accept modern conveniences, you lose this connection. Even Rodrigo. He sacrificed his connection to Pachamama to live between the worlds and to protect his people and our way of life. And, ultimately to protect the cosmos and the whole world."

Gabby nodded and the shaman continued.

"You are different. The spirits have told me to trust you and to help you."

"I don't know, I'm not special," Gabby said, but Chris just looked at her. "Tell them what I said."

Finally, Chris obliged. The shaman looked at Gabby, cocked his head to the side, and seemed to be contemplating something. Then he spoke.

"You're right. You are no more special than any other person, alone. The situation, the people, the cosmos brought you here. In this instance, you are special and will have…" Chris paused. *"O que você disse?"* he asked Rodrigo.

He nodded his head as Rodrigo spoke, this time slightly slower.

"Okay, got it," Chris continued, then turned to Gabby. "You're not special, alone. In this particular instance, you are special. This situation is special and it will have a dramatic effect on the future of all living beings."

Gabby wasn't sure how to react. She was humbled, slightly relieved, embarrassed, and scared all at once. She was relieved she wasn't placed on quite the pedestal she had thought she was, and sorry she hadn't quite understood the depth of wisdom the shaman possessed. While he understood things differently, his conclusions were no different than hers. She was embarrassed she ever assumed they thought she was special. And ultimately, she was scared. She had never in her wildest dreams or worst nightmares imagined this. They were on the brink of extinction. She could see that now, more clearly than ever before. The whole world was dying.

Gabby chewed her lip, then turned to Chris and said, "I will do whatever I can," then turned her attention to Chief Ëpë and the shaman. "I will listen to you. I will trust you. I will try to understand what the universe, or cosmos, needs." Gabby squinted and bit her lip again, struggling to find the right thing to say. She felt awkward using the term *cosmos*. She had always considered those new-age types inane and had never believed in such silliness, but things were different now and she had to accept that. She took a breath and continued. "I will try, but I can't promise it will help."

Chris translated. As Rodrigo told the shaman what Gabby had said, the shaman and Chief Ëpë smiled. Then the shaman spoke.

"We will try, together. That is all we can do. But for now, we eat, we nourish our body with a gift from our hosts."

The shaman and Chief Ëpë smiled and stood. As Gabby, Chris, and Rodrigo followed, they turned to see the tree villagers gathering in the space. A group of women stacked coconut shell bowls near the center of the platform. A light rain began to fall. While no drops reached them, the sound of the rain hitting their palm leaf roof was hypnotic.

The villagers gathered in a robust circle. Gabby, Chris, and Rodrigo found a seat in the ring and noticed Mayalú and her warriors sitting across from them.

Gabby heard chanting and singing coming from below. Soon a group of young boys carrying large palm leaves came up. With huge smiles, and small giggles of joy, they were followed by a teen boy that carried a hefty palm branch and wore bright parrot feathers and leaves around his shoulders. They chanted and sang while they shook and waved their palm leaves. They were so full of bliss as their families watched with proud smiles.

As the boys finished and sat with their families, a beautiful stoic woman came into the circle. She wore a headdress of long black feathers that framed her face. Her eyes were painted red and outlined in black. She carried a small bouquet of dried herbs and twigs that smoked. As she waved the bouquet around in graceful arches, she sang the most beautiful chant. Gabby had no idea what she was saying, but it didn't matter. The beauty of it was so moving, Gabby felt the sting of tears threaten to well up.

The woman finished her song and bowed her head. After a moment of quiet, a loud upbeat chant erupted. A group of girls wearing bright feathers joined the woman. They did a lively dance, they smiled, they sang, and they celebrated. Their dance was so full of cheer that they seemed to gracefully float from step to step. In between chants, Rodrigo said something to Chris.

"This is a ceremony to thank Pachamama," Chris told Gabby. "They are asking Pachamama to help them, to send Xapiri spirits from the mountains to dance and protect us."

"It's beautiful," Gabby replied. During her short time in the Amazon, she'd learned the indigenous people believed thousands of shamanic spirits, or *xapiripë,* inhabited the world, living in every plant, animal, rock, and stream.

As the ceremony finished, a group of men and women carried up hulking, steaming bowls and placed them in the center of the group. The chief of the tree village addressed the group. He pointed out Gabby and her group. Then Chief Ëpë said something, bowing his head.

Chris leaned in. "Rodrigo told me he thanked us for visiting and them for opening their homes to us."

Gabby nodded.

The women and men that carried the bowls up began passing out smaller servings of what appeared to be some sort of soup or stew. Gabby quickly recognized pieces of the snail chopped up in the stew. There was also some sort of greens and what looked like tiny yellow peppers. Gabby took a sip. The base was thick and creamy. It was delicious. With the next sip, she got a piece of the snail. The tender meat tasted like a cross between clams and chicken. The tiny yellow peppers added a burst of spice, while the greens were hearty, earthy, and a bit smoky. It was delicious.

"Do you want to know what you're eating, well, other than the snail?" Chris leaned over and asked.

"Yeah, it's delicious. These little peppers are amazing."

"They're wild peppers that grow here. The greens are the leaves of wild cassava plants, which have to be cooked for seven days so they're not toxic. The base is the yuca root of the wild cassava."

Chris smiled and took the last big slurp of his stew. "Tomorrow we will hike to another location and contact Michaela again."

Gabby felt warmed. Whether by his words, the stew, or the gathering of these amazing people — whatever the reason, at least for the moment, her heart calmed with the balm of hope that she'd lost earlier.

14 - ACUTE PHASE

Lucien was in his private lab at the electron microscope conducting a whole genome sequencing on Johnnie's post-treatment DNA. A few years ago, this process would take days to complete. Now it could be completed in minutes and analyzed in hours. Lucien clicked the computer screen on and took in the beauty of Johnnie's reactivated EVE-0 gene. Within minutes, the full analyzed report was complete.

Lucien immediately opened the report and scanned through the data. Everything was nearly perfect. Lucien gritted his teeth. The PGR, progesterone receptor gene, was a member of the steroid receptor superfamily of nuclear receptors and was located on Chromosome 11 and as planned there was a microdeletion at Chromosome 11q22. This gene needed to be switched off so the EVE-0 gene didn't continue to deactivate in the presence of bisphenol-a, BPA or other hormone-disrupting phthalates. That microdeletion indicated this gene had successfully deactivated in Johnnie, while his EVE-0 gene reactivated. This was perfect. However, there was also an almost undetectable synonymous mutation at Chromosome 22q11. Lucien knew this gene was a common deletion syndrome in terms of genetic disease and was also related to high incidences of schizophrenia. Could he have missed it in Johnnie's initial gene sequencing? Did Sy miss a history of schizophrenia in his medical background? Or, and the worst option of all, was there an unintended edit?

A light knock tapped on the closed lab door. Lucien hit a button under the desk and the door opened. It was Sy. He closed the door behind him and joined Lucien at the microscope.

"It looks good," Sy said as he took a seat next to Lucien.

"Almost fucking perfect. But look here," Lucien zoomed in on the view, "there's a synonymous mutation at 22q11," Lucien snapped.

"Oh... I didn't see that."

Lucien let out a breath of frustration. "Do you know anything about this gene?"

"Ah," Sy paused.

"Well?" Lucien snapped.

"A microdeletion at this specific location is known as DiGeorge syndrome, and it happens at birth. It increases a person's risk for schizophrenia by twenty-five percent. It doesn't always present with symptoms but it can cause issues in virtually every organ including cognitive delays."

"How the fuck did this happen?"

"Well, we did an extended family history ques-tionnaire, and Johnnie mentioned an uncle who had schizophrenia and heart disease, but he was also a drug user, so my assumption was his other issues stemmed from drug use. It's possible he may have had a partial 22q11.2 gene deletion. Meaning Johnnie may have carried a predisposition for this syndrome, which was exacerbated during this procedure."

"You didn't think it was important to mention that?" Lucien snapped.

"Most genetic instances of schizophrenia show up early and considering that his mental health was perfect. I didn't think it was worth mentioning. You don't think it's strange that it's a mirror reversal of the intended 11q22 deletion?"

Lucien glared at Sy. "Thanks to your misjudgment, we don't know."

"Well, if he did have a predisposition towards schizophrenia, the PEMF therapy could have set it off. It did hyper-activate his brain," Sy added.

"We need to test this procedure without the PEMF. That may have been an exacerbating factor."

"I will start looking for another subject."

"What's the status of Lt. Williams?"

"He's been sedated and is receiving antipsychotic medicines. We are going to bring him out of sedation soon and reevaluate."

The intercom in Lucien's lab buzzed. "Sir, General Holton is looking for you," a female voice announced.

"I will call him from my office," Lucien replied and turned off the intercom. "Let me see what he wants, then I will meet you in Lt. Johnathan Williams's room. Wait for me to bring him out of sedation."

Sy nodded and promptly left the lab as Lucien made his way to his office. Lucien took deep breaths to try to subdue the building frustration. He hated nature and its unending chaos. Science put things in order, and nothing angered Lucien more than these unexpected outcomes.

Lucien took a seat at his desk and opened the secure chat line.

"Lucien, I have wonderful news," Holton boasted.

"Well?"

"Our full team of extraction agents are set to leave tomorrow. We have a new SuperJet equipped with fifty full, sterile holding tanks that will transfer the specimens from the Amazon here. The tanks are removable and able to keep the specimens completely isolated throughout their transfer to the safe house tank."

"That's your good news? That you're finally able to do your job?" Lucien asked, rolling his eyes.

"No, I'm giving you an update. We also picked up on a satellite ping from the area."

"What?"

"We picked up on a ping. Someone is attempting to communicate from the area," General Holton repeated.

"Who?"

"We're assuming it's Lt. Silver and Dr. Gale, if they survived, which it seems they did."

"Who else could it be?" Lucien asked.

"There was that other unit, those religious freaks, tracking them, but according to our intelligence, they disappeared before our first team made contact."

"I know, so it has to be them."

"We are confident it is," General Holton said.

"So, you have a location on them?"

"Yes, we have the radius the ping originated from."

"Great, are your agents headed there?"

"They've begun scanning the area. My team will be more effective once the rest of the officers arrive."

"But, don't you have a location on them?"

"We've narrowed it down to a 2,000-mile radius," General Holton said.

"2,000 miles? Are you fucking kidding me? That tells us nothing new," Lucien snapped.

"It tells us they're alive, it potentially tells us the direction they're heading, and that they're communicating with someone."

"Who?"

"We don't know. The communication was encrypted."

Lucien clenched his jaw and closed his eyes for a moment. "How do you know it's not those jungle rats playing around with our equipment?"

"They've never seen a computer. Do you really

think that they could use sat comm?"

"Don't bother me again, until you have actual news."

"Wait, the more they communicate the more chances we have to decrypt their communications and find out who they are talking to."

"Put an intelligence team on it," Lucien ordered.

"We have and that's my call to make. My intelligence team thinks they can have the signal decrypted with three to four more communications," Holton snapped.

"Let me know when that happens," Lucien said, and promptly disconnected from the chat. He didn't have time to pat the back of incompetency.

Lucien took a few deep breaths, stood up, smoothed his shirt, and headed towards Lt. Johnathan Williams's hospital room. It didn't take long for him to reach Johnnie's room. The safe house had been designed around Lucien's quarters. He stopped in the PPE room, outside of the unit. Lucien had a personal PPE closet next to the main room. He punched his security code in and entered. Everything was sterile in the safe house, so the PPE requirements had been slightly relaxed. Lucien quickly threw on gloves, a gown, a cap, an N95 mask, and a face shield. It was more to protect him from Johnnie. Lucien was familiar with DiGeorge syndrome and schizophrenia, because when he was a graduate student, he had conducted a genome mapping study of mental health patients. While collecting a sample, a patient had covered Lucien in his spit and bodily fluids. He was so disgusted, he never got over it. He could still feel the splat of phlegm on his cheek.

Sy was already in the room with the two nurses and a doctor. They had the medicine ready to bring Johnnie out of sedation as soon as Lucien arrived.

"Dr. Smith, Sy, let's begin," Lucien announced.

On cue the team began to bring Johnnie out of sedation. His eyelids began to flutter, he started moaning and trying to move. His eyes fluttered open, then squinted shut again.

"Johnnie," Sy said, "can you open your eyes for us?"

He squinted again.

"Johnnie, we need you to open your eyes," Sy said. There was a nurse on each side of his bed, with Dr. Smith posted at the head, monitoring his vitals.

Lucien checked the digital clock above the television. It was 1 p.m., and his only lunch had been a series of bad news.

"Lt. Jonathan Williams," Lucien snapped, "we need you to wake up."

Johnnie's eyes shot open and looked directly at Lucien.

"Johnnie," Sy said as calmly as possible, "how are you feeling today?"

Johnnie just continued to stare at Lucien.

"Johnnie," a nurse said, touching his shoulder,

and he jumped, though he was still restrained.

"Don't touch me," Johnnie said, his speech still slow and slightly strained from the meds.

"How are you feeling?" Lucien asked.

"I know who you are," Johnnie slurred.

"I know you know me. We've spoken several times. Take a minute and let the medicine filter out of your system," Lucien said.

"No," Johnnie said, his voice becoming stronger, "I know who you *really* are."

"I'm Dr. Lucien Sabara. I'm working as hard as I can to save this country and the human race. We hope you're a step towards that goal," Lucien said.

"That's not who you are." Johnnie laughed.

"Is he on antipsychotics?" Sy asked.

Dr. Smith replied, "Yes, he's been receiving lithium since last night."

"Johnnie, try to focus. How are you feeling?" Sy asked.

"You're Lucifer. You can't hide from me," Johnnie growled.

"It's *Lucien*," Sy corrected.

Johnnie shook his head, squinting his eyes. "No... he's... not."

"Enough of this, Johnnie," Lucien ordered. "We have good news. We have successfully reactivated your EVE-0 gene."

"No, no, no, you can't fool me. The dragon in red, wears the clothes of man," Johnnie said through a clenched jaw, spitting as he spoke.

"Lt. Williams, you're having a psychotic episode. Do you have a history of mental illness in your family?" Lucien asked.

Johnnie growled, then moaned and screamed. "Ow! It hurts, take it out of me! Whatever you put into me hurts. Take it out, please." Johnnie began to sob.

"Lt. Silver!" Lucien snapped, and Sy looked at him. "Or, Lt. Williams, pull it together. You have a wife and daughter who need you. You are one of the most elite military officers of the United States of America."

Johnnie began to sob uncontrollably. "Please. Take it out. God, ow, it's melting my brain. It hurts so bad."

"Sedate him," Lucien ordered.

The nurse administered a quick shot. Johnnie's head fell to the pillow, his eyes closed, though he continued to mumble.

Dr. Smith offered, "I think we should switch up his meds. I'd like to add clozapine, though we will have to monitor his heart as there's a slight chance it will cause an irregular heartbeat."

"Fine," Lucien stated, "I will check in on him again tomorrow."

Lucien left. The day couldn't get any worse and he was stuck waiting. He returned to his office and decided he needed a massage. He rang his private masseuse. He knew exactly how to relieve Lucien.

15 – CLIMB

Gabby slept well for the first time in a while, and it was the first time she could remember dreaming in years. She saw Trent last night. She was back at home, in their apartment, but all their furniture had been replaced with plants. She was lying in a hammock when she heard a rustle and saw Trent sitting on a mat under a massive fern. She called to him, and he looked at her, but didn't say anything. She got out of the hammock and started walking towards him, but with every step she took, he got farther away. She tried to run, but her muscles wouldn't work and were suddenly extraordinarily heavy. Trent smiled at her. He was so beautiful. Then she woke up.

Gabby tried desperately to fall back to sleep, to see Trent one more time. But, the sun was coming up and she was wide awake. She lay there, listening to the cheerful sounds of morning, thinking of Trent. Even though they had both been so dedicated to their work, they somehow managed to find time to have fun. She remembered when they decided to try an intro-to-rock-climbing excursion outside of Philadelphia. They'd laughed at each other. They had been terrible and so awkward in their attempt to climb the red argillite slopes. When they finally made it up to the top, they were tired, satisfied, and beyond happy. It was the first time Gabby enjoyed doing something she was terrible at.

She knew they had a long day of hiking ahead of them, so Gabby decided to watch another video before they left. Chris was still sound asleep, so she tried to be as quiet as possible.

She quietly opened the computer, clicked open the folder, and realized this was the last video Trent made. As a wave of despair crashed down on her with the weight of losing someone all over again, her emotions boiled over and she began to sob. She cried silently but tears flowed from her eyes as if a dam had been breached.

She finally got control of her emotions, dried off the tears, and took care to ensure that no one saw her in this emotional state. She took a few deep breaths and decided to get ready for the day. She brushed her teeth, got dressed, and climbed down to the jungle floor to relieve herself. As she made her way back up to their platform, the sun had come up and Chris was waking up.

"Hey," Chris said, "I was about to go look for you."

"Chris," Gabby snapped, "you don't have to look

for me every second of every day."

"I was going to see if you wanted a cup of coffee."

"Oh, thanks. I'm going to watch another video before we leave. It's the last one." Tears threatened to break free as Gabby said that out loud, but she forced them back down.

"Sounds good. I'll see if I can scramble up some breakfast for us, too."

Gabby nodded and sat back down at the computer. She clicked open the file.

"Gabrielle, I guess you know this is my last video. Part of me was hoping I would've had a chance to talk to you by now, but I guess, deep down, I realized this is for the better. I don't know what's going to happen. The extraction team is here, and they are trying to get the specimens out. I'm doing everything I can to delay the process and mix things up, but I have very little control. They're not following my orders, they're reporting to someone else. One of the agents killed Kukua," Trent said, and paused to look towards the door.

"Gabrielle, I don't think I'm going to survive this. During the ayahuasca, I had a dream I died, and I'm ok with that." Trent paused again. "I'm ok with it, because in my dream, you survive. I love you, and before you say anything, I know what you're thinking. We're not the type to believe in these sorts of ridiculous things, but this is different. Things that were in this dream have already happened. I can't explain it and

I've given up trying.

"I hope you've made contact with Michaela. Remember that organization IFP? They're not the enemy. They're more powerful than you realize and they will be important. You are going to need as much help as you can possibly get, if you're going to stand a chance against AmCorps. Good luck, Gabrielle. I love you. And, please don't do anything stupid, like trying the treatment on yourself." Trent smiled. Gabby could hear a burst of gunfire. "I love you." There was a loud bang off-screen. Trent froze and turned his head towards the sound. He suddenly seemed concerned and quickly ended the video.

The abrupt realization that Trent recorded this video moments before she saw him for the last time hit her with such force it nearly knocked the wind out of her. The memory of him stepping in front of the bullet and taking his last breath in her arms kept vividly replaying in her memory with such clarity, it was as if she was reliving that tragic moment over and over. Her heartbeat quickened and her chest tightened. She saw all the blood.

"Gabs... Gabs... Gabrielle," Chris said, touching her shoulder, "are you okay?"

She looked up at him and was able to pull herself back to the present. She took a deep breath.

"Gabs, you're super pale, are you sick?"

"What?" she asked, as the fog was slowly clearing. She was drenched in sweat.

"Are you sick?" Chris felt her cheeks. "You're sweating, but you don't feel hot."

"I'm ok."

"Are you sure?"

She nodded her head. Her heart rate was returning to normal. She took a few more deep breaths.

"I found a few passion fruits and some nuts. And... dah... dah... dah... I heated up some water for a cup of hot coffee." He handed her a stainless mug. "That's the good news. The bad news is, we only have about a week of instant coffee packs left."

"That's going to be rough. I tried to give up coffee a couple years ago and the headache was so brutal, I quit after a day."

"I know all about caffeine headaches. We're not quitters anyway," Chris said, giving Gabby a silly, overly dramatic wink.

"Yeah, " Gabby replied, brushing off Chris's bad joke. "In the last video, Trent said we should try to contact IFP. "

"We need someone and they seem to be the logical go-to."

They quickly ate breakfast, then met Rodrigo, Francesco, and a few of Francesco's guys. As Gabby and Chris descended from the tree, Rodrigo signaled for them to remain quiet for a moment. Francesco and his guys were doing some sort of ritual around a small fire they had lit at the base of the main tree. They finished soon after and put the fire out. Rodrigo and Chris spoke as Gabby took a seat at the base of the tree. There was still a bit of a chill in the early morning air.

"Ready?" Chris asked Gabby.

"Yep," she said, standing. "Where are we headed?"

"Rodrigo said Francesco knows a place near a mountain. The people here are afraid of this area; they believe there are bad spirits there. They've already asked Pachamama for protection and promised the forest their intentions are good. Rodrigo said they're afraid Boitatá will consume our eyes if we," Chris said, pointing to himself and Gabby, "have bad intentions towards the forest. Though, they're most afraid of seeing Mãe-do-Ouro, a spirit so dangerous no one has ever survived it. They say it comes as a ball of fire. Follow their lead and try to be as respectful as possible. They're scared.

"Of course. Let's go," Gabby said. She appreciated their beliefs, but she was tired.

Chris nodded. "*Estamos prontos*, Rodrigo."

By now, hiking through the forest had become almost second nature to Gabby. It was far from enjoyable, but it was bearable. Though today, it seemed a little extra grueling. Gabby's legs quickly began to burn. She was exhausted. The monotony of the jungle was taking its toll on her mental state. She couldn't help but think about Trent. She missed him. There was so much she would tell him if she had the chance. She felt herself sinking into despair. Lost in sad memories, she crashed into the back of Chris with such force, she bounced back and tripped over a rock.

Stumbling back, she was able to break her fall with her hands, so the only pain she felt was a pang of embarrassment. She hadn't noticed that the group had stopped for a short break, and everyone saw her fall. She quickly jumped up.

"Are you ok?" Chris asked.

"I'm fine," Gabby said, brushing off her hands.

"We're stopping for a short break," Chris said, tossing Gabby a granola bar left over from their supplies.

"Thanks," Gabby said, taking a seat on a large root at the base of a tree.

Francesco's three guys took off into the forest. A few minutes later, one of the guys returned, crossed the path, stopped, smiled, and winked at Gabby, then continued through to the other side of the forest. As he stepped into the forest, Gabby could've sworn his feet were on backwards. She jumped up and tried to get a better look, but he was gone. She rubbed her eyes and sat back down. A few minutes later, all three of Francesco's men returned together from the other side of the forest. She quietly began to panic. *Am I losing my mind?* she thought. *No,* she told herself, *I imagined the first guy. It was a trick of the light. I'm not going crazy. I'm just tired. I recently experienced a traumatic event and stress hormones are flooding my brain. I'm fine. I'm fine. I'm fine.* She kept repeating it, trying to reassure herself as she would reassure a patient under similar circumstances.

She ate her granola bar in silence.

"Ready?" Chris asked. "It's only an hour from here, but it's the toughest part of the hike."

"Yeah." Gabby stood. "How do we know this is a good place for communications? Who told you that?"

"Rodrigo and Francesco both knew about this location."

"How do they know? I mean, they both live among people that shun modern living, which obviously includes electronics."

"They said they learned about this location when they trained with the Jungle Guardians."

"Do you believe them?"

"Do we have a reason not to?"

"Not really, but it doesn't make sense," Gabby said.

"Why?" Chris asked.

"Aren't we really deep in protected land? I thought the Guardians were on the outskirts. Rodrigo and Francesco both left the Guardians to rejoin their people."

"Yes, but they brought modern weapons, clothes, and other things with them. Maybe they've maintained their comm capabilities."

"I guess…" Gabby's voice trailed off. Her legs were on fire, and she was too tired to think anymore, let alone talk, and certainly too tired to argue.

Rodrigo suddenly stopped and excitedly called

Chris over. He pointed up in a nearby tree and shushed everyone. He leaned over and whispered something to Chris.

Chris put his arm around Gabby's shoulders and pulled her close. "Look, that's a little ocelot. Listen to it, it's mimicking the cry of a baby tamarin," he whispered.

Gabby peered up. She followed the sound and saw a small cat tucked behind some greenery on a low tree branch. The cat was cute. It had huge eyes and leopard spots, but it was small, not much bigger than a house cat. It was making the weirdest noise. It sounded like a cat attempting to poorly imitate a bird. Gabby started to laugh, but Rodrigo quickly quieted her with a stern look and finger over his mouth. She put her hands up and sheepishly smiled at him. Rodrigo returned the smile and pointed up in the trees, a little higher than the cat's post.

Gabby followed his finger and saw two tiny golden tamarins coming towards the sound. *Oh no,* Gabby thought. She instantly knew what was going on. The cat was imitating the distress cry of a baby tamarin to attract an adult tamarin. She didn't want to look, but couldn't help it. These adorable little tamarins were following the sound and heading right into the cat's reach. Gabby bit her lip. They were getting so close. She covered her eyes, but peered through her fingers. *Closer. Closer.* The monkeys abruptly spotted the cat and turned and ran, but it was too late. The cat lunged.

It caught one of the reddish-gold primates in its claws. They toppled to the jungle floor. The cat landed on top and quickly sank its fangs into the neck of the tamarin. It struggled for a moment, then went limp. The cat quickly dragged the limp body into the cover of the jungle brush and out of their view.

"Holy shit, that was cool," Chris said. "It's like we were in a nature video."

"That poor little monkey," Gabby replied.

"Gabs, it's nature. That's the perfect balance. We're lucky to have seen it in person."

"I guess."

They quickly picked up the pace again. Though, she was still sad for the little monkey. To be honest, she was slightly bothered by the fact that nature, something considered perfect, used deception, something she had always considered a human flaw.

The trail suddenly became steep and rocky. Much more of a climb than a hike.

"Almost there," Chris called down to Gabby.

As she looked up to answer him, she stepped on a loose rock and slipped, cutting her knee.

"Are you ok?" Chris called down as he carefully made his way to her.

"I'm fine. It's a scratch," Gabby said, blotting away the blood with the sleeve of her sweatshirt.

"You go ahead of me," Chris said.

Gabby rolled her eyes but didn't feel like arguing, so she continued on. They eventually caught up to the group, which had gathered ahead. The last part of the trek was a straight climb up a fifty-foot cliff. They were headed to an outcropping of rocks that sat just under the upper canopy and ran along a mountain.

Francesco took a long rope out of his bag and tossed it to Chris. Then, he and his guys quickly scaled the wall while Rodrigo and Chris were deep in conversation. Gabby couldn't believe that she had woken up thinking about the only time she had ever been rock climbing. Was it a coincidence, or could it have been something more? And, most of all, she remembered how terrible she had been with a rope attached to her, keeping her safe. Thankfully, this rock wall was jagged, which left plenty of outcroppings for her to use. She took a deep breath, reached up, and grabbed the first handhold and stepped up. The hold felt sturdy, although there was a lot of loose dirt on it, which made it slippery.

"Wait," Chris yelled, "we're climbing together."

Rodrigo quickly wrapped up his conversation with Chris and began his ascent.

"Rodrigo told me they don't like it here, but they use it when they need to. They believe there are malicious spirits here and that's why their signals have never been picked up." Chris paused. "I don't really believe this, but I'm going to tell you anyway, because it was so important to Rodrigo."

"What?" Gabby asked.

"Rodrigo said to make sure you disturb as little

of the earth as possible. Don't pick up anything. No rocks and especially no gold."

"Gold?" Gabby asked.

"I guess this area is rich in gold. They believe there's a spirit that guards the gold and the mountains. That's the Mãe-do-Ouro they mentioned earlier, the ball of fire. They believe once it appears, it's too late." Chris shrugged. "Just don't pick anything up. The guys are nervous enough being here."

"I won't."

"Let me tie this rope to you. It's just a precaution."

"What if you fall?" Gabby snapped.

"I've been climbing my entire life; do you have experience?"

"Not really," Gabby paused. "Give me the rope."

"Do you know how to tie it?"

She took a step closer to Chris and put her arms up so he could tie the rope to her. He quickly tied a figure eight knot.

"Let me start. I'm taking the more difficult but quicker line." Chris pointed out the path he would take. "You follow this line; it traverses a bit more, but it's a gentle line up." Chris pointed out the path Gabby would follow. "Ready?"

Gabby nodded. She rubbed her hands on her pants, followed the line she was taking one more time, and took the first few steps. It wasn't bad. There was plenty to hang on to.

"Great job," Chris called.

When she was about a third of the way up, the line became a little more difficult to follow. The handhold was just out of her reach, eliminating a three-contact reach. She remembered learning on her first climb she should always maintain three points of contact. Trent couldn't stop laughing when she'd whispered to him that she preferred two points of contact firmly planted on the ground. It was such a bad joke, but he'd laughed anyway. She would have to stretch up on one leg and let go with one hand to get it. As she was working up the courage to reach for the hold, she made the mistake of looking down. She was about thirty or forty feet up, but it seemed so much higher. Her leg muscles started trembling. It wasn't that she was scared; she was enjoying this. It took focus. It felt good to do something so physically demanding and reminiscing provided a blanket of comfort. Her mind was clear for the first time in weeks. Gabby took a deep breath. She closed her eyes and listened to the sounds of the forest. The symphony of soprano bird calls had become comforting to her. She made sure she had a tight grip with her left hand and a good hold with her right leg. She stretched up onto her toe, pulled with her hand, and reached till her fingertips gripped the next hold. She pulled herself up and made it.

When she reached the top, the team quickly followed a crevasse that wound around the edge of the mountain and curved up. It eventually opened to a cavern. They must've climbed to a hundred feet. As she looked out over the jungle, it was like she was at the top of a skyscraper. She saw a group of brightly colored macaws flying over the tree line. Suddenly, she heard a loud screech from the shadows. In a panic, she ducked down, and a brawny bat barreled over her head. It had a furry body, with big ears, a monstrously pointed nose, and leathery wings that stretched out to at least two feet. It opened its mouth to let out another screech, and Gabby could see its razor-sharp teeth.

A chill slid down her spine. It wasn't the bat. There was something in the atmosphere here. A *feeling*. It made the hair on her arms stand up. Chris shined a flashlight to the back of the cavern to make sure there was nothing else hiding in the darkness. Another bat screeched and took off. Then, they were left with only shadows.

Chris quickly began to set up the comm equipment near some very old equipment that had been left over. Chris took out a hammer to the secure the satellite.

"Pare... Pare!" Rodrigo yelled to Chris.

"Oh shit," Chris said, looking at Gabby and scratching his head, "I almost disturbed the earth. The satcom should work if I lean it against this rock." He took the backpack off and tried to use the rocks to counterbalance the satcom extension. After playing around for a few minutes, Rodrigo walked over and offered to hold it in place.

"Obrigado," Chris said. "I can't believe I did that.

They warned me at least a thousand times," Chris whispered to Gabby as he sat by her and the computer. They powered it up and quickly rang Michaela. The chat rang, and rang, and rang. The chat closed. *No Answer* appeared on screen.

"Try again," Gabby said.

Chris rang again. Same thing.

"Do you think she changed her mind?" Gabby asked.

"I don't know," Chris said.

"Try again," Gabby instructed.

Chris rang again.

"Hello... Hello... are you there?" a voice came through.

"Michaela? Are you ok?"

The screen slowly came into focus.

"Sorry, I was in my lab and didn't hear the ring," Michaela answered; she had glasses and her lab coat on.

Gabby let out a breath of relief. "Were you able to look through the files?"

"Yes," Michaela's eyes widened, "Trent gave incredibly detailed instructions. He made this very easy. With an active EVE-0 sample, I will be able to make the treatment incredibly quickly."

"Great," Gabby said.

"Did you look into IFP?" Chris asked.

"I was able to make an initial contact. In Metatron, Trent left the name of someone at IFP, so that's who I reached out to."

"Were they receptive?" Chris asked.

"I think they will be. They were just very vague. They probably want to check everything out. Although they did tell me Paulo wasn't an agent for them. They acted like they had no idea who he was. It was a little bit awkward," Michaela said.

"Are they denying they had an agent on this mission?" Chris asked.

"They were vague, but they didn't deny it. They said no one named or operated as Paulo was their agent."

"That's weird. They probably just wanted a chance to check us out," Chris said.

"Maybe. I'm talking to them again tonight. I will let you know next time we talk," Michaela said.

"Thank you. We will try to contact you again tomorrow," Chris replied.

"Thanks, Michaela," Gabby said.

"I'm so grateful I can help," Michaela replied.

"Stay safe. We're signing off," Chris said.

Michaela nodded and the chat ended.

Chris quickly packed up the gear and they headed back. The climb down was much more time consuming than the climb up. There was a small ledge that traversed the top two-thirds of the rock wall. It was only about ten inches wide, and it took them nearly two hours to make it that far down. They had to face out and slowly shuffle along the ledge. It was by far the scariest thing Gabby had ever done. Gabby used a small section of it when she climbed up, though if she had followed it the entire way up it would've taken her three hours. If she hadn't been so distracted by the prospect that Paulo hadn't been a double agent for IFP, she may have panicked. Once they were closer to the ground, they turned around and climbed down the rocky outcroppings closer to the base.

"Do you think Paulo really wasn't working for IFP?" Gabby asked.

"No, no way. He was obviously working for them," Chris said.

"You don't think it could've been someone else?"

"No, definitely not. Who else could it have been? Kukua?"

"You're right," Gabby said. Kukua, Patrick, Jim, and Bob had never spoken to anyone outside of Brazil till they met Gabby, Chris, and Trent. Gabby smiled, remembering their SpongeBob SquarePants-inspired modern names. They had been so smart and kind, and what little English they knew, they learned from SpongeBob. Gabby couldn't speak another language, yet these four young men, that up until the last few years had never seen a modern convenience, had taught themselves English from a silly cartoon.

The trek back was easier and quicker. They were almost back when they heard screaming. Francesco, Rodrigo, and the guys barreled off in a sprint. It was difficult for Gabby and Chris to keep up, but they managed to stay close enough to not get lost.

As Gabby broke through the last part of the trail and into the clearing under their encampment, she immediately wished she could've turned around. The heads of two of the tree villagers were on stakes driven into the ground at the base of their settlement. Their skin hung in jagged shreds. Coagulating blood still slowly dripped in gelled globs from the heads. The tree villagers were rushing down from their platforms. Some had thrown themselves on the ground, wailing at the base of the heads.

Chris and Gabby slowly made their way to Rodrigo. Tears streamed down his face as he tried to console a distraught Francesco. After the initial sadness rippled through the tree village, it was replaced by a palpable anger. The men began yelling and chanting. Gabby sat to the side of the clearing. She tried to sit as close to a tree as possible. If she could've, she would've disappeared.

"Gabs," Chris tapped her shoulder, "it was the other indigenous group that lives here. Francesco's guys went to make a peace offering today and to try to bargain, but this happened."

"Why?" Gabby asked.

"Why, what?"

"Why," Gabby pointed to the clearing and the heads, "did this happen? It couldn't be because they wanted to make peace. It was because of us."

"No. No, it's not. The other group sent a message that this is their land. This is their food. There's not enough to share. If Francesco's group doesn't leave, they'll all end up like..." Chris gestured towards the heads.

"It had nothing to do with us?"

Chris shrugged. "Not really."

"What did Rodrigo say?" Gabby asked.

"I don't think he would say we were the problem, even if we were."

"What are you not telling me?" Gabby interrupted.

Chris let out a breath. "Rodrigo did say it had nothing to do with us, but I've started to pick up on some words and in the letter, they condemned Francesco's people for helping the whites. Their enemy."

Gabby didn't respond.

"Rodrigo also told me they're going to retaliate. They tried to be fair, but..."

"Wait, what do you mean, retaliate? Like, attack?"

Chris nodded.

Gabby's head dropped. It was becoming nearly impossible for her to see a way through this without more bloodshed.

"This was going to happen whether or not we were here," Chris said. "Fighting is a part of human nature."

16 - THE BABIES

Lucien met Sy in the pediatric neonatal wing of the safe house. Lucien would finally get to examine the first line of AmCorps's children. While they were all only between two days and five weeks old, this was the first time Lucien had the opportunity to admire his work. Sy gave him regular reports, so he knew the babies were all perfectly healthy. In the short time they'd been on this earth, they were thriving.

Lucien decided to take the long way to the pediatric unit. It was after breakfast, and he wanted to walk for a bit. As Lucien moved through the concrete corridor, his heels clicked on the hard floor. He enjoyed the rhythmic announcement of his presence and did nothing to stifle the noise. He spoke to no one along the way. He never wasted time on small talk and the residents of this safe house knew not to approach him.

As he came around the final corner, Lucien saw Sy and Dr. Hollman, the head pediatric geneticist, talking outside of the entrance. Their conversation quickly fizzled out as Lucien approached.

"Sy, Dr. Hollman," Lucien greeted them, "are we ready?"

"Yes," Dr. Hollman answered, "they are waiting to meet you." Dr. Hollman's bushy dark hair and brows were speckled with grey, and he had a gap in his front teeth. Lucien always wondered why he never had it fixed. He was a highly intelligent, accomplished doctor and yet his gap-toothed grin made him look silly and stupid.

Dr. Hollman buzzed them into the welcome room. They were dressed in basic gowns and low-level protective gear; Lucien didn't want any of the nasty things that went along with babies to get on him. Then, Dr. Hollman opened the door to the nursery and held it for Lucien and Sy.

Lucien wasn't prone to emotion. At least, not in the conventional sense. Though he lit up as he saw the rows of babies, quietly lying in their specially-designed, unbreakable, borosilicate glass basinets. Their care team, lined up behind them, all wore light blue scrubs and matching gowns and caps. These perfect children were all there because he created them.

The babies were lined up by age. All wrapped in ivory cotton blankets. Lucien began his examination with the youngest, a two-day-old male.

"Would you like to hold him?" the nurse asked.

Lucien was momentarily stunned by this proposition; he wasn't accustomed to holding his work.

"Sir?" she asked.

"Yes," Lucien said.

The nurse placed this new life into Lucien's arms. With crystal blue eyes, he looked up at Lucien, made eye contact, and held it for a moment. The babe looked around the room. Lucien handed him back to the nurse and she returned him to his bassinet in the quiet of the nursery.

"There's no crying," Sy said, "is that normal?"

"Yes. We have them on a schedule. They are fed and changed before they sense discomfort, so they don't cry. Well, rarely cry," Dr. Hollman said. He looked directly at Lucien, "These are incredible children," Dr. Hollman beamed.

Lucien moved down the row, checking each baby as he walked by. He stopped at a three-week-old girl. She had red curls and green eyes.

"She's beautiful," Lucien said.

Her nurse picked her up and handed her to him. She cocked her head and looked directly at Lucien. Her eyes moved from the top of his head and over his face. She pulled her arm out of the blanket and reached up towards Lucien's face.

"Do they have names?" Lucien asked as he noticed their bassinet cards had just a number, their birthdate, and a sticker indicating their sex.

"Not yet," Dr. Hollman answered. "Now that all of the babies have been born, we're having a naming ceremony with the mothers next week. Since they have such little involvement with them, we thought it would be a nice thing to do."

"I suppose. As long as you remind them what their role is here and that they're serving a greater good. We want to be careful to not allow them to become attached," Lucien warned.

"Yes, of course. We have a psychiatrist that has designed the ceremony for this very purpose," Dr. Hollman replied.

Lucien nodded his head in approval as he walked down the row of infants.

Sy approached a four-week-old girl. The nurse handed her to him. He inspected her, checking her fingers and grasp. He examined her more as if she were a thing, not a child, and quickly returned her to the nurse.

Lucien made his way to the firstborn child. A five-week-old boy. He had big, round, deep-brown eyes. Thick black lashes highlighted their intensity. He had full cheeks, a tiny nose, and a perfectly formed mouth. Black curls swirled around the crown of his head. He was perfect. He looked more like a doll than an infant.

"Sir?" the nurse asked, moving towards the bassinet. Lucien nodded yes and she picked up the child.

"He's heavy," Lucien noted.

"Yes, he's remarkably strong for his age. It's a pattern we're noticing in all of the infants. They're meeting their milestones, both physically and intellectually, well before they should. This child in particular is doing extraordinarily well."

"Is he the genotype rs4950 child?" Lucien asked.

Sy answered, "Yes, I believe the oldest child was determined to be the rs4950 carrier and the birth order went exactly as planned."

Dr. Hollman nodded. "You're correct. He is. In fact, we did an experiment this morning. We held off their early morning feeding to see how they'd react. It took him eight minutes and thirty-two seconds to start crying. The other infants started crying soon after. We fed him first, and when he stopped crying, fifteen of the eighteen other infants also stopped crying, despite not getting fed yet," Dr. Hollman said.

"That's interesting. I didn't expect his leadership qualities to show so early," Lucien said.

Sy began counting the infants. "I thought all twenty of the children had been born. Are we still waiting on one?"

"Well," Dr. Hollman paused, "there is one infant that is not thriving like the others. She may have some sort of condition, but we haven't been able to identify it yet."

"Why haven't I been told?" Lucien snapped.

"She's only six days old and we're not sure yet… We suspect there may be an issue. Actually, we know there's an issue, we just haven't been able to diagnose it yet," Dr. Hollman said.

"Where is the infant?" Sy asked, looking up and down the line for a child that seemed different.

"We're keeping her in another area."

"Take us there," Lucien ordered.

Dr. Hollman spun towards the door, bowing his head towards the nurses as he left. "Thank you, ladies, keep up the excellent work."

The walk to the other room was not far from the nursery, but the scene was entirely different. The infant slept alone in her bassinet. The room was dark. The sound of monitors beeped incessantly. The nurse watched over the child from a station outside the room. The girl had very small eyes, a flattened bridge, and a small nose. The infant's arms were oddly skinny and her fingers were stubby and short.

"As you can see, this infant has several dysmorphic features, though nothing fits a singular diagnosis. We have mapped her DNA as well. We noticed several variables, though nothing that fits a known condition. For example, she has a tiny partial deletion on Chromosome 22, a 22q13.3, as in Phelan-McDermid syndrome. Then, some cells are missing an X chromosome like typical Turner syndrome, but not all," Dr. Hollman explained.

Lucien walked up to the bassinet. The girl was awake and stared up at him even though the skin around her eyes was so tight it made it difficult for her to look up. She stretched her scrawny arm out of the blanket.

"Sy, what are your thoughts?" Lucien asked.

"Clearly, there are issues with this specimen. She

should be studied to determine what went wrong. It appears almost as some form of mosaicism," Sy answered.

"If it were two or three of the specimens that turned out like this, I would agree. However, with only one anomaly, I wonder if it's worth our effort. Perhaps we should dispose of this failed specimen and place our focus on the others," Lucien countered.

"At one hundred children, this would mean five. At 1,000, can you even consider it an anomaly?" Sy said.

"Don't give me a fucking statistics lecture," Lucien snapped. "It's most likely an issue with the mother."

"We should find that out. Doctor, do you think studying this specimen will interfere with your work with the others?" Sy asked.

"No, we have a large staff and are fully capable of attending to each infant," Dr. Hollman answered.

Lucien cocked his head. "Because every other infant is perfect, it has to be an issue with the mother. Have you tested her for alcohol or drug use?"

"No, but these mothers were closely monitored during their entire pregnancies," Dr. Hollman replied.

"Check the mother," Lucien snapped. "If she has any alcohol or drugs in her system, dispose of the child and expel her from the safe house."

"Of course," Dr. Hollman said.

Lucien turned and left, with Sy following not far behind.

Once they were outside of the pediatric unit, Lucien turned to Sy. "Stay with Dr. Hollman and examine the mother. There has to be something with her that caused this issue."

Sy nodded and returned to the pediatric unit.

Lucien took the fast way back to his office. He had pressing issues to deal with. He made it back in five minutes and immediately opened his secure chat line.

"General, I hope you've made progress."

"Lucien, we are always making progress on our end."

"Well?"

"Our full unit has arrived. The base camp is fully operational. They are ready for extraction and have begun their location sweeps."

"Enough excuses. All I hear is that you have not located any viable specimens yet."

"In order to locate specimens, we need our team there and we need everything ready for extraction. I'm telling you that we are ready for extraction. We are now capable of full use of our equipment to locate specimens, swiftly move in, and capture them. We don't want to allow them an opportunity to pull off a stunt like the last one."

Lucien rolled his eyes at General Holton's semantics. "Let me phrase it differently. Do you have any idea of the location of any potential specimens?"

"Not yet, but today they will start using thermal tracking drones."

"Will that even work?"

"We have every reason to expect that they will."

"The Amazon is teaming with animals with thermal outputs similar to humans."

"Yes, and we've updated our analytics to reflect that. Most animals in the Amazon don't travel in groups. That will be another thing that our drones are sweeping for."

"And what about Trent? Have you located him or his remains?"

"Yes, we believe we have found his remains. They were buried in what appears to have been a western ceremony."

"What are you saying?"

"Dr. Gabrielle Gale or Lt. Christopher Silver likely were involved in his burial. In searching his lab, it appears as if an extraction agent may have accidentally killed him."

"What?"

"It seems that he may have been killed by friendly fire, though so much has been disturbed at the scene, it's hard to be sure."

"What are you saying?"

"Did you trust Trent?" General Holton asked.

"Of course. If one of your agents murdered him, you are more incompetent than I thought."

"We're not sure what happened, but rest assured that we're investigating everything."

"What exactly *did* you find, General?"

"There was an extraction agent that was found dead, shot in the back of his head in the lab. There was an imprint from a gun in the sand where he fell, though, no gun was found. There was also a copious pool of blood in the direction of the gun, where we are assuming Trent was killed. Our agents suspect that this extraction agent shot Trent, possibly because he was working with Dr. Gale and Lt. Silver, as he was attempting to secure the specimens for extraction. We also suspect that as this was happening, an insurgent working with Gale and Silver came in and shot this officer from behind. That has led us to assume that Trent was either helping Dr. Gale and Lt. Silver or was at the very least sympathetic to them."

"Let me get this straight. You have a pool of blood and a shadow of a gun, and you think Trent is a double agent?"

"Why would they have buried him if they were working against him?"

"Several reasons. You have no idea how these superstitious indigenous groups work. They may have been attempting to bury all of the bodies."

"Do they even bury their dead?"

"Yes," Lucien snapped. "Do yourself a favor and don't make any more assumptions. Just do your fucking job and bring some viable specimens here. Your handling of this has been pathetic. Your guy was the problem, not mine. If you even dare to suggest that again, I will have you thrown out of the safe house immediately. Remember General, I'm irreplaceable; you are not."

General Holton nodded, then clicked out of the chat.

17 – THE TREATMENT

The tree village was a flurry of activity. The villagers were extremely upset; some were crying while others appeared angry. They were gathering weapons in the main platform area. Mayalú and the warriors helped organize the weapons while Chief Ëpë spoke to the tree village's chief and the two shamans chanted over the weapons as the pile grew.

"We're in a bad position," Chris told Gabby.

"I know; the fighting will attract AmCorps," Gabby said.

"But we can't ask them not to."

"Do you have another idea?" Gabby asked.

"No," Chris said.

"I have an idea." Gabby paused. "Michaela can tell us how to make the treatment here. I'll give it to myself, then offer to go back to AmCorps. And, maybe, we can bring them doses of the treatment in exchange for them leaving the Amazon and its people alone."

"No fucking way!" Chris said.

"Hear me out. I will be the only one that's successfully taken the treatment and possibly the only one that knows exactly how to make and administer it. I'll be more valuable alive, as a study subject, than dead. I'll be protected."

"No, you won't. As soon as they have the treatment in their hands, they'll kill you, then come back here for more."

"I don't think they will and if they do, so be it. At least you'll have more time to figure out how to protect them."

"No, you're not doing that."

"We have to do something, or else all of this will be for nothing. We need to call Michaela tonight and figure out how to create and administer the treatment," Gabby pleaded.

"Trent didn't want you to do it."

"Part of him was probably still thinking there was a chance." Tears filled the corners of Gabby's eyes. "That... that we could still have a future. We didn't talk about it much, but when we did, we talked about having a family."

"I'm sorry." Chris hugged Gabby, then pulled her back. "But, you can't."

"Fine, maybe you're right. But we have to do *something* with the treatment and *something* with Am-Corps, so I thought if I intercept both, then you may have a chance to…"

"Slow down for a minute. We don't even know if it

will work. Let's call Michaela. We'll call from here. At this point, it doesn't matter," Chris said.

"So, we hiked today for nothing," Gabby replied.

Chris shrugged and began setting up the satellite equipment. "Things changed, I don't know what else to say. We had no idea tensions would escalate so quickly."

Gabby handed Chris the computer. "Ready?"

"Almost. Maybe you should look through Trent's lab equipment." Chris looked up. "We only have about an hour of light left; we should get an idea of what's in that pack."

Trent had packed up all of the essential lab equipment into one large backpack. Gabby carefully dragged it over to the sat comm setup. Chris opened the computer and rang Michaela. She didn't answer. Then a chat icon popped up. "Give me five minutes. I'm so sorry."

"Five minutes," Chris said. "I'm going to get an update from Rodrigo."

Gabby nodded. As Chris left, she went through Trent's lab pack. Everything was clearly marked and there was a set of step-by-step instructions. She also found an already made vial of the treatment that contained one dose of HAWA-317 genetic material that was good till November 15, ten days from now.

"Gabs," Chris called as he walked up to the platform, "they're planning to attack tonight."

"Tonight?"

"Yes, though Rodrigo is trying to talk Francesco into waiting a day. It makes more sense. They're most likely expecting an attack tonight."

"Listen…" Gabby paused, she wasn't sure why, but she stopped herself and quickly closed Trent's lab pack. She had been about to tell Chris about the vial she found, but decided to keep that to herself.

"What?"

"It's been five minutes, should we ring her again?" Gabby quickly clicked the chat open and rang Michaela.

"Hi," Michaela answered immediately. "I didn't expect to hear back from you so soon."

"We are dealing with some issues here and need to formulate our plan sooner than anticipated," Chris said.

"What sort of issues?" Michaela asked.

"The group we're currently staying with is fighting with another indigenous group, which we expect will attract the attention of AmCorps. It's also made it too dangerous for us to continue to run," Chris said.

"I spoke to IFP again; that's what I was doing when you called. They want to help. In fact, they're putting a team together. They've actually been working on this for quite some time. Besides their inside agent, who you thought was Paulo, they have others. But, their inside forces are extremely limited and can't do anything without assistance—which won't be able to deploy for at least a few weeks, at the earliest," Michaela said.

"I don't think we'll be able to last for a few more weeks," Gabby said.

"How sizable is their force?" Chris asked.

"They believe it's strong enough to stand up to AmCorps. They said they've been investigating AmCorps for years and have an intelligence unit in place, but they wouldn't tell me who their inside agents are. They don't have the EVE-0 formula and I didn't share it. Not that I won't, I just want to make sure they're fully committed to helping us and we can trust them, and I wanted your permission," Michaela said.

"How difficult is the formula?" Gabby asked.

"It's very easy, it's just dependent on the active EVE-0 genetic material. Although, the silver lining is, once some of the population has been rehabilitated, we may be able to use their genetic material to continue to make the treatment for the whole population," Michaela said.

"I think our only option is to hold out against AmCorps. We have to keep hiding." Chris said.

Gabby thought about disagreeing, as there was no way they could outrun AmCorps for another few weeks, but she let it go. She had an idea that was beginning to take root in the back of her mind.

"I have something else to tell you," Michaela said. "Trent administered the treatment to himself. It worked and there were no side effects, at least not immediately."

"That's great," Chris said, and Gabby nodded her agreement.

"How much genetic material is needed per dose and what is it, blood, right?" Gabby asked.

Michaela looked at Gabby for a moment. "I... I," Gabby stammered, "I'd like to have it ready so when it's time to go, we can leave quickly."

"Good idea. Yes, it's blood," Michaela said, "let me check." Michaela quickly read through a file on her computer. "Found it. Ok, from a standard blood draw of 8.5 milliliters, you'll take 1 milliliter of blood and mix it with 10 ml of 1X RBC Lysis Buffer. Mix it well. Let it sit at room temperature for 5 minutes, then put it in the centrifuge for 5 minutes. Decant the solution, and add 10 milliliters of PBS solution, the phosphate-buffered saline. Centrifuge again. Then you take the final solution and incorporate it into the treatment base. Trent said he has several of these bases prepared and AmCorps has even more. The base is an adenovirus vector encapsulated into a purified omega 3 nanoparticle. Let me do my math..."

Gabby had quickly pulled out a notebook and pen and jotted down exactly what Michaela said.

"...So, 1 ml of human blood is enough to make 10 treatments. That means that with a standard draw of 8.5 ml, you'll get about 80 treatments. So, if you bring home 50 vials of blood, that's enough for 4,000 treatments. But that's a lot of vials to transport."

"Got it. Thanks," Gabby said.

"Real quick," Michaela said, "how do you plan to bring back the blood samples?"

"I'm not sure, I still have to go through the equipment."

Michaela nodded. "I will let IFP know they may need to bring some blood collection equipment when they come to get you out. Considering that AmCorps wasn't planning on collecting blood, just specimens, you might not have the needed equipment to bring it back."

"Good idea," Chris said.

"Good luck. I will share the formula with IFP and keep you posted."

Gabby clicked out of the chat. "Why don't you go talk to Rodrigo and Francesco, and I'll put away the sat comm gear."

As soon as Chris left, Gabby grabbed the single vial of the treatment. Trent clearly marked it as a single adult dose. *He must've left it there for me,* she thought. She put it into a syringe. *Am I really going to do this?* Her palms were sweating. The sun was almost down. *I have to... I have to... Trent had a plan.* She closed her eyes, took a breath, and injected the treatment.

It burned as it went in, but only slightly more than any other vaccine. She could feel it as it spread through her arm. Slowly, the discomfort subsided. Soon, she felt nothing.

Gabby quickly cleaned up the lab equipment. She took a moment to look through the pack and found two kits for blood collections, which meant Trent must've been planning to collect blood. Each kit had a pack of blood collection bags, butterfly needles, tubes, bag sealers, a battery-powered fold out cooler, and a couple small instant ice packs. *Thank you, Trent,* Gabby thought. A sudden wave of sorrow washed over her. If only he had told her, things might've gone differently. He had everything so planned out and she had no idea.

She heard some talking nearby and quickly packed up the lab equipment. She left the blood collection equipment on top and began to take down the sat comm setup.

"Good news," Chris called. "They've decided to attack three or four nights from now. They are going to leave this village tomorrow before dawn, so the others think they've fled."

"That's good," Gabby answered as she nervously looked around to make sure she put the syringe away.

"The sat comm equipment's a little more complicated than it looks, huh?"

Gabby nodded. "Took me a little longer than I thought." She put away the last bit of equipment. "Where are they going to go?"

"They're going to the mountains near where we were. They're nervous about it and some don't want to go, but each family group finally agreed. The shamans are going to do a special ceremony to protect them from the bad spirits there."

"What about us?" Gabby asked.

"They've invited us to go with them, and I think that's our best option. It'll give us some time."

"Okay," Gabby said. "Trent packed several blood collection kits, so he must've been planning on collecting blood instead of specimens all along. When we're at the mountains, I'm going to collect some blood in case we need to leave fast."

"That's probably a good idea, but I don't understand why AmCorps was so set on bringing specimens back if the treatment could be made from blood."

"Insurance, a naturally regenerating source of the treatment." Gabby shrugged. "Maybe they're worried they won't be able to make the treatment from rehabilitated genetic material. I don't know, but I'm tired. When are we leaving?"

"Before dawn. Get some rest."

18 – THE HIDEOUT

"Gab... Gab... wake up," Chris gently rubbed her arm to wake her and a shot of pain cursed through her.

"Ouch."

"What's wrong?"

"Nothing," Gabby said, and avoided rubbing her arm where she'd administered the dose. "I slept weird."

It was still dark, the air was cool, and Gabby craved rest. The injection site on her arm was extremely tender, her whole body ached, and she had a headache.

"We're heading out. You have to wake up," Chris said.

Gabby pulled herself up. "When?"

"Now. Do you feel ok?"

"Yeah, I'm tired."

"Here," Chris handed Gabby a caffeinated nutrition gel, "we're running low on MREs. This'll do the job."

Gabby sucked down the pack. It tasted like chocolate but had the consistency of toothpaste. They loaded up and headed down to meet the others. The entire village was gathering in the clearing. They found Rodrigo, Chief Ëpë, Mayalú, the shaman, and the warriors already in the clearing.

"The first two hours will be difficult in the dark," Chris said as the group began their pilgrimage.

Gabby was exhausted. Her entire body ached. The jungle was pitch black. The large group moved surprisingly quickly through the tight trail. Parents carried the smaller children, while the older children helped with the supplies. Warriors at the front and back of the group had bows and arrows ready.

Gabby stumbled, and Chris grabbed her hand to keep her from falling. He squeezed it, then kept ahold. She needed something to hold onto, and Chris was there.

They marched through the darkness like that for the next several hours. If there had been something for Gabby to be afraid of, she couldn't see it. She had a strange sense of security in this moment. Moving through the jungle felt like something was getting accomplished. It was easier on the mind than waiting, though deep down, Gabby had a bud of guilt threatening to take root. She didn't want to deceive Chris. He had been her partner through all of this, and they had grown close. She knew he would do anything to protect her. She told herself that's why she had to do this. The first rays of light broke through the trees and Gabby looked at Chris. He could be so kind and devoted.

He caught her looking at him and smiled. "What?"

"Nothing." Gabby blushed.

He hugged her, kissed her head, and grabbed her hand again.

"You're a good person," Gabby blurted out.

Chris shook his head in disagreement. "If only you knew some of the things I've done... Where's all this sentiment coming from?"

"Nowhere. I... mmm... I appreciate you and what you've done for everyone here."

"Thanks," Chris said. "Gabs," he paused and pulled her closer to him, squeezing her hand a little tighter, "I've never met anyone like you. I love..."

"Don't," Gabby said, looking up at him. She threw her arms around him and buried her head in his chest.

He held her tight. "I love you, Gabs, that's it. I don't need anything back from you."

She loved him, too. She wasn't sure in what aspect, but they shared a deep bond, and she would leave it at that. Though that was exactly the reason she felt so bad for deceiving him. She took a deep breath, looked up, and smiled at him. He smiled and grabbed her hand again as they caught back up with the others.

The tree villagers passed around some passion fruit and nuts. They snacked but continued walking. They didn't stop once. Gabby could've collapsed. The only thing that kept her going was the group of women up ahead with toddlers tied to their backs and a baby or two tied to their fronts, who seemed to traverse the jungle like they were walking on air.

"I'm so tired," Gabby admitted to Chris.

"Me too. I'm embarrassed to admit it behind this group," Chris said, as the mothers happily chatted and passed snacks to their kids. Chris tossed her another energy gel.

The last hour was the worst. Gabby didn't think she would make it. It was a steady climb over rocks and roots. At one point Gabby tried to sit. "I need a few minutes," she pleaded.

Chris pulled her up. The sun was bright. The jungle steamy. Birds chirped. Monkeys howled. The forest buzzed. Gabby was done. The burning in her legs was so intense she thought they would give out on her at any moment.

Rodrigo tapped Chris. *"Diga a ela, estamos quase lá."*

"Rodrigo said, we're almost there," Chris translated.

Rodrigo gave Gabby a thumbs-up and smiled.

Gabby realized she must've looked as bad as she felt. If she had been any less tired, she would've been embarrassed.

Suddenly, the climb plateaued and they were engulfed in darkness. Moments ago, the jungle had been bright and teeming with life. Now it was dark and quiet. A shiver slid down Gabby's spine. Her senses heightened. Up ahead, Gabby could see a series of caves at the base of a mountain.

The tree villagers became quiet. They were notice-ably nervous. The mothers held their children close.

"They're terrified," Chris whispered to Gabby, "it's just the shadow of the mountains."

"Maybe," Gabby said. Though she had enjoyed plenty of time in the comfort of a shady spot, this was different. There was a heaviness in the atmosphere.

The shamans lit a small fire, then quickly put it out. They fanned the smoke over the villagers while they chanted. The shamans went to each villager. They placed their forehead to the villager's, then their hand to the villager's head, and moved on to the next.

Once they addressed each villager, they made their way to Chris, Gabby, Rodrigo, Mayalú, Roiti, and Kena. They said something to Rodrigo, then Rodrigo said something to Chris.

Chris turned to Gabby. "Our shaman is Menye Waempo, the Jaguar Father. His name is Pajé Dabi, and the tree village shaman is Pajé Amosina." He looked back to Rodrigo who spoke in Portuguese again, then said, "They have a blessing of protection they'd like to do for us."

Gabby smiled. "Tell them, thank you."

Pajé Dabi went to Gabby first. He put his forehead to hers and when he did, Gabby could've sworn she heard him say, "Trust your judgement." She pulled her head back and stared at him with her mouth open. He slightly nodded his head, smiled, then pulled her forehead back to his. Then he chanted. He pulled his forehead away, placed his hand on her head, chanted, then moved on to Chris. Soon, Pajé Amosina came over and did the same thing. When his forehead was to hers, she didn't hear words. Instead, she just felt care and sympathy, as if she was being hugged with no physical embrace. It was such a strange sensation. She wasn't sure if she was imagining it or if the shamans really did transfer thoughts and emotions straight into her brain. She shook her head. One thing she had learned in the jungle was how powerful the imagination was.

As soon as the shamans finished, Gabby leaned over to Chris. "Since we're all together, can you ask Rodrigo to ask Mayalú, Kena, and Roiti if we can draw some blood from them?"

"Now?" Chris asked.

"Yeah, I think we should be ready."

"But, why now?" Chris repeated.

"What if something happens? What if IFP comes to get us, what if the other group follows them and they get attacked, what if AmCorps gets too close? I think we should be ready," Gabby said.

"But what if nothing happens and we're waiting another three weeks? The blood will go bad, and we won't have the collection equipment when we do need it," Chris countered.

"The cooler is fully charged and will last at least a week once it's powered on. It also has a solar recharging panel. So, it will keep the blood good for as long as there's sun."

Chris looked down.

"Please," Gabby urged.

Chris nodded. *"Rodrigo, posso te perguntar uma coisa?"*

"Diga-me," Rodrigo said, and Chris asked him.

As Rodrigo translated to Chief Ëpë, Mayalú, Roi-ti, and Kena, Shaman Dabi rejoined the group. It was hard for Gabby to get a read. They looked hesitant. Then the shaman spoke. Their expressions softened and Chief Ëpë said something to Rodrigo.

"Sim, eles disseram que vão fazer isso," Rodrigo told Chris.

As Chris turned to translate to Gabby, she interrupted him. "They said they'll do it."

Chris nodded.

"While I'm setting everything up, can you explain to them it will seem like a lot of blood, but not to be scared?"

Chris nodded.

Gabby unfolded the cooler container and powered it on. It worked. There was a screen that kept track of the number of hours the cooler charge had. She pulled out the collection kit.

"Chris, can you tell them I'm going to take one pint of blood from them? Which is not very much, considering they have eight to eleven pints in their bodies. Their bodies will replace the blood within two days."

Gabby got everything set up and put on a pair of gloves. "Who wants to go first?"

Chris translated to Rodrigo, and Mayalú smiled and stood up. Gabby smiled and had Mayalú sit on a mat. She tied a rubber band around Mayalú's arm, wiped her elbow crease with an alcohol swab, then gently inserted the butterfly needle. Mayalú's brow creased as the needle slid in, but Gabby smiled at her and she relaxed. The shaman began chanting around them. Chief Ëpë placed his arm on Mayalú's shoulder. Gabby pulled the band off and Mayalú's blood began to fill the bag.

Her eyes grew as she watched blood leave her body. Gabby patted her knee and smiled. She remained nervous, though stoic. Roiti and Kena's blood draws went much the same. The shaman and Chief Ëpë remained by them for the entire process. When Gabby finished and got everything packed up, the shaman chanted over her and the blood.

Gabby got the sense that everyone was nervous. Mayalú, Roiti, and Kena sat huddled closely. No one was speaking. When Gabby looked around, the whole village was clustered in small quiet groups.

"What's going on?" Gabby asked Chris.

"Francesco and a few of the guys are looking for the best place to set up camp."

"We're not staying here?"

"No, they are looking for another cave near here."

"Why's everyone so quiet?"

"They don't want to attract the attention of any bad spirits."

"What's wrong with the cave here?" Gabby asked.

"They found a snake in it, which means it's a gateway to Ukupacha and Supay is here."

"Who's Supay?"

"He's the god of the underworld and evil spirits. He's like their devil."

"How do you know all of this?"

"Rodrigo told me while you were taking their blood."

"It's creepy here," Gabby said.

The shade was growing darker as dusk set in. The shadows began taking on a life of their own. They danced through the jungle, eating each other and growing like a gaggle of demons. She knew her eyes were playing tricks on her, fueled by her imagination. Nevertheless, her belly filled with nervous jitters.

The group stood and quickly began their march again. Gabby grabbed her bag and the blood cooler and thankfully followed the group out of the clearing. A few minutes into the hike, Gabby heard an excited chattering grow and spread through the group. She had no idea what was going on, but she welcomed the boost in mood.

Soon, they were back near the base of the mountain. While it was too dark to notice any unnatural gloom, Gabby didn't get the same uneasy feeling here. The group didn't waste any time gathering outside the cave, though the pace slowed as they condensed to move into the entrance.

The way into the cave was tight. Only one person at a time could squeeze through. The path weaved like that for what seemed like a long time. The ceiling was low and there were people in front of and behind Gabby. She was stuck moving in one direction. Pangs of claustrophobia threatened her calm. Just as panic wrapped around her chest, closed in on her neck, and started to squeeze, the cave opened up into a massive cavern.

It was incredible. At the center, towards the back of the cavern, was a sprawling, leafy tree. Rocks framed the tree on each side, turning it into an altar. The tree villagers had lit a few small fires and torches, giving the cave a soft, warm glow. Just above the tree, Gabby could see a series of small openings in the cave roof.

The cavern was so massive each family was able to have their own space. As Gabby's eyes adjusted to the soft, warm light, she could see vivid red paintings on the walls. The feeling Gabby got inside this cavern was unlike anything she'd ever experienced. The natural beauty made her almost cry. Light from the fires flickered off the towering rock formations like ethereal dancing angels.

The paintings on the walls looked very similar to others that had been found in the Amazon and dated to near the ice age. She remembered learning about their discovery when she was in grade school. These paintings depicted mastodons, giant sloths, and ice age horses that had been extinct for millennia—and now, here she was. To think she was in a cave that ice age humans may have lived in made Gabby realize the human race was meant to endure.

Gabby and Chris took a seat near a small rock formation they rested against.

"I've never seen anything like this. Did you notice the paintings?" Chris asked.

"It's... it's... I don't have any words. I've never been in a place that felt like this," Gabby said.

"Yeah," Chris said as Rodrigo joined them.

Rodrigo said something to Chris and Chris's eyes widened.

Chris turned to Gabby. "This cave is very special. It's been blessed by Pachamama. The tree is the manifestation of that blessing. Rodrigo said it's their equivalent of a holy place. It's protected their people since the beginning of time."

"It's incredible. Did they know about it?" Gabby asked.

Chris spoke first to Rodrigo in Portuguese, then said, "They have heard stories about it, but no one has ever seen it. They believe the caves and mountains are controlled by evil spirits and... *Rodrigo, qual você disse que era o nome dele?*"

"Supay," Rodrigo said.

"Right," Chris said, "they believe Supay controls evil spirits and lives here. The evil spirits are like demons. They come from under the earth through the caves, except, of course, this one. This cave is said to hold very special powers for protection and healing."

"It's a mystical place. I can see why they think that," Gabby agreed.

"They believe it's a sign, you know, that we found it."

"Sign or not, it is amazing."

"Definitely," Chris said.

"Estão preparando uma refeição, uma espécie de festa, vou ajudar. Avisarei quando estiver pronto," Rodrigo said.

"Obrigado," Chris replied as Rodrigo stood and left. "They're making a celebratory meal."

It was easy for Gabby to relax here. She felt truly safe and happy for the first time in years. When the pandemics started, there was a constant sense of fear that never left. She learned to live with it. And there were many moments of happiness, though they were always tempered by the thought of a sudden fever or a loved one getting sick. Becoming a doctor allowed her to tolerate this constant, nagging sense of foreboding. Though here, this fear melted away. She forgot how good it was to feel safe.

The villagers began gathering around the tree. Soon, Gabby and Chris were invited to join them. Once everyone settled around the tree, both shamans stood facing the tree. The tree, Gabby guessed, was close to thirty feet tall. It was lushly covered in bright green leaves that seemed to dance in the flickering light. Hanging from the branches were large pods that resembled a deflated football in shape. Some were bright orange and others had darkened to a burnt red color. They looked almost alien to Gabby.

The shamans joined each other in front of the tree. They faced away from the villagers. Together in perfect unison, they chanted. They lit a small bundle of twigs, then blew the smoke towards the base of the tree. When they finished, they stayed bowed in front of the tree, completely quiet. Every villager was silent. In this utter stillness, Gabby could hear the sounds of life. It was faint, yet carried on the breath of the people and in the beats of their hearts. She closed her eyes and tuned in. It was the most peaceful she'd ever been.

Gabby sensed movement and opened her eyes. The shamans gestured for someone to join them, and a group of women and young girls gathered under the tree. They sang the most ethereal song while the girls danced. It was similar to the welcoming festival from a few nights ago, but so much more sensual. When they finished, the men went up. Their song was strong and forceful. When they finished, everyone bowed to the tree while the shamans sang another chant.

When the ceremony finished, each family group took a turn going up to the tree.

"It's our turn, Gabs," Chris said, pulling Gabby from her trance.

"What?"

"It's our turn to approach the tree and offer our thanks. Rodrigo said this tree is a direct gift from Pachamama, and they believe we should ask for help and protection."

Gabby nodded. "Okay."

Gabby and Chris approached the tree. If she was being completely honest with herself, she felt a bit silly thanking a tree. Yet, when she kneeled under the leafy branches, that feeling disappeared. She was overwhelmed by a sense of awe. Praying didn't come naturally to Gabby, but she thought she'd give it a try. *Okay, thank you Pachamama. Can you help things work out how they are meant to?* she prayed. Please. Gabby heard a crack, then boom, and looked up. A dark red pod had fallen from the tree and now rolled towards her and Chris. Unsure of what this pod was, Gabby panicked and quickly scooted out of its way. Everything seemed to have poisonous teeth in the Amazon. The villagers erupted in laughter. Gabby quickly stood up, sheepishly smiled, and joined Chris back in their spot.

"Gabs, I had no idea you were so scared of chocolate," Chris laughed as they sat down.

"What?"

"You don't know what kind of tree that is?"

"No, but it looks poisonous."

"Really," Chris said, looking at Gabby with his mouth open, feigning shock, "you've never seen a cacao, a chocolate, tree?"

"That's a chocolate tree?"

Chris nodded, then laughed. Rodrigo leaned over and told him something in Portuguese.

"Rodrigo said Pachamama blessed us. That was another sign. The villagers are very happy," Chris said.

"Look at all the old pods underneath, it looks like they fall off all the time."

Chris smiled and shrugged.

Two women walked over to Chris and Gabby, handing them a sturdy leaf. There was a bright orange scoop of something resembling mashed carrots and two sticks skewered with what looked like roasted dates on top. Gabby immediately knew what they were... *grubs*. She had eaten grubs before, but not ones this big. The first time she'd tried grubs, they were tiny, more like peanuts. These were gigantic and Gabby could clearly see that it was, in fact, a grub she would be eating.

Chis leaned over. "In case you're wondering—"

"Nope," Gabby cut him off. She picked up a stick with one of the grubs; she could clearly see its little head and plump body. She tossed it in her mouth and bit down. It was delicious. The skin was crispy, while the creamy inside was rich and slightly sweet.

"They're called suri."

"The grubs?"

"They're actually a palm weevil. They're very fatty and full of vitamins. Dip them in the mashed aguaje."

The next suri Gabby picked up was so large she

couldn't fit the whole thing in her mouth. She dipped it in the mashed aguaje and took a bite. The aguaje tasted like a sugared carrot, which brought out the subtle sweetness of the suri. This meal was so rich and satisfying, it made Gabby immediately want to go to sleep. Yet tonight, she knew she needed to stay awake.

19 – FLOAT TANK

Lucien sat at his desk. He slammed his finger into the call button on his silver comm station. Each safe house had been hardwired for internal communications as an extra security measure.

"Yes, Dr. Sabara?" a female voice promptly came through.

"Find Sy, and have him come to my office."

"Yes sir."

He clicked the secure chat line on his computer. No answer. He rang the chat line again.

"Lucien," General Holton said, and clenched his jaw.

"Tell me you have an update," Lucien ordered.

"I told you I will let you know as soon as I have an update. I realize you have no idea how military operations work, so I will try to explain it again—"

"Don't fucking patronize me. Your ineptitude is pushing us closer to extinction every hour that you're incapable of doing your job."

General Holton rolled his eyes; lines had recently begun to show in his smooth, olive skin. "We've divided the area into quadrants. Each day we conduct a highly detailed search of a particular quadrant. So far, we have searched two quadrants and have not found anything. We are also trying to determine exactly what happened during the initial extraction attempt. There was a significant number of casualties on both sides."

"And?" Lucien asked.

"They had a very large force and most appear to have assimilated into the modern world, which is extremely strange. You can't assemble a force like this without planning."

"So, what are you saying, General?"

"I'm not saying anything, just reporting the facts."

"The facts are, you hired Captain Paulo and put a double agent with my team. Were you ever able to confirm he was working for IFP?"

"No. We've been more focused on the current extraction operation."

"Then focus on it. We have an organized and armed group working against us. I want to know who that group is. I'm getting very tired of waiting for you to do your job," Lucien said, ending the chat.

He took a deep breath in an attempt to calm himself. There was a knock on his door before Sy walked in.

"Have you met the mother?"

"I just left her," Sy answered.

"And?"

"I reviewed everything in her file before I spoke to her. She swears she did everything exactly according to protocol. Except, she almost didn't tell me this, but she broke down in tears and admitted she didn't take the prenatal vitamin we prescribed. She said the vitamin we prescribed had polyethylene glycol and she couldn't tell where the ingredients came from, so she purchased her own organic prenatal vitamins with traceable ingredients."

Lucien scratched his head. "Some people are so stupid, but do you think that could have even affected the outcome?"

"No," Sy answered.

"What do you think we should do?" Lucien asked.

"Clearly we can't keep the mother in our surrogacy program. Both she and her child are a drain on our limited resources. But I'm sure there's a lot we can learn from them. We can put the mother to work in the service department and run some more tests on both of them."

"We can't force her to stay in this new capacity. We need to give her the option to stay or leave. Explain to her that because she did not produce a viable child, she can no longer participate in the surrogacy program. However, if she'd like to work in another job, tell her she can stay in the safe house."

"Okay, and what about the child?"

"We'll get to the child. First, run some tests on the mother. Start with a comprehensive metabolic panel and full blood count," Lucien directed.

"Sounds good," Sy agreed.

"And how's Patient 13?" Lucien asked.

"I just left his room. His vitals are perfect. His EVE-0 gene has fully activated," Sy reported.

"And what about his mental state?"

"He's heavily medicated, so he's not violent anymore. But he is still having delusions and symptoms consistent with schizophrenia. Physically, the treatment has been completely successful."

"That's exactly what's so frustrating. Has he seen his wife yet?"

"No."

"Let's set up a meeting. She may be able to pull him out of this psychotic episode. Have her come here first. I want to prep her so things go smoothly. If she panics, she could make his mania worse."

"I'll go talk to her and the mother now."

"Thank you, Sy." Lucien smiled.

Sy was perfect, according to Lucien, and the world needed more people like him. Thanks to Lucien, it soon would. If it could survive long enough.

Lucien clicked on his computer and a camera view from the nursery came into view. The babies all lay in their bassinets. Not one was crying. Brain development mobiles had been placed above them. Lucien watched these special creations reach and swat at these mobiles, each with an attentive nurse. They were completely content. These were Lucien's children, and they were perfect.

Lucien zoomed in on the oldest child, the leader, as his nurse was teaching him sign language. The nurse showed the child a bottle of milk as she opened and closed her hand. She placed the bottle out of his view. He held his tiny hand up, opened and closed it. The nurse picked him up and fed him. When the bottle was almost gone, he held his small arms up with his palms facing him, then rotated his hands to face out. The nurse nodded, pulled the bottle out, and burped him before laying him back in his bassinet. This child was not even two months old, yet was capable of communicating. Lucien considered the fact that he may have created a human that was superior to himself. Beyond a genius. A natural-born leader. The most perfect human ever born.

The ringer chimed on Lucien's communications center.

"Yes?"

"Sir, I have Sy on the line. I'm patching him through," the familiar female voice said.

"Thank you," Lucien paused.

"Hello?" Sy came through.

"Yes, Sy."

"I just left the mother. She's not sure; she's thinking she may want to leave and wanted to know if she can take over care of the child."

"The answer is no, that child is ours. But take her to see the abomination, so she can see exactly the type of offspring she produces. Be gentle. Tell her we can help her determine if she has any health issues that led to this."

"Exactly what I was thinking. I will bring her by now. Where would you like to meet Patient 13's wife? I will set that up before."

"My office... No, scratch that. Have the coffee shop cleared. We'll meet her there. I think she will be more relaxed there," Lucien said.

"Perfect. It's 11:30, can we meet there at 1:30?"

"That's perfect."

Sy clicked off. Lucien could feel an elevation in his cortisol levels and needed to bring it down. His body would soon experience ill health effects if he didn't relax. This break in activity gave him the perfect opportunity to go into his sensory deprivation hyperbaric oxygen tank.

Lucien hit the ring button on his communication center.

"Yes sir?" the woman asked.

"I'm going into my chamber. Can you make sure that it's fully powered on?"

"Of course, Dr. Sabara."

"I don't want to be interrupted unless it's Sy and extremely urgent."

"Understood, sir."

Lucien heard his chamber power up in the next

room. It would take a couple minutes to ensure the water was at exactly ninety-three degrees. Just enough time for him to change. Lucien opened the closet in his office. Undressed. He hung each piece of clothing on its own hanger. Put on a robe. Shut the closet door and sealed it, before hitting the UVC light program in his closet. In five minutes, his clothes would be disinfected and refreshed while he was in the float tank. The safe house employed a UVC light system to disinfect its living quarters. While UVC light was completely safe to most humans, it was deadly to Lucien due to his genetic condition, xeroderma pigmentosum. Because of this, there were several safety protocols in place so the UVC system could not operate when Lucien, or any other human being, was in this area.

Lucien opened the door to his private lounge behind his office. The float tank pod was open. Lucien hung up the robe, stepped in, laid down, and hit the button to seal the pod. The water was the exact temperature of Lucien's skin. The salt content was so dense Lucien floated and felt absolutely nothing. Oxygen was pumped into the completely dark chamber, which raised the oxygen level from the normal 21% to 100%. Rather than silence, Lucien opted for white noise rain sounds.

Time melted away, and deep relaxation took hold. A sudden ring disrupted his meditation. This had never happened before and initially left him confused. The ring chimed again. Lucien felt for the button to answer.

"This had better be important. Sy should know better than to bother me in here if it's not," Lucien said as he reached for the chamber light button.

"Sir, it's not Sy."

"I told you to only disturb me if Sy needed something extremely important."

"Sir, there's a woman that's called in from a sat comm. She claims to be Dr. Gabrielle Gale. She said she needs to speak with you now and that—"

"It's Dr. Gale? Really?" Lucien said. "Dammit." He hit his head on the top of the chamber as he sat up, quickly finding the open button.

"What should I tell her?"

"Give me two minutes and patch her into my office."

Lucien jumped out of his chamber, quickly rinsed off in the nearby shower, and threw on his robe. When he went to open the closet to dress, the door had locked to complete the UVC sanitation process. Lucien attempted to abort the process, but the system froze. In frustration, he slammed his fist into the keypad. The lights began flashing. He tried his code again. Nothing. Again. Nothing. He slammed his fist into the keypad over and over. Finally, the code took. The system powered down and his closet unlocked. Lucien dressed as quickly as possible and ran to his office, smoothing his shirt and hair as he went.

He quickly sat down, took a breath, and hit the call button on his comm center.

"Connect her in, please."

"Right away, sir."

"Dr. Gale?" Lucien asked.

"Yes," Gabby said.

"This is Dr. Sabara. Are you ok? What happened?"

"Your extraction team killed everyone, including Trent," Gabby's voice cracked.

"Our last report from Trent was that you and Chris had absconded."

"No, you don't understand. The indigenous people despise the white man or any modern-living person. They want nothing to do with us. They have a full army of native fighters that once lived in the indigenous ways. Most of their families were killed by loggers or farmers or drug smugglers. They've been militarily trained and now protect the few remaining indigenous peoples. We thought they were going to kill us. It was terrifying, but we were figuring it out when your team got there. Thanks to Trent's plan, they had just started to trust us, and you ruined it."

"I don't understand."

"You will never bring them back with you. They will kill themselves before they go with you. One hundred years ago they promised to protect their way of life when the first missionaries started coming. Trent had a plan and was in the process of making a bargain. They were going to let him take blood, but your extraction agent killed him before he had the chance."

"I know the extraction team made some mistakes.

I had nothing to do with that. I'm as upset about Trent as you are."

"Then call off the extraction team."

"What?"

"I want to make a deal."

"I don't understand. I want to help you," Lucien said, "but you have to tell me what you need."

"I have enough blood to make more than 10,000 treatments."

"Wh—" Lucien started.

"Wait, I'm not finished. Did Trent tell you that he gave himself and me the treatment and successfully reactivated our EVE-0 genes?" Well, at least Gabby hoped her treatment had been successful like Trent's.

"What?"

"Right. Your extraction agent killed him before he could tell you."

"Dr. Gale, no one is as angry as I am about the extraction team."

"You're wrong about that, but I don't want to argue. I want to make a deal with you. If you leave the Amazon and leave these people alone, you can run all the tests you want on me and I will bring back enough blood to make 10,000 treatments. Trent also thought it may be possible to make treatments from the genetic material of people that have received the treatment and reactivated their gene."

"Ok. And what about Lt. Silver?" Lucien asked.

"What?"

"Lt. Silver?"

"Your extraction team killed him, too. You didn't know that?" Gabby snapped.

"No, they haven't recovered his body yet. Do you know what happened or where he was?"

"Not exactly. I was in Trent's lab with him in the village when the fighting started. Chris went to patrol the area. We heard gunfire, an agent came in and started shooting at us and hit Trent. Someone else came in and shot him. I think a Jungle Guardian. Then I don't know what happened. The next thing I know is it's morning and one of the locals got me. We buried Trent," Gabby's voice cracked again, and she paused, letting out a breath, "then the villagers fled and brought me with them."

"I'm sorry you went through that," Lucien said.

"Just leave the people here alone. You don't need them. Do you know an entire family with women and children killed themselves when your extraction team tried to capture them? That's how much they hate you."

"Yes, and I think it's terrible."

"Then call your dogs off. If you let them keep going, you will end up with no living indigenous people and no treatment. I'm offering you a deal. I have enough genetic material for at least 10,000 treatments and these people trust me. If we find we need more genetic material in the future, I can come and get it. You and your extraction team can't."

"Ok. I will talk to the President of the United States and General Holton. He's responsible for this mess."

"I will come to the extraction point within five days. If I get any word your teams are still hunting people, I won't turn myself over and I will dispose of the genetic material I've collected."

"You have my word. You will be welcomed into the safe house. Of course, you'll have to go through a quarantine period, but we will make sure your quarters are comfortable. We have a few such units contained within the safe house, so we'll be able to talk and immediately get to work."

"Fine."

"Dr. Gale, thank you."

The line immediately went dead.

Lucien's head was spinning. He'd never been confused like this before. *Can I trust Dr. Gale*, he wondered? He took a breath. The extraction team had been a disaster, that much was certain. The fact was, Dr. Gale had what he needed. If she'd survived this long, she wouldn't reach out to him with a lie, knowing that if she returned to the safe house without the genetic material she'd be jailed or worse. He made the decision to move forward with this plan.

He clicked open the secure chat on his computer and rang General Holton and President Spiegel.

General Holton answered first. "Lucien, I already told you I will let you know when I have an update."

"There's been a change of plans," Lucien replied.

President Spiegel clicked on. "General, Dr. Sabara, what's going on?"

"Your guess is as good as mine," General Holton scoffed.

"Lucien?" President Spiegel asked.

"I was just contacted by Dr. Gabrielle Gale. I'd like you to take the extraction operation out of General Holton's control and place it under me. We're in this mess because of General Holton. I want to place a hold on all extraction operations. Dr. Gale is in possession of enough genetic material to make at least 10,000 treatments. Trent also successfully gave her the treatment, before Holton's team murdered him."

"Absolutely not," General Holton snapped.

"If General Holton is allowed to continue on, the indigenous people and the genetic material we need will be gone. We need to pause our operations there, long enough to bring Dr. Gale back and reevaluate." Lucien countered.

"That's bullshit—" General Holton said.

"Enough, General," President Spiegel interrupted. "You've had more than enough time. I want the treatment here. Lucien, they are now reporting to you. You have my permission to pause all operations and handle things as you see fit. General, I'm extremely disappointed. I thought you possessed enough sense to treat this mission with more sensitivity than a standard military operation."

"I can't believe you actually believe—" General Holton began.

"Enough," President Spiegel warned, "or I will have your stripes removed."

"Fine. I hope for all of our sakes you're right, Lucien." General Holton left the meeting.

"Thank you, Lucien, this is the most relieved I've been in months," President Spiegel said.

"Thank you, Mr. President, me too."

"I will give the directive to pause all military operations and remain at the extraction point. I will also let the command know they are to report directly to you from now on. Commander Jones will be waiting on your directives."

"I appreciate it."

The president left the chat and Lucien let out a breath of relief. Finally, something seemed to be going in the right direction.

Lucien's communication center chimed.

"Hello," Lucien answered.

"I spoke to the mother again and she has decided to stay," Sy said.

"Great."

"The mother asked if I thought there was a chance the child could be cured. I almost said no, but this child provides us a unique opportunity to study and attempt to cure several genetic diseases. So, I said there's a chance and that really pushed her decision to stay. Besides, we will likely need to run frequent tests on the mother as well, so that opens the door for us to also have access to her."

"Perfect. Do we have any rooms in our staff quarters?"

"Yes. I will have her moved and find a job for her. I will see you in an hour."

"Try to find her a job that she will like so she remains cooperative," Lucien directed.

"Got it. I will see you in an hour." Sy hung up the phone.

Lucien leaned back in his chair. His sense of satisfaction began to fray with the realization he now had to wait five days to know whether or not his treatment would make it to him. He was forced to depend on one woman, alone in the Amazon Rainforest, to safely get it to him. *It's only five days. It's under my control. There will be no mistakes... It's only five days, it's under my control, there will be no mistakes.* Lucien repeated this mantra to himself over and over.

20 – WAR PARTY

Gabby slept more in the first night and day she spent in the Pachamama Cave than she had in months, if not years. The cave remained cool, the light soft, and she was bone tired. Chris went with two other villagers, Francesco, and Rodrigo to hunt and gather, but Gabby wanted to stay behind and nap. Gabby had been so exhausted that much of the day was wrapped in a haze. She had stayed up late the night before. She needed to make sure that Chris was deep in sleep before she snuck out to place a sat comm call, but then desperately reached for the comfort of sleep.

"Gabs," Chris shook her, "Gabs."

Gabby's eyes fluttered open. "What?"

"Are you ok?"

"I'm fine, why?"

"You slept all day."

Gabby stretched and finally forced her eyes to open. "I was catching up on sleep."

"Are you sure? You seem pretty out of it."

"I'm sure. I feel great. What time is it?"

"It's close to dinner time."

Gabby sat up, stretching her neck. "Oh, I didn't realize I'd slept that much."

"You're sure you feel alright?"

"Stop, I'm fine. It's comfortable in here and this is the first good sleep I've gotten in a while. I'll be right back."

"Where are you going?"

Gabby jutted her chin out and crinkled her brow. "I haven't moved in twelve hours, where do you think I'm going?"

"Gotcha, but it's been longer than twelve hours," Chris smiled.

"Don't follow me, I'll be fine."

"Someone woke up on the wrong side of the cave."

Gabby shook her head no, rolled her eyes, giggled, and walked away.

The air outside the cave felt nice. She was still grinning. Chris had a way of making her smile. She would miss him. That thought crashed into her much harder than she expected. In this moment, she realized that every part of her wanted to stay with him. She knew what she wanted, but she also knew what she had to do. She was done running. She was tired.

Gabby walked into the nearby woods. She found a quiet spot behind a group of trees to relieve herself. She stood and walked a little deeper into the trees. As the sun was setting, Gabby heard the familiar squawking of a flock of small green parakeets. Each evening when these birds were getting ready to settle into their tree for the night, they would cry out for their mate. Once they found them, they'd settle into their branch cuddled up to each other.

As this noisy colony settled, she closed her eyes and listened for sounds of the diurnal animals beginning to wake. She took a few deep breaths, attempting to use the air to bury her emotions. Once she was a little more composed, she opened her eyes and began to walk back to the cave.

In her distracted state, Gabby nearly walked into a big bear that came lumbering out of the trees. She froze. The bear noticed Gabby at the same time. It also stood directly between Gabby and the cave's entrance. The bear's fur was dark brown, but it had a blonde speckling on its face. While the bear's claws and sheer size were terrifying, it had an adorable face. Its light markings made the bear look like it wore glasses. Gabby couldn't tell if this was a ferocious beast or teddy bear—she knew better than to test it.

Gabby took a step back, very slowly. The bear cocked its head and looked at her. She took another very slow step back. The bear opened its mouth, let out a huff, collapsed back onto all fours, then shuffled off. She waited for the bear to disappear and sprinted into the cave. Not so much because she was afraid of the bear; she just didn't want to bump into anything else. Dusk wasn't a good time to be alone in the forest.

As Gabby barreled into the cave, she almost ran into Chris. She put on the brakes and slid to her butt.

"I was about to go check on you," Chris said, offering Gabby his hands to pull her up.

She laughed, grabbed his hands, and gave Chris a hug, "You're never going to believe what I almost ran into, other than you," Gabby said and laughed.

"What?"

"A bear!"

"What?" Chris felt Gabby's head and cheeks.

"I'm serious, I saw a bear," Gabby said, swatting Chris's hand away.

"Ei, Rodrigo, tem ursos aqui?" Chris yelled to Rodrigo.

"Sim, mas eles são amigáveis," Rodrigo answered.

"See, I'm not crazy," Gabby said.

"You might've seen a bear, but you're definitely still crazy. Rodrigo said the bears here are friendly," Chris said.

"Yeah, it was really cute, like you. It was about your size, too," Gabby smiled.

"Stop, you're going to make me blush," Chris said with a wink.

Gabby laughed, grabbed his hand, and leaned into his arm as they walked back over to their camp. They sat down and Chris wrapped his arms around her. There was something about being in this cave. Gabby couldn't explain it, but it felt good. As she looked around, everyone was smiling. Kids were happily playing and hugging their parents. Young warriors held the hands of their brides. Gabby wished she could stay here forever, but knew that was impossible.

"I'm glad that you're here," Gabby said, looking up at Chris.

He smiled. "I'm glad you're here too."

"I feel like, I... never mind," Gabby stammered.

"Gabs, I love you."

Gabby's eyes widened; she didn't know how to respond. "I, I love Trent."

"I would never take that away from you, or expect you not to. I just want you to know that I love you."

Gabby nodded and hugged him. She was so torn. She missed Trent, she loved Chris, and she knew that she only had a matter of days left with him. "I love you, too," Gabby said as tears streamed down her cheeks. Chris held her.

"Wait till you see what we're eating tonight," Chris said.

"Do I want to know?"

"If you can eat those grubs, you'll have no problem eating dinner tonight."

"The grubs were delicious," Gabby smiled. She realized Chris was trying to change the subject to make her smile. That's what she would miss most about him.

"Yeah, I can't believe I'm saying this, but, yeah, they were good. Tonight's meal will be totally different."

"Alright, what is it?" Gabby paused. "If it's monkey, don't tell me."

"It's not monkey. I think it's something like a wild boar. Then, we found all of these wild peppers and some sort of root."

"That sounds promising," Gabby said.

"I went hunting a few times when I was younger. Remember the girlfriend that I told you about, the vet that studied animals in Alaska?"

Gabby nodded.

"I went hunting there with a team of local expert hunters and the hunt today was completely different. Francesco and Rodrigo… I'm going to sound crazy saying this, but I swear they talk to the forest."

"A month ago, I would've said you're crazy."

"Chris," Rodrigo called, *"venha comer."*

"Dinner's ready," Chris said.

Gabby didn't want to move. She looked up at Chris and kissed him. It was simply a quick, sweet peck, but nevertheless he was stunned. His eyes widened. Gabby just smiled and stood up.

"Let's go," she said while Chris looked up at her with wide eyes.

There was something about being in this cave. It almost felt like a drug. She was happy, relaxed, content, and full of love. The doctor in Gabby rationalized that this feeling was due to a flood of endorphins following a break in the constant fight-or-flight existence she had been living. She knew it would have to end, but she was going to enjoy every second she had.

As Gabby devoured the small fire-roasted peppers that had been given to her, Rodrigo called Chris over. These peppers tasted like a sweet cross between shishito and bell peppers. They were bright shades of yellow, red, and orange. Each bite popped in her mouth and perfectly complimented the rich-tasting meat. Gabby had been so focused on these delicious peppers that she didn't notice Chris when he came back over.

"Gabs," Chris said. His brow furrowed as he sat down next to her.

"Yeah?"

"The war party is going to attack the village," Chris paused, "tonight."

"Tonight? I thought they were going to wait a few days?"

"A spy from here said that the village had been celebrating our departure all day and it would continue into the night. They will be very easy to overpower tonight." Chris paused. "They asked me to go with them. I had to say yes. It will be an easy fight, and we owe them."

Gabby nodded. "I thought we'd have a little more time."

"I did too. I kind of like it here. But, I'll only be gone for a day or two. You'll be fine."

"I'm going to miss you."

Chris looked at her for a second, and a brief look of concern flittered across his brow. "What? It's only for a day."

Gabby bit her lip. Hard. She smiled. "I know, just be careful." This was probably the last time that she would ever see Chris, which left her utterly hollow. It took everything for her to keep the space from overflowing with sadness.

"I will. Don't worry." Chris cocked his head. "Are you sure you're ok?"

"Yes," Gabby smiled. "I wish we could stay here, like this," Gabby leaned into Chris's arms, "forever."

"Just spend the next day or two like you did today. Ok? Don't go exploring or try to do anything stupid."

"I definitely need a couple days of rest, don't worry." Gabby smiled.

"I'll see you in a day or two, I love you."

"I love you too." Gabby kissed Chris. This time she lingered. A part of her felt guilty. Guilty for lying to Chris, though she was doing this to protect him. She hoped he would understand that. And guilty for loving someone other than Trent. She still loved Trent, she always would, but she loved Chris too. Like everything else in the jungle, emotions grew thick and dense quickly. This was the last time she would be with someone she loved, and she didn't want this moment to be tainted by guilt and by the things she wished she had said. In this moment, the comfort, warmth, and love outweighed the guilt.

"Chris," Rodrigo called, *"vamos embora."*

Chris gave Gabby one more kiss, hugged her, and smiled. "I'll see you in a day or two."

Gabby smiled back and nodded. Then, she pulled him in for one more kiss. "I love you."

"I love you too." Chris smiled and kissed Gabby's head before joining Rodrigo.

Just like that, she was alone.

A woman brought Gabby over another leaf of food, but she just smiled and shook her head no. She watched the villager carry it to a hungry child that happily gobbled it down. Gabby stood and went back over to their camp.

She started to gather what she would need for her trek back to the extraction point. She looked through Trent's lab equipment. She would leave that here for Chris. With Michaela's help, he could most likely create the treatment. She would leave Trent's computer as well. The only thing she really needed was the blood. The less she had to carry, the faster she could move.

Before she left, she grabbed a piece of paper and wrote a letter to Chris. She told him about the deal she made with AmCorps. She begged him not to come after her. She reminded him what was at stake: The people that depended on him to make the right decision—the decision not based on who he was in love with. She pleaded with him to be patient. Most importantly, she told Chris that she was truly and deeply in love with him and she was sorry.

Gabby left the letter on the top of Trent's lab bag. She grabbed her bottle of water and a handful of energy gels. She tucked them into a pocket on the outside of the blood cooler. She stood and spun to leave, only to run into Chief Ëpë and Shaman Dabi. She froze.

Chief Ëpë grabbed Gabby's hands, held them, and bowed his head to her. He took a bag tied to his waist and tied it to the blood cooler. Then, the shaman leaned his head into hers. She had a flood of jungle images, but nothing that made sense. Shaman Dabi looked at Chief Ëpë and shook his head no. Chief Ëpë let out a loud whistle. The shaman leaned his head in once again. Gabby was overwhelmed with a sense of gratitude and a vague idea that someone could take her most of the way. She crinkled her brow and looked at Shaman Dabi. As Roiti and Kena made their way over, she understood that they would help her get back to the extraction point and she was grateful. This time she leaned her head into Shaman Dabi's and tried really hard to say *thank you,* but then just opt-ed for a hug. They both seemed to understand. They bowed their heads to her and placed their hands on their hearts as she followed Roiti and Kena out of the Pachamama cave.

21 - DO NOT ENGAGE

"This is Jones," a gruff voice said.

"Commander, this is Dr. Sabara. Do you have any updates?"

"We've paused all search and recovery missions. My men know that under no circumstances are they to engage."

"Good. Any sign of Dr. Gabrielle Gale?"

"Not yet, sir," Jones replied.

"Have you recovered anything from the lab area?"

"A computer, well, parts of it. It was too damaged to retrieve anything from it. There was a printer and miscellaneous lab equipment, but everything's been completely destroyed. There's nothing to recover."

"Does it look like anything is missing?"

"It's impossible to tell, but in my opinion, if someone was going to take something, they would've taken the computer. Was there anything else with classified info in the lab?" Commander Jones asked.

"Not that I'm aware of," Lucien answered.

"They didn't take anything. If their motive had been to steal information, they wouldn't have left the computer. I mean, we're dealing with some pretty Neanderthal-like natives, literally," Jones said.

"They're clearly more intelligent than you've given them credit for. I don't have a read on Dr. Gale, but for the time being, I need her protected and alive. Do not engage. Do you understand?" Lucien asked.

"What if they attack? You realize there's a chance that this could be a setup, right?" Jones replied.

"Do not engage. Do you understand?"

"So, I should let my men stand there and get killed?"

"I would say to use common sense, but that's clearly lacking on General Holton's team. I will repeat myself one more time, DO - NOT - ENGAGE. That's a direct order."

"Yes, sir."

Lucien clicked off. He didn't have a great deal of confidence; he could just about hear Commander Jones rolling his eyes in his tone alone. What Lucien was certain of was that Commander Jones cared about his position and would take direction strictly to remain needed by AmCorps and the United States.

Regardless, Lucien could feel the sense of dread that had been a constant, buried deep in his gut, start to sprout the first blooms of excitement. This wasn't what he initially envisioned, but it was a possibility—or rather, a compromise he was more than willing to accept.

"Sir, I have Sy," Lucien's assistant's voice announced through his comm center.

"Put him through," Lucien replied and paused. "Sy?"

"Hi, I spoke to Johnnie's wife. She's planning on meeting us in the coffee shop in thirty minutes. It's currently getting cleared out. Does that still work for you?"

"Yes, that's perfect. Meet her there, get coffee. Make her feel comfortable. I'll meet you there."

"That works. When I told Johnnie's doctors to hold off on his sedative so that he's present when she sees him, they told me that he'd need to be restrained. How do you want to handle that?"

"Have him restrained."

Lucien needed something, anything, to pass the time while he was waiting for Dr. Gale, and trying to get to the bottom of Johnnie's sudden descent into madness gave him this wanted distraction. Currently, Lucien saw three possibilities. First, Johnnie may have been schizophrenic and kept his condition hidden until the natural stress of the procedure set off his full-blown psychosis. Second, he may have had a genetic predisposition and the procedure caused a sudden onset of schizophrenia. Third, the vehicle used to edit the EVE-0 gene mistakenly made a cut elsewhere in Johnnie's genome that caused his psychosis.

Lucien hoped it wasn't the third possibility. Though this was exactly the reason he'd pursued a career in science. His ultimate goal in life was to gain the ability to control nature. His entire life had been dominated by his own genetic condition. It had taken so much away from him. Most of all, he was forced to learn from a very early age that nature made mistakes, and he had been one of them. While most people with this condition didn't survive beyond middle age, Lucien thrived. He'd never seen a single ray of sunlight and that did not bother him in the slightest. In fact, he took pride in the fact that he was completely unaffected by a condition that most couldn't even survive. More than that, he was better because of it. He checked his watch, the Cartier his mother gave him when he graduated high school. It had belonged to his great-grandfather and always gave him a sense of comfort.

Sy and Johnnie's wife should just be getting to the café. If Lucien left now, Sy would have enough time to get her warmed up. Sy could be incredibly charming and persuasive, particularly with women. Lucien had never had this luxury. His looks were so unique they had a tendency to startle people. His walk took him along the main labs, an area closed to the public, where he saw his team of scientists preparing the infusion serum so that as soon as Dr. Gale arrived with the blood, they'd be able to make the treatments quickly. One of the scientists saw Lucien and gave him two gloved thumbs-up. Lucien nodded his approval and continued on his way.

When he got to the café, he stood outside for a moment and studied Sy and Johnnie's wife. The first thing Lucien noticed was that she was slightly overweight. Not obese, but heavy, and she was eating a cookie. Granted, the cookies were organic and made with heirloom wheat, dark chocolate, and maple syrup. Though, from the time he was young, he could never comprehend how so many people took their healthy bodies for granted. To Lucien, health was a gift, a gift he had never been given. He had to work and sacrifice for his health. It irritated him when people lacked enough self-control to appreciate this gift, but he had learned to tolerate it.

When Lucien walked in, Johnnie's wife looked up at him. Her face was beautiful. Perfect porcelain skin, red full lips, and bright blue eyes overflowing with sadness. Her wavy blonde hair grazed her shoulders. She stood as Lucien walked over to the table.

"Please stay sitting," Lucien said. "I'm Dr. Sabara," Lucien said as he took his seat.

"Yes, I know. I've heard so much about you. It's an honor to meet you," Johnnie's wife said as she sat down and nervously squirmed in her seat.

"This is Mrs. Williams," Sy said.

"Yes, of course, Johnnie has spoken very fondly of you," Lucien said.

"Please, call me Miranda. How's Johnnie? I'm so worried. I miss him," Miranda said as tears welled in her eyes.

"That's why we asked you here. He's ok and we'd like to take you to see him. We just want to get to the bottom of his psychosis, so that we're able to help him as best as we can," Lucien said.

"Psychosis?" Miranda asked.

"That's his mental state," Sy added.

"Oh, the delusions?"

Sy nodded.

"Does he have any history of mental illness?" Lucien asked.

"No, no, not at all," Miranda said.

"Are you certain?" Sy asked.

"Yes," Miranda said.

"No periods of anxiety or depression?" Sy asked.

"Well, I mean, everyone goes through periods of stress, especially these days," Miranda said, as she took a bite of her cookie.

"We'll come back to that," Lucien said, looking at Sy. "Do you know of any family history of mental illness?"

"Johnnie had a grand uncle on the Williams's side that was institutionalized. I don't know why, just that he hated visiting him when he was a kid. It could've been old age. I'm sorry, I don't know," Miranda said.

"Has Johnnie ever shown any signs of obsessive or paranoid thoughts?" Sy asked.

"Not really," Miranda said and took a sip of her latte. "When we first started dating in high school, he said his grandfather scared him. I vaguely remember him telling me a story about getting poisoned, or thinking he was going to. I don't know… I, I… it's hard to remember," Miranda said, her cheeks flushing.

"It's okay, Miranda, this is very helpful and explains a great deal," Lucien said.

"I want to help," she said as she tried to hold back tears.

"We know you do. Please don't worry, there's nothing that you can say or do that would be wrong. So, take a breath and relax. Would you like another latte?" Sy asked.

She nodded her head yes. "Thank you."

Lucien coaxed her further, "I know that all humans go through periodic episodes of stress and sadness, but think about Johnnie. Were there any times that he seemed to become distant?"

"Yes, I think so. Some days, you know, before we were in here, he would spend the entire day and night in the basement. I don't know what he was doing, but he didn't want to be disturbed. I just thought he needed some space. We all did," Miranda said.

"Early-onset schizophrenia is so difficult to diagnose because the symptoms do mirror so many other conditions and normal behaviors that people all experience from time to time. What makes it even more difficult is that schizophrenics have no idea that something is wrong, so they don't reach out to loved ones or doctors," Sy said.

The barista brought over Miranda's latte. "Thanks,

hun," she said.

"We suspect that Johnnie has been in the prodrome stage, which means that it was only a matter of time till full-blown schizophrenia developed. And the physical stress of this procedure coupled with his age may have finally pushed him into full-blown psychosis. This is the most common age for the disease to erupt," Lucien said. "Luckily, he's here and able to get the best medical and psychological treatment in the world."

"I guess that's a good thing, right?" Miranda asked.

"It was bound to happen, so yes, it's good that it happened here," Sy said.

"I'm sorry I didn't notice and get him treatment earlier," Miranda said as she broke down in tears.

Lucien consoled her. "This is not your fault. Family members are programmed to justify these behaviors, until those justifications no longer explain their behavior. This is all very normal. Though now, we want you to be a part of his progress. We believe that you hold the key to pulling him out of this psychosis."

"Okay, I mean, yes, anything I can do," Miranda sobbed.

"Take a few breaths. We need you to be calm when you see him. All we want you to do is talk to him and remind him, gently, of what's real and what's not. He needs to hear from someone he trusts," Lucien said.

"Okay," Miranda said, trying to stop crying. "No

one's ever really told me why he was quarantined in the first place. Did he have a breakdown while working?"

"In a manner of speaking, yes. Did we tell you the good news?" Lucien asked.

Miranda shook her head no.

"Johnnie," Lucien continued, "is the first American to be rehabilitated so that his immune system is now functioning again. The pandemics are no longer a threat to him. We suspect the emotional and physical response to this is what sent him into full-blown schizophrenia."

"He's going to say some very strange things, like his brain was melted or there's something inside him. Gently tell him that he's fine, his brain is fine, and there's nothing inside him," Sy instructed.

"Got it," Miranda said, nodding her head.

"Are you ready?" Lucien asked.

Miranda slowly nodded her head yes.

They made the short walk to Johnnie's room in complete silence. Lucien hoped that Miranda would be able to get through to him. As they walked through the corridor, Lucien's attention zoomed in on the wide sway of Miranda's hips. Most men would find her plump, curvaceous body attractive, but all he could think about was what sort of damage her diet had inflicted on her body on a genetic level. As Lucien's focus shifted from Miranda back to Johnnie, he wanted to believe that the uncle's genetic contribution to

Johnnie was at fault. But deep down, Lucien couldn't shake the doubt that Johnnie's psychosis was due to a mistake in the genome splice and repair. To be more specific, it was not due to a mistake in his science, but rather, a mistake in Johnnie's DNA. The procedure appeared to amplify weaknesses in DNA, and what human didn't have some weakness somewhere in their DNA? To date, this procedure had always result-ed in an unexpected reaction in the genome. It was completely unpredictable as these weaknesses were often imperceptible to science. It happened in the chimpanzees as well, but he'd hoped they may find a way around it—he knew better now. Lucien knew that this would only ever work if the gene used to repair the EVE-0 gene was already healthy, not one that was edited. In simple terms, the only possible treatment was still in the Amazon. He also wondered if they would, in fact, be able to create more treatments from rehabilitated individuals. Lucien was becoming frus-trated. He despised not having the answer and no way to get it. As they approached Johnnie's ward, Lucien was relieved to have something to distract him.

Sy used his card to swipe them into the control room. A shade had been pulled down and covered the window into Johnnie's room. The beep of monitors, sensors, and computers instantly made the room feel like a hospital.

"Hello, Mrs. Williams. I'm Dr. Saad. I've been overseeing the care of your husband. This is Dr. Faust, his psychiatrist. And these two gentlemen are part of his nursing team, Alex and William." Dr. Saad smiled, his perfect white teeth gleaming.

"Please, call me Miranda. How's Johnnie?"

"Physically, he's doing well. His vitals are perfect." Dr. Saad smoothed a wave of his coiffed dark hair into place. "The issues that he's dealing with are due to his current mental state."

"Yes," Dr. Faust chimed in. "He's, um, well…" He paused. He was short, balding, and he easily blended into the background of the small group. He folded his hands in front of his chest. "Frankly, we're having a difficult time controlling his current psychotic episode with tendencies towards violence."

"Violence?" Miranda asked.

Dr. Faust made an effort to wrinkle his brow and nod his head yes. "Unfortunately, this means that we've had to keep him restrained. Otherwise, he would hurt himself or someone else. The scratches that you'll see on the side of his face are from when we attempted to loosen the restraints. You see, he believes that there's something inside his body and that his brain is melting. He tried to get to it and scratched his face quite badly."

"Oh, dear God," Miranda said.

"The good news," Dr. Saad added, "is that episodes like this don't last. We just need to find the right combination of medication. We're hoping that when he sees you, you'll be able to get through to him. Calm him. Help him to understand that we," Dr. Saad gestured to the staff in the room, now surrounding Miranda, "want to help him."

"Okay, okay," Miranda said, becoming flustered.

"Miranda," Dr. Saad said, putting his hands on her shoulders, "I know this is difficult, but everything will be fine. We need you to be strong for Johnnie right now. Do you think you can do that?"

"Yes, yes." Tears started to break free from the corners of her eyes.

Dr. Faust handed Miranda a box of tissues. She wiped her eyes.

"We're going to let you go in alone," Dr. Faust said. "In Johnnie's current state, he perceives us as a danger to him. Our presence aggravates his psychosis. And we're hopeful you may be able to calm him."

"Okay," Miranda said as she took a breath and stood a little taller.

Dr. Saad rubbed Miranda's shoulders and flashed his model-worthy smile. "Are you ready?"

She smiled. "I am."

"He's right through that door." Dr. Saad pointed to the door into Johnnie's room.

Miranda nodded and walked over to the door. She paused momentarily, took a slow, deep breath, and walked in.

Dr. Faust quickly opened the shades so that Johnnie's room was in full view.

"Johnnie?" Miranda slowly approached his bed.

He jerked his arms, but they were tightly secured to the bed.

"Sweetheart?" Miranda took a few slow steps, inching closer to the bed.

Johnnie instantly turned his head to face Miranda.

"Oh baby." Johnnie's body sank, his head drooped, and he began to sob. "I'm sorry."

Miranda rushed over and hugged him.

"I shouldn't have done this," he said. "I'm sorry. I wish you didn't have to see me like this."

"No, it's okay. Johnnie, it's okay. I've missed you so much. I want you to get better and come home to me."

"Baby, you don't understand, they did something bad to me. They put something inside me. I think it's melting my brain, or... or... putting these bad thoughts in my head. I want it out. Baby, take it out, please." Johnnie began sobbing uncontrollably.

"John, listen to me. They are trying to help you. They didn't put anything into you. It's—"

"Get the fuck away from me!" Johnnie suddenly screamed and began thrashing in his bed. "They got to you."

"No. No. John, calm down." Miranda straightened up and looked directly at Johnnie. "CALM... DOWN."

Johnnie stopped thrashing and looked at her. She leaned in and whispered something to him. The speaker in the control room didn't pick it up. Johnnie didn't say anything in response, just nodded his head in agreement.

"It's going to be okay," Miranda said as she sat down on Johnnie's bed. She laid her head on his chest.

"I love you, baby. I love you and Emma so much. How is she?"

"She's good. She's so proud of her daddy. She loves you. We both love you."

Miranda whispered something to Johnnie again. He smiled. She kissed him. Then she leaned her ear over to him so he could whisper something to her. She smiled and kissed him.

There was a knock on the door. Miranda looked directly into Johnnie's eyes, nearly nose to nose. "Remember," she said, and kissed him again. Then she stood up as the door opened and Dr. Saad and Dr. Faust walked in.

"How are you feeling, Johnnie?" Dr. Faust asked.

"I was feeling okay, until you came in," Johnnie snapped. "My head hurts. What are you doing to me?" Johnnie screamed.

"Sweetheart," Miranda said.

"I'm trying, baby, but it's hard." Johnnie gritted his jaw, his face contorted in pain.

"I think Johnnie's had enough stimulation for today. He needs his rest. You're welcome to visit again in a day or two," Dr. Saad instructed.

Miranda nodded, her eyes filling with tears. "Johnnie, I love you. I'll see you in a day or two. Sweetheart, I love you so much." She leaned over and kissed his forehead.

"I love you. Give Emma a big hug for me." Johnnie gritted in pain again.

Miranda turned and left. The two male nurses walked in as she left and immediately gave Johnnie an injection. He let out a scream, then quieted down.

Lucien stopped Miranda in the control room.

"Miranda, thank you. You made a huge impact today. That's the most lucid Johnnie's been. This is great progress. What did you whisper to him? If we're on the same page, we can better understand what triggers him and what calms him down."

"Oh," Miranda blushed, "we just whispered some of the romantic things we'll do when he comes home."

"Got it," Lucien smiled.

"I also asked if he had been able to use a laptop. He's learning to be a computer programmer. After retiring from the military, that's what he wants to do. When he would get stressed out, he would write programs or apps or something. To be honest, I don't really know what he did, but he spent hours on his computer. I think that might be able to calm him. He's very bored."

"That's a great idea. I will get a laptop to him today. You've been incredibly helpful. Thank you, Miranda."

Miranda nodded, too close to the brink of tears to reply, and turned to leave the room. She paused. "When can I see him again?"

"I will talk to his doctors, but you should be able to see him every day or every other." Lucien smiled.

22 – SOLO

The jungle was so different without Chris. It was dark. She couldn't see anything. The first hour was extremely difficult. She had to maintain such a strong focus just to keep from tripping. Kena and Roiti were very hard to keep up with. After hours of this difficult trek, the trail opened up. Light from the moon trickled through the trees. The path was wide, flat, and easy to traverse.

Though with the ease of the route, Gabby's mind began to wander and sink into the depths of her feelings. She missed Chris. Her heart ached for Trent. Now, she was bringing the treatment right to the people that were responsible for everything that went so horrifically wrong. She had been so sure that she was doing the right thing in the cave. But now, she began to question everything. She told herself it was too late to turn around. Too late to change her mind. This was the chain of events that Trent set in motion. She had to hold on to that.

Out of the blue, Roiti turned around, grabbed Gabby's arm, and started running, pulling her along the trail so fast her legs could barely keep up. She was exhausted. Her muscles burned. She tripped and tumbled to the ground, hitting her head. Roiti and Kena pulled her up. They each grabbed an arm and kept running. She could feel a trickle of blood drip down her brow. They unexpectedly jumped off the trail and pulled Gabby behind a fallen tree.

It was quiet. Nothing happened for a few minutes. Then, Gabby heard a faint buzzing in the distance. It grew louder. A light appeared. It was an ATV towing a cart. As it came closer, Gabby could see that there were two guys on the ATV wearing tattered, modern clothes. Roiti pulled Gabby down. She slowly stretched up again to get a better look, just peeking her eyes over the trunk. As the vehicle passed, Gabby saw that they had three guys in a small cage on the cart they were towing. The guy on the back had an electric cattle prod and he continually shocked the prisoners, laughing loud each time their bodies tensed in the grip of electricity. As the cart passed, one of the prisoners made eye contact with Gabby. She froze, her eyes widened, and she started to panic. The prisoner slowly bowed his head to her. The maniac with the cattle prod shocked him and as his lips peeled back in a pain-laden contraction, Gabby could see most of his teeth had been knocked out.

This group looked like they had just crawled out

of some backwoods horror scene. They were filled with so much madness and violence that it seemed surreal. For a minute, Gabby wondered if she was actually asleep and having a nightmare. The tickle of blood slowly clotting on her forehead reminded her she was wide awake.

They stayed behind the trunk long enough to ensure they were safe. Gabby rolled onto her back and looked up. There was enough of a break in the trees for Gabby to see the night sky full of stars. She saw a flash of light dart across the sky and was reminded of all the time she spent staring at the stars with her dad. She knew the shooting star was a sign from him, though this just made her feel more desolate.

Kena tapped Gabby on the shoulder and motioned that they could move on again. He paused, pointed to the trees, and motioned a very slow walk with his fingers. He then pointed to the trail and motioned a very fast walk. Kena put his pointer finger up to pause, then made a gun with his hand and pointed back at the path. He also made a weird face. Gabby couldn't tell if that meant crazy or drugged. But, all in all, she figured that he was telling her that the path was much faster, but more dangerous. She guessed that it had been used by drug traffickers in the past. This made her think that the group that just passed were leftover runners that had been forgotten by the world and had clearly gone insane.

Gabby thought for a moment. The quicker she

could get to AmCorps and not have the option to turn around, the better. She wanted to run back to the cave, stay in the jungle, and hide from the world forever. She could feel her resolve weakening by the minute. Gabby pointed to the path. Kena nodded and they started to move again.

Gabby could tell that Kena and Roiti were nervous. They didn't like being on this road. They moved quickly. Too quickly. Gabby was struggling to keep up. Her lungs were burning. Her legs were on fire. She didn't think that she could make it much further.

"Stop," Gabby huffed.

Kena and Roiti looked back at her.

"I need to rest for a minute," Gabby pleaded.

They looked at each other. Gabby pretended to sleep. Kena and Roiti shook their head no and pointed at the horizon. Shades of navy had just begun to show. Roiti pulled a leaf out of a pouch tied around his shoulder and handed it to Gabby. By now, she was well aware of the burst of energy a coca leaf provided. Gabby stuffed the leaf into her cheek and gently sucked on it. Roiti pointed to the leaf and then the road, making the same gesture he made when the insane ATV barreled through. Next, he mimed planting and raking, like he was farming.

"Oh, they grow coca," Gabby said.

Kena and Roiti nodded, like they understood what she said. Gabby smiled. She stood, energized enough to continue. Her legs were so much lighter and her lungs had opened up. Her longing for Chris, though, had also been turned up by this herbal jolt.

The next few hours flew by. They were racing the rising sun and losing it second by second. The sun soon broke over the horizon and the path became too bright to travel on. Kena and Roiti broke off of the trail and back into the dense jungle.

The speed at which they could travel at night came to a pathetic crawl during the daylight hours. The trees, plants, bushes, vines, and leaves made an almost impenetrable wall. They inched their way through. The true torture though was coming face-to-face with everything else that crawled through this green casing.

Out of nowhere, Roiti shoved Gabby to the side, knocking her over. Kena pulled her up, but to the left of where she'd been headed. He pointed to a low-hanging branch that Gabby had been about to brush against. Gabby looked, saw nothing, looked back to Kena, and shrugged her shoulders. He pointed again. Gabby looked closer. She saw it. A huge, brown hairy spider the size of her palm. Gabby immediately recognized it from her antivenom guide. It was a Brazilian walking spider, or banana spider. She had the antivenom in her med kit. The kit she had left for Chris back in the cave. A banana spider bite would've put an end to her journey. It was the most venomous spider in the world and deadly without antivenom.

Roiti whistled and called them over. He found a

game trail heading in the direction they needed. This made moving a bit easier. It was still exhausting, but possible.

As the sun got higher, the jungle seemed to feel extra hot. The warmth of the sun was magnified in the tight forest canopy. It was humid and beads of sweat began to dampen Gabby's clothes.

Finally, after traveling for what felt like days, Roiti found a small clearing to take a break. Gabby was so tired she just collapsed on the dirt. She used her backpack as a pillow and laid down. Kena pulled out some nuts, seeds, and fruit and passed a handful to Gabby. She rolled onto her side, too tired to sit up, and swallowed down a mouthful of nuts. She laid back down and shut her eyes.

Next thing she knew, Roiti was shaking Gabby. The sun had begun its descent, which meant that Gabby must've fallen asleep for a couple of hours. Rested, but sore, Gabby struggled to get up. Her body felt like it was stuck. She had to slowly peel herself off of the hard dirt, every muscle crying out in pain as she did. Once she was up, she stretched, and slowly, life crept back into her body. The temperature had cooled to something more comfortable, and she was ready to move.

They clawed through the game trail for another couple hours, buying time until they could go back onto the large, cleared path. In this prison of greenery, Gabby grew anxious. She knew she was getting closer;

she didn't want to go with AmCorps. She realized that there was a strong possibility that they would kill her. Maybe not immediately. They would want to find out if the treatment had actually worked on her. She was curious about that as well. But, after they ran a few tests and secured the blood, they would likely execute her in some grand fashion. She had a plan to buy some time, a story she'd been working on. But they'd probably just decide to kill her anyway. That was their style.

With nothing to distract her but her thoughts, she began to worry about Chris. What if he had been killed when they attacked the other tribe? Maybe she should've waited, told Chris her plan, and together—with Michaela's help—they could've come up with a better plan. Hadn't she learned her lesson from Trent? If only he had been able to tell them everything earlier, maybe they could've worked together. Gabby swallowed down her tumbling thoughts. There were way too many should'ves and could'ves. At this point, all Gabby could do was fully accept her decision and hope for the best. Though, hope seemed like a silly luxury at the moment.

Finally, the sun set and they made their way back to the open trail. She had no idea how much further she had to go. Roiti suddenly put up his hand and they paused. They moved just behind the tree line and ahead slowly. They came to a field. It was hard to make out exactly what it was in the dark, but there was enough light to see that it appeared to be a clearing filled in with burly bushes.

Roiti slowly made his way out of the trees to get a better look. There was no sound or movement anywhere near, so Gabby assumed it had been deserted. Roiti gave the all clear and called them back out. While he was waiting, he started to pick leaves off of the bushes and stuff them into his pouch.

As Gabby got closer, she instantly recognized the leaves. It was coca. The field felt strange. It scared Gabby. Up ahead she could see the silhouettes of scarecrows watching over the field. That struck her as strange. She wanted to turn around. Even weirder was the flock of birds gathered on them. This didn't feel right. Roiti and Kena were too busy harvesting leaves to notice. Gabby tried not to look.

When she was almost past them, she made the mistake of taking one more look. She gasped and let out a high-pitched cry. They weren't scarecrows. The bodies of the men she saw in the cage the night before had been killed and placed on posts in the field. A flock of birds with huge black eyes were tearing away chunks of flesh. Their eyes had been eaten away, along with much of their faces. She could see the nasal bone and much of the jaw exposed. Gabby was only able to recognize them because she remembered the flannel shirt of one of the men that had dangled his arm out of the cage.

Roiti and Kena each grabbed one of Gabby's arms and took off running. The next hour or so was a blur.

The image of these men's bodies had been burned into her brain and that was all she could see. Gabby didn't know how much time passed, but suddenly she had to push Kena and Roiti to the side. She stumbled, collapsed to her knees, and threw up. She had nothing in her stomach but a little water, so her vomit came up hot and acidic. She rolled onto her back, took a few deep breaths, and before she knew it, Kena and Roiti were pulling her up again. They were on the move once more.

Gabby's legs kept moving. It seemed to get easier, or maybe Kena and Roiti carried more of her weight. Eventually, her mind calmed. Gabby wasn't sure how long they moved like that. They fell into a rhythm and Gabby was grateful for them.

It may have been an hour or three, but they eventually stopped. Kena and Roiti took Gabby to a small hidden clearing just off the path. They took a short break and Roiti gave Gabby some nuts, seeds, and a passion fruit. They didn't eat. When Gabby finished, they brought her back onto the path. Kena pointed to the horizon. Shades of navy streaked the sky. Then he pointed at Gabby and up the path in the direction they had been traveling. He pointed back to the horizon, traced his finger thirty degrees, and looked at Gabby with wide eyes. It took her a minute, but she understood. They were leaving her. She had about three to four hours before she would reach AmCorps's extraction point. Gabby nodded, then gave Kena and

Roiti a hug. They weren't sure how to react initially, but they hugged her back. Gabby's eyes filled with tears. She had never said a word to these two young warriors, but she would miss them.

Gabby turned and took off along the path. She hated being alone. While she had spent years feeling alone, after losing her parents young, she had never truly been alone. She always had her grandparents, a rotating list of roommates, and finally, Trent. She had never actually even lived alone.

She heard a branch snap to her right; she looked but didn't see anything. *God, please not again, please no more deadly animals, no more jaguars,* she prayed. Gabby picked up the pace. She felt like she was being watched, but knew that was just because she couldn't see into the trees. She remembered feeling like this as a kid, walking her dog at night near Wissahickon Park. The forested refuge just outside of Philadelphia was filled with dark trails. Every time Gabby walked by at night, she knew there were so many places for someone to hide. She always imagined someone watching her and ran as fast as she could to get past the street that bordered Wissahickon.

Here, she couldn't escape the feeling. She started jogging, but it was so difficult with the cooler bag and her supply pack. She stopped jogging, but walked as fast as her legs could go. She'd never been this tired. Every muscle in her body ached, her lungs were on fire, and her body became too heavy to carry. Without notice, her legs were suddenly swept above her head and she was hanging ten feet in the air.

It took a minute to realize what happened. Gabby had been snagged in a net—some sort of trap. She looked around, but no one was there. *Did AmCorps set a trap for me?* she wondered. *Or, maybe this was an old trap that had been forgotten?* She wiggled out of the awkward position that she had been caught in. She struggled to twist around so that she could try to dig through her supply pack. She hoped she had a knife in there. She thought she did; she prayed that she did. She managed to get herself turned so that her backpack was in her lap and began feeling through it. *Oh, thank God,* she thought as her fingers brushed against her folding survival knife. She gripped it between her pointer and middle finger, slowly wiggling it through everything else in her bag. Once she was able to pull it up enough, she gripped it, and pulled it out.

Out of nowhere, a loud whistle pierced the quiet just before dawn. Gabby froze. She didn't see anyone. Then, she heard the buzzing from the night before and her heart sank. Moments later, the ATV barreled out of a nearby trail offshoot. The maniac with the electric cattle prod stepped out from behind the large tree Gabby dangled from. He cackled with a devilish sneer. Gabby looked at him and saw evil. His eyes were extra close, small, and beady. There was madness in them. His lips curled into a hideously deranged smile, showing black, rotting teeth.

Gabby felt sick. She was so close. She gripped the knife tight. She placed her finger on the button that popped the blade open. She was not going to go down without a fight. The ATV pulled next to them. The driver positioned the cart with the cage right underneath Gabby, flipping the top of the cage open. Gabby dropped. She crushed her elbow on the metal frame as she fell and slammed into the hard metal base. Her body screamed in pain. She thought her elbow and tailbone might be broken. She frantically felt around for the cooler bag, which luckily was on top of her. Not that it mattered. The net that trapped her loosened and she clawed her way free—just as the top of the cage slammed shut and locked. As the driver climbed down, she could see that he was holding what looked to be a charred hand and forearm. He looked at Gabby, grinned, and took a big bite of meat from the muscled forearm. Meat hung out of his mouth as he cackled, chewed, and swallowed. *Please, please, please let that be a monkey,* Gabby wished. An abrupt tremor of searing pain made every muscle in her body tense, and her world went black.

When Gabby came to, her head was pounding. Everything hurt. Her vision was blurry and she couldn't remember what happened or where she was. She recalled that she had just parted with Roiti and Kena. She knew she was close to AmCorps. *How did I get in this cage? Did AmCorps capture me?* she wondered. She tried to sit up, but got dizzy. Gabby rubbed her head and laid back. When she closed her eyes, she was bombarded with images of the net trapping her and the fiends with the ATV.

She sat up. Her head flashed with shards of pain. She gave it a second to settle down, then took a quick inventory of herself and her things. She appeared to be alright. All of her things were there. She didn't think she had been touched. The cage was still bolted shut from the top.

Gabby looked around. The sun had just come up. The ATV had been pulled into a small clearing. There were a few very rough structures nearby. Some scrap wood had been used to make basic platforms with ramshackle roofs. There were some tarps tied around some of these structures, so she couldn't see into all of them, though she didn't see her captors or hear them anywhere nearby. The cage she was in was still on the cart, but the ATV had been separated and was not around.

Gabby tried standing. Her head was still spinning and she fell back. She took a deep breath and held on to the bars for support. She pulled herself up and tried to reach the latch, but there was a solid protective frame around the latch, so she couldn't get to it. There was nothing she could do. She had been captured and it was over. *No,* she thought, *no. I can't let that happen.* She would have to be patient. She could act hurt. Gabby quickly laid down in the corner of the structure. She picked up the knife and hid it in her boot. Where could these wackos have gone?

Gabby lay there and watched the sun climb higher in the sky. Finally, she heard them. They were behind her and sounded like they were arguing. Gabby thought they were speaking Spanish but wasn't sure. Gabby wanted to turn around and look at them, but they'd know she was awake and okay. So, she focused on listening. It was useless; she couldn't understand. She heard them getting louder and knew they were approaching the cage. Something hard jabbed into her back. She didn't move. It jabbed her again, harder. She didn't move. It jabbed her again, even harder, and this time she felt a sharp tingle of pain shoot through her back.

Gabby jumped up and spun to look at these two guys. This close up, she could see how disgusting they were. The nut with the electric cattle prod and rotten teeth snarled at Gabby, laughed, then held his nostril, and blew a repulsive green wad of phlegm out of his nose. Gabby could smell his rotten breath from this close. The other guy had both hands on the bars and was sticking his tongue out, pretending to lick Gabby. His skin was covered in pockmarked scars, puss-filled pustules of acne, and massive blackheads. Both men looked diseased.

They looked at Gabby and licked their lips, laughed, and walked into the clearing. They were building a huge spit. Gabby knew what it was for. She looked around their rough camp. She saw the ATV, finally realizing they had it hooked up to a portable solar charging station. She saw a few small bags. The wood on the shacks was rotting. She realized they probably hadn't been here for long. Her guess was that they had been drug smugglers or illegal loggers that were left behind. They had clearly gone mad, possibly from cannibalism, drugs, being left to their own devices, or just life in the jungle. It didn't really matter. What mattered was that Gabby knew how dangerous a psychotic individual could be. Gabby watched them. They moved in erratic, jerky motions. They seemed to lack focus, moving from one job to another without finishing any of them. They had a quarter of a fire circle built from rocks. They had one side of the spit started with rough timber. All of a sudden, they jumped on the ATV and took off.

Gabby frantically tried to reach the latch again, but couldn't. Everything was just out of her reach. She dug through her bag, searching for something that might be able to extend to the latch. There was nothing. She was trapped. She collapsed in the corner of the cage. She had been so close. She sat there exhausted, defeated, and despondent. Unable to even think, the teeth of rage began to eat at her from the inside out. Everything she had been through couldn't possibly come to an end like this.

She heard the buzz of the ATV; the maniacs were almost back. They were going to kill her and eat her. She couldn't imagine a worse way to die. She felt so stupid. She had walked right into their trap. She should've seen it coming, but was too focused on what she couldn't see in the woods that she didn't see what was right in front of her.

When the ATV pulled into the clearing, Gabby saw that they had collected more wood and rocks. They went back to work building the human-sized firepit and spit. Gabby hoped they would kill her before they cooked her. They seemed to be more focused now. Gabby saw them continually stuffing coca leaves into their mouths, which helped them work faster than before. Gabby ran her hand over the knife she had stuffed in her pocket.

23 – ENGAGE

Lucien sat at his desk. He clicked on his computer and rang Commander Jones.

"Jones here," he promptly answered.

"Hello Commander, any news?"

"No, sir. Dr. Gale is not here yet."

"Any sign of her?"

"Sir?"

"Any sign of her?" Lucien repeated.

"No, sir. We put a hold on all military operations."

"Yes, I know."

"So, how would we know if she was in the vicinity?"

"Aren't you surveying the area?"

"Sir, when you ordered us to cease all military operations... we ceased all operations. We had just picked up a visual of an ATV in the area with our drone surveillance, about thirty miles northwest of our camp. But we stopped when you told us to cease military operations."

"Was it her?" Lucien asked.

"Sir, it didn't appear to be Dr. Gale. It was two un-identified males."

Lucien gritted his teeth. "So, there are others in the area?"

"It appears so, sir."

"Are they dangerous?"

"The threat is unknown."

"So, they *could* be dangerous?"

"It's possible."

"Could they be a threat to Dr. Gale?"

"It's possible."

"I'm not sure if you're being passive-aggressive or if you're just stupid."

"Sir, you told us to cease military operations. We are trained to follow orders from our superiors, especially POTUS."

"My apologies," Lucien corrected, "I should be clearer in my directives. Keep a close watch on everything that is happening in the vicinity. Use common sense, but do not, I repeat do not, engage."

"To be *clear*, you want us to conduct surveillance, but not to engage in combat of any sort under any circumstance?"

"Yes, that's correct."

"We will resume surveillance immediately. What if Dr. Gale is in danger?" Jones asked.

Lucien rolled his eyes. "Protect Dr. Gale. If she is in danger, get her out of danger."

"So, we have permission to engage?"

Lucien let out a slow breath and closed his eyes. "Yes," he said, opening his eyes and focusing directly on Jones. "Please prove to me that you have common sense. Dr. Gale is to be protected. You are to bring her here, unharmed. Do not harm any of the indigenous people she has been in contact with. If there is some unknown threat that endangers her, use force to protect her. Is that clear enough for you?"

"Yes, sir. We're on it." Jones clicked out of the chat.

Lucien gritted his teeth. Why did everything have to be so difficult? It seemed that human beings' evolution had removed common sense in the last century or so. This just confirmed Lucien's drive to help the species, a species on the brink of extinction. It made perfect logical sense. Homo sapiens had beat out several other hominid species to become the only humans left standing. Many archeologists theorized that Homo sapiens rose to the top because of their need to be social creatures. It was their willingness and acceptance of others that allowed them to adapt, to work together, and to form strong communities, ultimately becoming the last (hu)man standing. Though now, Lucien couldn't help but think that this innate drive had evolved to become too important to human existence. That this social need had been replaced by herd mentality. Intelligence had been lost in an effort to have convenient, massive communities—no doubt spurred on more by social media. There were certainly instances of mass hysteria throughout history, like the Salem Witch Trials and the Dancing Plague of 1518. Though, those instances were limited. In the digital age, it seemed that no one was capable of thinking for themselves. Mass hysteria spread too easily and too quickly to be prevented.

Initially, this presented a problem for Lucien when he was formulating his evolved species. How could he create a race that was both inclined to follow directions and think rationally? He knew he needed to increase intelligence while tamping down emotion, but that wasn't enough. Lucien began to study Williams syndrome, a condition associated with hyper-sociability that was expressed through the deletion of twenty-five genes on Chromosome 7. There were some negative consequences to this condition, such as developmental delays, heart conditions, and other things that Lucien wanted to avoid. Though, he was able to manipulate the expression of these genes so that social acuity would increase without any unwanted side-effects. Creating socially aware and highly intelligent humans will usher in a new era and Lucien will be at the top of this empire. The second Renaissance.

Lucien knew this worked. Just over twenty-two years ago, Lucien created his first evolved species in secret. Genetic manipulation wasn't accepted by the scientific community, and it was also illegal, but that didn't deter Lucien. He just needed to do it secretly.

When an opportunity presented itself, Lucien seized it. A scientist that worked in Lucien's lab came to Lucien, desperate to have a child; Lucien knew he could help. Dr. Bastet Azazel had tried everything offered by modern medicine, but nothing resulted in a viable egg. Lucien had another idea. While it was not legal, both Bastet and Lucien believed in science. They realized the potential of genetic manipulation. Lucien and Bastet worked well together, they shared the same ideals, they were as close as two people with their intellect were capable of being, and they came to an agreement. Lucien would use genetic manipulation to produce a viable egg, Bastet would raise the child as hers, though she would share all decision-making with Lucien.

Their child was perfect and their arrangement worked flawlessly. Osiris "Sy" Azazel was perfect. He thrived in every aspect. He was social, well-liked by everyone, extraordinarily intelligent, an incomparable athlete, and simply perfect all around. Sy graduated high school at sixteen, college at eighteen, and received his doctorate at twenty-one. He received both academic and athletic scholarships. Unfortunately, Bastet passed away when Sy was seventeen, so she did not see how extraordinary he was. Sy joined AmCorps during his second year in graduate school. His work at AmCorps was allowed to compliment his graduate studies at Harvard.

It was during this time Lucien realized how incredible his creation was. He had gotten it perfect on his first try. Unfortunately, during that period of time between Sy and the pandemics, Lucien did not have any other opportunities to experiment. Well, that was until now. All but one of his specimens showed every indication that they were perfect. Of course, he had made a few more adjustments with this second batch that took into consideration what society would need as a whole, including genotype rs4950 and some additional adjustments on Chromosome 7. Lucien clicked the camera icon on his computer and chose the nursery view. He saw the perfect children. With the success of this program, Lucien decided to name his new breed of hominids, Homo osiris. They would be the rebirth of the human species. Because he and Bastet had been willing to take a chance, to break the law, to challenge the status quo, Lucien was now in the perfect position to save the human race. Those that would've condemned him were now begging him for his treatment, for his help, and he was able to deliver.

Lucien's comm center chimed. "Sir, I have Sy."

"Put him through, thanks." Lucien paused and waited for the secure line to chime, letting him know that Sy was patched through and his assistant had clicked off. "Sy, what's going on?"

"I found something interesting in the mother's genome that had gone unnoticed. She has a mutation on ABCD4 gene. That makes her body unable to process cobalamin, vitamin—"

"B12," Lucien inserted.

"Exactly. I think she may have late-onset cb1C disease, set off by pregnancy. I think the lack of B12 caused the birth defects in the child. The mother also presents with symptoms that confirm this. She appears spacey, slow, slightly confused. She's reported tingling in her extremities. She attributes these symptoms to bulging discs in her back and neck that were irritated by pregnancy. Though I suspect that it's actually a result of cb1C disease."

"That's great news," Lucien responded.

"That's why I wanted to let you know as soon as possible. It means that the problems with this child had nothing to do with AmCorps neonatal program. The program is flawless."

"Flawless," Lucien repeated, which was unusual in scientific or medical treatments. Lucien couldn't help but smile.

"I just stopped by the unit and the children are thriving. Every single one has surpassed expected milestones. They're incredible," Sy said.

"Indeed," Lucien added. "Have we been doing health checks on the mothers enrolled in round two?"

"Not really. We're monitoring their basic health. The checkups have been postponed until we have the EVE-0 treatment in hand. Then we will do the extensive posttreatment checkup, harvest the eggs, fertilize them, conduct the preimplantation genetic diagnosis, do the germline edits, and implant the embryos into the mothers."

"And what about the male donors?"

"Same, in terms of the health checks. Once they receive the treatment, we will do the full posttreatment check, then collect their sperm," Sy responded.

"I want them to be among the first treated. If all goes as planned, we should have the first doses ready within a week, which means we could potentially have our next round of embryos ready in six months. I want this program to take precedence."

"Over treatment distribution?"

"I don't think it needs to be over, but it can be equal to."

"Understood. Any report on Dr. Gale?"

"Not yet, but I'm hopeful that she will arrive to the extraction site very soon."

"Great."

Waiting with his thoughts and plans, Lucien hated feeling like his hands were tied. There was nowhere he could direct his frustration so he decided to resume his session in his hyperbaric float tank.

Lucien rang his assistant on his comm center. "I will be in my float tank. I don't want to be interrupted unless it's life or death."

"Yes, sir."

Lucien considered his hyperbaric float tank a necessity for him. It was like being suspended in nothingness. It was pitch black. Sometimes Lucien kept it silent, but usually he opted for either nature sounds, white noise, or instrumental music played at a frequency of precisely 741 Hz. Lucien believed that sensory deprivation, oxygen, and this frequency allowed the neurons in his brain to fire at their highest capacity and increase neurogenesis.

It took Lucien a little longer this time to reach a state of deep relaxation. He had a difficult time quieting his brain, but he was finally able to clear his mind. He focused on his breathing. Slowly inhaling and exhaling. He tuned into the frequency of the new age music.

"Excuse me, sir." His assistant's voice interrupted his relaxation. "Sir?"

Lucien was suddenly filled with rage. He took a breath before he spoke. "What is it?"

"I have Commander Jones on the line. He said it's urgent."

"Put him through."

"Dr. Sabara, our drones picked up some images of the two men we had been watching. They have a cage with someone in it."

"What?"

"We were not able to identify the individual in the cage. That means there's a possibility that it's Dr. Gale. The drones also picked up a few images of what appears to be a substantial fire pit and spit that they're building."

"Why don't you go there and see?" Lucien snapped.

"I wanted to check with you first, as you ordered

us to not engage in any combat activities with any indigenous people. We can't determine whether they are indigenous or not."

"Go fucking see. Bringing Dr. Gale back alive is your top priority. Use common sense to achieve that directive, even if that means engaging a threat to her. I told you this."

"Yes sir. We are approximately two hours away from that site. We—"

"You're two hours away from a site that has two men and a prisoner in a cage, that may or may not be Dr. Gale?"

"Yes, sir."

"Let me put it this way: if anything happens to Dr. Gale by your hand or any other, you might as well kill yourself. GET THERE NOW and let me know the second she is secured."

"Yes, sir." Commander Jones promptly disconnected.

24 – KURU

Gabby watched them meticulously build the spit. It was a simple design and they had it finished in no time. They made two tripods of what appeared to be bamboo, then tied it tightly with some sort of vine. They had a thin palm trunk that hung across the two tripods. They started to light the fire and Gabby thought this was it for her. *Wait,* she thought, *how can I have been so stupid? Where is my Chief's Special? Please, let the gun still be there!* She felt for the small handgun in her bag. It was still there.

The maniacs managed to get a huge fire going quickly. They had a stockpile of wood set up next to the flame. Then, they disappeared into a nearby shack. She couldn't see what they were doing, but she heard some yelling and banging. They came out dragging another man. He was badly bruised, bloody, and barely conscious.

"Eramos amigos. ¿Por qué estás haciendo esto?" the man cried.

"Eres molesto y temenos hambre," the man with the cattle prod spit.

"Te has vuelto loco," the man cried.

Gabby realized they were speaking Spanish and understood bits of the conversation. Just enough to know that they weren't from here, they had been friends, and the maniacs had, in fact, gone crazy.

The man with the cattle prod peeled his lips back from his rotten teeth, broke out in a fit of laughter, threw his head back, and began to howl like a wolf. The other maniac joined in. While still howling, he jammed the cattle prod into the man and shocked him unconscious. They stripped his clothes. The man's bowels had emptied.

"Mierda! Tomo un poco de agua y lavarlo," the cattle prod maniac yelled, and the other scurried off.

He quickly returned with a bucket of water and threw it on the unfortunate friend of these two. He reflexively gasped for air, though barely conscious. The cattle prod maniac took the heavy metal prod and swung it at the man's head, leaving him completely comatose. They laid the thin palm trunk next to him and tied his hands and legs around it. They each grabbed a side, heaved it onto their shoulders, and scooted it in place over the fire. The man dangled like a pig. It was the most dreadful thing Gabby had ever seen. Her brain struggled to comprehend what was happening. The guy's face slowly began to contort in pain as the flames began to bubble his skin. The pain was so intense that it pulled him from insentience. His eyes shot open in horror and he screamed. Gabby wanted to take the gun and shoot him in the head to put an end to his torture, but if she did that she would lose what little element of surprise she had.

"Dios," the man cried, *"por favor ayudame."*

The leader with the cattle prod began sniffing the air with a disgusted expression. *"¿Hueles eso?"* He sniffed some more, while the man wailed in pain. *"Huele a mierda. No puedo comer eso. Sácalo."*

The other guy, "the rat," as Gabby viewed him, scurried over to the one side of the palm trunk, while the other guy grabbed the other side. They heaved him off and dropped him in the dirt on his melted skin. He made one last jerk of pain, then went still. They untied him and dragged his body to the side of the clearing.

"Ella sabrá mucho major," the leader grinned, looking over at Gabby and licking his lips. The rat giggled and licked his lips too.

Gabby felt for the hammer and cocked the snub-nosed revolver. She took a breath and steadied herself. She had one chance at this. Timing would be everything. She waited. The psychopath came towards her, his cattle prod leading the way. When he was a few steps away, she pulled the gun out, aimed through the bars, and pulled the trigger. It jammed. She pushed down on the hammer. Then pulled the trigger again. It was stuck. She banged the revolver on the bars of the cage and it fired. The bullet sailed past the maniacs.

She cocked the gun again and fired. The psychopaths dove out of the way. She missed. She cocked the gun again. She saw the rat scurrying away from her cage. She aimed and pulled the trigger. The bullet hit him and lodged in the back of his leg. He cried out in pain and began to whimper. Gabby heard a noise behind her and spun to see the cattle prod coming towards her. She ducked out of the way, cocked the gun, and pulled the trigger. The bullet barely skimmed the cage, sparking, and lodged into the leader's shoulder. He didn't make a noise. Just reached into the wound, pulled out a bloody finger, licked it, and laughed. She cocked the gun and pulled the trigger. Nothing. Cocked it again. Pulled. Nothing. Her chest turned to stone as she realized that she was out of bullets. A sudden surge of intense pain stiffened every muscle in her body and her world went black.

It was dark, but Gabby felt like she was on a boat that was rolling in the ocean. Sharp pain in her shoulder pulled her out of her daze. She moaned and felt an urgent need to open her eyes. She struggled to reach out and grab onto something, but her body refused to move. She finally wrenched her eyes open. She was lying on the hard dirt ground. The maniacs grabbed her and dragged her towards the fire and dropped her. She remembered the knife she had put in her pocket, hoping it was still there. The maniacs were untying the twine from the dead guy's hands and feet.

Gabby quickly stuffed her hand in her pocket and

found the folded-up blade.

"Ve a quitarle la ropa," the leader yelled to the rat.

Gabby knew *ropa* meant clothes. She stuffed both hands in her pockets and spun. As the rat approached, she began kicking him. He tried to grab her legs to pull her pants off. She got a few good kicks in. He backed up and tried to get to her arms, but she spun again. Gabby used her legs to sweep and trip the rat. He went down.

"Maldito idiota no puedes hacer nada," the leader barked as he approached Gabby.

She rolled almost onto her stomach, away from the leader. She used her body as cover to pull out the knife. She popped the blade out and waited. The second the leader grabbed her shoulders, she rolled to face him and jammed the blade into the back of his calf and pulled hard. She sliced through as much of his calf muscle as she could. He screamed and fell back. Then the rat stepped on her, pulled his leg back, and kicked her. She rolled towards him, grabbed his leg so he couldn't kick, and sliced through his Achilles tendon. He didn't make a noise, but his face turned completely grey, and he collapsed back. Gabby spun back towards the leader, ready to send the blade in. She saw his quad coming towards her. She lifted her arm and sent it towards his thigh. The blade broke through the surface of his leg, then her muscles went rigid, shooting pain blinded her, and her world went black.

25 - SHADOW WARRIORS

Chris, Rodrigo, Francesco, and the tree village warriors moved through the jungle quickly and silently. Chris struggled to keep up. These men were at home here. They didn't need their eyes to see where they were going. They knew the way the ground felt. They seemed to sense every rock, tree stump, and fallen log. Chris was more like a wrecking ball, crashing into everything in his path. He likely sounded like one to these men as well. Rodrigo eventually came up with a system to help Chris. He told Chris to stay close behind him. He would make a clicking noise when there was a low obstacle in their path, and he would let out a short, high-pitched whistle when there was a larger obstacle. This worked. Chris was able to keep up and stay relatively quiet.

They made it to the tree village in three hours, a quarter of the time it took them to flee to the Pachamama Cave. It was dark and quiet. They found a handful of rival villagers sleeping in their tree house. It looked like several more had started to move over to the tree house, but hadn't gotten there yet. It was just the war party that had been tormenting them. Their faces and bodies were still painted black. Chris remembered these warriors. The black paint made them look as if they were constantly in shadows, even in the dark of night. *The shadow warriors,* Chris thought. Their bodies lay passed out, practically on top of each other. They had clearly been celebrating. Chris remembered their cold, hate-filled glare as they threatened Francesco's people. The heads they left on stakes in the clearing below for their families to find. The tree warriors moved swiftly, quietly, and without remorse. They killed each shadow warrior as they slept, never waking them up. A few opened their eyes when the spear broke through their chest, but they were dead before they realized what had happened. Chris just stood back. This wasn't his fight, and he would only insert himself if needed.

They threw the bodies out of the tree village and dragged them into the jungle. They cut the heads off of the two men who had done the same to their warriors that tried to bring peace. They used the same spears that had delivered their loved one's heads and took them as they left. This was the same violence and revenge Chris had experienced in almost every battle he'd ever fought. At their root, human beings were all the same. He didn't like it, but this violence was part of human nature.

They were quickly on the move again. They made it to the shadow warrior's village in just over an hour. Everyone was sleeping, except one young child. The village was in disarray. There were gourds the size of mixing bowls scattered around. In the center of the village were three large hollowed-out trunks that looked like skinny canoes. There was a trace of liquid left in them.

Rodrigo leaned over to Chris and whispered, *"Caxiri."* He quietly explained that the village was drunk. Chris had seen some of these bowls scattered around the tree village as well. No wonder the men hadn't awakened. The child was about four years old, Chris guessed. He was holding his head like it hurt. He didn't notice them watching him. One of the warriors took out an arrow and placed it on his bow. Chris put his hand on his shoulder, stopping him.

They pulled back into the shadows of the forest and moved out of the village square. They found the Chief's *maloca* or hut. It was abnormally long, so it likely housed several people under its thatched roof. The plan was to move in, capture and secure the chief, and kill only those that got in their way. Francesco held his hand up, readying them. He brought his hand down and they charged in.

In the first open room, people were sleeping everywhere. They didn't seem to notice them come in. Some stirred and groaned, but that was it. They were so drunk, Chris almost felt bad for them. Francesco accidentally stepped on one of the sleeping bodies, a young man. He sat up, didn't realize what was happening, and Francesco swung his club at his head. It knocked him down, but not out. He managed to get out a gurgled scream and others began to wake up. Rodrigo and Chris stayed in that room while Francesco and the warriors moved on to capture the chief.

It was chaotic. There were no weapons in the *maloca*, so it was not difficult for Chris to fight off any threat. The villagers' festivities from the day and night before made things even easier. Chris felt a slight pang of guilt at the realization that this stirred something in him that he enjoyed. His pent-up stress was melting away with each punch he landed. A loud whistle pierced the *maloca* and the fighting stopped.

The chief walked into the main room, his hands above his head. Two tree village warriors carried the spears with the heads of their slain warriors. The chief addressed his people. Rodrigo leaned over to Chris and in Portuguese said, "He's telling his people that this is his fault. There is enough forest here to share. His selfishness and need for power has caused their demise."

"Is it really this easy?" Chris asked.

"For now. We have the chief, so it's done. They were stupid and greedy," Rodrigo said.

Francesco and the warriors marched the chief out of his *maloca* and through the village. They held torches and the retribution heads while the chief proclaimed their surrender. Out of nowhere, an arrow lodged into the arm of the warrior holding the heads. Then another whizzed by. Chris followed its trajectory and saw three men with arrows behind a small *maloca*. Chris pointed them out to Rodrigo and pulled out his gun. They were readying their bows again. Rodrigo nodded to Chris, and he fired. The bullet struck the shoulder of the man on the outside flank position. They all dropped their bows. The chief yelled something, and they came out from behind the building.

They continued their march through the village, waking everyone up with loud war cries. The parade finished in the village square. They waited for everyone to slowly gather there. When the clearing was filled with wary and hungover villagers, Francesco pushed the chief down on his knees. With his head bowed, the chief remained completely stoic. Chris couldn't understand what was being said, and Rodrigo wasn't able to translate. Francesco addressed the crowd. He made a show of asking the chief a series of questions with no emotion. The chief answered each question. Francesco pulled his gun out and showed it. Rodrigo pulled his two guns out and held them up as well. He leaned over and told Chris to pull his gun out and show the crowd. Chris made a show of it and they each fired a shot in the air. Francesco held his gun up to the chief's head. The villagers gasped. He addressed the chief and the upset villagers, many of which were crying. He pulled his gun away from the chief and holstered it. Francesco pulled the chief up. The chief said something to his people. Then, Francesco and the chief embraced.

Francesco began to walk away and his warriors placed their heads down gently to follow him. A group of men from the village followed behind Francesco's warriors, and finally Rodrigo and Chris walked at the rear of the group. They headed back to the tree village. On the hike back, Rodrigo explained that Francesco spared the chief's life because he agreed to never bother them again. They agreed to share their land for hunting and to be peaceful.

The villagers cleaned up their belongings from the tree village, gathered the bodies of the war party that had been there, and brought them back to their village to bury. It went as expected, or even a little better. The sun was just starting to come up when they began their trek back to the Pachamama cave. Chris thought they'd be gone for a couple of days. Instead, they'd make it back in less than twenty-four hours. He couldn't wait to throw his arms around Gabby.

They definitely weren't traveling at the same pace they were last night. They were exhausted, but the adrenaline from the easily won battle made everything a little easier. The air was a comfortable temperature and the birds were singing. Chris didn't know what the future held, but right now all he wanted was to see Gabby again.

They made it back in just under five hours. Chris

was ready for a long nap, right after he wrapped his arms around Gabby. Chief Ëpë was waiting outside and grabbed Rodrigo. Chris didn't understand what they were saying, but he could tell by their expression that it was serious.

"What happened?" Chris repeated in Portuguese several times before running into the cave.

Please let her be alive, Chris repeated as he made his way into the cave. As he barreled in, everyone turned to stare at him. He felt his pulse quicken, dread filled his entire core, and he felt sick. *Please, God, please let her be alive,* he repeated to himself. Nausea crashed into him when he saw her camp had been cleaned up. He clenched his jaw and closed his eyes to calm himself. He walked over to where their camp had been. Wait, he slowly realized, *why would her pack and the blood cooler be gone?* He looked around and saw the letter. He snatched it up, his eyes racing across the words.

Chris, the letter read, I *told AmCorps that you're dead. This will buy you time to work with Michaela and potentially get the treatment out to the world. Then, and only then, come for me. Or, at the very least, save you. But, if you do something stupid and AmCorps learns that I lied to them, we'll both be dead, and you won't have the space to accomplish anything.* Gabby signed the letter with, *Please, please, please don't do anything stupid. I love you, Gabs.*

Every ounce of dread was instantly replaced with

rage. The only problem was, he had no one to direct it at. He wanted to be mad at Gabby, but he loved her, and she had sacrificed herself for him. *What the fuck was she thinking!*

Chris quickly began to pack up his bag. He grabbed another gun from his pack and some ammo. Rodrigo put his hand on Chris's shoulder. "Are you okay, friend?" Rodrigo asked in Portuguese.

Chris didn't answer. Instead, he picked up the pace packing his things.

"Chief Ëpë filled me in," Rodrigo said. "Gabby did a very kind, honorable thing."

"That's bullshit. I'm going after her," Chris snapped.

"Not now."

"I'm going. When did she leave?"

"Last night."

"The extraction point's at least a two- or three-day hike. I can catch up to her," Chris said, and threw his bag on his back.

"No." Rodrigo stepped in front of him.

"Get out of my way."

Chief Ëpë and the shaman came over and said something to Rodrigo. He nodded and stepped out of Chris's way. "Fine, but I'm going with you," he said.

Chris shrugged and started towards the cave's exit.

Chief Ëpë said something to Rodrigo. "Chris," Rodrigo called out. "Wait, Chief wants you to know something."

Chris paused and turned.

"Chief says that you should trust Gabby's plan. He knows it will work."

Chris smiled and nodded. He quickly continued on his way.

As soon as Chris stepped out of the cave, he lost every sense of direction he had. He couldn't figure out north, south, east, or west. His adrenaline pumped, clouding his usual ability to function efficiently as a seasoned warrior. He took a few calming breaths to get oriented. He realized that if he didn't know which way to go, Gabby didn't either. She could've wandered off in any direction. How would she know which way the evacuation point was? He was totally lost.

"I don't know where to go," Chris said.

"Follow me," Rodrigo said.

Moments later they were back on the trail. Chris estimated that Gabby had about a fifteen-hour jump on them, which at the pace he was going, meant he should be able to catch up to her by tonight or tomorrow morning, at the latest.

Chris felt like he was on a hamster wheel, running as fast as he could but getting nowhere. The jungle all looked the same, though it was a different place without Gabby. He couldn't believe she'd done this. They were better together.

26 – SAFE

Gabby's head was spinning. She could hear someone calling her in the distance but couldn't get there. She couldn't make out the voice, but she wanted it to be quiet so she could rest. She was so tired. She heard it again. The blackness was nice. She wanted to drift off into it, but that annoying voice wouldn't quit. She struggled to open her eyes.

"That's it, come on," the voice called to her.

She tried a little harder. Her eyes cracked open and pain and light flooded in, forcing them closed again. "Ouch," Gabby moaned.

"I know, but if you wake up, we can make you feel better," the voice calmly offered.

Gabby tried again, this time blinking several times. Her vision was extremely blurry, but there was a figure standing over her, gently rubbing her head.

"That's really good," the voice said.

Gabby rubbed her eyes. Her body throbbed in pain and she winced. The figure brushed some hair off Gabby's face. "You're almost there," the voice said.

Gabby blinked some more, her world slowly coming into focus, though she didn't immediately know where she was or what was going on. As her eyes were finally able to focus, she saw a man sitting with her. He wore black tactical gear. In a panic, she sat up. The pain was so intense, she collapsed back and the man caught her. "Slow down there. You had quite the experience. But you're safe now."

Gabby slowly worked her way to a seated position and looked around. There were several men all dressed in the same black tactical gear. Gabby looked around and suddenly remembered where she was. She saw the leader and the rat, dead. She saw the cage that she'd been in turned on its side.

"My things," Gabby said, "where are my things?"

The man waved over another agent.

"This is what we found near you," he said, and the man placed her things in front of her. Her pack was there and so was the blood cooler. Gabby checked it; there were still five hours left on the charge and it looked untouched.

"Where are we?" Gabby asked. Her mouth was so dry it felt like it had been stuffed with straw.

"We're about two hours from the extraction site."

"You're AmCorps, right?"

"Yes, ma'am. Dr. Gale, we're so glad we found you when we did."

"What happened?"

"What's the last thing you remember?"

"They're cannibals," Gabby said, pointing to the leader and the rat, "they were going to put me over the fire and, I think, eat me. I was trying to fight them off."

"You caused a lot of damage. When we found you, this one had tried to shock you, but you had stabbed him with the blade of a metal knife, so he shocked himself as well. You're lucky the knife had a metal handle. You passed out from the shock and so did he."

"I thought they were going to kill me," Gabby said.

"If you weren't so tough, they probably would've."

Gabby's head pounded, but she wanted to get out of here. She forced herself to stand but wobbled a little. The agent reached out and steadied her.

"Thanks. What's your name?" Gabby asked.

"Commander Jones, ma'am."

"Nice to meet you."

"You too, Dr. Gale."

Gabby tried to smile. "When can we get out of here? I need to charge or plug in the cooler as soon as possible."

"Whenever you're ready. You and I will take that ATV over there and we'll meet the others at the extraction point. The planes are powered up and ready. You can plug your pack in there."

"I'm ready," Gabby said, grabbing her bag and the blood cooler. She quickly peeked in to make sure that everything was alright. The cooler was still cold and the blood packs were all perfectly intact.

The ride to the extraction point was rough. Every bump, and there were a lot, sent shocks of pain through Gabby's body that echoed in her throbbing head.

"Dr. Gale, can I ask you what happened with the original extraction?"

Gabby took a breath. "The people that live here made the choice to reject modern living. For the last hundred years or more, they've been tormented by missionaries carrying disease, illegal loggers destroying their land and killing their families, and drug smugglers causing havoc. The only reason they trusted us was a pure stroke of luck. When your guys came in, they destroyed the delicate understanding we had formed. The extraction team murdered our guide, Kukua, just because he got in their way. They killed Trent, their mission leader. I was scared. I'm still scared that you'll just kill me, too. You have to understand that it's very hard for me to trust you," Gabby knew she would face a slew of questions, so it was essential that she was very careful with everything she said.

"We're a completely different team, ma'am. Under completely different orders. We're not going to hurt you. You can trust me. We are here to protect you. But," Jones paused, "can I ask what your stroke of luck was? How you made friendly contact with the natives? Why they trusted you?" Jones looked at Gabby when he said that. One eyebrow and the corners of Jones's mouth lifted slightly, giving away his mistrust.

"It's going to be hard for you to believe," Gabby said.

"Try me," Jones smiled.

Gabby bit her lip. "Okay. While we were trying to find one of the native villages to make contact, Trent was bit by a bushmaster. It was bad, so we were camped out near a river. It was our second day there, and Trent started to feel better. We were planning to leave the next day."

"Keep going." Jones smiled. Gabby wanted to hate Jones. She definitely didn't trust him, but there was something likable about him. He was rough, and it showed in his sandy, greying hair, thick neck, and gravelly voice. But he was also charming. She realized that could be a weapon of its own. She chose her words carefully.

"All of a sudden, Kukua and his guys, Patrick and Bob, started packing up camp. They told us to grab our stuff quickly. Out of nowhere, the river started flowing faster, then it started rising. Before I knew it, the water took over our camp and we fled. I don't know how it happened, but I got separated from everyone. In a split second, it was like they disappeared."

"Seriously?"

"Yeah, they were gone. I yelled their names. I searched everywhere and couldn't even find a sign of them or the camp. I heard a twig snap, looked up, and a huge jaguar stepped out from behind a tree. I froze. I could see every muscle in its body tensed and ready to attack. I thought I was dead. I tried backing up slowly and it followed. Another minute and it would've eaten me. But then something whizzed by me and a dart stuck into the jaguar's shoulder. It whimpered, turned, and fled. A group of Matsés warriors had been tracking this jaguar and found me. The jaguar holds mystical powers for them, and they believed the jaguar brought them to me for a reason. It was pure luck and silly superstition, but it allowed us to make a connection with them."

"That's crazy and *very* lucky."

"I told you, you wouldn't believe me."

"I do believe you," Jones smiled. "So, that's how you got to their village?"

"Yeah."

"The other thing that I don't understand is how you were able to raise such a large force to fight Am-Corps's initial extraction team?"

"We didn't raise a force. They're the Jungle Guardians, a sort of ragtag army. Most of the members were indigenous people whose families had been killed by illegal loggers or drug smugglers; mostly loggers though. They had some horrific stories, entire families just brutally murdered. Their purpose is to protect people like themselves. They are highly trained in jungle warfare. They came to the area because they thought that the extraction team was a new logging operation moving in."

"No shit. Who would've expected that?"

"Yeah."

"Do we need to worry about the Jungle Guardians now?"

"No, the few that survived left with the Matsés."

"Where'd they go?"

"All different places, but I'm not going to tell you. These people protected us and helped us. They'll never go with you. To be honest, I don't trust you either. AmCorps, our own team, your extraction unit, killed Trent, Kukua, Patrick, Bob, Chris, everyone—except me. And that's just because the guardians and the Matsés protected me. I really didn't want to come here, knowing you're probably going to kill me too, but I owe it to them."

"No, Dr. Gale, please, you can trust me. General Holton has been removed and we've been directed to approach this mission much more sensitively. I can't speak for the other unit. I don't know what they were thinking or what their orders were. All I can tell you is that it's been made very clear that we are not to engage under any circumstances. Our only directive is to get you back to the safe house alive."

Gabby had to remind herself not to believe him.

He looked down at the ATV's gauges. "The battery is running low. Don't think this thing gets very far on a charge. We may have to walk the last bit," Jones said, breaking the silence that had settled.

"That's fine." Gabby checked the timer on the cooler. "We have three hours to get this cooler plugged in."

Gabby could feel the ATV getting slower and slower.

"I think we can walk faster than this. You good?" Jones asked.

"Yep."

"We only have a couple miles to go. My estimate is about a forty-five-minute walk."

Gabby nodded and grabbed her bags. Jones reached over to take the blood cooler.

"No, I've got it," Gabby snapped.

He held his hand up, palms out. "That's fine. I just wanted to lighten the load for you."

"I'm fine."

The trail looked familiar. Gabby recognized some of the trees and thought of how Kukua told her that's how he knew his way around the forest. She had been on this trail before, but it was dark. Gabby saw a spot of darkened earth and burn marks on a tree. This was where the mortar round exploded. Gabby began breathing quicker.

Jones turned around. "Are you okay?"

She nodded her head. "I just need a second." Gabby felt sick. She was hot and sweaty.

"We're almost there; there's a shortcut right up here."

Gabby took a few deep breaths and steadied herself. "I know the shortcut."

She did; it was the game trail she'd followed the

jaguar into. The trail that took her back to Trent. That was the worst night of her life. The anxiety that had exploded in her chest just minutes ago had already been replaced with sadness. They followed the trail and were soon back in the Matsés village. Seeing this empty village brought a flood of memories back. Being back here was much harder than she expected. She put her head down as she walked. She began to wonder if she was doing the right thing. She hadn't really thought this through. It was such a rash decision. She missed Chris. She hoped that he would understand her decision, the decision that she was currently trying to understand herself.

Gabby made the mistake of looking up as they walked past Trent's lab. Her heart felt as if it turned to stone, rolling down her chest and taking out everything in its path, leaving her hollow. Then, a large, iridescent blue morpho butterfly, like the one she saw when she was leaving, flitted across her path and something changed in her. It was like she could feel Trent there. A warmth melted over her. While she was still immensely sad, her resolve was bolstered. She remembered her purpose. The help that Trent had given her. The strings that he pulled and the events that he put in motion. She couldn't explain it, but she knew she was in the right place.

They made it to the extraction point. The old planes had been cleared off the runway and lay in a pile of rubble. It appeared there had been a massive bonfire, then Gabby noticed the pile of bones in the ashes.

"You burned the bodies?" Gabby asked.

"We had to. The smell was unbearable, animals were coming here, and we couldn't risk the threat of disease from the rotting corpses."

She asked, "Did you identify any of the bodies?"

"Some. We were able to account for all but five officers from the original extraction unit."

"Did you find Chris?" Gabby asked.

"No," Jones shook his head. "Do you know where he went down?"

Gabby nodded her head and pointed. "Over there. He was part of the first charge. He was already gone by the time I was able to reach him."

"There were a few bodies that were too damaged to identify. Animals also dragged a couple into the forest."

Gabby put her head down and let a few tears break free.

"I'm sorry."

"It..." Gabby paused. "It didn't have to happen. That's what makes me so angry and sad."

"I agree. Though in combat situations, you don't always have the luxury of time to figure things out. In life-or-death situations, it tends to be shoot first, figure it out later."

"It didn't have to be life or death."

As they approached the planes, a group of extraction agents came out to meet them. They saluted Commander Jones.

"At ease," Jones ordered. "This is Dr. Gale. Unfortunately, Dr. Gale crossed paths with some leftover drug smugglers on her way here. She did a solid job on her two captors but needed a little assistance. We got there just in time."

"They had gone insane from being cannibalistic. And I somehow managed to walk right into a trap they had set." Gabby admitted, in an effort to seem as personable as possible.

The soldiers' eyes widened. Whether from the idea of cannibals or her survival from their hands, she couldn't tell.

"Glad we were able to get to you, ma'am," a young soldier offered.

"Me too." Gabby smiled.

"You must be exhausted. We have a special area set up for you on the smaller jet," Jones said, pointing towards the lead plane.

"Special area?" Gabby asked. She recalled with a shudder the cages the first extraction team had used for the natives she and Chris had rescued.

Jones smiled. "Comfortable travel accommodations. It's actually a luxury jet. You, me, and a few of my men are on that plane. This is a military transport aircraft. It's very uncomfortable and slower."

Gabby smiled. "I am exhausted and I want to get out of here. How long until we can leave?"

"My men should be an hour behind us, at most. Then it's wheels up. You hear that, boys?" Jones directed his attention to his men. "Get everything ready so we can leave as soon as everyone is back."

"Yes, sir," the soldiers answered in unison. They saluted Commander Jones, then left.

Jones brought Gabby onto the plane. It was either the same plane that Gabby took to Brazil or exactly like it. That seemed like a lifetime ago.

"There are some beds in the back if you'd like to rest."

Gabby nodded and made her way back to the beds. She collapsed onto the closest one. She would feel better when they were in the air.

She plugged the cooler in and secured it under her bed.

27 – TAKE OFF

"Chris," Rodrigo pleaded, "we need a break."

"I have to catch up to her."

"You will tomorrow, when the sun comes back up."

The trail that Chris and Rodrigo were on was very difficult. Every step was a struggle. Rodrigo found a small clearing with a few boulders and moss. He sat down and rested against the rocks.

"Is this the trail she took?" Chris asked as he reluctantly sat down.

Rodrigo shrugged. "I don't know, man. All I know is that she headed back to the extraction point."

"If she was on this trail, we should've caught up with her by now. She does not move well on trails like this."

Rodrigo didn't answer. Chris looked over and found him already asleep.

Chris debated moving on alone but realized that would be impossible. He didn't have a map or any navigation tools. He'd never get there if Rodrigo didn't lead the way. Chris found a spot of soft moss growing up a rock and laid back. He'd been awake for nearly forty-eight hours. To function at his best, he needed a short rest.

Chris took a sharp inhale and opened his eyes. He didn't remember falling asleep. He had been just going to take a short rest. The next thing he knew, the sun was up.

"Rodrigo, get up, we have to go," Chris said, jumping up.

Rodrigo forced his eyes open and stretched. "Oh shit, we slept." He jumped up.

They grabbed their things and were on the move. The difficulty of the trail didn't ease. They maintained their pace from the morning to the late afternoon. They didn't talk, they didn't stop for any breaks, they just moved.

Finally, Rodrigo broke the silence. "Chris, there's another trail we can take. It leads right to the extraction point but it's open. AmCorps will definitely spot us if they're anywhere in the area or doing any kind of surveillance. It's extremely risky and goes against everything that Gabby wanted."

"I don't care."

Rodrigo shrugged. They crossed onto the open path as dusk was setting in. Their trek became much easier. They moved quickly, but cautiously. They hugged the tree line. They passed the coca field. Rodrigo quietly grabbed a few leaves for his pockets, and they moved on. A shiny reflection abruptly caught Chris's attention. Light from the setting sun was catching on something metal in a small clearing up ahead. As Chris got closer, he saw a few abandoned shacks through the trees.

"This field has been abandoned for years. We chased the growers out a long time ago," Rodrigo said.

"Someone's been here," Chris said as he jogged ahead and turned into the clearing. The metal that was reflecting through the trees was a cage. Then, Chris saw the legs of two bodies behind some sort of huge fire pit. He sprinted over, relieved that he didn't recognize them.

Rodrigo caught up, then stopped suddenly when he saw the bodies. "They look like drug smugglers, but no one's been here in years."

"They're not guardians, right?"

"No, definitely not. And that cage was never here. That's strange."

Chris looked from the bodies to the tipped-over cage and cart. "Oh shit," Chris said, running towards the cage. He bent down and picked up a small revolver. "This was Gab's gun."

"Are you sure?"

"I'm 100% sure. I was there when she picked this gun." Chris looked around, bent down, and picked something small up. "She fired it. Here's the shells. Check the shacks."

Rodrigo ran into one shack, while Chris ran into the other. Rodrigo screamed, and Chris ran over.

"Don't come in," Rodrigo said, but Chris didn't listen. He burst through the plywood door. Inside were pieces of a body hanging in the corner, an arm from the shoulder down and a leg from the hip down. They looked like they had been cooked. The skin was charred. Chris put his hand over his mouth.

"It's not her," Chris whispered, "it's not her."

Rodrigo walked over and took the leg off the hook.

"What are you doing?" Chris was on the brink of tears.

Rodrigo didn't answer. He put the foot of the limb flat on the ground, next to him. "It's not her," Rodrigo said, "look, Gabby was shorter than me. This person is taller."

Chris let out a breath and walked over and stood next to the leg. "You're right, this person was around my height. This is definitely not Gabby." Chris let out a huge breath. He had never been so relieved.

"Do you think Gabby killed them?" Rodrigo asked.

Chris shrugged and said, "I don't know," then walked back out to the clearing. He examined the bodies first. They both had been shot by high-caliber rounds in their heads. Chris instantly recognized the military-style executions. "AmCorps was here."

"How do you know?" Rodrigo asked.

"Look at their heads."

"Ah, got it," Rodrigo said as soon as he noticed the gaping wounds in the back of their heads.

"I think that's an electric cattle prod," Chris said as he kicked what resembled a metal bar with a grip on one end and two prongs on the other.

"It is," Rodrigo agreed.

Chris looked at the cage. There was a game net tangled in the bottom and a metal cable. "I think they caught Gabs in a snare trap while she was on her way to the AmCorps extraction point," Chris said.

Rodrigo nodded his head.

"I need to know if she made it to them. I don't care if they see me," Chris added.

"That's a little selfish, don't you think?"

Chris didn't respond. He just spun around and headed back to the open path. He had an idea of where to go. That's all he needed.

"It will be dark soon," Rodrigo relented, "so we just need to be careful." Rodrigo followed Chris out.

They made it to the village in just under two hours. The sun had gone down, and it was pitch black. They clung to the tree line, but the village was empty and they eventually moved in.

"Wait," Rodrigo said. He reached into his bag, pulling out a couple bandanas and hoods. "Put this on."

It was eerie and deserted. Memories of its tragic past hung heavy in the vacant walkways and homes.

If Chris hadn't been so focused on Gabby, the sight of the ghost village would've saddened him.

A sudden loud noise pierced the quiet. It took Chris a second, but he recognized it. It was the sound of a jet engine powering up. Chris took off running. He made it to the tree-covered path that led right to the extraction point surprisingly fast. Rodrigo sprinted and tackled him with every ounce of force he could muster. They bounced off of a hard tree trunk as they tumbled. Chris had at least fifty pounds and six inches on his friend, but that didn't matter. Chris went down and Rodrigo used all of his weight to hold him in place.

"What the fuck are you doing?" Chris snapped as he tried to free himself from Rodrigo's surprisingly strong hold.

"Just stay down."

"I don't want to hurt you," Chris warned.

"You're being stupid and selfish. They will kill her if they find out you're still alive."

"Get off of me," Chris huffed.

"No! I need you to find your common sense."

"I'm not going to tell you again," Chris growled.

"You're her only hope. Gabby's obviously alive if they're leaving. If you love her, you need to listen to me."

The words cut his heart. Yes, he did love Gabby. More than anything. Chris calmed down and stopped trying to break free of Rodrigo's snakelike grip. He craned his neck up enough to see the lights of a plane lift over the tree line. He heard another engine power up.

"You can get off now," Chris said.

Rodrigo didn't move.

"They're gone," Chris continued.

Rodrigo finally got off as the engine sounds headed off in the distance. Chris sat up and watched the second plane's lights disappear over the trees. He jumped up and took off sprinting, skidding to a stop just before breaking into the clearing. The field was empty.

Rodrigo caught up to him soon. Chris turned and punched him in the face, then instantly regretted it. "I should not have done that. I'm sorry," Chris said.

"It's alright. I deserved it," Rodrigo said, blotting his lip with the sleeve of his shirt, "but remind me to teach you how to punch."

"I'm sorry." Chris smiled. "Fix your bandana. We should sweep the area for any surveillance devices AmCorps may have left."

The area was clean. AmCorps seemed to have left in a hurry.

PART III

"Nevertheless so profound is our ignorance, and so high our presumption, that we marvel when we hear of the extinction of an organic being; and as we do not see the cause, we invoke cataclysms to desolate the world, or invent laws on the duration of the forms of life!"

-Charles Darwin
The Origin of Species, 1859

28 – EPIGENETICS

Lucien sat at his desk. He was pulling up data on genetic diseases in the last fifty years. In just a single generation, multiple genetic diseases had risen by anywhere from 70% to 200%. Genetics alone could not account for this increase; it was clearly influenced by environmental factors. Several scientists, activists, environmentalists, and anyone with a soapbox moaned and groaned about this fact. Yet nothing had ever been done. There was too much profit at stake to get industry behind it. Besides, the masses refused to lose a hair of modern convenience. Lucien didn't blame them. Who would want to regress to darker eras?

None of that mattered now; science provided a way around all of that. Actually, Lucien provided a way around that. With the power of genetics, there was no need to suffer through imperfection, disease, and aging—well, the last one would have to be tightly controlled, so as not to have a negative effect on the population of the world. Though, that would not be a problem again for many generations to come. When Lucien reflected on his life, his genetic condition, the pandemics, everything had led up to this moment. It was perfect. This was what he was born for.

Lucien's comm center buzzed. "Sir, I have Commander Jones on the line."

"Put him through."

"Sir, we have Dr. Gale and the genetic material she promised."

"How is she?"

"A little bruised and beat up, but she's fine. We got to her just in time."

"What's her mental state like?"

"She appears to be fine. She's made some pretty severe claims about the initial extraction attempt."

"Do you believe her?" Lucien asked.

"Her story fits with what we found. When we exhumed Trent's body, the bullet that killed him matched up to the agent that had been killed in the lab. It would be extremely difficult for her to have lied about that. Everything seemed to match with what she said."

"So, everything she said checks out?"

"She claims to be the only survivor from the team. We were able to identify everyone's bodies except Chris's. We also did not find Jim or Paulo, but we were told they died prior to arrival here."

"Were you able to account for all of the dead extraction agents?"

"All but five. There were some bodies that had been too mangled by animals to identify."

"So, it's possible that she's telling the truth?"

"I guess it's possible, but it's hard to believe that she was the only one that managed to survive and that she was fully embraced by the primitives. She had this ridiculous story about a jaguar. I..." Jones paused. "She's either insanely lucky or lying."

"Interesting. Where is she now? I'd like to talk to her."

"She's resting. I recommend waiting till the morning. We're only five hours away."

"Fine. There's a small quarantine and decontamination unit attached to this safe house. That's where I want Dr. Gale and you. The rest of your unit can quarantine in the detached isolation barracks. I will have techs ready for you when you get here. The pilots have their own quarters, so don't worry about them."

"Yes, sir."

Lucien could breathe for the first time in what felt like an eternity. He would be out of this unbearable waiting period in a matter of hours. Lucien clicked open his file on Dr. Gale. Thanks to Trent, AmCorps had mapped Gabby's genome a few years ago when Trent was worried that Gabby would inherit early-onset Alzheimer's disease. He had been working on a genetic treatment for Alzheimer's, which had essentially cured the disease. Well, not cured the disease. Rather, it taught the brain to make its own medicine, which stopped the progression of the disease. After seeing the effects of the disease, Trent began to worry about Gabby and wanted to ensure that she could be treated if need be. Luckily, she did not carry the APOE e4 gene, which increased the risk of disease. She also did not have any mutations on her APP, PSEN1, or PSEN2 genes. Although, if she ever began to show symptoms, like both her grandparents had, Trent could treat her. As Lucien read through her file, he remembered Trent explaining all of this to him, and how relieved he was when her results came back clear. That was so typical of Trent; before there had been a problem, he had the solution. He would be missed at AmCorps.

As Lucien quickly scanned the rest of her file, he was pleased to see that her genetics were as good as a modern human's could be. If she and Trent really did give themselves the treatment and it worked, then Dr. Gale would be an endless possibility of genetic experiments. To start, she could be his first treated mother in his IVF program, and possibly the mother of the modern human race. The other mothers in the program were at least six to eight months out. They would all have to receive the treatment, first. The Alpha group had all recently given birth, so they'd have to wait at least six months before being impregnated again. The Beta group were all about three to five months into their pregnancies, so they'd have to wait even longer. But, Dr. Gale had already received the EVE-0 treatment, she'd never been pregnant, and was, therefore, the perfect subject. His groin tingled and he was becoming excited just thinking about the possibilities. Though he forced himself to calm down, he was getting slightly ahead of himself.

He picked up his comm center and punched the direct line to Sy's office.

"Yes?" Sy answered on the second ring.

"They are approximately five hours out. Have the techs start to get the quarantine unit ready? Then they will need to go out onto the tarmac to bring them in. Make sure they are in full protective gear and go through the extended decontamination process. I want to run a full genome sequencing on Dr. Gale as soon as she arrives. Understand?"

"Yes. We will be ready."

"Any update on Johnnie?" Lucien asked, looking for something to help pass the next five hours.

"He is doing better. He was given a laptop. He's still suffering delusions, but is maintaining better control and is no longer violent."

"Good. Is he still sedated?"

"No, he's obviously medicated, but not sedated."

"Can you meet me there in five minutes? I'd like to talk to him again."

"Sure," Sy responded, and clicked off the chat.

Lucien didn't really care that deeply about how Johnnie was doing. It was more of a distraction to pass the time. Mental illness had always intrigued Lucien. The thought of your brain betraying you was incomprehensible. Lucien's condition had been clearly physical. He realized he looked different—people stared and he enjoyed the fact that he was completely unique. His brain had carried him through. His intelligence, resilience, and guile made him extraordinary. Someone like Johnnie—who appeared physically strong and perfect, but so mentally diseased—was almost entertaining to Lucien, at least because of the irony.

Sy was waiting outside of Johnnie's unit.

"Sy," Lucien greeted, "shall we?"

Sy opened and held the door for Lucien. Johnnie's team was expecting them.

"We're making great progress," Dr. Saad said, brushing back a glossy wave of black hair.

"Yes," Dr. Faust added. "He's still having delusions, but learning how to manage them. He's no longer violent and we've been able to take his restraints off."

"Is it safe for us to go in?" Lucien asked.

"I think so. The nursing staff will quickly sedate him, should something trigger him," Dr. Saad said.

Lucien nodded and Sy opened the door to Johnnie's room.

Johnnie didn't appear to notice them come in. He was sitting at a desk facing the wall, set up in the corner of his room and rhythmically tapping on the keyboard of his laptop.

"Hello Johnnie," Sy said.

Johnnie didn't turn or seem to acknowledge

their presence. Sy, Lucien, and the nurses slowly approached.

"Johnnie?" Sy called.

The keyboard tapping slowed, but Johnnie still did not respond to them.

"Johnnie, we'd like to see how you're feeling," Sy said.

The keyboard tapping stopped, but Johnnie still didn't turn. He sat there, frozen.

"Johnnie?" Lucien called.

Johnnie abruptly spun his entire wooden chair around. It made a loud screech on the concrete floor. Lucien and Sy reflexively cowered back.

Johnnie was completely expressionless as he sat, perfectly straight and still in his hardbacked chair.

"What do you want? I'm very busy," Johnnie said.

"We just want to see how you're doing," Lucien replied.

"Okay, but make it quick," Johnnie said, directing his attention to Lucien.

"What are you working on?" Lucien asked.

"A very complicated computer program."

"Can I see?" Lucien asked.

Johnnie nodded his head yes and held his laptop up for them to see. Lucien had a very basic understanding of computer languages, and he knew enough to tell that Johnnie had just typed a very erratic set of characters onto a blank document.

"Impressive," Lucien replied, "that does look complicated."

"It is," Johnnie said, setting his laptop back down.

"And, how are you feeling?" Lucien asked.

Johnnie suddenly shot his focus from Lucien to the back corner of his room and erratically shook his head no.

"Johnnie? Are you okay?" Sy asked.

"Don't worry, I'm not going to do it. I already told him I wouldn't," Johnnie said.

"Do what?" Lucien asked.

"Kill you?" Johnnie said. "But don't worry. I won't do it."

"Who wants you to do that?" Lucien asked.

"Zadkiel. He's over there," Johnnie said, pointing to the corner of the room. "You can't see him, though."

"Oh, well thank you," Lucien said. "Do you mind if Sy and I stay in here for a bit? Just to watch your work. It's very fascinating."

"You can stay, as long as you don't talk to me."

"Great; thank you, Johnnie," Lucien said.

Johnnie turned back to face his computer and immediately started tapping away.

Lucien sent the nurse staff out. Sy comm-sealed the room. This was the only room in the safe house that could be completely sealed. The vast majority of areas in the safe house were wired for communication throughout the building, which made it slightly vulnerable to someone listening in. Due to the experimental nature of this room, it was not hardwired for communication. The control room was, but this area could be sealed off from the control room, with a code that only Lucien and Sy had.

"Safe?" Lucien asked.

Sy nodded his head yes.

"Dr. Gale's story appears to check out, but Jones still doesn't believe her," Lucien spoke very quietly, in almost a whisper.

"What do you think?"

"I can't imagine her coming here with the treatment if she was lying. She's been clear with her intentions, which align with her story. Something doesn't seem right, though."

"Is it Lt. Silver?"

"Precisely."

"You don't think he's really dead?"

"If he was actually working for IFP, he could've flipped Dr. Gale and this could be a setup."

"But she *is* bringing enough genetic material to make thousands of doses of the treatment."

"Yes. Like I said, her story appears to check out." Lucien confirmed.

"Why don't you test her?" Sy asked.

"That's exactly what I was thinking," Lucien replied. "If she actually took the treatment and her EVE-0 gene is reactivated, she could be the first mother to test out our in vitro fertilization method. The mothers in our program won't be ready to test the procedure for at least six months."

"If she says no, we'll know that she's not invested in AmCorps mission and likely lying about every-thing."

29 - OSIRIS

Chris and Rodrigo made it back to the tree village in a few days. They took their time. Chris was moving a little slower. Not intentionally, but the weight of grief was a heavy companion. When they got back, Chris found his things placed back in the platform hut that he had last shared with Gabby. A comfortable bed had been set up for him. He also saw the remnants of where they had secured the sat comm equipment and the case placed right under it. Chris had been dreading his next call to Michaela. He didn't know how he was going to tell her about Gabby.

When he unzipped the sat comm equipment case, a note fluttered out. It was from Gabby. He unfolded it. *Chris, I hope you understand why I had to do this. I miss you terribly already and I will think of you every second of every day until I see you again. But, till then, I need to tell you one more thing and you need to pass this along to Michaela. I gave myself the treatment about a week ago and I think it worked. Trent made two treat-*

ments. He took one at the Matsés' village. He confirmed that it worked and he left the other one, I presume for me. I gave myself the treatment so that AmCorps would be more likely to keep me alive, if for nothing else than as a study subject. It's not much, but at least it's a little insurance. Tell Michaela that I had no adverse reactions at all. Slight soreness at the injection site. I was slightly fatigued for a day, but that's it. Please stay safe. I love you, Gabs.

Chris had to admit that she was smart. Her plan made sense, but it was risky. Trent had better be right. Chris now moved a little quicker in setting up the sat comm. He had a lot to talk to Michaela about. This letter reminded Chris that he had a purpose, but more importantly, it let him know that Gabby had a plan and hope for the future. She didn't just give herself up to AmCorps; she put a real, multifaceted plan into motion.

"I'm here," Michaela answered on the first ring. "I was getting worried. Where have you guys been?"

"I'm still in the Amazon, but Gabs is on her way to AmCorps."

"What?" Panic widened Michaela's eyes.

"It's a long story." Chris told Michaela every detail of Gabby's plan: what he knew, and what he thought was likely.

"HO-LY shit," Michaela said. "Well, I have just as much to tell you. First, you're not going to believe this, but IFP's inside guy was Trent."

"What?"

Michaela nodded. "Yeah, he's been working with them for almost three years. As you know, the treatment has an expected 95% chance of making women infertile. Well, not infertile, just unable to conceive naturally. Did Trent mention that part of Lucien's plan was to use this to his advantage, so that as parents went to clinics to become pregnant, this would provide them a chance to edit embryos, in order to erase disease and undesirable characteristics?"

"Yeah, I remember Trent saying something about this."

"So, a few years ago, Trent met Lucien's first fully edited child. This kid, Osiris Azazel, was like eighteen or nineteen when he began working with Lucien. On paper, he was perfect. He was a genius and could've gone pro in either baseball or football. But Trent was not enamored with him and believed Osiris had the potential to do something horrible. Trent referenced a few examples of inhumane behavior with lab animals. He was, without a doubt, a sociopath. He didn't experience emotions, though he seemed to completely understand them. A world of Osirises terrified Trent, and that's when he reached out to IFP."

"Wait, Lucien was capable of this more than twenty years ago? Was that legal then?"

Michaela shook her head no. "Trent turned to IFP because he learned IFP had been overseeing an ethics panel for the European Union regarding how to handle the pandemics, as well as how to fairly distribute vaccines and treatments and international medical access, presuming a treatment would, one day, become available."

"How did a faith-based organization become so powerful and so unknown?" Chris asked.

"Faith-based is a bit misleading. Their whole foundation was built on determining paths towards an understanding that's inclusive of multiple faiths. I pulled that from their mission statement," Michaela paused, "and they have representatives from every religion as well as atheists. Faith actually has very little to do with what they do, other than acknowledging the power that it holds for others."

"How'd they become so involved in health policy?"

"During the pandemics, conflicting faiths began to create these divides and barriers towards reaching some communities. IFP became very important in bridging these gaps. They also employed a team of scientists that worked with different faith representatives, which put them in a position to become essential to them all. Particularly during vaccine rollouts and quarantines."

"Smart."

"Thanks to Trent, IFP has been quietly building an international crimes against humanity charge against AmCorps. They've already presented it to the Sixth Committee of the United Nations General Assembly."

"Are you kidding me?"

Michaela shook her head. "Wait, it gets better. IFP has been building safe houses as well that have been working. They're spread throughout Europe. They used a lottery system to choose occupants in addition to government officials and other necessary people. And they have a military."

"When are they going to bring those charges against AmCorps?"

"Here's the thing. Trent encouraged them to work on the treatment first, and then to deal with Am-Corps."

"Okay, so where's that leave us?"

"Well, I poured through Trent's files. All I need to make the treatment is—"

"The active EVE-0 gene."

"Yes, so this is what I'm thinking. IFP's forces, you, viable blood, and me all need to come together. IFP is in Europe, you're in Brazil, and I'm in Canada. IFP can pick you up and as much blood as you can carry, then head to me and my lab. Then, we can move in on AmCorps."

"How long will it take till we can get to AmCorps?"

"With this new plan, IFP is ready to move. It could be a matter of weeks. Check back with me in twenty-four hours."

30 – DECON

The AmCorps jet slowly pulled to a stop. Gabby had no idea what to expect. She couldn't see anything. They were on a large, open runway. From her window, all she could see were grey skies and empty trees. She was scared. The door to the jet slowly unfolded. The sting of cold air prickled her skin. She'd almost forgotten the feeling. She grabbed her bag and the blood cooler. It had been fully charged during the flight. Two people in full hazmat gear were waiting for Gabby and Commander Jones.

"Follow us," a male voice said from behind his hazmat hood and mask.

He led them to an unmarked door on a large grey building. Inside was a small empty room with three doors—the one they came in and two others on opposite walls.

"Do you have the genetic material?" the man asked.

"It's right here. The cooler is charged but it needs

to be transported to a proper storage container."

"Give it to me."

Gabby hesitated. Commander Jones nodded at her to hand it over.

"We will get it to the lab and into refrigeration. Dr. Sabara is waiting for it."

"Okay," Gabby said, finally handing it over.

"Thank you," the man said. He then handed it to the other hazmat-suited individual.

Gabby couldn't tell if it was a man or woman. They wore a full white jumpsuit, mask, hood, and shield. All that Gabby could see was a sliver of their eyes. The man opened the door, and the other safe house worker disappeared with the blood. She soon heard a soft hiss sound that sounded like an airtight seal opened. This was followed by a ding.

"Okay," the man said as he opened the opposite door. "Please go in here."

Gabby and Jones walked into another small holding room. On the opposite side of this room was an airtight door. It was painted grey, but a slightly warmer shade than the walls. The door had a keypad and screen built into it, a long, vertical silver metal handle, and a round, thick glass window. The man punched a code into the keypad. A red light above the door came on. The light turned green, and he grabbed the handle and pushed it into a horizontal position. There was an audible hiss, and he pulled the door open.

"Please take a seat inside this room and wait for

instructions. When the airtight seal secures, you may notice a slight change in air pressure. This is completely normal. Don't worry."

Gabby and Jones stepped over the ankle-high threshold and walked into the small room. They took a seat on the cold metal bench and waited. The man closed and sealed the door. The pressure in Gabby's ears rose; she yawned and they popped.

"Welcome, Dr. Gale and Commander Jones," a male voice came through a speaker, "my name is Dr. Azazel. I will be taking you through your decontamination process. To begin, do you have any personal belongings that you feel strongly about keeping?"

Gabby opened her bag and quickly looked through it. The only thing she had that she wanted to keep was her copy of *Jurassic Park* and Chris's copy of *On the Road* that he let her borrow when their trip was just beginning.

"I'd like to keep these two books," Gabby said.

"That's not a problem. There is a fumigation bin in the next room. As long as that's all you want, it will be very easy. There is also an incineration bin. Dr. Gale, I will guide you through first, please grab all of your belongings. I'm going to buzz you into the next room. Commander Jones, please wait where you are."

Gabby picked up her things and waited by the door. She heard a buzz, followed by a hiss, and the door opened. She stepped inside and the door closed behind her. This room was smaller than the others.

It was bright white. There was another door on the opposite side and two small bins along the wall. One was labeled *Fumigation* while the other was labeled *Incineration.*

"Dr. Gale, go ahead and place your books in the fumigation bin. Try to spread them out and drape them over the two bars inside."

Gabby did this and closed the bin.

"Okay, now please place everything else into the incinerations bin, including your clothes and shoes. Check for any hair ties. There should be nothing remaining. Are you okay with this?"

"Yes," she said as she opened the incineration bin.

It was much larger than the other bin. She dropped her bag in first, then her shoes and clothes. She stood completely naked in the middle of the room. She reminded herself that she was a doctor, all too familiar with the naked human body. She had been through similar, though less intensive, decontaminations before. Yet part of her felt oddly exposed for the first time in this stark room, and she wondered if the man behind the voice could actually see her. Maybe he was just giving instructions without the need for a camera. She could only hope.

"Please close your eyes. We are going to flash you with a few short bursts of UVC light. It's completely safe for you. Just keep your eyes closed, please."

Gabby closed her eyes.

"That was two. Can you flip your head over, as if

you're touching your toes?"

She did.

"Okay, you can stand up again. Do you think you're able to hold your breath for twenty seconds?"

"Yes."

"Great. Take a few slow, deep breaths. The room is going to fill with a copper solution. It's safe to breathe, it just may be slightly uncomfortable. I personally prefer to hold my breath."

"Okay."

"Ready?"

"Yes."

"3-2-1."

A mist filled the room. It stung Gabby's eyes slightly, so she closed them.

"Ten seconds... and it's complete."

Gabby opened her eyes. She saw the last bit of mist get sucked out of the room through a small vent in the corner. She took a small, shallow breath. The air was clear.

"Okay, Dr. Gale, please grab your books and walk into the next room."

The next room was grey and concrete, with a metal drain in the middle. There were two showerheads equally spaced in the middle of the room.

"Place your books in the bin. They will be fumigated one more time. Then, please stand under the first showerhead."

Gabby looked around but didn't see a bin.

"It's on the opposite wall. You will not get your books again until you're dressed."

Gabby looked over and saw it, by the next door. She placed her books in it, then walked under the showerhead.

"The first showerhead, please."

"Oops, sorry," Gabby said as she moved under the other showerhead. Well, she had her answer: there was definitely a camera somewhere.

"No need to apologize. A soap solution is going to spray you. Keep your eyes closed and please make sure that you scrub every part of your body— face, ears, private areas, and hair. It's actually a mild, all-natural soap that uses grapefruit seed extract and thymol. Ready?"

"Yes."

A warm, sudsy soap solution poured down on her. It felt good. This was her first real shower in months. She scrubbed every square millimeter of her skin.

"Okay. I'm going to start the water. Just take a step forward when you're ready and you will be under the water."

She heard the shower come on. She reached her arms out, found the water, and stepped under the spray.

"Okay, when you're ready, step forward, and a fan will dry you off."

She stepped forward and a powerful fan came on. She quickly dried and the door to the next room opened. This room had lockers along one wall and a door on the opposite end.

"Find the locker with your name and open it."

Inside the locker was a metal hanger with a top and pants. Underneath were two shelves. One held undergarments and socks; under that was a pair of shoes. Every single thing in the room was grey. The walls, the lockers, the clothes, the undergarments, and the shoes. Gabby quickly dressed. The clothes were soft, loose, and comfortable. The shoes were made of a heavy canvas with rubber soles.

"Does everything fit?"

"Yes, perfectly."

"You have completed the decontamination process. You will now enter the quarantine quarters. Grab your books, exit the dressing room, and find the door with your name on it. Once you're settled in, please click on the computer screen. Dr. Sabara and I are looking forward to speaking to you."

Gabby was surprised by her quarantine quarters. She expected a jail cell, but what she walked into was more like a modern luxury condo. She had a living room with a large-screen television, a work area with a computer, a full kitchen that was stocked, and a comfortable bed. The closet was stocked with clothes, all in shades of grey. She had everything she needed. She also noticed that there was no plastic in the apartment. Everything was either metal, glass, or fabric.

She sat down at the desk and turned the computer

on. It powered up and had her name on the screen. As she was clicking around, a notification for a chat request popped up. She clicked on it, and Dr. Sabara flickered onto the screen.

"Dr. Gale, you have no idea how relieved I am to have you here."

"Thank you."

"How are you feeling?" Lucien asked.

"Okay," Gabby replied.

"Are you up to talking for a few minutes? I'm trying to fill in some gaps. I'm extremely upset by Trent's death and the initial extraction team's action. Trent was an integral part of this organization, but he was also like a son to me."

"I know. He looked up to you," Gabby replied.

"The last few reports we had from Trent were erratic. It started with a report that you had identified the mole, Paulo, and dealt with him. Then he reported that you and Chris had flipped and that he had you both secured. I saw him question you both. Then you escaped, and all hell broke loose. Based on this intel, General Holton issued a kill order on you and Chris. At that point, Trent became very difficult to get a hold of. I'm assuming that's when the chaos started."

"Trent never told you about the ayahuasca?"

"Ayahuasca? No."

"In order to gain the trust of the Matsés, the chief and shaman insisted that we do an ayahuasca ceremony. It's a hallucinogenic drink that they believe shows your spirit. There was about a six- or eight-hour period that's a bit fuzzy, during which we all had mild hallucinations. Chris thought he saw angels. For me, everyone started turning into animals, and Trent thought Chris and I flipped. We all started the ceremony out together in the lab; maybe that was when you saw Trent question us. To be honest, a lot of the night is foggy. I woke up in a hut near the jungle. We all talked about it the next day and tried to fill in the pieces."

"Then what happened?" Lucien urged her to continue.

"The next day is when things got out of control. Trent came to us in a panic and said that the extraction team had issued an order to kill us on sight. He tried telling them to cancel those orders, but they wouldn't, so he told us to run."

"He did try to cancel those orders," Lucien admitted.

"When we fled the village, we bumped into the Jungle Guardians. They were going to kill us, too, but then Chris explained what was happening. The next thing I knew, things started to explode and fighting broke out everywhere. I got really worried about Trent, so I ran back to the village. We were hiding in his lab when an extraction agent came in." Gabby started to cry. This part of the story was true. It took no acting to show her emotions.

"It's okay, take your time," Lucien said.

Gabby took a few deep breaths. Trent was a genius; he orchestrated everything so perfectly. She missed him. In this moment, she fully understood the sacrifice that he made.

"When the extraction agent came in, he kept yelling at Trent to step away from me. Trent tried to tell him that I was coming back with them, that this was a mistake, and he ordered him to stand down. The agent told Trent that he had orders that superseded his, and he fired in my direction. Trent pushed me behind him and the bullet hit him. Then someone came into the lab and killed the extraction agent. I'm assuming it was a Jungle Guardian, but I don't really know. I was trying to treat Trent. But the bullet hit his liver and he died."

"I'm very sorry, Dr. Gale. The orders that superseded Trent's were from General Holton. He's been relieved of his duties, and I'm advocating for the president to bring formal charges against him. His arrogance almost cost us everything. Can I ask, what happened to Lt. Christopher Silver?"

"He was killed in the fighting near the extraction site. When the fighting stopped, I saw his body in the field near the airstrip." Gabby wiped some more tears. "He was already dead. There was nothing I could do."

"You have nothing to worry about any longer. You're safe here. You will be an integral part in how this operative moves forward," Lucien said.

Gabby just nodded her head.

"One more thing. You said that you and Trent

gave yourselves the treatment?"

Gabby nodded her head yes. "Trent took it first when we got to the village and identified an active EVE-0 gene. A day or two later, he was super excited and told me that it worked. Then he gave it to me, but with everything that happened, I never found out if it worked."

"Did he tell you the expected side effect in women?"

"Yes; it would likely stop menstruation and make conceiving difficult or impossible without medical assistance."

"Right. I'd like to send a lab tech over to collect some blood from you today. Is that alright?"

"Yes, definitely. I'm anxious to know if it worked."

"Great, I will send him over now and let you know as soon as I find out."

"Thank you."

"No, thank you, Dr. Gale. I'll be in touch soon." Lucien disappeared from the screen.

Gabby laid on the couch and turned on the television. It was strange to have the luxury of modern conveniences again. She felt guilty as she scanned through movies. She thought of Chris on the hard ground, eating grubs and monkeys, and she smiled. Even in those terrible moments, she had found joy.

There was a knock on the door.

"That was fast," she greeted the lab tech in full hazmat gear.

"Can you come down to the meeting room?"

"Sure," she said, pulling the door shut behind her.

There was a conference room at the end of the hall with a wooden oval table and chairs, and nothing else.

Gabby took a seat and rolled up her sleeve. The tech took several vials of blood without exchanging a single word. The tech finished up, put a fabric bandage on her, and put everything away.

"Thank you, Dr. Gale," the tech said before disappearing through a coded doorway.

As Gabby made her way back to her room, Commander Jones stepped out of the last stage of the decontamination process, completely naked.

Gabby blushed. "Oh my gosh," she looked at the ground, "I'm so sorry."

"No need to apologize; they forgot to put clothes in my locker." Jones smiled and politely covered what he could with his hands. "Please go ahead."

Gabby quickly scooted by, her head down. "Thanks."

"No problem. So, does this mean it's just you and me together for the next couple weeks?"

"Not together. We each have our own quarters. I don't think we're supposed to be in contact with each other during the quarantine period." Gabby wasn't sure if that was true or not, but she was going with it.

"That's too bad, darlin'. Enjoy your break. I'm right here if you need me," Jones said as he disappeared into his unit.

31 – MED KIT

Chris laid on his bed mat for twenty-four hours straight. He had no reason to get up, although, he didn't sleep. He just thought about Gabby. His mind raced through every possible scenario. Was she alright? If she wasn't, he knew he couldn't survive without her. The day dragged by. Every hour felt like ten. Chris was utterly miserable.

Finally, enough time had passed that he could call Michaela again. He quickly set up the sat comm and dialed.

"Chris," she answered. "I need coordinates. IFP has a jet ready to go. They will pick up you and any blood you can collect."

"Okay, wait a minute; let me see if Rodrigo has the coordinates."

Chris sprinted off to find Rodrigo and luckily bumped into him on the main platform. Even luckier, he knew the exact coordinates of the runway.

"I'm back." The camera view was empty. "Michaela... Michaela?"

"I'm here." Michaela answered, then sat down.

"Are you ready for the coordinates?" Chris asked

Michaela nodded her head yes, though she looked a little preoccupied to Chris.

"5°21'32"S 70°59'10"W. Did you get that?"

"Yes," Michaela replied, "and I already sent it to IFP."

"We need two days to get there," Chris added.

"Okay."

"And can you make sure that they bring several blood donation collection kits and a refrigerated storage cooler?"

"Got it; they've already confirmed."

"Brilliant," Chris said.

"See you soon." Michaela smiled.

"Michaela, stay safe."

She nodded, said, "You too," smiled, and clicked out of the call.

Chris packed up the sat comm equipment and went to find Rodrigo. He was sitting on the main platform with a group of his warriors. They were happy, relaxed, and in a deep conversation that only paused for hearty laughter.

"Rodrigo, amigo, I have a favor to ask," Chris said in Portuguese.

"I'm listening," Rodrigo said back in Portuguese, smiling.

"I need to get back to the Matsés's village in two days."

Rodrigo threw his head back. "Are you kidding me?"

"That's not it," Chris smiled, "I need some warriors or young villagers to come too, so that when the plane lands to pick me up, I can collect some blood, like Gabby did."

"Okay, let me see who I can round up. I will also let Chief Ëpë, Shaman Dabi, and the crew know. I'm sure they'll give you some more blood. When do you want to leave?"

"As soon as we can."

Chris went back to his platform to pack everything up. He paused for a minute on Gabby's med kit. Then, he opened it and looked through what was left. He had never been the sentimental sort, but this kit brought a rush of memories that washed over him. He felt himself stitching Gab's chin, then saw her tending to Trent's snakebite, and remembered how much pain she had been in when she was bitten by the bullet ants. He felt this need to protect her. It was a drive like nothing he'd ever felt before. A purpose. He took a breath and continued. There was a lot of stuff still left. Bandages, antibiotics, antiseptic, painkillers, and a note. Chris unfolded the paper. It was Gabby's handwriting. She simply wrote, *everything will be okay.* It must've been a little reminder that she had left herself. A mantra—her mantra. He smiled and put the note in his pocket. The rest he would leave with Rodrigo.

"Pronto para ir?" Rodrigo leaned into Chris's platform. "Ready to go?"

"Yeah. Did anyone agree to come with us?"

"Yeah, they're down there waiting." Rodrigo pointed over the railing.

Chris looked down and saw dozens of villagers ready to make this journey with him.

"You're the best," Chris said.

"They all wanted to come just to give their blood."

"Seriously?"

"Yeah, since Mayalú did it, everyone wants to." Rodrigo smiled.

"I have some stuff for you." Chris waved him over. "This is Gab's med kit." He pointed out everything. "And I want you to keep the sat comm. I'll show you how to use it and how to reach me."

Rodrigo gave Chris a hug, then helped him grab everything. They joined the rest of the group as they made this journey for the last time with Chris.

32 – QUARANTINE

Gabby divided her time between the bed and the couch. She spent as little time on her feet as possible. Physically, her body needed the rest. Mentally, the quiet was eating away at her. A few days had gone by; she wasn't sure if it was two, three, or four. She had completely lost track of time. Somewhere around the fourth or fifth day of her quarantine, her computer rang. She made her way over and noticed that she had a chat request from Lucien.

"Hello," she said as the chat screen flickered on.

"Dr. Gale, you look rested. How is your quarantine going?"

"Fine," she smiled, "I've never had this much time to relax."

"I have great news," Lucien announced.

Gabby's eyes widened. She wasn't sure how to respond. "Oh," was all she could muster.

"Yes, your EVE-0 gene is fully functional."

"That's great." She smiled. She was relieved, happy, and then it hit her—the sadness. "I wish I could tell Trent," she blurted out.

"Me, too." Lucien smiled.

"I have more good news. We've already been able to make 3,000 doses of the treatment and have administered 100 doses within the safe house."

"Trent would be happy," she said. Though her thoughts began to tumble. *Would he be happy?* she wondered. *Was this part of his plan, or did I make a mistake? Should I have stayed?*

Lucien nodded. "You only have two more days left in quarantine, then we can bring you into the main unit. I'd like to show you around then."

"I thought the quarantine period was two weeks?"

"It is."

"I've only been in here for a few days."

"Today is the twelfth day."

"Really?" Without windows in the quarantine area and no clocks or calendars, she felt disoriented.

"It's hard to keep track of time in there," Lucien acknowledged, "but before I go, do you need anything?"

"No, thank you. I'm fine."

"We'll talk soon." Lucien clicked out of the chat.

Gabby laid back down. She lacked the will to do much of anything. She missed Chris, she missed human interaction, she missed her freedom, and she even missed the jungle. Boredom was picking at these invisible lesions. With nothing else at her disposal, she used creature comforts to dress her wounds. She ate her way through the supplies, slept, lay on the couch, and did as little as humanly possible. She considered the possibility that she was being monitored, so she attempted to maintain some level of neatness. This existence was eating away at her mental state much quicker than she had prepared herself for.

She had no idea what day it was or what time it was when she got a knock at her door. She dragged herself off the couch, smoothed her hair, and opened the door.

"Hello, Dr. Gale," a woman's voice greeted her. She was completely covered in hazmat gear. "I'm here to clear you from the quarantine."

"Okay," Gabby said.

"Do you have any symptoms? Sore throat, fever, cough, congestion, stomach pain, or any other unusual symptoms?"

"No."

"Great. I'm going to take some swabs of your nose, throat, fingernails, and ears. Okay?"

Gabby just nodded. The woman was not gentle with her swabs, but Gabby was unfazed. She felt little these days.

"It will be five minutes. Is there anything that you'd like to bring to your new unit?"

"Ah..."

"Did you bring any personal items in? You will have all new clothes and hygiene accessories. Did you bring any jewelry or anything like that?"

"Oh, yeah. I had two books."

"Go ahead and start to gather your books. Did you want to change or brush your hair or anything?"

Gabby shrugged.

"You'll probably go to a few meetings, explore the safe house, get to know some of your neighbors. You'll probably feel a little better if you get dressed and brush your hair. Those are technically our pajamas. Would you wear pajamas out in public at home?"

Gabby shook her head no. She assumed she should feel embarrassed but lethargy had come over her these last two weeks—*had it really been that long?* Part of her seemed to hardly care anymore while another part, deeper down, clung to the woman's words, trying to orient herself, to ready herself for whatever lay ahead.

"We've found that the society in here operates much better when we abide by similar customs. A vast majority of our members are wealthy, successful, intelligent, and..." the woman paused, cocked her hooded head slightly while giving Gabby a hint of her side-eye, "formal. They present themselves in a professional manner. So, why don't you take a few minutes while your tests are processing and pull yourself together?"

"Okay." Gabby's shoulders slumped a little further; she was fatigued at the very idea of needing to get moving.

"I will wait right out here."

Gabby nodded and dragged herself to the closet. She hadn't even looked at the hanging clothes once. She pulled a pair of pants off the hanger and grabbed a soft sweater. She pulled her hair into a low ponytail and tried not to look at herself for too long.

Gabby heard a soft tap on her door, grabbed her books off of the table, and opened the door.

"Much better," the woman said. "Your tests have all been processed and you're cleared. Follow me."

The woman took her to a doorway at the opposite end of the hallway. Gabby hadn't noticed it before, as it was flush with the wall. She hit a button on the wall, pulled her hood and visor off, then positioned her eye for a retinal scan. The door opened and she pushed her cart in. She pulled her hood, visor, and mask off, shook out her wavy, shoulder-grazing red hair, and smiled at Gabby.

"Ugh, am I glad to have that off." She unzipped the top of her jumper, then keyed in a code. There was a soft hiss, followed by a pop, and the door opened.

She moved into the next room. "Pull that door shut behind you, please."

Gabby pulled the door closed. The woman entered a code. "It will just be a minute while the air circulates and filters." A light in the room glowed red, yellow, then green. There was a hiss, followed by a pop.

When this door opened, Gabby knew that she had just walked into the safe house. The light glowed in soft, rosy hues. The walls were painted with impressionistic pastel murals. Elegant men and women bustled through the streets. Gabby felt like she had just arrived on vacation. She saw people's full faces. They smiled as they passed her. They were walking in groups.

It eventually dawned on Gabby that she had inadvertently viewed these massive windowless hallways as streets. It stunned her that the strangeness of this faux-city wasn't her first observation. As she was beginning to grasp the immensity of where she was, she was half-filled with dread and half-filled with wonder. While she tried to bury it, she had hoped that one day Chris would show up and rescue her. She now saw that conquering this fortress would be impossible.

"Dr. Gale, welcome," Lucien said as he rounded the corner. "Thank you, Beth. I will take it from here."

Gabby spun to face him.

"Nice meeting you, Dr. Gale," Beth, who'd brought Gabby in, said as she pushed her cart down the hall.

"You too." Gabby attempted a smile.

"Would you like a tour?" Lucien asked.

"Sure," Gabby said.

"Great, follow me," Lucien said, directing Gabby down a far hall. At the end of the hallway was another short hallway that made a sharp turn.

"Is that the way out?" Gabby asked.

Lucien laughed. "No, that's where I spend most of my time. It's my office area. The safe house is constructed without a way out, as you put it. The entire building is sealed, for pathogenic safety reasons," Lucien answered, then quickly changed the subject. "This is Restaurant Square. People are able to dine here together. It's been years since this was safe to do." Lucien proudly grinned.

Parties of people sat in a replica of a city square. They laughed. Deep in conversations, waiters bustled around. It was such a familiar scene, but so distant. There was a marble fountain surrounded by three restaurants and a café with tables that fanned out.

"Wow," Gabby said. Seeing this brought back a flood of happy memories of better times.

"All of our food is organic and grown on property. We have large indoor, organic, soil-free, hydroponic grow houses. Our meat is also lab-grown, so it's cruelty-free and has zero impact on the environment. Are you hungry? Would you like to grab lunch?"

"I'm okay right now." Gabby smiled. "Does the staff live here too?"

"Of course, and their families. We wanted this to be a fair and true representation of our society. You either had to buy your way in, or take a job. This was an extremely expensive undertaking. Those that bought their way in provided much of the funding for this. Each safe house is completely self-sustaining."

"That seems fair," Gabby said, but was it fair? There was so much to take in, Gabby's mind struggled to keep up.

Lucien looked at her. "Did you expect that it wouldn't be?"

"Oh, it was just something that Paulo said."

"The spy that was trying to steal the treatment?" Lucien asked, though he knew the answer.

Gabby smiled sheepishly and shrugged her shoulders.

"In line with keeping things fair, I have a job proposition for you," Lucien continued. "Would you consider being an on-site doctor? We do have doctors, but we could use another one."

"That would be nice," Gabby said.

"Of course, we will give you some time to adjust and heal. But, when you're ready, we have a job for you."

"Thank you."

"Of course," Lucien smiled. "We're coming up to your living quarters. Dr. Osiris Azazel is meeting us there. He is going to get you situated and give you the basic rundown. Sy worked with Trent and knew him well. They were close."

"Really?"

"Yes, but everything was top secret, so there was a lot that Trent couldn't tell you. Well, until you joined our team, but then things happened so fast. You'll learn a lot of great things about Trent here."

Gabby smiled. She was becoming more confused with each minute she spent here. She'd had this image of an evil outpost and was struggling to align what she'd thought with what she was seeing as they walked toward the housing area.

This area had glowing walls and a glowing ceiling, like artificial daylight, but without windows or clocks, she felt in limbo, ungrounded, and now, in view of this wondrous place, perplexed as well. She could feel herself getting sucked into the deception. It was like an industrial utopia. Everyone was so happy and everything was so perfect. It would be hard to resist the charm of this place. Every fiber in Gabby's being was suddenly electric with the realization that this place was very similar to the cloud village from her ayahuasca dream. Her skin prickled as anxiety left her hollow. While the cloud village was set in nature, with perfect walls constructed of stone and outdoor gardens fed by sunlight, and the safe house was entirely artificial, the way she felt in each was identical. Déjà vu was never pleasant, but this was terrifying.

"Sy," Lucien called, "this is Dr. Gale."

Sy flashed a warm, big, perfect smile at Gabby. His charisma was palpable, and she couldn't help but smile back.

"It's so nice to meet you," Sy said, and held his hand out to shake Gabby's.

"You too," Gabby said, shaking his hand.

They stopped in front of a natural wood door, with a metal key plate on the silver handle. Sy punched a few keys. "Dr. Gale, enter a four-digit code that will be your key code."

She nodded her head, then punched in her code. Sy hit two keys. "Okay, put that same code in one more time."

Gabby did. The light on the keypad flashed yellow three times, then turned green.

"Perfect, okay Dr. Gale, now enter your code."

Gabby entered the code, the light flashed green, and the door unlocked. Sy opened the door, then stepped to the side, and invited Gabby in.

The apartment was beautiful, modern, and luxurious. The color scheme was black and white, and there were clean lines, comfortable linen sofas with down cushions, modern abstract paintings, and a glass dining room table with ample space.

"Wow," Gabby said.

"Does this work for you?" Lucien asked.

"It's beautiful," Gabby said.

Sy explained, "We took the liberty of stocking the closet with clothes for you. The kitchen is fully stocked. We also have a food delivery service. All of that information is in your welcome packet by your comm center and computer."

"Thank you."

"Do you have any energy left? I'd love to show you my favorite part of this safe house," Lucien asked.

"Sure."

"Perfect," Lucien said and opened the door.

"Wait," Sy interrupted, as he walked over to the desk, "her watch." Sy picked up a stainless-steel smart watch.

"Oh right," Lucien said.

Sy held the watch out to her. "This will help you find your way, at least in the beginning. If you're trying to find your way somewhere, hit this button," Sy pointed to the button, "and say where you are trying to go. For example, home or Restaurant Square or the gym. The watch will communicate with the safe house and a small path of fiber-optic lights will light your way." Sy put the watch on Gabby's wrist.

Gabby was instantly grateful for this bit of an anchor, both in time and place. Part of her realized it was also a leash, though she needed something to hold on to and gladly wore it.

"Why don't you give it a try?" Lucien suggested as he opened the door and held it for Gabby. "Hit the button, then say nursery."

"Nursery," Gabby said to her watch.

Immediately, golden fiber-optic lights glowed in front of Gabby's feet. The lights then spread ahead a few feet. With each step they took the lights moved forward, gently guiding them. Gabby felt like a kid; it seemed like magic. As she followed the lights, she found herself falling head-over-heels for this place. The lights sparkled around a corner, then stopped in front of a door. They twinkled momentarily, then faded. They were at the nursery.

"Pretty cool, right?" Sy said.

"Very cool," Gabby said.

"I'd like to take credit," Lucien started.

"But, it was all my idea," Sy interrupted. "We knew that coming into the safe house and learning the way around was going to be frustrating and difficult. We didn't want those frustrations to grow into problems. Little touches like this serve a deeper purpose than it appears on the surface."

"Smart," Gabby said.

Lucien keyed a code into the numeric pad just outside the door, then went in.

"Dr. Hollman, how is everything going?" Lucien asked.

"Incredible, wait till you see." Dr. Hollman smiled.

"Fantastic. This is Dr. Gale, our newest resident." Lucien motioned to Gabby.

"Nice to meet you, Dr. Gale." Dr. Hollman nodded towards her.

"You as well," Gabby smiled.

"Follow me, you are here at a great time." Dr. Hollman beamed.

The nursery was bright and white. The babies were lined up in perfect rows, with individual nurses stationed behind their bassinets. It was so quiet. This room made Gabby uncomfortable. It was too orderly and quiet for a nursery. In an effort to ground herself, Gabby checked her watch; it was about one minute before noon. Though it was so hard to tell, there were no windows apparently anywhere in the safe house. Then Gabby noticed the babies had seen them come in and were staring at them. She had another flash-back to her ayahuasca dream; the children with no expressions, sitting at their desks in a perfect lineup.

Precisely at 12, the baby at the end of the row held his tiny, plump hand straight up in the air. Then the other babies all did the same. They formed their little hands into horizontal C shapes. They faced their palms in and put their hands in front of their necks and moved them down towards their bellies. *This is so weird,* Gabby thought.

"We've taught them sign language," Dr. Hollman boasted. "That means they're hungry."

The nurses stood, picked up the children, cradled them, and placed a bottle in their mouths.

"Dr. Gale, would you like to feed one?" Dr. Hollman asked.

Gabby felt both a fascination and discomfort at the idea but kept her expression unreadable. "Sure. How old are they?" Gabby asked, stepping a little closer.

"Primus is our oldest at seven weeks old. Why don't you hold him?" Dr. Hollman pointed her towards Primus as the baby's nurse stepped around the bassinet and placed him in Gabby's arms along with his bottle.

"Isn't that young to use sign language?" Gabby asked. She stared down at the child. He was perfect.

"It's extremely young. The earliest babies typically learn to sign is around eight months," Dr. Hollman replied.

"Wow," Gabby said, though her focus had waned.

She had quickly become consumed with Primus. "Hi, little one," she cooed. "You are just the cutest thing ever... yes, you are," she said, her voice going up several octaves.

"Dr. Gale, I know this is hard, as it's very tempting to do, but we don't use baby talk with these children. They are far too advanced."

Gabby's cheeks flushed and she could've sworn that little Primus rolled his eyes at Dr. Hollman. He finished his bottle. He held both hands up and flipped them from palm out to palm in.

"That means he's finished," Dr. Hollman said.

The nurse came over and took the bottle, "Do you know how to burp a baby?" she asked.

Gabby smiled and nodded, then lifted Primus over her shoulder and gently patted his back. He let out a loud belch and she cradled him again. Gabby smiled at him and he smiled back. He reached his tiny hand up and placed it on her cheek.

"It's time for their afternoon nap," Dr. Hollman said, and Primus's nurse took the baby from Gabby and laid him back into his bassinet.

"Thank you," Lucien said to Dr. Hollman.

"Anytime."

"We could use another doctor here, if Dr. Gale is interested in helping out. Even if it's just a couple days a week." Dr. Hollman turned to Gabby with a raised eyebrow.

"I'd like that," she replied.

"Great," Lucien said as they made their way out. "Dr. Gale, before you head back to your quarters, would you like to grab a cup of coffee with me?"

"Okay."

Lucien and Gabby sat down in the coffee shop. Gabby got a black coffee and Lucien ordered tea.

"I…" Lucien paused. "This must be very difficult for you."

Gabby nodded her head, and wiped a tear.

"Did he tell you about the unavoidable side effect of the EVE-0 treatment?"

"Yes, of course."

"That was silly of me to ask. I know how close you were and how much you loved Trent. There's still a piece of him here at AmCorps."

"I loved him very much. I appreciate you acknowledging his presence here."

"Yes, of course. He was instrumental in this achievement, but that's not exactly what I'm saying."

Gabby looked at him. She didn't understand what he was trying to hint at. "What do you mean?"

"I'm trying to tell you that we have Trent's sperm. This may sound odd to hear from me, but Trent often talked about what a great mother you were going to be. He couldn't wait to start a family with you. You can still have his child, if you want. And, as the first rehabilitated woman on the planet, it would be a great service to the future of the human species. Procreation will look different, better, if you ask me, but different. You will be an example, no, an inspiration to everyone."

"Ohh." Gabby caught her breath. She wasn't expecting that.

"Don't answer now. Just think about it," Lucien said.

The barista dropped off their coffee and tea.

Lucien looked at his watch. "I'm afraid I'm going to have to leave you here to enjoy your coffee without me. I have a meeting." Lucien stood.

"Umm." Gabby wasn't sure what to say. "Thank you." Her tone rose unintentionally, as if she was asking a question, giving away how truly confused she was.

Lucien smiled. "I know it's a lot to take in. Get some rest and we'll talk soon."

She waited for him to leave. Then she hit the button on her watch and said, "home."

33 – STEALTH

When Chief Ëpë and Shaman Dabi arrived at the Matsés village, the shaman lit a small bundle of leaves. He carried them through the deserted village as he chanted. Mayalú started to cry.

"É difícil." Rodrigo leaned over to Chris. "It's hard for them to see their home like this. Let's gather some firewood."

Chris nodded. As they walked through the forest between the extraction field and the village, collecting wood, Chris heard a jet in the area. He handed Rodrigo the wood. "Wait for me in the village. If you hear a gunshot, flee."

"You don't trust them?"

"I do, I just know enough to know that anything is possible." Chris paused. "It's just a precaution."

"I should go with you," Rodrigo said.

"No, you should keep everyone else safe. I'm almost sure it's fine."

Chris walked into the clearing and saw the jet fly

over. Shit, he thought, *I hope I didn't give bad coordinates.* The plane circled back. This time it flew over much lower. It circled one more time, then landed.

Chris hung back while the plane taxied to a stop. It was a stealth aircraft, which made him feel much better. Chris had been worried that AmCorps would pick up their activity on radar, but this made that unlikely. He made his way towards the plane. He had no option but to trust them. They were obviously intelligent. As he waited for someone to come out, nothing happened. No doors opened. The plane just sat there. Chris started to get nervous. He put his hand on his gun and got ready. Finally, the door cracked and opened very slowly. A figure covered in hazmat gear stood in the doorway. He unfolded steps, then descended. Chris waved, then slowly approached.

"Hiya mate, you must be Chris," said a male voice, with a crisp British accent. "I'm Oliver."

Chris nodded. "Nice to meet you," he said as he approached.

"We've been in quarantine. We're pathogen-free. Though we want to be as careful as possible with the local community here. We think it's important for us to minimize contact."

"Definitely," Chris agreed.

"We'll unload the supplies. Let you collect the blood and wait for you here."

"Sounds good," Chris said, as another person carried a mini-pallet of supplies off the plane. He handed the pallet to Oliver.

"These are the blood collection kits. Thomas is getting the cooler."

Thomas came out with a large backpack cooler. "It's fully charged and will stay cold for eight hours, but we can plug it in on the plane."

Chris took the backpack from Thomas, then the mini-pallet from Oliver.

"Thanks. I will be back as soon as possible," Chris said, then headed back into the forest, moving as quickly as he could.

Rodrigo was relieved to see Chris. He had a fire lit, and everyone gathered around it.

Chris opened the pallet. There were thirty kits, with thirty stainless steel trays.

"Can you lay a tray next to each person donating blood?" Chris asked Rodrigo.

Chris placed a PVC-free blood bag in each tray. Next, Chris tied a rubber strap around each arm. Rodrigo followed with an alcohol swipe. Then, needles were in.

Chris and Rodrigo worked so well together. They had become good friends and Chris would miss him.

As the bags slowly filled, Chris went down the line and removed the needles, while Rodrigo put rubber band-aids on. He placed the blood bags into the cooler. They had collected twenty-seven pints of blood. Chris placed the used needles into a stainless-steel collection tin and secured the top.

Chris hugged Rodrigo. "You're a good friend and a real badass." Chris grinned.

Rodrigo laughed. "Thanks for everything."

"Keep in touch, man."

"I will. Stay safe, brother."

Chris nodded, then said his goodbyes to the villagers. Lastly, he bowed to Chief Ëpë and Shaman Dabi. The shaman held his hand over Chris, blessed him, and put his forehead to his. He heard the thought, *Life is a balance between intellect and emotion. Give power to your ability to be understanding. Use patience to save Gabrielle.* Chris pulled his head back; the thought came through like any other thought of his. It was in his voice, but it wasn't his thought—or maybe it was. He bowed.

He placed the now very heavy cooler on his back and headed towards the plane. The steps were down and ready for him. Oliver and Thomas sat in the doorway. They stood when they saw Chris come into the clearing. The plane powered up as he boarded the plane.

"That was fast," Thomas said. "You can secure the blood in there," he pointed out a spot in the galley with straps, "then make yourself comfortable."

Thomas pulled the steps up and secured the door, then he joined Oliver in the cockpit. Within minutes, the plane was in the air.

"Just shout if you need anything, mate," Thomas said, peering out from the cockpit. He had removed his hazmat gear. Thomas had short sandy-blonde hair, slicked back. He was muscular and looked like he had been in more than one fight. He had tattooed arms that attempted to camouflage several scars.

"Thanks," Chris said, "how long is the flight?"

"Ten hours," Oliver yelled back.

Chris reclined his leather chair all the way back so that it was a bed.

"Chris... Chris..."

Chris felt a tap on his shoulder, then opened his eyes.

"We're landing." Thomas stood over him.

"Oh shit," Chris said, rubbing his eyes and sitting up.

"You had a nice rest."

"Yeah," Chris said, stretching.

He leaned over and opened the window shade. It was dark out. It looked like they were flying over trees, but he wasn't sure.

After a bumpy landing, the plane taxied to a stop. Then, everything started happening really fast. Several planes were already waiting. Chris was ushered into a waiting SUV. A freezing cold wind blew drifts of snow to the sides of the runway. Chris had on light khakis and a tee shirt. The cold stung his skin.

Chris kept the blood close the entire twenty-minute drive to Michaela's compound. Chris guessed that they were in a remote part of Canada. Towering evergreen trees, piles of snow, and narrow winding roads were not the easiest to traverse. They pulled off the road and onto a trail that barely seemed big enough for the car.

Soon, the trail opened and Chris saw an opulent house just ahead.

"We're here," Thomas said, and turned off the headlights.

"Chris, you're staying in the main house," Oliver said.

"Just me?" Chris asked.

"The rest of our unit is divided between a few guest houses on the property. They will be arriving throughout the week. Once everyone's here, we'll introduce you to the rest of the team. Everyone has been strictly quarantined and tested," Oliver said.

Chris nodded his understanding.

"Take the blood and your belongings, Michaela's expecting you," Thomas said.

The SUV crept to a stop in front of the huge stone mansion. It was completely dark from the outside, so Chris couldn't take in its full stature until he stepped out of the SUV. The only light came from the clear night sky and full moon. The house looked empty.

"You're sure this is it, right?" Chris asked before grabbing his things, as he stared at the pitch-black home.

"Completely sure mate. Just head to the front door," Oliver said.

Chris smiled, grabbed his bags, and headed to

the front door. Oliver and Thomas pulled out without turning the headlights on, and headed to the back of the property with the rest of the convoy.

The snow crunched under Chris's boots as he made his way to the front door. He was going to need some different clothes as soon as possible. It was freezing. He let out a deep breath, mentally willing his body to be warm. His breath, visible in the cold, circled his head as he picked up his pace. The extra-large, dark wood front door didn't have a lever or handle. Just one long bar and a keyhole greeted him. Chris tried to push and pull the door, but it didn't budge. He looked for a doorbell, but it was too dark to see in the towering shade of the mansion. Chris knocked, then stood back. Nothing. He knocked again, then put his head to the door to see if he could hear any motion inside. Nothing. Chris stood back and looked around. He was completely alone.

Chris turned around. He saw the trail the cars left in the snow. He was planning on following that to find someone when he heard a click. He spun to see the front door crack open. He pushed it and stepped inside. It was a dark foyer. Chris closed the door behind him and heard the lock engage. Then, a light came on. There was a closed door at the opposite end of the foyer, but Chris was still alone.

"Hi Chris, I'm so glad that you're here," a voice piped in through a ceiling speaker.

"Michaela?" Chris asked, looking for a camera.

"Yes, it's me. Look in the right corner. Do you see the tray?"

Chris sat his bag and the blood cooler down. "Yeah."

"There are three swabs. With swab number one, you're going to swab your nostrils. Do five full circles in each nostril. With swab number two, you're going to swab the back of your throat, both sides. With swab three, you're going to swab under your fingernails. Behind each swab is a solution. Remove the lid and stir the solution with the swab, then leave it in. If the solution stays clear, you're pathogen-free. If it turns blue, you're not."

"Got it," Chris said, and sat down in front of the tray.

His palms were suddenly sweaty. It was almost as if he had forgotten the pandemics and the threat they posed. This invisible enemy caught Chris off guard. His hands shook, just slightly, as he picked up the first swab. He instantly remembered how much he despised doing this. He stuck the swab in and fought back the urge to sneeze. His eyes watered. He stirred the solution. Clear. Chris let out a breath of relief. Next was his throat. He hated this the most. He gagged every time. He took a deep breath, swallowed, then swabbed both sides. He gagged and had to swallow hard to keep from throwing up. He stirred the second solution. Clear. *Thank God,* he thought. Finally, he swabbed his nails and stirred the solution. Blue.

"Oh shit," Chris said.

"It's ok. Don't panic," Michaela said. "The solution is extremely sensitive. It's probably just reacting to some dirt or soil. Look to your left. There's another tray. There's sanitizer and two more swabs with solution. Clean your hands and under your nails really well, then swab them again."

Chris soaked his hands with sanitizer. His heart was racing. He fanned them to dry. Grabbed a swab and retested them. Clear. He let out a breath of relief.

"Awesome," Michaela said.

A door at the opposite end of the foyer unlocked and cracked open.

"Grab your things and come in. I'll meet you there in two minutes. Close the door behind you," Michaela instructed.

As Chris stepped inside of Michaela's home, he closed the door and set his bags down. Michaela's home was magnificent. A massive stone hearth warmed the sprawling living room. Light from the flames gently flickered off the stone and soft surroundings. Billowy wool blankets were draped over the back of the oversized taupe linen sofa. Black wood beams crisscrossed the tall ceiling. It was the nicest house that Chris had ever been in. Chris made his way over to the sofa and readied himself to melt into it.

"Chris," Michaela called.

Chris spun to see Michaela walk into the room behind him. "Michaela," Chris smiled, "you're smaller than I expected... I didn't mean it like that. It's... it's... just you've been such a larger-than-life scientist and—"

"It's alright, I get that a lot," Michaela said, and smiled. At most, she was five feet tall and a hundred pounds. She wore loose jeans and flannel shirt.

"Your house is really nice," Chris said.

"Thanks. Abe and I built it. We started small and just kept adding. We wanted it to be our family compound one day."

Chris smiled at the thought.

"Want a quick tour and I'll show you to your room?" Michaela asked.

"Sure."

"You have the blood, right? We'll stop by the lab first."

"Right here," Chris said, and picked up the heavy cooler. "We do need to get it into a refrigerator soon."

"Great. I have a walk-in lab fridge; we'll put it there. Follow me," Michaela said.

"I marked Mayalú's sample. We know that she was AmCorps's prime choice, and we know that she has an active EVE-0 gene. The rest you'll need to sequence to make sure."

"That works. How much blood did Mayalú give you?"

"About a pint."

"Oh, that's plenty to start with. I think when Gabby asked, I figured that that makes about a few thousand treatments, which is more than enough to treat everyone here. I should be able to have the first doses ready in a couple of weeks."

Chris nodded and followed her down a long hallway, then up a set of stairs. The space opened to a carpeted den. There was a game table in the corner, a pool table, and a big television built into dark wood cabinets. On the far side of the den was a large window that looked into a state-of-the-art lab. There was a group of people working in the lab. When they saw Michaela and Chris, they quickly make their way to the den.

"This is my lab," Michaela said. "That's Jay, Lulu, Aston, and Luke. We were the original founders and inventors of the life tattoo."

"Nice to meet you. Do you all live out here together?"

"We all moved out here after my husband died; I guess we've been quarantined for longer than it's been cool. Luke, can you grab the blood from Chris and get it into the fridge?"

"We've heard a lot about you, Chris. We're glad that you're here," Luke said as he took the blood cooler from Chris. Luke had short sandy-blonde hair and wore black framed glasses.

"Me too," Chris replied with a smile.

"Your room's this way," Michaela pointed. "I put some warm clothes in there and some snacks. There's a bathroom and shower."

"I haven't had a hot shower in months," Chris said.

The bedrooms were up another flight of steps. There was a voluminous, king-sized bed in Chris's room, piled with down blankets and comforters that proffered the aesthetic of an upscale hotel in a trendy mountain town, which was ironic, because hotels had shut down years ago or had been taken over by the government. Chris took a much-needed shower, laid down in bed, and turned on the television. As he lay in his luxurious bed, his mind quickly found its way to Gabby. He prayed that she was still alive.

There was a soft knock on the door and Michaela walked in.

"Is everything alright? Do you need anything?" she asked.

"It's perfect. Thank you," Chris said.

"I just got a message from IFP. I thought you'd like to know," Michaela said.

Chris sat up in the bed. "What is it?"

"They said they received some intelligence that Dr. Gale has made it into the safe house and she is okay."

A rush of relief poured down on Chris. "How did they find that out?" Chris asked.

"I'm not sure," Michaela said, then added, "Well, I will let you rest. We have a busy day tomorrow. Help yourself to anything that you need. My home is yours."

Michaela closed the door behind her. Chris was beyond relieved to know that Gabby was still alive.

Though this sent his mind racing. *What is she doing, right now? Is she safe and comfortable? What is the safe house like?*

34 - CHILD OF MINE

Gabby couldn't sleep that night. She couldn't stop thinking about that beautiful baby in the nursery and the possibility of having her own. Her heart jumped at the possibility of getting a piece of Trent back. She wasn't prepared for this. A baby wasn't something she'd realized she wanted so badly. *Wait, what am I thinking?* her mind suddenly screamed. She knew this was a bad idea. She didn't trust Lucien, but she could feel her subconscious slowly starting to find reasons why she should. Her own mind's ability to justify such an insane proposal scared her. She knew she was supposed to hate AmCorps, and she did, but maybe that was when it was under General Holton. Maybe it did care about the good of the world. *No—stop,* she told herself, *Dr. Lucien Sabara is an evil, manipulative, powerful person.* Although, she had to admit, he didn't come off so bad. He seemed nice and genuine. Gabby didn't see the monster that Trent did, but she trusted Trent. She would tell Lucien no. She had to tell Lucien no. She reminded herself that he was most likely lying and if he did in vitro fertilization, he would probably implant in her some genetically modified creature, not Trent's child. Gabby made up her mind: she would tell Lucien that she wasn't emotionally ready to be a mother right now.

A chat request pinged on Gabby's computer. She checked the time; it was 2 a.m. *Strange*, she thought. The chat pinged again. Gabby got up and made her way to the computer. It was a message request from USER12712: *Dr. Gale, please accept this chat request. I have something urgent to tell you.* Gabby reread the request. It was from someone that knew her name. She thought about ignoring it. She stood to go lay back down in bed, but the chat pinged again. She sat and approved it, then typed, *Who is this?*

You don't know me, but I have important information for you.

Gabby just sat there. She could see that USER12712 was typing.

Dr. Sabara and Sy are testing you. If you do not agree to the in vitro fertilization, they will kill you. They don't trust you and you will be of no use to them.

What? How do you know? Gabby quickly typed.

I don't have time to explain any more. If you want to survive, you will do as Lucien says. There are others, like me, that know this is wrong. If you want to survive, you'll listen to me. I have to go.

Wait, what do you mean? What is wrong? I'm

confused. Please tell me more... Gabby was still typing when she noticed the chat had ended. Gabby's computer screen flashed, then went blank. It powered back up after a moment, but the chat window was gone. She couldn't find it or any evidence of it anywhere on the computer.

Gabby laid back down in bed. She felt like the butt of a cruel joke. Was this mysterious chat a manipulation by Lucien to get her to agree, or was it some sort of sick test? Could there really be someone inside the safe house that was against AmCorps? Gabby's mind was caught in a tornado of thoughts, doubts, and what-ifs.

Morning came surprisingly fast, despite Gabby not sleeping. As predicted, the comm center in Gabby's apartment rang. It was Lucien's secretary.

"I hope I'm not bothering you too early," Lucien said.

"No, no, not at all," Gabby said.

"How are you feeling? Dr. Hollman asked if you're planning on working in the nursery."

"I'm feeling good. I'd like to work in the nursery and start as soon as possible," Gabby said.

"Wonderful. Have you had anymore thoughts concerning our chat?"

"Yes and yes," Gabby said. After a sleepless night, she was no closer to an answer—yes was just what came out.

"That's fantastic. Why don't you meet me at our

OB-GYN center in an hour? We can get the process started today. I will talk to Dr. Hollman and see if you can start there this afternoon."

"Okay. Thank you so much," Gabby said. While she heard those words come out of her mouth, she almost couldn't believe she had said them. But what were her other options? She realized she wanted to survive. She didn't want to disappear here, inside of the safe house. But, could she give up her body for the sake of surviving?

Gabby made her way to the OB-GYN unit. She found it easily with her watch. Lucien was already there and introduced her to the head obstetrician, Dr. Jason Malik.

"So, I hear that you'd like to harvest some eggs today?" Malik said.

With his strong features and deep, big brown eyes, he reminded her of Chris and how intensely she missed him. "Is that possible?" Gabby squirmed in her chair.

"Of course. It's a very simple and painless treatment. We've come a long way in the past ten years. We no longer need medicine to prepare the ovaries. We have a thick needle and we'll numb you; it's painless, since we stick it into your ovaries. This needle has a very slight electromagnetic charge that attracts and catches your eggs. We're capable of harvesting about five eggs at a time."

"Wow, I didn't realize that I would do it today. I thought it was a longer process."

Malik shook his head. "It's incredibly easy. I can check the viability of your egg today, have them fertilized by tonight, and could have it implanted tomorrow, technically speaking. It's the editing process that takes longer."

"Editing?"

"Yes; what eye color, hair color, nose shape, face shape, any specific skills you want your child to have, musical inclinations, things like that. The more specific you are, the longer the editing process."

"I don't want to edit at all."

"Oh, really?" Dr. Malik looked at Lucien—Lucien nodded in agreement.

"Then in that case, we can possibly have you pregnant tomorrow. Let's get those eggs out, then we'll know for sure. Follow me."

Gabby did not expect it to move this fast.

"What if I decide that I would like some edits, how long would that take?" Gabby asked.

"Oh, that could take anywhere from days to weeks," Dr. Malik said.

"Trent was very specific in his desire not to have his offspring genetically altered, so that's off the table. Are you having second thoughts?" Lucien asked Gabby.

"No... no, I was just curious." Gabby added, "Trent and I actually had these conversations."

"Perfect," Dr. Malik said, "follow me and we'll get started."

Gabby stood and followed Dr. Malik down a short hallway and into a procedure room. She told herself that these procedures often took multiple tries; she had time.

Lucien spoke up as he prepared to leave her in Dr. Malik's hands. "Dr. Gale, I spoke to Dr. Hollman this morning and he asked if you can start today? He's eager to get another caretaker in with the children."

"Okay."

"I will let him know to expect you shortly. Thank you so much." Lucien smiled and left.

The procedure was, physically, much easier than Gabby expected. Mentally, she couldn't believe that it was actually happening. *There's no way it will be successful,* she told herself as she lay on the procedure table.

"All done," Dr. Malik told Gabby. "I'm going to give you a quick hormone injection to prepare your uterus. Stop by later this afternoon and I will let you know about the viability of your eggs."

She left the OB-GYN wing and stopped by the café before heading to Dr. Hollman's neonatal pediatric unit. She ordered a coffee and an organic breakfast bar from an unmasked barista. She was in a daze. After years of pandemics and mask-wearing, suddenly things were so different. She looked around the café at groups of people talking and sitting close. She took a bite of her breakfast bar, but realized she had no appetite. She tossed her bar away and used her watch to find her way to Dr. Hollman's unit.

She rang the buzzer and Dr. Hollman opened the door.

"Thank you for agreeing to work here a couple days a week. I have your badge ready. Follow me," They stepped back outside the door. "The first time you scan your badge, it will ask you to put a code in, here." Dr. Hollman scanned it. "Go ahead." She put her code in. "Okay, now try it."

The doors clicked open. "It's official," Dr. Hollman said.

"What would you like me to do?"

"We want to start to broaden the individuals that these children interact with. So, that's where you come in. Just spend a little time with each child. Talk to them. Interact with them. You can pick them up and hold them. Speak to them like adults. Try not to baby them. We want to explore their bonding mechanisms."

Gabby spent the rest of the day moving between the children. They all looked like perfect dolls. They were beautiful. A few seemed interested in her, while others barely looked at her until they wanted something, with the exception of Primus. He actually engaged with her. At one point, he used a sign to ask Gabby to pick him up. She was drawn to him, as were the other babies. They watched him and imitated him. Gabby couldn't help but become enamored with him.

Four o'clock was here before she knew it. Dr. Hollman asked her to come back again tomorrow and she happily agreed; she enjoyed the distraction these babies offered.

Gabby slowly made her way back to Dr. Malik's. He was waiting for her and brought her right into his office. "I have a video to show you," he told her. He turned on a large flatscreen, then clicked a button on his computer. An image of a microscope and an egg came onto the screen. There were five round shapes, then one by one, a round tube grabbed each shape while a thin needle partially pierced the other side.

"Tell me," Gabby said, too afraid to assume anything.

"Those are yours and Trent's. You have five viable eggs." Gabby's mouth dropped open. "Tomorrow will be the perfect time to implant your blastocyst."

"Tomorrow?" Gabby asked. She thought of Trent and missed him. She thought of Chris, and missed him, too, but she knew that she'd probably never see Chris again.

She had made a sacrifice and it seemed to have worked. AmCorps had left the Matsés alone. People were receiving the treatment. The safe house seemed fair, odd, but somewhat fair. Gabby had to stay in here so she could continue to protect the people that had given so much for her.

"Yes. Can you come first thing in the morning?" Malik asked.

"I'm supposed to work with Dr. Hollman again tomorrow," Gabby said.

"That's no problem. The procedure tomorrow is easy and takes about an hour. If you come at 7:30, you'll be finished by 8:30, 9 at the latest."

"Okay," Gabby agreed.

"Great. I'm going to give you one more hormone injection, then get a good night's sleep and I'll see you tomorrow."

A strange stir of excitement began to bloom from the back of her mind. She might be a mother soon. Then a twang of guilt took a bite at her. She felt as if she were betraying Chris and Trent, but she had no choice—did she?

"Dr. Gale," Sy said, walking up behind her, "can I talk to you?" She turned and he stood a little too close. It was almost threatening.

"What's going on?" Gabby asked, taking a few steps back.

"Our intelligence unit picked up on some sat comm pings coming out of the area of Brazil that you just left. How's that possible, since you've been here?"

"I left the sat comm for the Jungle Guardians in case we ever needed to reach them or they needed us. They saved my life from AmCorps's first extraction team. It was the least I could do," Gabby snapped. She tried to sound tough, but wasn't sure how it came across.

"Huh, so these primitive humans that can't even use a phone, suddenly are capable of using a highly technical sat comm system?"

"The guardians are experienced with technology. They've trained with the Brazilian army."

"If you say so." Sy took a step back so that he no longer had her cornered. "Have a nice night, Dr. Gale. Thanks for clearing that up."

Gabby let out a breath. She did not like Sy; she could see what Trent was saying. He scared her and she got the direct impression that he didn't like her. She hurried to her apartment and locked the door behind her.

She ordered dinner, took a long shower, and went to bed early. She had the craziest dreams that night. She was swimming in the ocean and this huge hook got tangled in her hair, pulling her out of the water. Lucien looked over the side of the boat, and she tried yelling for help, but couldn't. Then he disappeared for a moment and came back with a gaff hook and tried to stab her. Trent reached over the boat and cut the line and yelled, "Gabrielle, swim! Don't let him hook you. Swim!"

Gabby woke up, drenched in sweat. *It was just nerves... It was just nerves,* she told herself. Though she tried to push the nightmare out of her thoughts, part of her was also glad to see Trent. She missed him. She looked at the clock: 6 a.m. She took a quick shower and got ready.

She heard a knock at her door. *Please don't be Sy,* she thought. She opened the door. It was Lucien. "I brought you breakfast," he said with a smile.

"Thank you. Come in."

"Black," Lucien handed her a cup of coffee, "and a grain-free banana nut muffin. I..." Lucien paused and looked down. He was hard to read, he seemed so genuine. "I miss Trent. He was my first intern, he was brilliant, and he became like a son to me. I'm worried that I may have inadvertently..." he paused again, "that my grief may have led me to inadvertently influence you. I don't want you to do anything that you're not sure of."

"Oh, no, you didn't. I made the decision on my own," Gabby replied, caught off guard by the sadness and sincerity that this powerful man willingly revealed to her. Could he be telling the truth, or was this part of his game? Gabby was reeling. She didn't know what to think, who to believe, or how to feel. The worst part was that she wanted to believe this. She wanted the safe house to be safe. She wanted it to be fair. She wanted this all to be true, but she knew better. She forced a smile.

"Of course," Lucien said, "I just wanted to catch you before I go to my office, and let you know that whatever you decide, you have my full support. There's no rush."

"Thank you, but I made the decision on my own," Gabby paused, wondering if he was playing some sort of malicious game or truly sincere, "I'm heading there this morning."

"Oh, that's fantastic. It will be so wonderful to

have a piece of Trent in this world again."

Gabby caught the slightest squint in his eyes when he said that. She wasn't sure why, but his expression betrayed his sentiment. It was fleeting, but it was there. Gabby smiled and looked down. "I know," she replied, looking back up at Lucien.

Lucien looked at his watch. "I have to go. If you need anything, just let me know." Lucien patted her shoulder and left.

Gabby threw the muffin and coffee away, then headed to Dr. Malik. She didn't want to admit it, but the fleeting pang of excitement had fully morphed into regret and now guilt. Was she being too passive? Was she too eager to survive? Was she somehow undermining Trent's mission—the very things that, in the end, he had come to believe and ultimately give his life for? Was she less of a person than Trent, because she wasn't throwing herself in front of a bullet? She reminded herself that this was a different kind of battle. She told herself she had made her mind up and that was it. Luckily, for Gabby's mental state, the walk to Dr. Malik's was fast, and she didn't have enough time to change her mind.

"Dr. Gale, you look rested. Are you ready?" Gabby nodded her head yes and he guided her to the procedure room.

"Go ahead and take off your clothes and put this gown on. I'll be right in," Dr. Malik instructed.

She quickly undressed and laid down on the table.

Dr. Malik knocked, then walked in.

"How many eggs would you like to implant in the procedure? The more you attempt, the better your chance for a successful pregnancy, but the higher your chance of having multiples."

"I don't know."

"Do you want twins?"

Gabby shook her head no.

"Then let's just try with one. Your eggs are all very healthy, genetically speaking, so we should have no problem with just one."

"Okay," Gabby said.

"Are you alright? You seem nervous. This procedure is easy and painless."

Gabby smiled and nodded. "I'm fine."

As she lay on the table, her feet in stirrups, she felt sick. The dark thoughts in her mind told her that she was weak for allowing her body to become a vessel just so she could survive a little longer. Worst of all, she felt guilty that there was a part of her that wanted to be a mother. Not like this, not in this world, but the desire was there. In this moment, she hated herself. Though, physically, she was fine. The procedure was easy, painless, and fast. She didn't feel any different; maybe a little bloated, but that was all.

After dressing, Gabby made her way to Dr. Hollman's unit. She keyed in her code and the door opened. She walked into the nursery but didn't see him anywhere. She heard him yell from another room, "Can someone come in here? This thing won't stop crying today."

Gabby walked into the other room where the wailing of a child interrupted the usual quiet. "Hi Dr. Hollman, I got here a little early today. What can I do?"

"Oh, Dr. Gale," he jumped and tried to stand in front of the single bassinet in this room, "you are early. Can you go check on the other babies?" He motioned back toward the nursery.

"Sure, but what's in here?" Gabby stepped to the side and craned her neck to see what was in the bassinet and gasped. A red-faced, squalling baby shook its stubby hands in the air, its oddly shaped facial features even more contorted by its wide-mouthed crying.

"Ugh," Dr. Hollman's mouth frowned in disgust as he stepped to the side and turned to face this child, "this thing is the result of a mother's undiagnosed genetic condition."

"Here, let me try," Gabby said, reaching down to pick up this child. The card on her bassinet said *girl #16*; that was it.

"Don't waste your time on this one."

Anger flashed across Gabby's face.

"Fine," Dr. Hollman relented as he left the room, "try to get it to shut up, please."

Gabby picked up the baby and instantly the cries turned to gasping tiny breaths. The little girl strained to look up at Gabby. She reached her little hand to Gabby's face and rested it on her cheek. Gabby immediately fell in love with this child. She squirmed and whimpered. Gabby lifted her to her shoulder and patted her back. She let out a huge burp, and her entire tiny body relaxed. She moved her back to the crook of her elbow and rocked her. The baby fell asleep in her arms and slowly, gently, Gabby laid her back down in her bassinet.

The day flew by again. Gabby was torn between spending time with Primus and the little girl that was separated from the rest. She hadn't been given a name, so Gabby started calling her Angel. She was so neglected and tucked away while the perfect babies were proudly displayed. This whole place was wrong. As much as Gabby wanted to melt into the comfort of the safe house, she couldn't. These babies had charmed her, but there was something odd about them, or maybe it was this place, this situation. Gabby wished she could do more, but she was chained. She was alone. Or, was she? She needed to find the mysterious messenger. She was done waiting around.

35 – DIVERSION

More of IFP's team began to show up at Michaela's compound. When the forces grew too big to fit in her guest quarters, they opted to stay outside in a hefty, heated tent. From Chris's bedroom window he could see out over their encampment. He watched the initial forces grow into a mini barracks. It seemed like their numbers doubled every other day. He watched the men sit around fires during the day. They played cards and laughed. They patrolled the property and the surrounding woods.

The days dragged on like that. Waiting. Watching. Wondering if Gabby was alright. Wondering if he would see her again. Wondering if the world would survive. Waiting. Torture. Wondering if Gabby loved him. Chris lacked the motivation to spend much time out of bed or with anyone else. They had been at Michaela's for almost two weeks and not much had changed. Michaela was working on the formula, and she was close and gave Chris regular updates, but there was nothing he could do to help. There was no reason for him to get out of bed. The only person that needed him was hundreds of miles away. A prisoner.

There was a soft knock on Chris's door. Michaela walked in. Chris turned the TV off, expecting an update. "Is the formula ready?" Chris asked.

"Close. I think we'll be able to administer the first doses tomorrow."

"That's good," Chris replied, and laid back down.

"But, that's not why I'm here," Michaela said, and Chris sat back up. "Commander Frei just arrived. He will be leading the safe house strike and wants to meet with you."

"When?"

"Now."

"Where?"

"He's waiting downstairs."

Chris jumped out of bed. "Alright, thanks," he said, and disappeared into the bathroom.

He brushed his teeth and washed his face. He couldn't remember the last time he did that. He changed out of sweatpants for the first time in weeks and found jeans and a sweater that Michaela had left for him.

Commander Frei was standing in the living room, watching the flames of the fire.

"Sir," Chris said, and saluted Frei as he turned. Chris noticed a thin scar down the side of Frei's face.

Frei returned the salute. "Chris, I've heard a lot

about you. It's nice to meet you," Frei said. His English was perfect. Chris detected just the slightest accent but couldn't place it.

"You as well," Chris said.

"I'd like to introduce you to the rest of the team and get your input on our plan."

"Yes, sir," Chris said, and followed Frei, noticing how big he was. He towered over Chris. He imagined Frei standing at the helm of a longship, covered in fur and wearing a horned helmet. Chris guessed Frei to be somewhere in his fifties, but more fit than most thirty-year-olds.

"We have soldiers from more than fifty countries, including the United States. Though most are European," Frei said.

"IFP has its own military?"

"Technically, we're the NRF. Do you know what that is?"

"Yes, the NATO Response Force," Chris said.

"Right. We've been working closely with IFP for the last five years or so."

"I haven't heard about NATO in so long. Didn't the U.S. pull out a while ago?"

"Yes," Frei said.

"How do you have U.S. soldiers?"

"They've been with us for almost ten years. When the U.S. pulled out, they opted to stay and become Swiss citizens," Frei said.

"Chris, mate, where have you been?"

Chris looked ahead and saw Oliver standing outside of the substantial tent.

"Waiting for my invite to come and hang out with you," Chris smiled.

"Well, welcome," Oliver said. He quickly saluted Frei, then pulled the tent curtain door open for them.

There was a control room set up with a few tables, several computers, and a communication center. Beyond the control room was an area with long tables set up and groups of men sitting around playing cards. At the far end of the massive tent, Chris could see rows of cots. It took him back to his days as a PJ.

Frei pulled out a chair for Chris in front of the main computer and sat down next to him. He clicked open a chat request, encrypted, of course.

"Sir, I have Lt. Christopher Silver... Chris this is Jan Saltzenberg, NATO's Secretary General," Frei said.

"Lt. Silver, it's nice to meet you. We are deeply appreciative of your service and your willingness to do what is right, even if that means defying your own country," Jan said. He smiled. His rectangular glasses lifted just slightly and framed his gentle blue eyes. Though what he said caught Chris off guard.

"I," Chris paused, "I never thought of it as defying my country. My goal has always been to protect my country, its citizens, and to do so with minimal loss of life. I—"

"My apologies. I didn't mean to offend you. Sentiments are often lost in my translations. I just meant to say that it takes courage to go against your superiors, in rank that is, so thank you," Jan said. Like Frei, his English was perfect with just a slight hint of an accent.

"Of course," Chris replied.

"We would like your input. We have the crimes against humanity charges ready. We plan to file them in two days. Then, once everyone has been treated, the forces will go to the safe house to officially make the arrests," Jan said.

"No," Chris blurted out.

"What?" Jan said.

"I don't think you should announce them until we are there. If you do, I think they'll kill Dr. Gale and perhaps destroy any evidence of what they have done."

Jan let out a quick, "hmm…" He paused for a moment, then asked, "You don't think we should let them know that we are aware of what they're doing? That may put pressure on them to pause their operations."

"No, not at all. If anything, that will make them speed up their plan and endanger any evidence and," Chris paused, "well, Dr. Gale."

"Do you feel this is what's best for the mission, not just what's least likely to harm Dr. Gale?"

"Yes, they are very powerful. If they have time to mobilize, you will not be able to make those arrests. Forgive me if this sounds cliché, but no one will be safe until Dr. Sabara is stopped," Chris said.

"I agree," Frei said, "this is the United States of America we're talking about. We need as much help as we can get and I think we need the element of surprise. It will also give them and us time to rehabilitate more people, which I think is important."

"Okay, it's settled then," Jan said. "We will bring the charges when you are at the safe house and we will simultaneously broadcast it to the public."

"Thank you," Chris said.

"Just be aware, there's been quite a bit of activity with moving the unit to you. I'm sure their intelligence has picked up on it. A few countries have reported it to us," Jan said.

"Do you have any pilots and planes available that can create a diversion?" Chris asked.

"Not much, but we can arrange something. The problem is most of our available pilots and planes are at our designated distribution site, which I don't want to bring any attention to. I will figure something out," Jan said.

36 – DECEPTION

Instead of going right home after work, Gabby decided to stop by Lucien's office. She had no idea what she would say, but maybe she could learn something. At least get a direction to move in. When Gabby tried to put Lucien's office into her watch, nothing came up. She would have to try and find it by memory. She tried to remember her first day here and the tour he gave her; although she didn't see his office, she remembered him pointing it out. She traced her steps by the café past Restaurant Square, back to the café, and back by Restaurant Square. Then she spotted the small hallway that took her to the café and made the turn.

"Can I help you?" came a voice from a nearby speaker. Gabby looked around, but saw nothing.

"Excuse me, can I help you?" the voice repeated.

"Umm, I'm trying to find Dr. Sabara's office," Gabby said.

"Do you have an appointment?"

"No, I just wanted to stop by."

"You have to have an appointment. This area is not open to the public."

"I just want to stop by. Can you call him now?"

"I'm sorry, that's not possible."

"If I go back to my apartment and call him, I'm going to explain how you prevented me from speaking to him. I'm going to tell him how rude and difficult you were," Gabby said.

There was a pause. "Dr. Sabara will see you now. Please proceed."

A door at the end of the hallway mechanically opened. Gabby walked into a reception area, though it was empty. The receptionist must have been located somewhere else.

"Please take a seat. Dr. Sabara will be with you momentarily," the receptionist announced.

Gabby sat down. The waiting room reminded her of the conference room she sat in at AmCorps Lab when she learned about the EVE-0 gene. If only she knew then what she knew now. She thought about the way the lab looked so innocuous from the outside. Just a small, grey concrete structure, a basic industrial shed. But inside, the lab sank down into the earth. Levels and levels of this massive structure lay hidden beneath a gentle landscape of lawn and evergreens. It was so deceptive and misleading. Some might argue that it was simply a mechanism of protection, but to Gabby it seemed a perfect description of what AmCorps and those that backed it stood for. Deception.

As Gabby sat there, she remembered the little ocelot that mimicked the cry of a baby tamarin to attract its prey. *Am I the cat or the monkey?* she wondered.

"Dr. Sabara is ready to see you," the receptionist's voice announced as a door at the far end of the reception area opened.

"Dr. Gale, what a nice surprise. To what do I owe the pleasure?" Lucien said.

Gabby took a seat at Lucien's massive oak desk. She sank into a comfortable fabric chair. The seat forced her to look up to Lucien, but now, she knew this was something she could use to her advantage. She cowered even lower, raised her eyebrows, and opened her eyes a little wider.

"I... I just... I'm worried. What happens when you, when we, run out of the blood to make the EVE-0 treatment?" Gabby asked.

"That's where you come in. I know that it's very important to you that we protect the people in the Amazon. So, you will work with them to decide how we proceed."

"Have you tried any other treatments after the patient that I saw?" Gabby's pulse quickened as the image of her hand pushing through the patient's flesh as his skin dissolved flooded her brain with panic.

"I know that was traumatic for you to witness. I'm sorry. We have actually, with much more success, though there were still some unforeseen side effects. I can introduce you to him, to Patient 13. I think you should see what we're up against and how important the active EVE-0 gene specimens are."

"Is Patient 13 alive?" Gabby asked.

"Yes, he's healthy—physically, at least, and his EVE-0 gene is active. But he is suffering some severe delusions and has become schizophrenic. In the few weeks that you've been here, we've already been able to successfully rehabilitate two-thirds of the safe house with the genetic material you brought to us. When you see what he is dealing with, I think you'll understand the importance of the genetic material."

"Okay," Gabby said. She didn't know where this would go, but the more she could learn and the closer she could get to Lucien, the better.

"Follow me," Lucien said, standing. "I almost forgot. How are you feeling after your procedure?"

"Great, just a little anxious to find out the results." Gabby smiled and meekly looked down.

"I can imagine."

Lucien led Gabby out of his office and down a hidden hallway that she'd never seen before.

I am the cat. I am the cat, pretending to be the baby in need. I'm not the monkey. I'm the cat. I'm the cat, Gabby repeated to herself on the walk over. She was nervous. Watching Patient 12 die such a violent, horrific death was something she would never get out of her mind. She watched the pure and complete physical breakdown of a body. Now she was going to see Patient 13 who'd had a mental breakdown. *Why is life so cruel?* she wondered.

"When we go into his room, stay aware and keep a good distance between you and him. He's been prone to violent outbursts in the past. He's familiar with us, but you're a new face. I'm not entirely sure how he'll react," Lucien said.

"Okay," Gabby replied, but what she wanted to say was, "Forget it."

"Here we are," Lucien said as the long hallway dead-ended into a set of metal doors. Lucien keyed in a code and opened the door.

"Dr. Sabara, we weren't expecting you," Dr. Faust said as he jumped up from a table in the control room. Dr. Faust and his nurse staff had been deeply engaged in a game of poker. Since there was no money in the safe house, they had made twenty-dollar promise notes out of paper.

"Don't get up," Lucien said. "This is Dr. Gale. She is the newest resident here and brought us the genetic material to make the treatment. You can thank her for your newly reactivated EVE-0 gene. I want to introduce her to Johnnie so that she can see the result of our most successful reactivation without the active genetic material."

"It's an honor to meet you Dr. Gale," Dr. Faust said.

"How is Johnnie doing?" Lucien asked.

"About the same. He sits at his computer for hours. He's still having delusions and engaging with them."

Gabby looked through the window and saw Johnnie. He was sitting at a desk in the corner of his room with his back facing them.

"I'd like to take her in to meet him. Is he showing any signs of violence?" Lucien asked.

"He hasn't had any violent outbursts in quite some time. Though, I'd better send Mike and Matt in with you, just in case meeting someone new sets him off," Dr. Faust said.

Mike and Matt, the nurses, put their hands down and quickly got up. They opened the door and held it for Lucien and Gabby. Johnnie didn't turn around when they came in.

"Hi Johnnie, there's someone I'd like to introduce you to," Lucien said.

Johnnie put his head up, but didn't turn around.

"We'd also like to see how you're feeling," Lucien continued.

Johnnie put his head back down and continued drumming keys on his computer. Gabby noticed he was doing this in a distinct *da-dum-da-dum-dum* rhythm.

"Johnnie, can you look at us?" Lucien asked.

Da-dum-da-dum-dum... da-dum-da-dum-dum. SCREECH... Johnnie's chair abruptly spun to face them. Gabby inadvertently stepped back and tripped over Matt's feet. He caught her. When she regained her balance, she looked up. Johnnie was sitting straight up, completely rigid, staring at her.

"You're new," Johnnie said.

"I'm Gabrielle," Gabby cleared her throat, "Dr. Gabrielle Gale."

"Mike, you're here. Matt's here. Dr. Sabara is here. Is Dr. Gabrielle Gale here?" Johnnie asked, without taking his eyes off of Gabby.

"Yeah, Johnnie, she's here," Mike said.

"And what about him?" Johnnie asked, and pointed with his thumb to the side of the room, by his hospital bed, though he still had his eyes pinned to Gabby.

"No, John, there's no one there," Mike said.

"Revelation 12:7-12. Then war broke out in heaven. Michael and his angels fought against the dragon, and the dragon and his angels fought back. But he was not strong enough, and they lost their place in heaven," Johnnie said.

"Okay, Johnnie," Mike answered.

Something clicked for Gabby. Something was familiar, but she couldn't quite place it.

"The great dragon was hurled down—that ancient serpent called the devil, or Satan, who leads the whole world astray. He was hurled to the earth, and his angels with him," Johnnie said.

"Johnnie, can you talk to us for a little while? We'd like to see how you're doing," Lucien asked.

"But woe to the earth and the sea, because the devil has gone down to you! He is filled with fury, because he knows that his time is short." Johnnie's voice had become much louder.

"Johnnie, I enjoy Revelation 12, as well," Gabby said, trying to break the uncomfortable stare.

"I want to see my wife. When is she coming?" Johnnie asked.

"Johnnie, it's Thursday. You know that on Thursdays she comes at 5:30," Mike said.

"Yes, Miranda comes at 5:30 on Tuesday and Thursday." Johnnie looked down and began rocking. "Then she goes to the café. She has a coffee. Grabs dinner for her and Bella. Then she goes home. They watch a movie. Miranda gets Bella ready for bed—"

"Johnnie," Lucien interrupted, breaking his train of thought, "can you tell us how you're feeling?"

"Johnnie is fine. Johnnie is good. Johnnie is fine. Johnnie is good. Johnnie is fine..."

Johnnie kept repeating this pattern, his eyes transfixed to a spot in the distance.

"Okay Johnnie, we just wanted to check in with you. Let me know if you need anything," Lucien said, then looked at Gabby. "Ready?"

She nodded.

"Johnnie is good. Johnnie is fine. Johnnie is good. Johnnie is fine. Miranda comes here at 5:30. Then goes to the café. Johnnie is good. Johnnie is fine."

Gabby could hear Johnnie—Patient 13–continue to repeat this as they left.

Gabby and Lucien walked in silence for what felt like forever. They wound through hallways. Revelation 12:7-12 kept repeating in her mind. There was something so familiar about it, but she couldn't quite place it. Lucien paused in an empty hall and turned to Gabby.

"Dr. Gale, Gabrielle, I want you to understand something about me. My life has shown me the worst in humanity. As a child, kids were so mean and so filled with anger towards me, simply because I looked different. They threw rocks at me, they called me names, would't come near me because they didn't want to catch what I had. I didn't understand why they hated me, so my mom protected me. She found me one friend, our housekeeper's son, and that was the only childhood friend I ever had," Lucien explained.

"Oh, I'm sorry," Gabby replied.

"Because of my condition, I was only able to go outside at night. I saw horrible things. I saw a mother hysterically crying over her twenty-one-year-old son's body that had been killed in a meaningless bar fight. I saw drug addicts living on the street; prostitutes beat by their pimps. We can do better than this. Humanity can be better. Trent had a difficult upbringing as well. He had a very abusive father, as I'm sure you know. We both didn't want others to suffer as we had. Together, we wanted to cure diseases of all kinds, physical and mental."

"I see," Gabby replied.

"Follow me, I want to show you one more thing."

They rounded one more corner and were spit out into the middle of Restaurant Square. It was packed.

Groups of people sat with smiles so big it almost seemed comical. A symphony of laughter.

"Do you see these happy, healthy people? Their immune systems are functioning. They know they can soon return to normal life. They are happy. And that's all thanks to you. In a matter of weeks, they've been rehabilitated. You are their savior," Lucien said.

As if on cue, one man in the crowd noticed Lucien and Gabby standing there. He stood up and started clapping. Everyone took notice and joined him. People were crying happy tears, yelling their sentiments of gratitude.

"You see," Lucien leaned over, "this is why we need your friends in the Amazon."

Her insides felt as if they had just turned inside out. She couldn't get Revelation 12:7-12 out of her head. All of these people were staring at her. Cheering for her. It was so uncomfortable. This was not what she wanted. What was it with Revelation 12:7-12? She felt dizzy. Lucien grabbed her hand and held it up to the cheering crowd. She chewed her lip.

"Smile," Lucien leaned over and whispered, "I know it's a lot, but just smile."

Gabby smiled. Lucien put his hand to his heart, bowed his head, then stepped to the side and held his arms towards Gabby, presenting her.

She smiled and waved to the crowd. Lucien waved, then grabbed her hand and led her out. As they left the area, Gabby heard the cheering quickly quiet and the chatter pick up.

"Do you understand?" Lucien asked.

Gabby nodded her agreement. "I do," she said. Her mouth felt like cotton.

"Thank you for joining me. I feel like that was illuminating. Can you find your way back?"

"Yes," Gabby said.

"Lucien," Sy yelled from down the hall, "I've been looking everywhere for you. Why didn't you answer my calls?"

Sy barreled past Gabby, bumping into her hard as he went by. It seemed intentional.

"I was busy," Lucien calmly answered.

"Intelligence has picked up a flurry of flight activity," Sy said.

"Where?" Lucien asked.

"Can we go to your office to talk?" Sy asked, flashing Gabby a hate-filled glare.

Lucien nodded and they vanished down a long hallway.

37 – CHEERS

Chris sat on his bed. Commander Frei had given him five rough satellite pictures of AmCorps's suspected safe houses. NATO's intelligence had identified five locations, but they weren't exactly sure which location Gabby was in. They narrowed it down to the two eastern locations, one in Maine and the other in West Virginia. They hadn't been able to track the plane from the Amazon and IFP's inside agents couldn't say exactly where they were. Every safe house resident had been picked up and driven in a specialized vehicle that was pathogen secure and didn't allow the passengers to see out. The inside agent in the safe house Gabby was located in had been picked up in Washington D.C. and had driven for roughly eleven hours.

As Chris studied the West Virginia and Maine locations, the West Virginia site stood out to him. It was massive, over twice as large as the Maine site, but it was only a few hours outside of D.C. It was also shaped much different than the other safe houses. The typical safe house was a rectangular structure that measured one mile by two miles and butted up to a half-mile by half-mile square. The West Virginia structure featured a central square edifice that was one mile by one mile, then two rectangular offshoots on opposite sides that were each one mile by two miles. That had to be where Lucien and the U.S. officials were.

NATO and IFP were sending forces to each location, though Chris was able to choose which safe house he would go to. His gut told him the West Virginia location. He would join Commander Frei's division.

Each safe house had a small runway on the property with a hangar and additional barracks. There were no windows, barely any doors. It was going to be nearly impossible to reach Gabby without placing her in an insane amount of danger. They couldn't let Am-Corps or the U.S. know that they were there to rescue her. They would have to treat her like any other resident until they could get her away from the property. Chris would have to hang back and keep his presence completely unknown.

"Chris," Michaela knocked on his door.

"Yep?"

"I have the first small batch of treatments ready. I made six. Would you like to join my team and me in being the guinea pigs? It's the exact treatment that Gabby took."

"Sure."

"As long as there are no issues, we'll be able to manufacture them much quicker after this."

"Great, so what do you think, about a week?"

Michaela nodded. "Maybe not even. Trent said that the treatment takes effect immediately. I'll be able to tell by tonight if it worked."

"That's fast."

"Come on." Michaela gestured, and Chris followed her.

Jay, Lulu, Aston, and Luke were sitting around the card table, just outside of the lab. They had pulled up six chairs. In the middle of the table on a silver platter were six syringes and alcohol wipes. Michaela and Chris took their seats. "Ready?" Michaela asked.

"Yes," Lulu said, biting her red lip, nearly squealing with excitement.

"Are we injecting ourselves or the person to our right?" Michaela asked.

"Person to our right," Aston suggested.

"We've all given shots before, right? Chris?" Michaela asked.

"Of course. I was a PJ." Everyone just stared at him. "Pararescue." Their faces were still blank. "A medical combat rescue specialist. I didn't just give shots, I gave other medical treatments in active war zones while under heavy fire."

"So, you can give a shot." Michaela winked. "Ready?"

"Wait," Luke said, "this is a big moment, shouldn't

you say something?"

"Fuck AmCorps and Lucien Sabara. Cheers!" Michaela held up a syringe.

"Cheers," everyone echoed.

They administered the shots.

"Does everyone feel alright?"

"I don't feel anything," Lulu said.

The table broke out in a roar of laughter, but the joke went over Chris's head.

Luke leaned over to explain, "Genes don't have nerves so they don't feel anything."

Chris still didn't get the joke.

That night, Michaela learned that the treatment had been successful in all of them. She and her team worked through the next three days and nights to make enough treatments for IFP's entire military force. During those forty-eight hours, Chris decided the best way he could help was to make sure that Michaela and her team could devote every second of their time to making the treatment. Chris ensured there was always fresh hot coffee, and he made breakfast, lunch, and dinner. He checked in frequently. Too frequently. Michaela finally asked Chris to give them some space.

He set up his post at the card table just outside of the lab. He brought the satellite images of the five safe houses. He focused on the largest one. It was as big as a small city. There was no way that Chris would be able to reach Gabby in time. He had no idea where she was located. Her only hope was to get word to IFP's inside agent, if that was even possible. Chris checked in the lab. They were busy working. The coffee was fresh. There were still plenty of snacks. He grabbed his coat and went to find Commander Frei.

It was bitterly cold out. The wind seemed to blow right through Chris. It was a chill that hurt from the inside out. Much too cold for March. It dawned on Chris that he had started this mission a year ago. Though it had been nearly a decade since life had been normal. Could things really be on the verge of returning to normal? If Gabby didn't survive, he—no, he didn't even want to consider that. She would survive. That was it.

Chris found Frei in the control room. There were four other men standing around a makeshift conference table. They didn't notice Chris walk in.

"Commander?" Chris said. The full table looked up.

"Chris, perfect timing," Commander Frei said, "we're just going over the plans for each safe house mission."

"That's what I wanted to talk to you about," Chris said.

"Great," Frei said, as the men made room at the table for Chris to join them, "we plan to arrive at each safe house at the same time, bring the charges, then go in. We are sending the largest force to the West Virginia location for obvious reasons. According to the size of the barracks, each safe house has a small unit guarding it."

"Do we have enough troops for that?" Chris asked.

"No," Frei replied, "we are currently deciding if we should go to every safe house or focus on a couple, then deal with the others later."

"We should focus all of our forces on the safe house that holds AmCorps and the ranking officials," Chris said.

"Agreed, but the problem is we don't know exactly where they are. According to our very limited intelligence, Lucien and the high-ranking officials are not housed in the same location. Though we know they are both within driving range of D.C., so I think we should focus on the two eastern safe house locations," Frei said.

"The other reason I'm here is that Dr. Gale will be in a tremendous amount of danger as soon as we show up. Probably even before, as soon as they pick us up in route. Can we get word to her or the inside agent?" Chris asked.

"I don't have access to the intelligence unit. I can make a request, but I don't know. They have extremely limited contact," Frei said.

Chris nodded. "Put the request in."

Chris turned to leave, but saw Michaela and her team walking in.

"They're ready," Michaela said. "Can you help us administer them?"

38 - PRESS CONFERENCE

"Something is going on," Sy said as he paced back and forth, inside of Lucien's office.

"What are you talking about?" Lucien asked as he calmly clicked open his computer home screen.

"Check your email," Sy demanded.

Lucien saw an urgent message in his folder. It was an intelligence report. A major uptake in flight activity had been picked up in Europe and Canada. POTUS had tried to reach Lucien.

"Why didn't you find me earlier?" Lucien snapped as he scanned through the emails. "Quickly fill me in."

"Our intelligence suspects that Europe, possibly NATO, is planning something. They may have learned that we have the treatment and want it. Though what bothers me most is that several planes have landed in Canada near Michaela Kelstrum's location," Sy said.

"That's extremely bothersome," Lucien agreed, "were there any planes to leave the Amazon after Dr. Gale was picked up?"

"Our intelligence didn't pick up on anything. There was one unusual blip near the extraction site but nothing that could be confirmed. Something is going on. Dr. Gale is lying. She should be taken care of now, before it's too late."

Lucien clicked open his secure chat and rang POTUS.

"Lucien, I've been trying to reach you," President Spiegel snapped.

"So, I see. I apologize, I was securing our contact to the specimens. In order to harvest genetic material as needed, we must have Dr. Gale's full support," Lucien said.

"Fine, but none of that will matter if we are attacked. We are readying our full defenses."

"You think that we're going to be attacked? For what, the treatment?" Lucien asked.

"Did you read the full intelligence report?" The president flashed an angered look at Lucien. "Europe, likely NATO or whatever's left of it, is planning something," President Spiegel said.

"You think they're going to attack?" Lucien asked again.

"Yes," Spiegel replied.

"Why don't we make an announcement that we've identified a successful treatment that affects the immune system and stops each pathogen in its tracks," Lucien suggested.

"I am," President Spiegel snapped. "But we need to

offer to share some doses of it with Europe and other nations around the world. How many can we spare?"

"Not many. We're still not sure if we will be able to utilize rehabilitated genetic material and it will take some time to go back to the Amazon to harvest more genetic material."

"How much treatment do we have on hand? Can we offer a small amount to EU's leaders to prove its success and to buy us time?"

"We don't have much. We don't even have enough to treat all of the safe houses. We can send over 500 treatments at the most, if you think that will make a difference," Lucien said.

"I have the press conference scheduled for this evening. I'm positioning the statement in a manner that says we have isolated a cure. We need the support of the world in order to deliver it. If Europe, any other nation, or organization intervenes, they are essentially blocking this treatment from the world. I will close the announcement with the offer of 500 treatments to be distributed by the World Health Organization. Ready those treatments, we will talk again after," President Spiegel said.

"I want to be part of the press conference. In fact, you should have several staff in the background. No masks. You want this announcement to prove that we've identified a cure and we're ready to share it with the world, as long as we have their support."

"Can you get over here in an hour?"

Lucien nodded and clicked out of the chat.

"Dr. Gale is behind this," Sy spoke up, "her and Lt. Silver."

"Keep a close eye on her," Lucien said, and stood to leave.

It was almost five miles to get to POTUS's side, which had been sealed off from AmCorps's side. There was a 2500-acre indoor farm between each independent side. The farm section housed its workers separate from the two safe house sides. The air was on its own filter and the workers distributed the food to each side through a specialized UV conveyor system that went through a series of hermetic seals and UV disinfection chambers.

Now that both sides, as well as the workers, had received the EVE-0 treatment, it was no longer necessary to keep the hermetic seals engaged. Though they hadn't had any reason to disengage them either. There was a tunnel that ran underneath the entire six-mile compound. Lucien was one of five individuals that possessed the code to access the tunnel and he was the only person in it. It was strange to be alone in such a huge space. The tunnel had a motion-activated lighting system so it was completely dark, except for a small section around Lucien. Lucien loved it. He'd never enjoyed being around people. He tolerated it, but they inevitably irritated him.

Lucien wished it took longer to reach the bureaucrat's side than a measly twenty minutes. He reluctantly made his way up to the president's quarters. This safe house was identical to AmCorps's side in appearance. However, the president's quarters were in the place of Lucien's and instead of the AmCorps labs there were extra living quarters for the Secret Service, key politicians, and certain military officials.

Lucien keyed in his code and was immediately greeted by two Secret Service agents.

"Dr. Sabara, the president is ready for you. Do you know where the studio is?"

Lucien nodded. Of course he knew where the studio was, he designed this entire compound. He didn't waste words explaining this to them. The president had given weekly status updates. It was always just him, talking to anyone that still cared to listen, anyone that had somehow managed to survive. He pleaded with them to remain strong, remain isolated, that a cure was on the horizon. Now, Lucien would tell the world that he was delivering it. He was bringing a return to normalcy after more than a decade. *I know it's hard for you to remember what normal is,* Lucien rehearsed in his head, *but soon you will be free to socialize, to go outside, to go shopping and to not be afraid of a deadly enemy that you can't see—that's good,* he told himself.

"Lucien," President Spiegel greeted him as he entered the Oval Office studio. "We saved your spot. I'm going to have you here, right behind my right shoulder as I give the address." Spiegel was sitting at his desk. General Holton was placed directly behind him. The first lady was right behind his left shoulder. The vice president and secretary of state were next to General Holton.

"I'd like to say a few things," Lucien said.

"Right; we didn't get a chance to talk about that. This announcement is rushed. We need more time to prepare our full address. This is going to be short, sweet, and to the point. We just need to make the announcement now. We'll have a full press conference in a day or two." The president snapped his fingers. "I will be sure to announce that. And, don't worry, I'm going to give you all of the credit. Are we ready?" President Spiegel asked, looking around the room. "Ready?" he said, looking directly at his press secretary who was manning the tablet that would broadcast the announcement. "Is everyone in their places?" The press secretary, a young, attractive, dark-haired woman, nodded. The press secretary held up her hand to show 3–2–1 and she pointed to the president.

"Good evening, America, it brings me great joy..."

Lucien forced a smile, though he was boiling on the inside. This should be his announcement.

"And this is all thanks to the work of Dr. Lucien Sabara and AmCorps Labs. I beg you to remain strong for just a little longer. We will have the treatment to you soon. Good night and God bless."

"And... we're out," the press secretary announced.

"Thank you everyone. Lucien, let's talk tomorrow and we'll work on the logistics of your address. Haley,

I want you to look through our engagement numbers and figure out the best time for the press conference. I'm starving. Shall we, sweetheart?" President Spiegel stood, took the hand of his first lady, and made his exit.

"Lucien," General Holton said, scowling at him and walking out of the office, followed by the rest of the staff.

It was just Lucien and two Secret Service agents. "Sir, can we help you find your way out?"

"I know where I'm going," Lucien snapped.

39 - REVELATIONS

Gabby felt sick to her stomach. Her head was pounding. She had been so desperate to get away from Lucien and Sy that she took off in the first direction she could and kept walking. Now, she had no idea where she was. She wasn't sure how long she had walked for. She stopped walking, took a few deep breaths, and tried to get her bearings. but it was useless, She was lost. Worst of all, she could not get Revelation 12:7-12 out of her head. Why couldn't she get that out of her head? It was driving her crazy. Then—it clicked. She felt sick. Revelation 12:7-12... User12712. *No. No. No,* she thought, *he can't be User12712. Johnnie can't be User12712.*

Gabby stumbled back and steadied herself against the wall. Johnnie was completely insane. She hoped there were others inside; in her mind she had pictured a small resistance. Now she realized that it was just the ramblings of a psychotic person. *But, how would he know about the in vitro fertilization?* Gabby wondered. She remembered Johnnie mentioning his wife. She had to find her. She looked at her watch, hit the location assist button, and said "café."

The lights on the floor glowed. She followed them. They led her back past Restaurant Square where a large group of people were gathered, waiting for a table. Gabby checked her watch; it was just after 6 p.m. When Gabby reached the crowd, she put her head down. The lights on the floor must've sensed the horde and the lights spelled out *café*, then pointed an arrow to the left. Gabby scooted around the gathering and the lights picked back up.

She made it to the café and looked around. How was she ever going to find Johnnie's wife? She didn't know her name. She didn't know what she looked like. And, she didn't know anything about her. All she knew was that she came here after her visit with Johnnie. The café was nearly empty. Two men sat at a corner table.

Gabby ordered a coffee and sat down. A young man and woman came in, ordered drinks, then sat. A tall, very fit dark-haired woman came in. She looked tough. She carried a book with her, *Grit: The Power of Resilience.*

Could this be her? Gabby wondered. Gabby started at the woman. She definitely looked like someone that would be part of a resistance. The woman noticed Gabby staring at her. Gabby smiled. The woman looked confused and uncomfortable; she quickly smiled back at Gabby, then looked away. *Not her*, Gabby thought.

"Oh sweetie," Gabby heard from the entrance, before a curvy blonde walked in, "make mine a double today."

"You got it Miranda," the barista answered. "How are you doing today?"

That's definitely not her. She's too loud and friendly to be part of a secret resistance, Gabby thought.

"Oh, you know, I've been better. Johnnie's doing well. I just miss him so much," Miranda said, fighting back tears.

There's no fucking resistance. There's no agents inside. I'm a fucking idiot, Gabby thought.

"Hi, there. I haven't seen you before. I'm Miranda. Mind if I join you? I don't like drinking coffee by myself," Miranda said, stopping at Gabby's table. "Samantha back there appreciates her quiet time. Hey Sam." Miranda waved to the brunette that came in just before her.

"Umm, sure," Gabby said, "I'm Gabrielle, Gabby."

"Nice to meet you, Gabby," Miranda smiled. "So, what's your story? Oh," Miranda dug into her bag, "before we start talking, I just finished this book. It's one of the best books I've ever read. Do you like to read? Do you want to read it?" Miranda pulled out a book.

"Umm, what's—"

"You'll love it," Miranda said, cutting Gabby off

and passing Gabby the book.

"Thanks," Gabby smiled.

"Don't open it till you get home." Miranda paused and gave Gabby a slight nod. "Once you start, you won't be able to put it down."

"Sounds great," Gabby said, and placed the book securely on her lap.

"What do you have there?" Sy asked, surprising Gabby and Miranda.

"Hi Sy, I didn't see you come in," Gabby replied.

"Dr. Gale, Miranda, mind if I join you?" Sy asked.

"Doctor? So impressive," Miranda smiled. "Of course Sy. Pull up a chair."

"So, what do you have there?" Sy asked again.

"Oh, Miranda gave me a book she just finished."

"Can I see it?" Sy asked.

"I haven't read it yet, but I'll give it to you as soon as I finish," Gabby said.

"Once you start, you can't put it down. It's so good. It's a thriller," Miranda said.

"Thanks," Sy said.

The barista brought over a latte and cookie for Miranda and a black coffee for Sy.

"Thanks sweetie," Miranda said.

"I think I'm going to excuse myself," Gabby said, "I have a headache. I hoped a coffee would help, but it doesn't seem to be. Miranda, it was a pleasure meeting you. Thank you for the book. Sy."

Gabby quickly made her way to her apartment.

Sy terrified her and she was crushed. She didn't realize how much hope she had placed in User12712. She realized how badly she wanted to get out of the safe house. Miranda was a bubbly, talkative, emotional wreck and User12712 was psychotic. There was no resistance. Gabby felt like a complete idiot for concocting such a ridiculous story. She wouldn't let her mind consider the fact that she might be—she couldn't even bring herself to say it. She thought she was buying time, part of some conspiracy, and valiantly gave her body to the cause. She had never been so mad at herself and so full of regret.

Gabby made it to her apartment, tossed the book on the coffee table and collapsed on the couch. She was exhausted. Physically and mentally drained. She must've fallen asleep. She suddenly sat up with a major crick in her neck. She looked around and was still on the couch. It was almost four in the morning. She decided to turn on the television and reached for the stainless-steel remote. When she did, she noticed the corner of a piece of paper hanging out of the book Miranda gave her.

Dr. Gale — You need to avoid Lucien Sabara and Osiris Azazel. We will do our best to protect you. This will be over soon. Follow your normal routine, but be very alert and keep as much distance between you and Lucien and Sy. If you hear any commotion, take cover. Hide. Do not wear your watch. Dissolve this note in water. Your friend, X.

Gabby sat straight up. Sy had come so close to seeing this note and she was oblivious. What if she had dropped it? *Holy shit,* Gabby thought, *that was beyond lucky.* She jumped up and ran the letter under the water. It quickly dissolved.

Gabby made a huge pot of coffee even though she felt energized and decided she'd head over to the nursery early today. The nursery was unchanged. This morning functioned exactly to the second like every other morning she had spent here. Though, today Gabby felt different. She kept checking the time. Minutes felt like hours. The day seemed to drag on. The initial comfort she felt when she was with Primus and the other babies had frayed to nothing. Everything was so structured and so rigid; it was almost like life had been bred out of these children in favor of machine-esque qualities. It was so different from the chaos of the jungle, which was so full of life. At first, being in the safe house was relaxing. There wasn't something that could kill her lurking at every step. In order to survive, she'd been in a state of hyper-alertness for almost a year. Walking into the comfort and routine of the safe house had felt good—at first. Now, as she held Primus in her arms, she realized the threats that lurked here were much more malevolent.

Precisely at 1 p.m., Primus held his little hand open over his eyes and pulled it down. It was nap time. Before Gabby laid him back in his bassinet, she nuzzled him and kissed his baby-soft cheek. Primus did not like this. He pushed her away and stuck his tiny fist up. He held up his thumb, pointer, and middle finger, then closed them—the sign for no. He wouldn't look at Gabby after she laid him down.

Gabby then went to check on Angel. She changed her diaper and fed her. She was burping her when Dr. Hollman came in.

"We're finishing early today. You can go home," Dr. Hollman said, surprising Gabby in Angel's unit. He never came in here.

"What? Why?"

"We have some internal business to wrap up today, so you can go home early."

"Okay," Gabby said, then picked Angel back up to burp her again. Gas tended to collect in her abdomen.

"I told you to go home," Dr. Hollman snapped.

"I'm just going to burp her one more time."

"No!" Dr. Hollman screamed. "Leave now."

Startled, Gabby laid Angel back down, gently patted her belly, and left.

As she walked into the hall, the entire building was in a frenzy. Guards that she'd never seen were charging through the walkways.

"What's going on?" Gabby asked repeatedly, but no one answered.

Suddenly her body slammed into the wall, then someone grabbed her hair and started dragging her. "What's going on?" she screamed. She managed to get her footing and spin to see Sy. He shoved her to the ground. "Get up," he spit, reached down, grabbed Gabby's hair again, and dragged her. They moved against the stream of people. No one looked at her, let alone helped her. He pushed her through a doorway, slamming the door behind him.

"What's going on?" she cried.

Lucien spun around in his desk chair. "You don't know?"

"No, tell me, please," Gabby begged him, fear clawing at her mind.

Lucien turned his computer monitor towards Gabby. Onscreen was the camera view of the field outside of the safe house. A crowd gathered, calm but with determination on their faces, and numerous cameras pointed at the door. Lucien hit another button and pulled up the press conference.

"If your boyfriend, Chris, is in that crowd, I'll kill you myself, right now," Sy sneered.

"I told you, he's dead," Gabby cried.

"You fucking liar." Sy swung his fist right into Gabby's jaw. She flew back into a chair. Her vision became fuzzy. Then tunneled. She clung to any bit of consciousness she could.

40 – IT'S A GO

Chris was on the plane with Thomas, Oliver, and Commander Frei. They were on the second plane to land at AmCorps's main safe house. The first plane included several officials from the United Nations, European Union, and NATO. They had already started their press conference, which was broadcast across all available channels at this very moment as well as online.

The plane was stopped; they were just waiting for their cue to assist NATO's forces as they entered the safe house. Chris had never been this nervous for a mission. They got their signal and the door flung open. The team rushed off the plane and flanked the officials as the press conference was underway. Chris hung back.

The President of the European Commission, Dr. Helga Von Batten, pounded on the unmarked steel door to AmCorps. She turned to address the row of cameras.

"We are here to serve AmCorps, Dr. Lucien Saba-ra, President Spiegel, current President of the United States of America, General Holton, and Dr. David Benjamin with crimes against humanity charges, as well as charges of attempted international kidnapping, violence against indigenous peoples, withholding medical treatments, and unfair distribution of lifesaving medicine. It's time for the American people and the world at large to hold them accountable for these atrocities."

The door swung open and a barrage of automatic gunfire erupted. Caught in the crosshairs, Dr. Von Batten jerked as a bullet caught her and she went down. An IFP agent quickly pulled out of the way as other NATO soldiers returned fire. From behind them, someone tossed a grenade into the doorway and hollered, "Down!" The building shook but held, blowing much of the blast in ripples of energy back out, throwing a few of NATO's soldiers to the ground.

Secretary General Jan Saltzenberg took over, "To the American people and soldiers inside. We are here to help you. If you surrender now, we will not hold you accountable and you will be freed from the tyrannical control of your government. If you decide to fight, you will be charged with the same crimes." The first line of soldiers charged in. Chris went in with the second wave. There were a few bodies inside the entrance, but not many. AmCorps's forces had pulled back and were waiting to surrender. When they surrendered,

Chris heard the highest ranking AmCorps officer tell NATO's forces that information had recently begun to circulate inside regarding what AmCorps had attempted to do and when the time came, they had already decided that they wanted to be on the right side of things, well most of them, anyway. *Wow*, Chris thought, *the power of inside agents*. They were quickly led out by a NATO unit.

The halls inside the safe house were completely dark. Chris's unit used flashlights to weave their way through the long empty corridors. An alarm blared. In between sirens, a male voice urged residents to seek immediate shelter inside their housing units and to remain calm, that this would be sorted out shortly.

They stumbled upon General Holton's quarters first.

Chris found Holton sitting at his desk. "You're being brought up on charges of international crimes against humanity," Chris said.

"You dumb-shit, you'll never get away with this. I will try you for treason against your country and execute you myself. You stupid asshole," Holton said from behind his desk, careful to keep his hands visible.

"Where's Dr. Gale?" Chris asked.

General Holton began to laugh hysterically.

"You heard him. Where is Dr. Gale?" Thomas repeated.

"All of this for her? She brought the treatment right to him. Asshole, she doesn't care about you.

Newsflash, fucker, she got tired of running around the jungle and sold you out."

"Where is she?" Chris said, moving closer to Holton.

General Holton laughed harder. Chris jammed the back of his gun into Holton's stomach. He gasped for air. "I'm too old for this shit. You're at the wrong safe house, moron."

Chris looked at Thomas and Oliver who now had Holton by each arm; they shrugged. "You fucking imbeciles, you didn't know that, did you?" Holton shook his head.

They marched Holton out as President Spiegel and Dr. Benjamin were also being escorted out.

A phone in General Holton's inside jacket pocket rang. Oliver reached in and picked it up. He pulled it back looked at the screen, then looked at Chris. "It's for you, mate."

Oliver handed Chris the phone. Lucien's face filled the video call. His jaw clenched as his eyes held a spark of triumph.

"Lt. Christopher Silver, another one of Holton's mistakes. I just wanted you to have a chance to say goodbye to your girlfriend." Lucien turned the camera to face Gabby as Sy clasped his hand around her neck.

"Stop!" Chris screamed.

"Oh, and we want to tell you the good news. Your girlfriend is pregnant with Trent's baby. It's such a shame that we will have to waste this miracle." Gabby's face was bright red. She couldn't breathe.

"What are you talking about? Leave her alone!" Chris cried.

"Let her tell him about it." Sy said and let go of Gabby's neck.

"Chris, I—"

"Tell him," Lucien demanded.

"They gave me an IVF treatment with Trent's sperm."

"Who wanted it, who made the decision to get it?" Lucien snapped.

"I did, but I had no choice."

"I call bullshit." Sy cackled and backhanded Gabby.

"The only liar here is our sweet little Dr. Gabrielle Gale. It seems that she manipulated everyone in her path to get what she wanted."

Gabby just cried.

"I'm coming to get you," Chris said.

"No, don't, please, just—" Gabby cried.

The phone cut out. "Where is she?" Chris growled to no one in particular, his frustration taking over his senses.

Thomas pointed, and Chris saw Oliver at a table, poring over a picture of this structure he'd pulled from their planning session.

"Look," Oliver said, "we're here, but there is a mirror building over there. It's clearly separated down the middle, but there is no indication of an opening between them. AmCorps must have that side."

"You're right," Chris said, and took off running. Oliver and Thomas handed Holton over to a couple of NATO's soldiers, then ran after Chris. They followed the stream of incoming NATO's forces and quickly found their way out.

A chaotic crowd was growing outside of the safe house. Chris knew it would take too long to go by foot, so he pushed his way through the crowd to the building that sat near the runway. He prayed there was a vehicle they could take inside. This building must've been used to house an external guard unit. Luckily, it was empty; NATO's first team had already cleared the building.

Right inside was a small garage with several Ranger ATV's. There was a locker on the wall. Thomas ran over, discovering it was unlocked.

"Is there a number on the vehicle?" Thomas asked.

Chris looked and found a small number near the ignition, "Three."

Thomas grabbed the corresponding key and ran over.

The ATV started, Oliver opened the garage, then jumped in.

They were able to find a small path around the crowd and made their way onto a rough trail that ran along the massive building. Thomas had the ATV flying as fast as it would go. It was so bumpy that Chris had to hold on so he wasn't thrown out of the vehicle.

Oliver requested backup, but with all of the chaos currently at the President's side of the safe house, it would take the support team some time to get there. That meant they would be all alone.

They finally came across another door, identical to the first. Oliver placed a blast bomb on the door and detonated it. The door shook, but didn't open. They placed another one. This detonation loosened it enough that they were able to kick it down. Inside was a small room with another door. An alarm blared, *warning, hermetic seal breach, warning, hermetic seal breach,* while a bright red light flashed. They only had one blast bomb left. "I'll do it," Oliver said. "Wait out there."

Chris and Thomas took cover on each side of the door. Oliver ran out and took cover. Nothing.

"What's going on, mate? " Thomas asked.

"Give it a minute, " Oliver said.

BOOM, it blew. They waited a second for the smoke and debris to clear, then went in. The heavy metal door was hanging by a single hinge. Chris and Thomas pulled it down with a heavy crash.

They walked in slowly. It was an incredible, massive indoor farm. There were rows and rows of stacked metal trays growing crops. Chris had read about vertical farms but had never seen one in person. In here, nature was under industry's full control. Artificial UV lamps hung from the ceiling. It was massive. Chris, Oliver, and Thomas ran through the rows, but it was so massive, they quickly got turned around. Oliver held his hand up. They froze. He made a left turn and found a group of farm workers hiding.

"Have you received your treatment?" Oliver asked.

They nodded their heads yes.

"You're not in danger. We are here to help you. Slowly make your way to the exit. NATO is there and will help you reacclimate."

They nodded.

"How do we get to AmCorps's side of the safe house?" Oliver asked.

"Follow me," a young man with his hair in long locs offered, then led them through a maze of vertical crops to a door. He keyed in a code and the door opened.

They came up on a guard, watching the action on the surveillance system that he was manning. The high ranking AmCorps officer from the other side of the safe house had joined the press conference and was currently addressing those still inside the safe house. He urged the other guards and residents to cooperate with NATO. He immediately surrendered, as many of the soldiers had already decided to do.

Holton's phone rang again. It was Lucien. "You realize that you'll never find us. I see everywhere you go, and if you get any closer, Sy will squeeze every ounce of life out of your precious little Dr. Gale."

"Okay, okay," Chris said, stopping. "Don't hurt her. Just leave. Escape before you're arrested."

Lucien laughed. "Arrested for what? For helping the human race survive? Arrested for helping the human race reach its full potential?"

"You're creating monsters. Trent, your right-hand guy, knew this was wrong. Did you know that Trent had been working with IFP and NATO to stop you? He is the one who gave them all of their information."

Lucien's mouth twisted. "You're lying."

Chris smiled. "No, I'm not. He made videos for us telling us what to do. He had us contact Michaela Kelstrum. How do you think we knew to reach out to her? She made the treatment for us. We've all successfully reactivated our EVE-0 gene. In fact, she's improving the formula as we speak."

"You're lying. Kill her," Lucien commanded, turning to Sy.

Sy smiled and squeezed. Gabby's face turned bright red. Her eyes bulged. There was a sudden bang, then the phone cut out.

41 – SPECIAL AGENT

Gabby collapsed back in the chair, gasping for air. Her vision had holes as she struggled to hold on to consciousness.

"Johnnie, what are you doing here?" Lucien asked.

"I have been waiting so long to do this," Johnnie said.

"Calm down, Johnnie, calm down," Lucien pleaded.

"You have to be stopped. What you're doing is wrong for humanity," Johnnie said.

"John, you have been experiencing delusions. Do you remember? You have a history of schizophrenia in your family," Lucien said.

"Yes, I remember. What you weren't aware of, is that because of my family history with the disease, my parents opted for an alternative preventative treatment to train my brain to recognize delusions if they were ever to appear, and they did from time to time. Your treatment definitely exacerbated something. But that's not why I'm here. I am here because of those children, those monstrosities. They're not natural," Johnnie said.

"He is right. Free choice—" Gabby said.

"Shut up," Sy took his hand, placed it over Gabby's whole face, and shoved her head back. "How do you know about that program?" he asked.

"Let me introduce myself. I'm Special Agent Johnathan Williams with Allied Command Operations. My specialty is cybersecurity. My wife, Miranda, is higher ranking than me. There isn't a computer system that we can't get into."

Gabby rubbed her head, trying to cling on to everything that was happening, "Look out," she screamed as she saw Sy grab a heavy glass paperweight from Lucien's desk.

It was too late. Sy swung the paperweight into Johnnie's temple. Johnnie stumbled back and Sy lunged. He was on top of Johnnie, pummeling him with blow after blow. Gabby lunged at Sy with all of her weight and tackled him. He easily tossed Gabby off, smiled, and swung, connecting a left hook right to her jaw. Her legs immediately crumbled under her. Her vision went black, but she could hear Sy laugh somewhere in the distance. This anchored her, and gave her something to hold on to. She let her anger surge and pull her back.

This brief attack gave Johnnie enough time to get up and face Sy on even ground. Johnnie swung, but

Sy easily dodged the punch. Johnnie swung again and skimmed Sy's chest.

"You're going to have to do better than that," Sy said, and swung back at Johnnie but missed.

"Boys, boys, boys... Johnnie, I've been looking everywhere for you. Now is not the time to mess around," Miranda said from the doorway to Lucien's office. She stepped in and closed the door behind her. She held a tablet in her hand.

From the ground next to Lucien's desk, Gabby saw Lucien frantically dig through his desk. He found what he was looking for and pulled it out—a gun. Gabby lunged at him with every ounce of strength she could muster. The gun fired, but Gabby was able to knock it out of Lucien's hands. The gun skirted across the office floor and slid under a corner cabinet. Sy and Johnnie lunged for it.

"Now, would you all quit moving for a second? We're going to take a quick UV bath," Miranda announced, keying a code into her tablet. "Close your eyes."

"No," Lucien screamed, "that's impossible."

Slats on the ceiling of Lucien's office opened up. There were a series of bright flashes of light. Gabby closed her eyes. She could hear Lucien scream. Then she heard something that sounded like a tree branch snap before everything went dark. Gabby opened her eyes. Lucien had collapsed on the ground near where she sat. Half of his body was contorted in a partial seizure. Though he was still alive. She quickly scanned the room. Miranda and Johnnie were locked in an embrace. Sy lay in the corner, motionless. His eyes were open, but his neck was bent at an unnatural angle and a syringe stuck out of his arm.

Gabby pulled herself up. "I have to find Chris," she said. "I owe you my life. Thank you."

"Of course," Miranda said, and smiled. "How about that close call last night? Girl, you about gave me a heart attack."

"I realized that this morning," Gabby smiled, then hugged Miranda. She looked for Lucien's phone that he had called Chris on and picked it up. She tried to open it to call Chris, but there was a lock screen code.

"Hand it here," Johnnie said. Gabby passed the phone over, and he keyed in a code that unlocked it. He redialed the last number and Chris's anxious face appeared on the screen.

"Chris, where are you?" Gabby asked.

"I'm here, Gabs. I'm in your safe house."

"Look around, do you see any signs?"

"Neonatal/Pediatric," Chris said.

"Stay there. I'll find you."

The halls were empty. Despite the billions of dollars that the guests paid for their place here, they were anxious to return to normal and left at the first opportunity. Gabby started to run. She ran as fast as she could. She ran by the empty Restaurant Square. Half-eaten plates were scattered everywhere. She ran past the café and the abandoned coffee cups. She turned the corner, then froze. She saw Chris. He turned and saw her. A visible wave of relief washed over him as his rigid stance softened.

He wrapped his arms around her. "Gabs," he let out a breath and pulled her in closer.

"I missed you," Gabby said and smiled up at him. She was not going to leave him ever again.

THE END

To find out the fate of Dr. Gabrielle Gale,
Lt. Christopher Silver, and Dr. Lucien Sabara
visit DanielleGomesWrites.com